CW00429270

The Ev

in red and white

a novel by

Steven Kay

FastPrint Publishing

www.fast-print.net/store.php

THE EVERGREEN IN RED AND WHITE
Copyright © Steven Kay 2013

All rights reserved

No part of this book may be reproduced in any form by photocopying
or any electronic or mechanical means, including information storage
or retrieval systems, without permission in writing from both the
copyright owner and the publisher of the book.

All characters are fictional.
Any similarity to any actual person is purely coincidental.

The right of Steven Kay to be identified as the author of this work has
been asserted by him in accordance with the Copyright, Designs and
Patents Act 1988 and any subsequent amendments thereto.

A catalogue record for this book is available from the British Library

ISBN 978-178035-758-4

First published 2013 by
FASTPRINT PUBLISHING
Peterborough, England.

Author's note

In 1894 Rabbi Howell became the first Romany to play football for England. I have never believed the accounts in the club's history books of what happened in 1897-98: a pivotal season for him. My research led to what I believe to be as close to the truth as is possible. This is a fictional account based on what facts that can be gleaned.

The glossary contains Romany and dialect words, should the reader wish to know exact meanings.

The Evergreen
in red and white

I don't know exactly what Howell is made of, but he is an acrobat and I believe if he were standing on his head he would somehow get his kick in, and the ball would be picked up by one of his side. — Free Critic, Athletic News, January 1898

Chapter 1

Rab took the little leather bag containing the fairy's foot from around his neck and placed it in his kit bag. He looked up to where Needham stood at the rain-streaked window; those steely eyes gazing out beyond the sodden cricket pitch. Angry Peak skies were trying to drown little Glossop huddled and cowering in the valley bottom beneath the sullen moors that had encircled her. Chimneys struggled to expel their smoke away from greasy grey slate roofs as first it rose then swirled back down to make anyone venturing out cough and curse even louder than they were already.

'We can't go out in that – it's sileing it down!' Rab said to no one in particular. 'The only ones of God's creatures out there are the bloody sheep and they'd be in if they had a choice.'

'Rab's right, Nudge, go tell 'em we ain't bloody sheep – and we ain't built no sodding ark neither!'

The United team were sat hunched on wooden benches in the pavilion: the distinguished United team. The team of goalkeeper, William "Fatty" Foulke, Ernest "Nudger" Needham, Rab Howell, and Walter "Cocky" Bennett. *The* United – Championship runners-up to the Villans.

Rab saw Needham's brow lose its furrows as he turned to his men who were all sat, elbows on knees as if mimicking each other, woollen jackets over their red and white jerseys against the cold, illuminated only by what light from the grey skies made it through the line of windows.

'We're professionals: it's our job. We're men – we've played in worse. What about that time at Perry Bar.'

'Yeah Nudge, but that counted for summat – this means nowt to no bugger – not even the folks of this blooming town can be bothered to shift from their fireplaces. And we were promised a big crowd and a game of football, not a mud fight in front of half a dozen,' Rab replied.

Bill threw in his not insubstantial weight to the argument: 'Aye, and even tha nearly fainted wi' cold – and some of the Villans played in overcoats – and Charlie Athersmith had his umbrella up! Didn't tha bring the red and white striped umbrellas?'

Needham could see he had to cut his losses. 'I'll see what's going on – see if we can't postpone it.'

He was soon back with trainer George Waller at his side.

'Mr Stokes says we're going out in ten minutes no matter what. He's agreed with Mr Wood that we can play just half an hour each way, but we just have to get on with it. Anyhow it's perhaps slowing a bit.'

'Bugger it is!' someone muttered from a bench away to Rab's right.

Everyone was silent. Needham sat down on the bench next to Bill and Rab; he bent down to tighten his laces. George Waller stood in front of them stroking moisture off his moustache, water still dripping off his tweed cap worn at an angle.

'Look 'ere lads we've a job to do so let's do it eh? And let's put on a show for them poor buggers what's paid their sixpences to see the United – let's show 'em what the United are all about. You all know what you need to do. Let's win this and then we're done.'

Rab's jersey clings cold to him and the cold dribbles into his stockings as they jog over the cricket pitch to where the Enders line up, equally enthusiastic, by the looks of them. A few spectators stamping their feet on the banking by the railway, pipes well charged with tobacco against the weather, try to raise a cheer – as much for their own sakes; then a black engine puts them back in their place as it puffs its way across the bridge and passes behind, enveloping them in steam.

Let's get this bloody thing over wi'. Go on Cocky, play up! Corner. Push up. Ball sticks in the mud, hoof it out, mud everywhere, in boots, in ear, up knickers. Bill saves and sprawls: a trout on a riverbank. Nudge not in red and white no more; rain can't wash that clean. Stick to your man; mud sticks. Get the ball. Penalty. Jimmy blasts it wide, daft sod. Walls makes up for it, stinging shot; stinging rain. No stopping that. Half time one-nil, half way over.

Rain slows, so do we. What's the point. Nowt in it for no bugger. Let's go home. Damn him; good stop Bill.

Enders' free kick. Bill has no chance, wind must've caught it. Then the best United chance and Cocky fires over. Again back down our end and the same bloke passes Harry and strikes it past Bill again.

Kicks off again, he won't get away. Ball stops in pool of water. Feet fly in, water sprays. His leg tangled round, his sweat, his breath, mud, water, sky pewter grey; looking up. Ref's whistle. I'm a'reight Nudge. "Here!" – Nudge's hand, warm, wet, gritty. Other bloke still down, clutching his leg. Sorry mate – it were a fair challenge. His grey eyes look beyond at grey sky. Carries him back to the pavilion.

Down to ten. Knee aching. Dull. Run it off.

Ref's whistle – about bloody time – get back inside.

They scraped off the worst of the Derbyshire mud. Stinking brown leather boots and shin guards were scattered like tannery floor offcuts interspersed by mounds of sodden, brown red and white jerseys, and brown and blue knickers.

'Lend us thi' comb Nudge, eh?' said Bill.

'I'm not thi' father,' Needham said as he reached in his pocket. 'Here have it.'

'It's like the Crimea in here lads,' said George Waller, 'let's get straight before Mr Stokes comes in – he wants a chat.'

Rab sat in his shirt-tails, legs stretched out in front of him, poking at the fleshy bit above the knee. George Waller came over. 'Everything all right Rab?'

'Yeah, just a bit stiff, maybe a bit of Grattans on it and I'll be reight tomorrow, tha knows me, takes more than that.'

'Tha did go into him a bit heavy though.'

'Ah but there were nowt wrong wi' it – it were fair.'

'That's not what the ref thought.'

'Ah, what's a nob like him know about owt.'

'Come on, let's have a look then.'

Waller felt his knee and compared it to the right one. 'Where's it sore? There is a bit of swelling I reckon. Tha's done summat to it.' He got out some embrocation from a shiny tin and rubbed it in to Rab's knee – the thick vapours rising up almost visible as they were released in wafts by George's work. Needham came over, waistcoat unbuttoned, getting the ends of his tie the right length for tying. 'Tha all right?'

'Yeah champion. How's the other feller?'

'Worse 'n thi I should imagine – tha didn't half clock him one.'

'Well I tries not to do owt by halves.'

'How is 'e George? What's tha reckon?'

'Might take a few days. Might not be right for *the Wednesday* game, that only gives us two days. Doubt that's enough.'

'I'll be reight George, tha needs me to chase Freddy round.'

'We might not be able to risk it Rab; we want to put a strong side out at the Grove so as to win the Sheffield league. If tha's not fit tha don't play – we don't want to play wi' just ten men if thi knee gets worse.'

'George's right,' said Needham, 'we can bring in Harry.'

'What put young Harry up against Fred Spiksley, he'll eat him.'

'No, Harry Hammond, he can play at half too, and if Tommy's back that's more than enough to stop 'em coming forwards. Anyhow young Harry didn't play too bad out there.'

'Except for that goal: that showed lack of experience – he should've played the man not the ball.'

'Aye – like what tha did tha lundy sod.'

'Ah gi' o'er! he should've got out o' t' way quicker.'

'Tha'll do Rab,' said Waller, 'Get thisen dressed. If tha's not right for Monday tha's not right. Just get some rest. Put thi leg up. It's Easter. Spend Monday with the family instead. Come down the Lane on Tuesday and I'll look at thi again and we'll see whether tha's fit for the tour next week.'

Charles Stokes, respected dental surgeon, known to some in the room as "the Tooth-yanker," walked in, bowler-hatted and wearing his Chesterfield buttoned up tight. 'Not good enough that, men. Not enough commitment, not enough by far.' Everyone looked at something other than the speaker: the small pool of water gathering at the tip of Stokes's umbrella that he had leant against the wall, a raised knot on a floorboard, or a mashed piece of mud and grass, punched through with a hole from a stud, like a power-press offcut. Only Waller and Needham held their heads up.

'You are paid good wages. Good wages. Good wages to do a job of work; you therefore are required to do that job and do it well, to the best of your ability, whether you feel like it or not. Whether it's raining or not. It's not for you to decide on which occasion you should work your hardest and when you should not. I have been making excuses on your behalf to Mr Wood. Mr S H Wood is, as you know, an influential man. He has put up a not inconsiderable sum of his own money that this game might go ahead. I have had to make excuses for you: that it has been the end of a tough season etcetera, etcetera, but quite frankly it rang somewhat hollow.'

Some of the players glanced up as the Tooth-yanker unfastened his coat revealing the gold watch chain beneath. He removed his hat, took a handkerchief out of his pocket and dabbed his brow. Then the floor became interesting again.

'As you know we at this club are ambitious. We are not satisfied with second place. We require performances to match, nay supersede those of the other Sheffield team. They have won the Cup; we must do the same. What they do we go one better.'

One or two heads nodded. Some shifted weight from one buttock to the other on the hard wooden benches.

'We will look to improve next season. And that means bringing in players who share our vision of success for this club. Myself, Mr Wostinholm, and the Committee invest a great deal in this club and we do not wish to be disappointed and let down by men who work when it suits them; we want men who share our ambitions. On Monday we face *the Wednesday* and we want to win the Sheffield league – both they and we will field our strongest teams. I do not need to remind you of the importance of beating our rivals.'

With the thumb and forefinger of his left hand he raised his watch out of his waistcoat pocket on its yellow chain, then cradled it in the palm of his other hand and smiled back at its golden face. 'I shall be conducting our little tour south myself next weekend. It will

9

be an ideal opportunity to show that you have a future in this club, to show off your talents to spectators not used to seeing first-rate football; but also an opportunity to enjoy fresh Norfolk air, good food and fellowship. You will continue to report to Bramall Lane all this week as instructed by Mr Waller. Thank you men. Have a good journey home. A peaceful Easter to you.' He turned, put on his hat and went on his way to tea with his host.

George closed the door to the weather as Stokes departed. 'The train goes at ten to seven,' he said, 'that gives us an hour to get tea at the Station Hotel before us train. Let's get a shift on eh?'

The team gathered up their bags and went back out into the rain, pulling up the collars on their jackets, and those with mufflers pulled them tighter as they turned the corner into Howard Street and headed into the squall.

Bags were piled into the guard's van and two compartments invaded; other passengers suitably deterred. Needham and Waller sat conspiratorially next to each other, and Foulke sprawled opposite, pulling his cap over his eyes more as a sign of his intent than to shade his eyes from the feeble light cast by the compartment's gas light. Rab sat by the window, opposite his old friend Mick Whitham. The grey skies darkened further as the dusk set in. Through the rain-dotted window, lights from farmhouses punctuated the greyness as the train rattled and bumped its way up the darkening valley. The train whistled as it plunged into the earth at Woodhead. Rab saw his own feint image appear in the glass, as the only existence left was theirs inside the gloom, steam and smoke of the carriage. He saw his furrowed brow and relaxed his face to make it go; stared at his own eyes looking back. How old was he? He told different people different things, twenty-eight usually, a good age to be that, for a footballer, experienced, nobody's fool. But he was still at Ecclesfield when he married Selina and he'd have been twenty then, one season at Ecclesfield, one at the Swifts, then seven and a bit at the United. Ah stick to twenty-eight Rab! The train came back into the world and the smoke cleared from the window as the train slowed down for a station. A man in railway uniform stood watching as a few passengers got off the train, stepping out of the platform's pools of light and away into the night. The uniformed man glanced over and, catching Rab's eye, touched the brim of his cap as the train jolted forward again. Rab came to.

'How long does tha think we can keep playing Mick?' he said. 'I mean how long can a professional keep being a professional?'

Mick, who had opened his eyes when the train pulled in at the station, shrugged, 'I dunno. Thing is I suppose nobody knows – in the old days amateurs would just stop when they felt like it. But for us it's different – we're like thoroughbreds – train regular, fed well, looked after. As long as we're still winning races they'll keep paying us.'

'Aye and then we'll be sent to the knackers!'

'I suppose I'll have to go back to grinding blades or summat leastways one of these days.'

'Well they'll not get me back down t' pit, sweating away in hell. I'd sooner go to the knackers.'

'Thi and me we're the first generation of proper professionals. No reason why we can't keep going a bit yet. But we'll have to stop some day though, even if we don't get nobbled – or worse.'

Rab glanced down at his knee and stretched it out, 'Yeah but I'm still getting better – wiser, and we keep fit through training. I ain't done quite yet.' Mick was looking straight ahead, arms folded, a look almost of contentment on his face. Gentle eyes for a hard man.

'What's tha think he meant then, the Tooth-yanker, about bringing in new players?' Rab said.

'He means up front, goals, that's what we need, at back and half-back we're as good as there is. You, Nudge and Tommy – the legendary midget half-backs! Nowt to worry about there.'

Rab looked at his friend – United's first ever international player. He saw a bloke much heavier than when they first played together in the Ecclesfield days. Not as quick as he used to be; he worried about his chances; Bob and Harry were much sharper.

*

The wind and rain were not quite so fierce on the right side of the Pennines, but Lake Street in Brightside seemed aptly named that

11

evening as ripples blew across pools of water in the unpaved street and yard at the back. No one cared much about the street at the front – it was only used rarely as a route by the children to bunk over the end wall to get to the river's bank. Normal human traffic passed through a wooden gate on the Alfred Road side and across the shared yard. The terrace was only thirty-odd years old, but looked older; it was never well built, and the landlord had always believed money spent on its upkeep a waste. From the yard you stepped straight into the living rooms of the six two-up, two-downs in the middle of the terrace. But the house at the end, number twenty-four, was slightly more desirable, having as it did a separate scullery extending out at the back, making five rooms altogether.

In the living room of number twenty-four Selina was sat in front of the range to one side; her mother Jemima sat on a Windsor chair at the other side with the mending box on the rag rug in between them. The room was not a large one, appearing even smaller by everything in it: a deal table in the centre covered with a plain oil cloth, not large enough for the whole household to sit round at once, a sideboard against the wall between the door to the cellar and the door leading to the front room and the stairs. The range was well polished, a copper kettle was warming and the largest pots and pans were stored there. The mantelpiece had two brass candlesticks and a wooden clock with a brass and silvered face and some porcelain ornaments of pastoral figures. On the walls, yellowed like the ceiling by smoke and cooking, hung some framed lithographs of landscapes, and opposite the fireplace was a gas light usually illuminated only during teatime in the winter and a round mirror in which you just caught sight of your head and shoulders on your way through to the scullery or "slop-kitchen." A window overlooked the yard and the privy block, but was hidden behind a thick, faded, maroon curtain. The outside, though, refused to be shut out completely and sent reminding gusts to rattle the sash and the scullery door. An oil lamp on the table with a red glass reservoir cast just enough light for them to see where they were putting their stitches. Every now and then a small pother of smoke from the fire blew back down the chimney before being sucked back up again just as it threatened to spill too far into the room.

This was the best part of the week for Selina, even better than the peace that descended over her in the church pew on Sundays. The house was quiet: her father was round at the Blucher, the children were upstairs and her brother Charlie was out doing whatever it was that fifteen-year-old boys did on a Saturday evening. Mother and daughter had cooked supper, cleaned and put away; the flags had been scrubbed. They had been down Brightside Lane to do their marketing: the scullery shelves filled with flour, jars and little brown-paper parcels of groceries; the children had been sung to and tucked up: Little Selina and Lizzie in the small bed and Little Rabbi in the big iron bed keeping it warm for his parents when they turned in. They were both in a little homely bubble before the men came back and burst it. How things had changed. This house, three wages coming into the household. 'Would you go back to the old life *Dei*?' she said.

Her mother smiled and it was like she looked beyond Selina, her gaze somewhere else. 'I miss having all my family around me – now we're all spread out – our Sarah Ann in Walkley, Eliza in Darnall, George and Jimmy in Attercliffe, and the others further still – just Henry nearby. We've no space even for us to all sit round together and just be. Your *Poori Dei*, *Kooshto Doovel* rest her soul, never could get used to living in walls: to being a *keiringro*, but we have to move with the times.'

Selina looked at her mother who was still partly somewhere other than the here and now. Her skin bore the signs of thirty odd years of outdoor life: her fingers and hands were those of a peg maker despite not having split a willow for many years, her body was shaped by years of sitting cross-legged and carrying baskets over her shoulder from door to door. Her hair was grey, with remembrances of her former dark tresses. Selina had noticed occasional silvery strands in her own dark hair and wondered how long before plucking them out became impossible and she became like her mother. Not the skin though, fresh air and sunshine were more things of her childhood life than her life in Brightside: despite its name it was never ever bright.

Her own memories of outdoor life were few. They had moved to live amongst *gorgios* in Ashover when she was young; when her

13

father had to finally let go of the old ways and support his family by going underground. She had images and feelings, like it was from a previous life, not from this one: the fires with hanging cooking pots, the cosy feeling of snuggling next to all her sisters in the tent whilst the rain beat outside, horses, gathering wood, and the singing and dancing: the magical singing and dancing – fiddles and voices, laughing, swirling figures and smoke, and orange sparks rising up into the night sky. She knew well that it was only the fondest of her memories that came to mind.

Her mother's focus seemed to shift back into the room. 'We've not had a proper get together since Sinamenta's wedding. But it's not the same. We used to keep an eye on everyone, now they go their own ways and the old traditions are being lost. But we've got a home, a fire, food, so we are blessed.'

They sat quietly again, as they rhythmically weaved their stitches and thoughts.

Their bubble burst when the latch to the scullery door clunked and Selina heard the sounds of her father entering the house. The door to the room opened; Jemima was already on her feet, giving up the chair by the fire to her husband. He slumped into it without speaking.

'*Bokalo shan?* Would you like a slice of bread and scrape?' Jemima said, as she squeezed round the back of his chair to avoid stepping in front of him.

'I would that,' he said. '*Pariko toot.*'

Selina folded her work away and packed up the mending box.

'Your fella back from playing his schoolyard games yet?'

'Not yet Dad, I 'spect he'll not be long now.'

'Then he'll be off on his holidays with his chums leaving you and the kids. When's he off?'

'Next week. Down to London, I think; then Norfolk.'

Jemima passed him the plate. 'May you eat in health,' she said as they left him to wolf down the bread.

'I'll just cross t' yard then I'm heading *opre woodrus*. I've got a woodenly thick head,' he said.

Jemima followed her husband upstairs. Selina sat for a while watching the little jet of gas hissing out from a fresh lump of coal in the grate, then reached down for the pair of bloomers she had been reattaching the lace to.

At Victoria Station Rab said his goodnights and slung his bag over his shoulder and headed down the long flight of steps emerging into the bustle of Saturday night underneath the Wicker Arches. Women in shawls with large baskets, heading from their marketing, vied for seats on the next tram with railway passengers and grimy workers heading home. The first two trams went past before he finally got a seat up top; he found a damp blanket on a seat and pulled it over his knees.

When he got off the tram at the terminus there was a group of men outside the Wellington. One of them recognised him.

'Eh up Rab. Tha been playing? Tha win?'

Rab shook his head and rounded the corner into Alfred Road. His knee was by now painful to walk on and causing him to hobble as he crossed over Lake Street and through the gate into the back yard.

When Selina heard Rab's footfall her ears followed his progress in to the house. She heard the scullery door open and waited for the thump of the bag on the floor.

'You all right?' she said in a raised voice.

His head appeared round the door, 'Aye not bad love, 'cept we lost, but to be honest, I ain't bothered. Shouldn't have made us play in that – it were awful.'

'You need a wash? I've got some water on.'

'Well I've not had one, so that'd be good.'

Selina got to her feet. 'What about food: you hungry? There's some cold beef in a pot and some bread under the cloth in there.'

'No, I'm a'reight – I'll mebbes have summat before I turn in, but we had chops for us tea. I wouldn't say no to a cup of tea though.'

'You eat like you're at a banquet at the Cutler's Hall, you lot.'

'I'm sorry Lina, but we have to keep in shape,' he grinned as he posed like a prizefighter.

She left Rab sitting by the fire and went through to the scullery to get the bath off the hook; then she placed it in a space created by moving the rug. Using a tin jug she poured a little cold water into the bath first, followed by water from the kettle, saving some for a pot of tea which she placed on the floor next to the bath. Steam rose and was drawn up the chimney. Rab undressed and knelt at the side of the bath and dipped his head in, rubbing it with coal tar soap.

'You're right muddy; I'm not looking forward to dealing with your bag.' She scooped out some water with the jug, poured it on his head, then filled it again. 'When do you need your stuff for?'

Rab wiped his face with his hand. 'Don't think I'll need it till the weekend, when we go away.' He stepped into the bath and sat in the inch or two of water. 'George said I won't be fit for Monday's game and I think he's reight – mi knee's a bit sore from a tackle.'

'Does that mean we get to see you for Easter?'

'Yeah, looks like tha'll have to put up wi' me – I've been ordered to rest it.'

'I'll fetch you a towel.'

She sat with the towel on her knee watching him soap his legs.

'It's this knee here, it feels a bit swollen. Needs kissing better, but I wouldn't let George do that.'

His eyes flashed as he looked up at her and gave a broad smile.

Shaking her head, she pulled up her sleeves and took the soap off him and rubbed his white back. She worked away at his shoulders and down to the very bottom of his back. There was pleasure in getting things clean. Then she got the jug and poured it over him. He stood up, enlivened by her touch, unashamed, and wiped himself with his hands to get the worst off, then she rubbed him hard with the scratchy towel. He grabbed hold of her.

'Hey you're getting me wet, you chump.'

He burst out laughing and wouldn't let go. 'How's about kissing this knee better then?'

'Rab no, our Charlie's not back yet!'

'Oh he'll not be back for a while. Tell thi what I'll flip the bolt on the back door at least; then we'll have time.' She watched him tiptoe brazenly across the cold flag floor, and heard the bolt on the door to the yard grind shut.

Then he came back, pushed the bath to one side, replaced the rug and sat down on it in front of the fire. He pulled her body towards him.

Chapter 2

Rab didn't go with them to church the next day. He stayed in bed until late. He had slept badly. He was unable to get comfortable with his leg and Little Rabbi, as usual sleeping splayed out like a butchered duck, had deprived him of his share of the bed. No matter how many times he had shoved him over to his mother he had kept shifting back. So, when the others went down for breakfast he rolled over and slept. He had to steady himself against the wall when he eventually went down the stairs, and had to keep his left leg straight leading with his right in descent. He spent most of the day sitting doing nothing, his leg resting on another chair, worrying, and getting cross with his knee, or for a change of scenery sitting stretched out on the battered old horse hair couch in the window in the front room strumming his Spanish mandolin – although he soon tired of sitting on his own, ignored in that room, and it was cold without a fire. He would have to be more careful. He couldn't bear the thought of having to stop playing. He would not go back underground, and besides he wanted recognition: he wanted to win the English Cup, he wanted to play for England again, against Scotland, not just against bloody Ireland. And his time was running out.

He asked his mother-in-law whether she had anything to put on his knee to take the swelling away. She got some jam jars out and warmed up some bits of stick she called cat's foot with some chickweed in some wax and paraffin oil and wrapped it round his knee with some strips of rag. He sat out in the yard and smoked his cutty clay pipe listening to the clunk of a ball against the outside wall where the kids had scraped a wicket on the brickwork using a broken bit of pipe clay or, better still, one of their mums' donkey stones, if any of them dared to 'borrow' one. There was a lot of noise from the girls too, as they played skipping games; and then the arguments that followed as to how far away from the wicket they should stay. Little Rabbi would occasionally wander up to him and ask him to play and use his raised leg as a bridge to crawl under but would soon get bored of his dad's inaction and wander back out of the yard into the street to find the girls.

'That's what tha' bloody well gets for playing silly buggers' games,' Dennis said, stood over him, unshaven, shirt sleeves rolled up over thick, hairy arms, slopping tea from his cup onto the yard.

'It's just like any other job,' said Rab, 'down t' pit tha could just as easy get laid up: tha knows it just as well as me. How often are you having days off wi' bad backs, else ricked elbows or whatever, especially on Saint Mondays.'

'Tha cheeky bugger, hewing coal's a man's job; look around,' he said swinging his arm round, slopping tea again, 'this bloody place, *Chooreste-gav*, would grind to a halt; wi'out us we'd all starve or freeze t' death. Running around playing games does nowt for no bugger.'

'Fuck off! I shifted as much coal in a day as tha ever did, but never again. Tha can keep it. I addles good money; more 'n tha does. What I do is gi' poor buggers wi' nowt in their lives summat to look for'ads to on a Sat'day. When they're bored out of their heads at their hammers or trundling their carts about all week, they can escape; and they know even when they never come out on top agin their gaffers, and are ground into the dirt – they know their team could well win, and gi' 'em summat to shout about for a couple of hours. I get respect. Tha gets shitted on.'

'*Beng te lal toot!*'

'Don't tha devil me with thi Romany *rokkerpen*, or tha'll regret it.'

Selina heard these threats from behind the scullery door where she was getting the jam for tea. Such hard, cruel words! Words that cut, that hurt. Rab had come in and gone through to the front room; he had not seen her behind the door. She stood, not knowing what to do. Should she try to soothe her father's anger or her husband's? She went to the front room. Rab was sat in the window with his eyes shut as if nothing had happened. He didn't open his eyes as she approached.

'I wish you wouldn't speak to him like that,' she said.

Rab opened his eyes slowly and looked up at her unsmiling. 'He should keep his bloody trap shut then. He can't just let me be. Always judging folk he is. Never short of an opinion on others' business.'

'It's just his way.'

'Oh don't stick up for him! Didn't tha hear what he said?'

She stood not knowing what to say.

'I'd go for a walk to get out of the way if it weren't for this bloody knee!'

'Must you use such language on a Sunday – Easter as well?'

Rab closed his eyes again.

'I'll give your leg a rub down, see if it helps.' She went to get the ointment then knelt at his side, rolled up his trouser leg and worked the ointment into his knee; his muscular leg warm under her hands. She thought of Mary Magdalene going to the tomb with oils to anoint the body and then how the disciples had not believed her. That's men for you – always have to find out for themselves, make their own mistakes.

'You missed a lovely service this morning,' she said.

He opened his eyes. 'Best not walking too much yet. Following George's orders.'

The muscles round his knee slipped under her thumbs.

'Ah! that's the sore spot,' he said.

'Rab, why do you think that no-one recognised Jesus when he rose from the tomb?'

Rab grinned at her. 'Don't ask me. Per'aps 'cause it weren't him after all. I dunno.'

'Rab!'

'Well all that about him rising up into the clouds seems a bit far-fetched to me. Just as if he sailed up and the last thing they saw was his feet disappearing! Nah.'

Selina stopped and rolled his trouser leg back down. 'I wish you'd come to church more often Rab,' she said.

*

By Tuesday Rab was glad to be getting out of the house. Dennis and Charlie had left for work early; Rab had waited until they had gone before getting up. The two women hurried everyone out of the house, keen to get shut of them, the sooner to start their wash-day, delayed by Easter. The scullery was already steamy from the set pot, and the dolly tub, ponch and lumps of black-fissured soap were lined up. Rab left the house with the two girls heading for school; they kissed him and hurried hand in hand towards the bridge, and he went the other way onto Brightside Lane to get the tram in.

He got out at the bridge and walked up into town to get the tram from Moorhead – walking easier but still not right.

Most of the lads were already in the pavilion clubroom when he arrived.

'How were it yesterday?' he asked.

'Lost two one,' said Tommy. We could've done wi' thi as Freddie's shadow. He gets all over that un. 'I got the goal, not a bad un. Headed it in from long shot: Nudge were having a pop from twenty yards but I got on it – ball just trickled over past Massey, he should've had it by rights.' As he talked he made little half movements to illustrate the action. 'Their second goal were bad. There were this long pass that Bill rushes out to and he just missed it, clean missed it, over his head it goes right to Davis and he heads it down and it bobbled over the line.'

Rab wandered over to watch Bill and Needham at the billiard table. 'Catching practice today Bill is it?'

'Fuck off!' was the terse reply.

'All right Rab, how's thi leg?' said Needham.

'Not bad, had some of mother-in-law's gipsy magic on it.'

'What's that then?' said Bill, 'powdered hedgehog liver mixed wi' the blood of Christian babies?'

'Oh yeah summat like that, nice fat little bastards from Blackwell, I think they was. We goes out there special in the middle of the night and steals 'em from cradles. Makes us magic extra strong. Right little fat uns, Blackwell babies.' Rab patted Bill on the gut, then not knowing how, found himself upside down over Bill's shoulder and being swung round in the air.

'A'reight, I give in, tha wins, put us dahn!'

Waller came in and Rab was put the right way up, a bit dizzy. Bill smiled at George like a naughty schoolboy and straightened Rab out like a mother would to a child on the way out of the house.

'That'll do. You lot have got work to do. Cricket season doesn't start for you lot till after you get back from the tour. We're playing Clowne tomorrow in a charity match, then you've got six matches away starting in Luton on Saturday: early start from Midland station. Tommy will be captain for that game 'cause Ernest is playing for the English League against the Scotch. He'll join us after in London to play against Woolwich on Monday. They're no mugs, for a southern side, up and coming, we shouldn't underestimate 'em.'

'Yeah but there's not a southerner amongst 'em,' chipped in Needham.

'That's why they're not mugs. They could be a team for the future. Then we're up and down East Anglia wi' a match each day, finishing at the seaside in Lowestoft, where you'll get a nice fish supper after the game; some sea air.

'Plenty of goals if you don't mind, to entertain the paying customers, then back 'ere the following Sat'day. Mr Stokes is conducting the tour so it'll be bed by ten, and no mucking about – and best behaviour. You heard what he said about bringing in new players who want to win, he'll be keeping an eye on you on and off the pitch. Them's as don't impress won't be back in September. Right ho! Walking round the pitch, not fast, but not dawdling neither, till I say stop. I'll get you all weighed later. Off y' go. Rab, tha stay here.'

Everyone clattered out of the room.

'Trousers off and on the table Rab – let's see how tha's doing.' George felt round both knees and bent and unbent them several times. 'It's still not right, there's still fluid behind it at the back here. How's it to walk on?'

'Not bad, I've had a poultice on it and it's easing off.' Rab fastened his trousers and sat back up.

'Well tha's not playing tomorrow and I doubt tha'll be ready for Sat'day's game, there's no point in the cost of taking thi just for the train rides.'

'Aw George tha's not going to leave me here, I was looking for'ards to a little bit of sea air.'

'There's no point risking it Rab. We need thi for next season. Push this too hard now and who knows what'll happen. Gentle exercise, a mile a day to start with, on the flat, then build it up to two, then three and do a bit of hill work – get up to the woods or summat. Then when you're doing five no problem, then you start a bit of sprinting. I'll see thi when tha picks up thi money on Friday anyhow and then I'll have thi back here, what'll it be, the first Monday in May. We'll see how tha's doing but tha should be reight by then. We'll bring thi back a kipper. Go and do a couple of laps of the pitch nice and slow. We're not going to do much today. A bit of ball work after dinner. Tha can watch. Off tha goes.'

Rab went down the steps onto the cinder track round the pitch and set off walking. Needham caught up with him, then slowed down to his pace. 'What's the verdict Rab. Tha looks glum.'

'Yeah, Nudge. Got to stay here instead of coming on holiday wi' you lot. Serves me reight I s'pose. I'm going to be more careful, I ain't getting any younger: if I can stay out of trouble, tha's not seen the best of Rabbi Howell.'

'I believe thi Rab. Tha's right about staying out of trouble an' all. This is dangerous work. If tha breaks a leg tha's done for, and tha might be dead after. Tha's to show no fear but judge it right – get the ball or get the man but time it right and tha'll not overload muscles or joints. There was a kid got killed at Tamworth last week – read it in the paper, just from a heavy challenge.' They walked on a few paces. 'How was Easter anyhows?'

'Ah, not bad.'

'Me and Mary went to our cricket club ball Monday night – good do it were: all us players were in our whites, instead of us Sunday best – still had grass stains on mi knees from last year though!'

'I couldn't do owt wi' mi knee playing up but they looked after us I suppose – just a bit boring stuck in the house, and the little un pesters, and I wish I weren't stuck living in the same house as the in-laws.'

'I find it works well enough. More money coming in.'

'Tha's lucky, mine don't get on wi' me, I'm not good enough for their daughter. I don't have enough of a care for the old ways or summat; it's a bit the same wi' my own folks too. It's the little stuff as really gets yer though. It's how the father-in-law grunts like a pig when he takes snuff, and spits in the fire. It's nowt much but it makes me want to chuck. And the hairs growing out of his ears and nostrils!'

'Tha knows what's the worst thing is in living wi' the in-laws?'

'What's that Nudge?'

'Having a constant reminder of what yer lovely wife, what my Mary, will look like in thirty years time.'

'Oh don't! Bastard! – crozzled and bent and smoking a pipe! What's tha have to put that in my head for!'

'Cross mi palm wiv silver young sir!' he said with a smile and strode off.

After several laps round, and having been overtaken by everyone several times, and after a bit of a piggy back off Bill, George came out to keep an eye on things. 'Take a rest Rab,' he shouted from the steps of the pavilion. Rab didn't need asking twice. He sat down on a wooden bench by the pavilion, polished smooth by shuffling moleskin trousers, overlooking the ground. Steam and smoke rose up from the brewery and mingled over St Mary's Church, obscuring the tower intermittently; and just a bit further off started the edge of the forest of tall chimneys. The grass was looking good again. It was over three weeks since they'd used it and it was now a cricket ground and surprisingly peaceful – right next to the noisy town; this enclosure, this oasis: sweet like the feeling of dropping off easily to sleep even though life around you is shit. The only noise the crunch of cinders as those sportsman walked round; how could that be? He fingered his pipe in his pocket, ran his finger over Gladstone's clay nose, slid it back into his pocket and got up and wandered round the other side to the bowling-green. Happy Jack was out with his mower, tending his beautiful bit of grass, trundling up and down in stripes. Rab greeted him and Jack called back, 'First cut of the year Mr Howell, does y' good dun't it, knowing spring's here?'

'You could say that Jack but it's a long old wait for us – we're looking for'ards to September already.'

'Oh don't say that Mr Howell, it's going to be a lovely summer you see, and Her Majesty's coming soon, and the town'll be done up grand.'

Rab shook his head slowly.

There was a delivery cart outside the pavilion with a well-groomed chestnut horse. Rab, thinking it unattended, went over to take a look. As he got near a young man of around nineteen or twenty years bobbed up from where he was stooped at the rear of the horse.

'Morning!' he said, 'you took me by surprise sneaking up on us like that.'

'No, sorry, I wasn't… I didn't see you there, I just came to look at the horse.'

'He's got summat up wi' his leg I reckon.'

'Let's have a look. I know a bit about horses.' Rab felt the horse's leg and lifted its foot. As he bent over he became aware of a woman approaching: out of the corner of his eye he caught sight of a dark skirt and white apron coming over from the building.

'Is anything the matter Jim?' she said. She was a pale skinned woman in her early twenties with red hair tied at the back beneath a straw hat, a round face and lively eyes.

'This here gent's just looking at Parnell's leg – I thought he were limping a bit before. This is mi sister, Ada. Ada this is… sorry I didn't catch yer name.'

'Rab Howell, I play here – football. 'cept I'm not right now 'cause I've got a gammy leg like this 'un,' he said nodding towards the cart-horse.

'Is something wrong with him then? We can't do without him,' she said.

'I reckon, but it's nowt much, it's not bad yet but you'll need to see to it before it gets worse. See that sore there: gitts I think. He probably got a thorn in his foot or a bit of stone what's worked its way up, then got the gitts. You need to keep washing it wi' lots of clean cold water and strap on a poultice made of bread and crushed up Way Bread leaves, rat's tail some folks call 'em. If that don't do

25

the trick there's also some kind of ointment mi dad used, can't remember what were in it.' He then did a sort of bow, he didn't know why, and then felt colour rise in his neck.

'Sounds daft to me but I guess it's worth a try, before we call in the vet, eh Ada?'

'What are these leaves though; where do we get them?'

'They grow everywhere in the grass, like little mandolins they are, but wi' the strings on the inside, when you pull 'em up slowly the strings pull out, an little flowers like vestas in the middle.'

'I think I know the ones. We can't manage without Parnell, so it is worth a try,' she said. 'So you know about horses then Mr Howell?'

'Not really; well a bit. I was brought up wi' 'em sort of. Mi father did a bit of buying and selling.'

'So if we needed some of this ointment of yours, where would we get it?'

'I'd have to find out what it were first. They'll know at home. Ask for us down here if you like. They'll know when I'm in.'

'Well we deliver here regular, so if we need your ointment, Mr Howell, we'll ask for you.'

Rab looked at the cart – there was white writing on the green painted sides; he looked for clues as to what was on the back but couldn't see inside. He searched around for something to say next but nothing came. He smoothed the horse's flanks instead. The brother climbed onto the back of the cart and moved some boxes or crates around.

'So you play football Mr Howell?' Ada said.

'Yes Miss.' Again he tried to think of something else. '"cept I'm injured – but leastways it's the end of the season nearly.'

'So what will you do until it starts again?'

'Well we starts training proper again in August: until then nowt much – get fit again, fresh air and exercise, come down here a bit, that sort of thing.'

'Sounds like the life of one of those country gentlemen in a story.'

'Oh I don't know about that.'

'We ready then Ada?'

'Yes Jim, Sheaf House is the last one this morning.'

'See yer then, don't forget the lots of cold water bit as well as the poultice.'

'Perhaps see you again Mr Howell. Thanks for the advice.' She said and smiled at him.

Rab stood back as the young woman turned the horse round and climbed up onto the cart, took the reins, and headed up to Cherry Street; her brother lounging on the back. The tail-board was down and Rab noticed stalks of what looked like cauliflower on the back. Ah, a greengrocers then, that made sense. He watched them turn up onto Bramall Lane, then wandered back round to the front of the pavilion; Happy Jack still trundling on his straight green paths.

He looked across the ground, the morning's exercise was winding up, a few pigeons wheeled round looking for somewhere safe to land. He tried to imagine the stands full of noisy supporters but today it was hard to believe it was the same place. Perhaps Jack was right: pale watery sunshine was diluting the grey clouds – he'd get out on long walks, eat well, get fit – next season would be his best yet.

Chapter 3

Rab slotted himself into a new routine. He got out of bed when he felt like it; often it was after the girls had gone to school. Then not until getting out on the street would he decide whether to go left or right. He was more often than not drawn to the river and stood on the Abyssinia Bridge for a while. There was green on either side of the river, dotted with yellow of buttercups and patches of dandelions. But this was not a pure, cleansing, life-giving river like he played in in his boyhood. This was the Don – starting life as virginal rivers on the moors and then forced and sullied and abused by many fat dirty fingers before being discarded by Sheffield and handed over to Tinsley, only to be abused again and handed over to Rotherham. The river at Abyssinia was, through half-closed eyes, capable of an illusion of beauty, but no more than a whore seen from a distance whose illusion is created by make-up and lace and feathers. And she stank: she stank of humans, animals and machines, all mixing their filth, and blood and fluids in her waters. And her voice was ruined, not the light notes of clean waters, only a dull churning, accompanied by the constant rumble from the armour plate works, the low-pitch hammering of massive drop forges and the ringing manual blows of steel on steel drifting back up the river. He would then head away, to walk round the park or to walk along to Broughton Lane Bridge and along the canal, out to the green fields of Shepcote Lane or through Tinsley Park woods. When his walks got longer he would get Selina to pack him some butties and a bottle of cold tea and stay out the best part of the day or head back through Darnall to call in on his brother Charlie after his shift at the colliery.

Charlie Howell was four years older than Rab. He was the one who always looked out for Rab, the one person who Rab felt had any pride in what he did. Charlie had lent him status as a boy; he was Charlie's brother, so he was all right, he could join in the games: he might be small but he's a good little footballer, he can be on our team. Charlie made sure he got noticed when Ecclesfield were looking for players. Without Charlie he'd still be down the pit. Charlie defended him from the big ones: William and Wilhelmina were much older than Rab and Charlie, and he had always bracketed them as big ones with the adults; both worked and left home when he was young. They were still separate – they were both still in Ecclesfield near their parents and were like a different family. Charlie was the only person he had to advise him in life. Nudge was full of advice on the field, as was George on all matters sporting, but you couldn't tell them stuff in your head. He had lots of mates, you couldn't be a team unless you were mates, but Charlie was a friend and the only person who he could ask about private things, about head-stuff. Charlie was interested in him and asked him things that no-one else seemed bothered about; not just out of politeness but because he really wanted to know. He wanted to know what had gone on on the pitch and about the rest of the team and what they were all like; what Rab thought and felt. He got along to matches when he could, to watch Rab, but he struggled for money. Rab got him tickets, which he told him were free.

Sometimes he'd mistime his visits to his brother's and Charlie wouldn't be back yet so Eliza would be on her own: their little Clara being at work in a shop some afternoons since she'd turned twelve.

Eliza always seemed pleased to see him: he was her Charlie's brother, and he was a news-bringer. But Eliza had her good and bad days; she lacked energy, she was thin and pale and sometimes when her breathing was bad she didn't want to talk, and Rab just sat opposite her watching her concentrate on taking each slow breath with her eyes closed. She was a more wintry reflection of her sister. Rab had often been attracted to her as he had to Selina, they had shared the same essence, though something in Eliza had never grown as strongly, she was always the weaker stemmed of the two flowers growing side-by-side: but there had been something in that fragility. That former attraction though was now gone. What's going on at *Dei's tan*, she would ask, and Rab would tell her what he knew of her mother and Selina's routine, what they'd cooked for tea, if they'd bought any new clothes, what new words Little Rabbi was coming out with. He would praise the way they turned the girls out, always '*rinkeni*.' On these occasions, when she was ill, knowing that she didn't like to waste her breath on speech, he didn't say anything that called for a reply other than a nod or half smile. Charlie would then have to sort his own bath out. Once he was clean and dressed they might share a bit of tobacco twist, or Charlie would walk part way back with Rab, perhaps as far as Pot House Bridge or towards the aqueduct where they might go to the fried fish shop to get a greasy chip butty or stop for a drink and a game of shove ha'penny at the Pheasant.

They talked about Eliza and how hard Charlie was finding it, sometimes getting home to find nothing had been done around the house and no food ready; Clara could stay home but they'd miss her money coming in, small though it was.

'I think it's a blessing we've never had more than one. Besides her not being strong enough to bear 'em, I think looking after 'em would've been the death of her.'

'It's a pity Dennis and Jemima couldn't come and live wi' thi; tha'd be welcome to 'em.'

'That'd be the death of *me*. I'd rather struggle on ta.'

Rab grinned. 'But seriously, they oughta be where they're needed; we don't need 'em. I sometimes think they just want to keep an eye on us. They get Lina on their side and chip away at us and at her.'

'What's tha mean chip away?'

'It's like he's still working in his stall hacking away, bit by bit waiting for enough to go before they kicks away the spraggs, 'cept it's me, not the bloody seam. It's like they turn her agin us. They don't think I've got a proper job – and it's rubbed off on her. Tha's seen what it's like down at the Lane – they sing that they wish they were me. Thousands of people think I'm summat. I reckon, but for her folks, she'd look up to us too, but I just hands over mi money and that's it. And it's the same wi' the kids. They don't look up to their dad. I wish they could see us being cheered at the station. I could be doing owt for all they knew. Sweeping crossings or summat.'

'But she loves thi don't she?'

'Yeah of course, but I wonder sometimes exactly what it is. Is it really for mi own sake?'

'I'll switch places wi' thi then. I wish I had half the talent tha's got. Tha's an ungrateful bastard. Idolised, nice house, lovely kids, spend all day laiking about.' Rab knew he wasn't angry with him, he was just trying to provoke him into seeing things from his perspective.

'I know, I'm sorry Charlie, but if I can't talk to thi, who can I talk to. Anyhow I started off worrying about thi and Liza and Clara.'

'We can manage. We don't need the in-laws. And besides we've no room for 'em. Anyhow, now summer's coming she'll be better, it's the cold that makes it worse… and when she gets the influenza or summat.'

'At least they could pop round and help her out a bit though. Poor Liza seems to miss 'em.'

'Ah that's true enough, when she's bad she can't get very far.'

'We see the other members of the Smith tribe often enough: always round, but it's like they expect them to come to our place all the time. I'll have a word and see if they can't come over to help out a bit.'

'Thanks Rab. That'd be good for her. She natters to neighbours in the yard but tha knows what it's like, she's always a bit wary of folks knowing too much about where she's from. Right I'd better be heading a-gatewards. I'll be seeing thi Rab.'

'I'll pop round again soon.'

As the days warmed into May, the city started to develop a collective obsession: every citizen thinking about the approaching visit of their monarch. On payday Rab headed up into town on his way to the Lane. A small crowd was round the monolith and there was a certain excitement rippling through them. Up on the steps, a man was addressing the crowd:

'..our Christian brothers the Armenians being slaughtered, Crete blockaded, and what do we do about it? I'll tell you. Nothing. We stand by and let it happen. Our imperial might, our military system propping up tyrants, not freeing the oppressed. Instead of rising up and demanding change all we are bothered about here in this unpretentious, industrious, no-nonsense city is dressing ourselves up with tawdry decorations and frills, spending thousands of pounds to make ourselves look stupid, like putting a silk hat on a collier at the pit head. Instead that money could feed the children of the poor.'

One man shouted "'ere 'ere!" only to have his neighbour knock his hat off him in response and pushing and shoving started before a policeman pushed through the crowd and pulled away the speaker from the steps of the monolith and the crowd melted away.

The town hall entrance was hidden behind canvas, Rab didn't know why, and town was busier than usual with workmen unloading timber and constructing stands, and arches being erected at various positions. It certainly seemed that a great deal of money was being spent. Sheffield was being done up like a shop window at Christmas.

He picked up his wage packet. Pinned to it was an envelope. There was his name written on the front: "Howell" he could recognise. He opened it, inside was a single sheet of paper with several lines of writing on it. At the bottom was A..d..a, – Ada! He quickly stuffed it inside his jacket. He went to chat with the others about the tour and interrogated them on who had played well and who had disappointed. He couldn't ask any of them about the letter.

'I saw this fella get arrested outside the Town Hall earlier.' Rab said to Bill. 'He were going on about how this Jubilee's a waste of money and summat about Armenians being slaughtered.'

'I dunno about Armenians but he's reight that it is a waste of money, what's going on, I'd say. There's nowt wrong wi' a bit of a parade but she don't need no more spending on her – it's all so as them toffs can show off to the rest on us. Ain't that reight Nudge?'

'What's that then?'

'I was just saying, spending all that money so that toffs can show off in front of the Queen ain't reight. I'd say they've spent enough on building t' Town Hall, never mind sprucing it up even more.'

'Tha'll get carted off to t' Tower!' Needham said.

'I told him Nudge, that the police carted off this bloke that was spouting off at folks outside t' Town Hall.'

Needham sat on the arm of a chair. 'I'd say it's more about taking pride in the city. Showing a bit of respect and honouring a queen that's served sixty years and has overseen a vast improvement in her country. It's about showing a bit of loyalty to the nation – showing her that us northerners are as much a part of the nation as London.'

Bill started a rendition of "Rule Britannia" on an imaginary trumpet as Needham was finishing speaking and got a clip round his ear as a reward.

George kept them all behind in the club-room. Mr Stokes wanted a word before they departed. When the Tooth-yanker entered the room he was closely followed by Mr J B Wostinholm, once Joseph to his mother – club secretary, stockbroker, freemason, Sunday school teacher, overseer of the poor of twenty years standing, believer in bricks, frequent guest of the Lord Mayor, after dinner raconteur; and unbeknownst to him, known by others in the room as "the Philanthropist," though some of them didn't know what it meant and assumed it meant something like "miserable bastard." Their entry was accompanied by the scraping of chairs and the rapid tailing away of conversations. The two committee members went and stood with their backs to the fireplace as though to warm their backsides even though it wasn't lit.

'Gather round please gentlemen,' George said, taking up a place near to the two bearded officials, though not too close, half with them and half with the players as if wanting to be afforded recognition by both: authority, but still one of the lads. The team gathered, some staying seated and some leaning against their seats.

Stokes spoke first. 'Congratulations again on a successful tour. The splendid reception we were afforded everywhere we went was a testament to your sporting prowess and gentlemanly conduct. I was proud, proud indeed, to lead you. I do not believe even a team of gentlemen players could have had a better reception. You were a credit to the professional ranks of the game. You now have the summer to recuperate and to get in shape for next season's challenge. Not all of you will remain with us and to those players we extend our gratitude for their service to the club, we will part on good terms and we wish them well in the future. They will be notified individually of our decision after the committee has met to discuss our plans for next season. Mr Wostinholm would also like a word.'

Rab's mind was elsewhere. He felt unsettled. The letter in his pocket presented him a problem and anxiety; but to receive a letter was novel and made him want to hold his head a little higher.

Eyes turned to the Philanthropist, stood with his thumbs in the waistcoat pockets of his Irish tweed suit, his patriarchal eye surveying the room of followers. 'I add my own tributes to those paid by Mr Stokes, not only for your conduct as ambassadors of this club whilst on tour, but also for the season past. We hope for even better next season. To encourage you in that endeavour we shall be discussing at the committee the arrangements for a bonus pot to be shared out at the season's end, based on the matches won.'

There were one or two nods of approval round the room which his roving eye sought out. 'You are reminded that you must not engage in any behaviour which may bring the club into disrepute. If you must drink, though you would do wise to abstain entirely, you shall only do so in moderation; as in all things, moderation. You shall not pursue any sporting activities, other than those approved by the Committee. Cricket is acceptable.' Needham and Foulke nodding. 'Engaging in any football for entertainment purposes is not. You should not need reminding that any player engaging in exhibition matches will be brought before the committee and dismissed. You are still being paid to do a job even though you have no matches for a while. Part of that job is to keep fit, eat healthily and rest, no late nights. Mr Waller will direct you. We will find out should you stray; so be warned.'

Rab wondered about asking someone in the street to read the letter to him. If he chose the right person they wouldn't know him or his name; an elderly lady perhaps. What about Charlie? It would likely just be about the horse, but he didn't need Charlie's advice which would surely follow.

The Philanthropist ended with some remark about her Majesty, and the splendid celebrations and looking forward to their return in August in fine fettle.

They ate together, beef and onions followed by stewed rhubarb – Rab wondered whether it had been delivered fresh that morning.

After dinner he poked his head round the kitchen door and spoke to the cook. 'Nice bit of rhubarb that Mrs Meeks. Where d'y get it from?'

'What's d'y mean where do I get it from? From a shop, it don't grow in the corner of the pitch does it.'

'I mean which shop. I might get a bit for my missus to make a pie.'

'We get all our fruit and veg from McGrail's on Bridge Street.'

'Ta missus.'

He walked back up to town up South Street. All the way up to Moorhead, shops were readying themselves for royalty. A man was busy boarding out his small front garden raised above street level and enclosed by iron railings. Rab had obviously looked at the man a bit queer because he explained: 'perfect viewing platform this'll be – half a crown a person – that's got to be worth at least a guinea, don't y' reckon?'

'Dare say it'll be an even nicer harvest than them plants you're crushing leastways!' Rab said laughing.

As he headed down towards the river he had the idea of just going round to McGrails' shop on the off chance: that way he could bluff his way round the letter. Should he? Nowt to lose he thought and went left after the Old Town Hall instead of heading over the bridge. He wandered along Bridge Street past a cart laden with castings, its horse straining, its driver cursing, looking out for a greengrocer's shop and spotted what might be it as he turned the bend in the road. There was a shop with a green awning and a trestle outside and, as he got nearer, he saw it displayed bunches of carrots, spring cabbages and a box of gooseberries. An archway at the side led through to a yard at the back. He looked back, but carried on and walked purposefully past the shop. Then down the street he stopped when he got past the row of shops and the pub. There were hissing sounds on the other side of the brick, factory wall behind him and he felt the deep queasy vibrations travel up through him as the machinery worked on metal. He walked back again and feigned to look at the cabbages and tried to see inside the window but couldn't make out if anyone was in. A woman came to the open doorway of the shop with her arms folded across her fierce bosom, grey hair tied up behind her head.

'Can I help you sir?' Irish, Rab thought. Could be the mother.

'I came to see if Miss McGrail was in,' he replied, then immediately wished he had just bought a cabbage.

'And which one of them will you be wanting, if you don't mind me asking?' she said.

'Er, Ada, missus.' He was being given the eye, so he had to explain. 'I, er, gave her a tip about her horse a fortnight since, and I thought I ought t' see if he was a'reight now.' She looked down on him from the step.

'Oh did you now. Well you'd better come through, so you did. She's out the back boxing up.' He followed her as she shuffled inside. 'I said it were mad, so I did, bread and weeds on a horse, whatever next. Whether it were that I don't know, but the old lad seems to be better for it, so he does. Ada! Young gentleman to see you! That horse magician.'

Rab went through. The woman stood at the side of a door opening in to the yard from the back of the shop. She still had her arms folded as he sidled past her with an unrequited smile. 'Thanks missus.'

Ada appeared into the yard from another doorway. She was wearing a full-length apron and had her sleeves rolled up. Her red hair was uncovered and her cheeks glowed healthily from her exertions.

'Mr Howell, if I had known you were coming…' she said, looking down at her garments, a little embarrassed.

He held his hand out. 'Good afternoon miss.'

She half stuck her hand out in response, then pulled it away and showed him the palm covered in dirt. 'Potatoes,' she said.

Rab kept his hand out. 'Dun't matter miss.' She took it – her hand was cold.

'Been scrubbing 'em ready for sale tomorrow,' she said, 'They fetch a ha'penny a pound more scrubbed.'

He patted the breast of his jacket. 'I got your letter today when I called in for mi money, thought I'd stop by on mi way home to see how your horse were doin.'

'It's kind of you to think of us. As I said in the letter it seems to have healed over. Do you want to have a look?'

She went to the back of the yard and Rab followed her into the small stable. A pleasing, warm smell of animal and hay filled the space. The horse was stood at the back and the large treacle eyes turned to see who had entered. Rab greeted him with a slap on his flank and stooped to look at his hoof. 'How long've the bandages been off?'

'Not long – a few days. We did as you said – got the weeds as mother called 'em from a bit of grass when we were delivering to the Drill Hall at Hyde Park.'

'I went there for a bit. I were in the Hallamshire Rifles. But I were chucked out 'cause I were too tall for 'em.'

Ada laughed and Rab noticed how her face wrinkled at the corners of her eyes, and dimples appeared in her cheeks.

'Looks like it's healed over nicely to me. Keep an eye on it though. I found out what tha needs if it comes back: make up an ointment by warming marshmallow root in a bit of pig fat and keep it smeared on.'

'Much obliged to you Mr Howell.'

'Call me Rab. All mi mates do.'

'Thank you Rab. Mother said Parnell wouldn't get better with weeds but I reckon there's something in your remedy.'

'My folks've allus had a way wi' horses, I s'pose, passed down from old. Why's he called Parnell, odd name for a horse.'

'Oh that was my dad, God rest him, he called him that, an Irish thing.'

'Oh, I'm sorry, I didn't…'

'No, it's fine. Just me and Jim, who you met, and my sister to help mother out now.'

They wandered back into the yard.

'You going to be making money out of this here Jubilee then, everyone else seems to be?'

'I doubt it – we're losing a day's trade on the day – no one'll be coming here and we won't be able to deliver even if folks wanted us to. No one'll be able to move round here. We might make a few bob in supplying the Jubilee parties in a few weeks though. They say the town's going to look a treat when it's ready, lights everywhere, flags, and those arches going up! I'm looking forward to seeing it, if I can find someone to take me.' She looked him straight in the eyes.

'Yeah, you're right, a lot of work's going into it.' Something surged in his chest. 'I could take you if you like.'

What had he said that for? Like a stupid kid blushing in front of some girl in plaits, sat on a gate swinging her legs as she spoke.

'Thank you, I'd like that very much. They say the night before will be the best. I'll finish 'ere about eight; there's no half day closing on the Thursday,' Her cheeks had flushed. He recalled stories from his boyhood, sat around the fire, about princesses long ago whose skin was so fair that you could see red wine go down their throats when they drank.

'I'll meet you this side of Lady's Bridge about eight then.'

'You can go out this way – see you next week!'

She showed him to the little door inside the large yard door leading straight onto the street. He was glad she had spared him going past the bosom. He smiled and touched the brim of his cap and she closed the gate behind him. What was he thinking of? He couldn't accompany a woman round town. Bloody fool! He'd have to find a way out.

Chapter 4

Selina had done the cleaning and ironing and her mother had taken Little Rabbi out to the park – he'd been getting under their feet all morning, and on top of that had become tired and fractious but would not lie down for a nap. Selina needed the time to work on the girls' dresses. They were not good enough to wear to Norfolk Park next week, they were a bit short for one thing. What if the Queen herself should see them paraded in front of her; they had to be perfect and no one was to look down their noses at her girls. She needed two yards of white muslin, some white braid or lace, and their hats could be made to look new with a bit of gluing of the brims and a bit of crisp satin ribbon, pale blue or lilac. She got down a small tin off the top shelf in the scullery, and took out two shillings, carefully hiding the tin away again. Whilst standing on the stool she checked the jar containing lime flowers, she was still feeling nauseous despite the lime flower tea she had been sipping that morning – there was still plenty in the jar, enough to last until the trees flowered again in a few weeks. They would have to get out and collect elderflowers – they would be out already – she wondered if she could find time that afternoon to head up towards the woods. Fresh elderflower tea would do her good – perhaps that would work better than dried lime. As she was pulling her shawl around her shoulders and pinning her hat on a brief panic hit her – what if it was typhoid? She had heard that a young girl on Windmill Street had died, it was doing the rounds again. No, she would have been feverish by now, and she had no other symptoms other than an odd taste in her mouth. She could get some liquorice root. Another thought stayed at the back of her mind that she might soon be buying linseeds for making linseed tea.

As she headed back along Brightside Lane from the shops she

couldn't get the thought of fresh elderflowers out of her head. She could smell them: their sweet musty scent; the tiny beetles crawling around on them; she felt sure that they would calm her stomach. That metallic taste: was it in the air – the taste of engines and metal dust swept over the wall from Brightside sidings? Hot sweet flowery tea would purify. She would wander up to the edge of the wood and get some. She hurried from the ringing of metal in the works on one side; under the bridge as it threatened to collapse in with the rumbling train overhead, and out into Upwell Street where there definitely was a taste in the air from the chemical works and the gas works. The air cleared past St Thomas's and the first green things came into view, past the graveyard and up to the wood's edge.

Looking back, chimneys, joining earth with sky, stretched away, and the noise of the city was a constant drone, an orchestra of sounds of metal on metal, and metal on stone; instruments she imagined played by half-naked men, powered by black rocks dug out by wholly naked men, like her menfolk somewhere under the ground over there beyond the smoke. It was a horror and magnificent: brains, toil, heat, sweat, motion turning rocks into knifes, guns and ships. Mastery of the mysteries of fire and earth by tender flesh. She felt warm and adjusted her shawl.

She found the bush she had sought with its hundreds of little creamy lace flowers crowded together so much that you couldn't appreciate them individually as you should. She pulled off a dozen, exactly, and put them at the bottom of her basket underneath the paper containing the trimmings for Lizzie's and Little Selina's dresses. She had wasted enough time and hurried back.

When the girls burst through the door, home from school, Selina was sat serenely with one of the best china cups sipping sweet flower tea, deciding how best to arrange the ribbon around their straw hats and how big a bow to have.

'Mummie, Mummie – look what we've got!' they chorused.

'We've got medals!' said Lizzie.

'They're from the Queen!' said Little Selina.

'They're not from her! They're to wear when we sing for her!'

'We're going to get buns!'

'And lemonade!'

'And we're going to wave little flags!'

'We've been practising today!'

'We've been singing "There's no Place Like Home" and "Rule Britannia." It's ever so hard! All those words!'

'Look they've got writing on them!'

Selina had got to her feet and had a daughter under each arm, but they were not to be stilled. She was passed both medals to admire. 'Well it's a good job I chose blue ribbons for your hats – it will match quite nicely. What do they say then, read them to me.'

This was Lizzie's job. She read the words slowly, 'In comm… er… comm…enting of the the loving welcome given by the children of Sheffield..'

'That's us!' piped in Little Selina.

'Shut up Lina! …to Queen Victoria in Norfolk Park, Sheffield, May 1897. 1837 Diamond Jubilee 1897.'

'How far is it to Norfolk Park, Mummie? We're going to have a ride on a tram!'

'I've never been before,' said Selina, 'I think it's where the Lord Mayor lives, the Duke of Norfolk, so I dare say it's very grand.'

The door opened and Little Rabbi rushed in, not wanting to miss whatever was causing the excitement, and leapt at his mother's apron.

The full account of the medals had to be gone through again for the benefit of their grannie.

'Sing us one of your songs then.' Jemima said.

Little Selina and Lizzie stood side by side, and the two girls for whom a tram ride to Sheffield was a great adventure, and neither of whom had been further, sang about roaming amid pleasures and palaces and when they came to singing 'Home! Home! Sweet, sweet home!' truly meant it.

Rab heard their voices as he walked up the yard; he stopped short of the window and listened. They sang, "Give me them with the peace of mind dearer than all," and finished with "there's no place like home!" He couldn't go in yet; he shuffled back intending to walk once more round the block, but, as he turned, Dennis and Charlie came through the gate.

41

'A'reight Den, Charlie, just got back misen,' he said turning back again as nonchalantly as he could. They looked at him and acknowledged him before following him in the house. Little Selina and Lizzie then had the whole excitement to go through again. 'Daddie, Granda, look what we got!'

Rab went into the front room with the girls whilst pit muck was washed off hair and backs, and stew and dumplings were warming on the range.

'Daddie, will you be able to come and see us sing to the Queen? We're going to Norfolk Park on the tram!' Lizzie asked.

'Well you'll be getting two trams actually because the rails don't go all the way through town, so you'll have a walk in between. Norfolk Park's not far from where I go to train and play football.'

'Do you know the Duke, Daddie?' said Little Selina.

He laughed. 'No but I have met Mr Ellison, "the Squire" we call him, he looks after the Duke's estate for him. He's almost as important as the Duke and 'as the big 'ouse in the park. He's the President of Sheffield United.'

'So will you be there Daddie?'

'Yes I'll try and make it. I've got another idea too. How about going into town to look at all the decorations?'

They squealed. 'Oh can we? What are they like?'

'Well there's lots of grand archways and banners being put up and lights and stuff. Go and see what you mother thinks. She could come too.'

They squeezed round the table as usual for their tea, their relative ages having no bearing on their height at the table, the girls high up on stools and Charlie set back a bit lower down on the Windsor chair. Little Rabbi, wearing one of his sisters' old dresses, sat on the rug, clutching his wooden boat with a small bowl in front of him, the potatoes getting prodded by the prow of the boat. Occasionally he'd get up and selectively bother the grown-ups for attention or extras in his bowl. At the table the adults were animated.

'It's all very well having a day off but how's a working man s'posed to pay for *chobben* for his family; a man's not an ostrich and can't eat nails!' said Dennis. 'And there's no work Saturday neither, so some folk'll go wi'out their Sunday dinners thanks to her Majesty!'

'Oh Dad don't blame her! She's done nothing but good for this country; look how much better things are even in our lifetime. It's the bosses that should be paying their men, they can easy afford to pay the holiday.'

'Selina's right Den,' said his wife. 'There's a bargain struck: on your side you give up Heaven's free air, and sweat, and on their side they give you enough to live off. Any less than that and it ain't right.'

'Aye tha's reight, it's only what's our due,' said Dennis. 'But they won't give up wi'out a fight. They're running scared, the Miners' Federation's demanding eight-hour days, and they know how bloody minded we can be, we showed 'em four year ago.'

'But look where that got us! Only Rab's money coming in for four month. Poor buggers living on thieved scraps o' turnips and handouts.'

'But they didn't beat us.'

Rab, who was never early into these teatime discussions, chipped in: 'if we bide our time things'll change, folks say that we're coming to the end of an era don't they?'

There was a silence for a while with just Little Rabbi mithering his mother and the sounds of cutlery on crockery. Rab had expected this to start a new thread of conversation, but it took Selina to say, 'Well, she's made it to sixty years and I don't s'pose she can go on much longer.' There were nods and sighed consent. Jemima got the teapot and poured out more tea.

'She won't die before we can sing to her will she?' said Little Selina.

'Nay lass. Reckon she'll be reight for a few more years!" Dennis said smiling.

'Oh good. I would be very sad if she didn't come because she was dead.'

'Ay, it would put a bit of a damper on t' party!' said Rab.

'Dad said he'd take us to town to see the decorations Grannie. Have you seen 'em yet?'

'No I haven't lass, I've not been up to town for a while. Reckon we'll save it for the day itself, make it more of a surprise.'

'Will you and Granda come and see us singing?' said Lizzie

'We're not sure Lizzie. We'd get lost in the park and we probably wouldn't see you and might not even get close enough to see the Queen. They say there'll be thousands of children and then there's grown-ups on top of that. We might be best going and seeing her open the new Town Hall.'

'But hasn't it been open for ages?' said Lizzie.

'It has,' said Rab, 'but she's going to do it official. They're doing summat fancy to it, so I've heard, 'cause it's all hidden behind canvas so as no one can see what's going on. And what she'll do is open it wi' a special key – she won't even get out of her carriage.'

'How can that be then? Doesn't she need to turn the key in the door to open it?' said Lizzie.

'No, it's like a magic box, all electric; so they give her this box, she puts the key in and the gates open by electric too, that's what I heard.'

'I don't understand this electric stuff,' said Jemima, 'I don't see how as they'll make the trams go without horses. Not sure I'd feel safe.'

'But that's what I mean about everything changing. Don't y' think it's exciting?'

'Well I think it's a worry.'

'Hey talking o' decorations have you heard what they're doing at Cammell's?' said Charlie.

'Is the Queen going there too?' asked Selina.

'Yeah, it's to show her steel plate being rolled,' said Dennis.

'Anyhow, they're laying turf all along the sides of the road her carriage will go into the works on, and they're planting flowers and bushes, and hiding all the coal carts and stuff! What d'y think to that!' he said slapping the table edge and laughing.

'So she'll think that Cammell's looks like the Botanical Gardens! I s'pose we'll be hanging lace curtains at the pit head next!' Dennis roared.

'And roses growing on the colliery tip to hide the stench!' added Charlie.

'Well I think it sounds nice!' said Little Selina, who often spent hours in the summer decorating the back yard with heads of dandelions and daisies arranged in rows and circles. 'I think they should make it look pretty with daisy chains!'

The conversation drifted, as so often it did, to reminiscences of country lanes, fields, and family, and food. To the girls, talk of eating and sleeping outdoors was magical. The stories swirled round in their heads with those they heard at school and church of the Israelites in their tents, and quails, and manna from heaven.

Selina was bemoaning not having eaten freshly caught rabbit for a long time, and Dennis was praising trout straight from the river.

'There was this little river we used to stop by with a deep pool, and when I was younger it was my job to go up the river and bring back trout for tea.'

'*Shoonta!* You can keep your trouts and rabbits. I don't care what anyone says, the finest meat, given to us by *Kooshto Dooval*, given to us and not the *gorgie*, is the *hotchiwitchy*!' said Jemima. She had slapped her trump card down on the table and paused to let the effect settle. Lizzie wanted her to go on. 'Tell us the riddle, Grannie!'

'As I was walking down the lane the other day, I met a man coming through the hedge with pins and needles on his back. Who was he?'

'The hotchiwitchy!' shouted Lizzie.

'Hedgehog!' shouted Little Selina.

'That's right!'

'And did you really eat them Grannie?'

'Yes lass, that we did. Lovely they are too, roasted or boiled.'

'I've never seen a hedgehog Grannie. Can you buy them in the shops?' said Little Selina.

'*Ei!* No lass. Given to us free they are. Us old folkie know how to catch them – how to spot their nests. You take a long stick and crawl him out. Then you toss him on the fire and get all his prickles off. Then you cuts him open along his back and give him a good wash. Then you sprinkle lots of salt and pepper in him and roast or boil him.'

'I'm not sure I like the sound of that!' said Little Selina, 'I like pork best.'

'Tha takes after me lass!' said Rab. 'Nice bit o' pork belly or a slice o' cold bacon. Better than tough old hedgehog!'

'You've never had one o' mine that's for sure!' said Jemima.

'No that I ain't, but I dare say they're much of muchness. The worst one was this stuff I remember as a boy. I remember having to collect snails for mi mother and she would boil up this milky stew wi' 'em and make us all eat it until there were none left!'

'Snails, yuk!' said Little Selina.

'*Bourri-zimmins!*' said Jemima. 'It's delicious! I don't know what Grannie Lizzie did with it but your Great Grannie Lizzie, your Mummie's grannie put special herbs in it to make it nice. You also had to starve the snails a bit before you cooked 'em. That's the trick!'

'Tell us where Mummie was born,' said Lizzie; and she listened in a reverie to the tale she had heard many times about how it was a cold winter and how their Granda had stayed up all night holding up the tent to stop the blankets blowing away because the stones weren't enough to hold them down in a gale, and how they'd had to go and live in a farmer's barn where her mother was born on the straw. Lizzie pictured her mother in a manger.

After tea Rab plucked his pipe out of his jacket and announced he was taking Mr Gladstone for a walk. 'Lend me a bit o' tobacco for my own *swegler*, will you love?' said Jemima. At least she had the decency to only smoke indoors he thought.

He wandered down to the bridge; a young couple pulled apart on hearing him approach and sauntered off. He turned Mr Gladstone round to look him in the eye – he looked back sternly – and ran his thumb over the chipped nose. Then he filled the inside of his head with bits of leaf ripped off the tobacco twist which he then screwed back up and shoved into its leather pouch. Cursing, he wasted several vestas before it took. He was alone on the bridge. Just him and Mr Gladstone. He took the letter out of his pocket and looked at the writing. It said something about the horse but there was a pageful of words. He thought of her smiling at him in the yard, her hands covered in muck, her red hair tied up showing the pale skin on her neck. He drew on his pipe, the tobacco glowed and he shut his eyes, and leant against the wooden parapet. He should just throw the letter in the river to add to all the other shit and remnants of lives down there and just go home. Back to Selina and the girls with their beautiful smiling faces and their innocence and their joy at all the little things. And Rabbi, his fat little arms, who he'd take to the rec and teach to run with a ball so that they'd not be able to turn *him* down; who he'd watch from the stand as he played against Scotland. He went back over teatime in his mind and the talk of the old ways, an image of Dennis' pot-sitten face and Jemima's eyes drilling holes into you.

He tucked the letter in his pocket and wandered back as the light faded around him and cool air blew up the river.

*

The evening they had set to go to town arrived. The girls had put on their dresses and hats and woollen shawls. Rab wore his match-day suit. Little Rabbi was left behind with his grannie.

The girls were beside themselves when one of the new trams, crimson with gold decorations, approached the Wellington terminus and was turned round.

'Can we go outside Daddie, please?' said Little Selina.

'You'll catch cold Lina,' said her mother, 'we'll go inside.'

'She'll be 'reight, there's rugs,' said Rab. 'I'll go up wi' 'er.'

Selina threw him a look which said "how dare you interfere."

Little Selina pleaded to Rab with her big brown eyes, he looked towards Selina but she was already heading inside holding Lizzie by the hand. He nodded towards the ladder and she almost skipped up it. She sat at the front and Rab got a rug and threw it over her but she pushed it off and he compromised with it over her legs. Leather creaked and the horses right below them strained and got them underway. She snuggled under his arm.

'It's very high up,' she said. 'Is Mummie cross?'

'Don't worry,' he said. 'Look, that horse on the left it's just like the one that pulled your Grannie's *vardo*, her wagon.

'Who? Grannie Jemmie?'

'No Grannie Lizzie, my mother, don't you remember seeing the *vardo* looking all sad and abandoned in the field round the back of theirs?'

'No.'

'I suppose it's a while since you've been.'

He pointed out the river before they went under the railway viaduct and came out on the other side; on and on past vast black buildings towering like mountains over them. Deep inside the mountains the sounds of war being fought, thumping and squeezing metal according to man's will. Little Selina snuggled closer.

'These're the biggest steelworks in the world Lina. Queen Victoria wouldn't have an empire wi'out 'em. That's why she's comin here – over there that's Cammell's – where they're making it look pretty for her wi' grass and whatnot.'

'I'm glad they are, it's too horrid for a queen.'

Rab laughed.

Then they turned a corner into the long straight stretch of Saville Street and Little Selina gasped. Decorative masts stretched away on both sides of the road with garlands draped between them and they were heading under a canopy of flowers and huge crowns, and there were real flowers growing in baskets on the masts, and union jacks and banners and bunting.

'Look that's the way into Cammell's,' said Rab.

Little Selina laughed at the decorations on the front, of camels and battleships.

They went in to the tunnel of flowers.

'Read the banners to me eh?'

'Welcome to … Victoria … Queen and … Emperors.'

'That one?'

'She has …worried? … her people lasting good.'

Rab laughed.

'Look Daddie, little pictures of the Queen!'

'What does that one say?"

' "Our steel…shell … guard and loyal heave-ets shall praise," I think. And that says "God Save the Queen!"'

Rab laughed again.

Little Selina squealed as they approached Wicker Arches draped in red cloth and streamers, with decorated shields and banners and flags. As they emerged on the other side there were more masts and garlands and flags and Japanese lanterns and pennants in blue and gold hanging from the tops of buildings.

Little Selina was nearly popping, it was so far beyond anything in her experience and had forgotten her fear of how high up she was so that Rab had to hold her down to stop her jumping up and risking falling off.

'That says "Well Played! 60 not out!"'

'That's like in cricket – when tha gets sixty runs they say tha's sixty not out, and she's been going sixty years.'

She wasn't paying any attention: she was just trying to make sure she saw everything.

When the tram stopped at the bridge Little Selina couldn't wait to get down to tell Lizzie all about it. 'Oh you should've been on top, we went right underneath!'

Rab got another look to reinforce how irresponsible he had been.

'Which way shall we go?' he said.

'I don't mind. It's up to you,' she replied.

'Shall we go straight up in to town girls? Let's go this way then,' he said.

The girls headed over the bridge hand in hand.

'Does that suit Lina?' he said, 'or would you rather…'

'Whatever you think,' she said. 'Stay close girls, it's very busy. I don't want you to get lost.' She went and took their hands leaving Rab to follow.

The ostentatious decorations started again when they regained what would be the royal route. Every now and then they passed a working man heading home in moleskin or corduroy, with neckcloths tucked into buttoned jackets or waistcoat fronts. Some would greet Rab with an 'Eyup Rab!' or 'How Do!' or 'A'reight Rab.' Rab would just nod at them politely.

'Who are those men Dad?' Lizzie turned to ask.

'Dunno, just football supporters,' he replied.

Reassured and unimpressed Lizzie went back to her sightseeing. The girls stood open-mouthed as they looked up at the blue and purple velvet and silk canopy arching over the roadway on top of gilded columns with golden cherubs holding a crown. Rab too was amazed at the transformation since he had last been through town just a few days earlier. There was if anything too much to appreciate it all; after a while it was like a large spread put out on a table at a club fundraising do – by the time you got to your pudding you just didn't take as much pleasure in it as you would have if you'd had your pudding first. It would be nice to see it at night – all lit up by the lights. Selina was holding tightly on to the girls' hands. She seemed less vexed now but her focus was on them – he might as well not be there following them around. When had she last walked proudly at his side holding on to his arm.

'Look at Coles' love, ain't it done up lovely?'

'Yes,' Selina replied.

They stood and looked up at the flowers draped all over the shop, crimson cloth edged with gold along the lines of windows, and shields with flags behind them in between the windows.

'Look at those flags!' said Little Selina pointing to the top of the building. 'That's our one, but what's that other one with the stripes Daddie?'

'I think it's the American one Lina,' he said.

'And look at that pretty crown on the top – it's like diamonds!'

They went up Fargate, Rab still following behind, weaving their way round other people who were not looking where they were going either, and past carts of traders trying to do business as normal despite everything. Tall columns like in lithographs of ancient temples lined the street, linked together with real ivy; more shields and flags, and topped with wreaths. Banners stretched over the street and the shops competed with each other like ladies descending from their carriages to attend a reception at the Cutler's Hall.

Lizzie and Little Selina discussed their favourite buildings. Lizzie went with the Albany Hotel and Yorkshire Penny Bank with its flowers and a large crystal at the centre with words over it, which she read out: 'God Bless our Queen.' Little Selina chose Mappin and Webbs with, she counted, thirty coats of arms and the same number of crowns all set out in an array with crimson cloth, flags and evergreens. They went through the triple arch into Barker's Pool: only when Rab tapped the hollow sounding side did the girls believe it was not made of stone. Past the Albert Hall where the public conveniences on the corner were hidden behind arches, draped in cloth and capped off with a red and white bell, they turned down Cambridge Street and the magnet factory and emerged onto Pinstone Street. They pushed past the crowds milling around the new Town Hall which the girls had never seen before.

'Is that the Queen's palace?' Little Selina asked; and they walked under more arches that looked like they were made of stone.

As they headed back to the tram, Rab bought everyone a baked potato from a stall, with a shake of salt into the newspaper to hold it in. The girls were happy with this, to be able to walk around and eat – something not normally allowed.

'Food always tastes better out of doors don't it?' he said. Selina was still not herself. He could tell she was not wanting to spoil the girls' evening, she'd probably have shouted at him otherwise. She kept chatting to them, but he knew he was still out of favour; and all over the tram thing. Not much he could do about it now. She would come round in her own good time. It was probably that time of the month – *mochardi*. She wouldn't say anything about it of course.

As they were stepping on the tram back, Little Selina said, 'Sheffield must be the most beautiful place in the world!' Rab shook his head and laughed. Even Selina smiled at that. Rab was glad. It was a good idea of his to come.

This time they all went and sat inside, the cool evening air was coming in anyway. Little Selina and her father sat in front and Lizzie and Selina behind them. The motion of the tram clattering along the track made Selina feel queasy. In front, the father of her children, and her youngest daughter were poking each other in some sort of game. She looked at the short hairs tapering down his neck beneath his cap. She could run her finger down them. She felt Lizzie shuffle closer to her. She put her arm round her beautiful daughter. A tear rolled down her cheek which she brushed away, straightening herself up and turning her head to look out of the window. This was the first time they had been out as a family for such a long time, other than to church occasionally. He was never around, always living his life away from them. Those men greeting him in the street – claiming him for their own; strangers to her, being so familiar with her husband. She couldn't understand; why would they do that; what had he to do with them? His focus was not on them: his family, on her. He lived for this other life, where his passions really were; his joys were not for them, with them. She did not really know what he got up to on all those nights away. He couldn't even behave nicely to her when he did take them out. She had looked forward to this outing. She was dressed as well as anyone that evening but he hadn't even noticed her: her best velveteen blouse and the skirt she had trimmed herself with black gimp edging. And she was angry with herself for feeling this way – he was her husband after all and she had no right to doubt him, to judge him – she was to be in subjugation to him; to call him lord – and yet she couldn't help herself. He couldn't wait to get away from her onto the top seats of the tram. How reckless to expose Little Selina to cold – if she fell ill with a cold, or worse, she could never forgive him. And making her sit up there, a young girl, with the men; and she could have fallen. It was not fair to Lizzie either. All the way to town Lizzie had been straining to see out of the window and she knew Lizzie was blaming her, not him, even though she bore it like the saintly child she was. Lizzie would never chide her openly. She really felt for her when they got off and Little Selina had been all over her with excitement. She knew Lizzie bit her lip and didn't let herself be provoked. It could have been such a special outing; town looked so beautiful. He could have offered her his arm and they could have been together, and as a family. And then there was the potato. He did not ask. He did not consider whether she would have preferred one of those ice creams in the little glass cones – she would have – no, he just went and bought potatoes because that's what he fancied. She had taken a sniff of hers but felt sick. It usually grieved her to waste good food but she had just left it when no one was looking on one of the posts for the wooden barriers erected along the street. She hoped some hungry person would be glad of it. The tears continued to roll down her cheeks; she was glad that the girls were still, even Little Selina was calm; both too overwhelmed to want to see yet more decorations. She didn't want them to see her tears.

She put the girls to bed by herself when they got home and kissed them both on their warm, scented foreheads. They, at least, were blissfully happy. She made tea with bread and jam for Rab's supper then took a candle upstairs while he ate. She hung up her embroidered blouse and her skirt then poured some water out of the jug into the wash-basin and splashed some on her arms, and cooled her face. She crossed her boots on the floor for luck and sat on the edge of the bed. Little Rabbi's dark hair was sweated across his forehead. She stroked it away, blew out the candle, put her arm round him and closed her eyes.

Chapter 5

The day before the Queen's visit was dry and warm and there was only a slight breeze blowing up the canal bringing with it a faint odour of sulphur from the coking kilns. Rab had stopped by Tinsley locks for a drink of Jemima's herb beer from a corked bottle and was watching some boys splashing about and swimming in the water, their voices getting lost when a train, pulling its long load of coal wagons, trundled slowly past. Selina, he thought, had still been punishing him before he left that morning. He had gone to bed hoping for a little affection but she did not stir when he went up, already asleep or pretending to be. Women! Hard to fathom out sometimes. Didn't one of the lads say that's what made them fascinating? Perhaps, but a few clues every now and then would be good. Could be time of the month. But then wasn't it her that made him some supper not Jemima? Unless she was trying to poison him? Not that he believed that load of old gipsy crap.

He thought he would go tonight – there was nothing in it, he could show Ada the decorations and have a chat, and a bit of pleasant company, nothing wrong with that. He had no other motive.

He pulled Gladstone out of his pocket, turned him round a few times, then got up and continued his walk out past Tinsley Bridge and back round by Wincobank.

After tea he changed into his match-day suit, put on a tie and said he had to go to Bramall Lane for an evening-do to raise money for one of the Philanthropist's charity things. He was far too early, so decided to walk slowly into town. He asked the time when he reached the Wicker – half past seven – so he picked his way past theatre-goers heading over Blonk Bridge for the evening's performance at the Alexandra. He stood for a while and watched the two different coloured rivers mixing where they met, then headed to Lady's Bridge to look at the water tumbling over the weir. Fearsome women with large baskets were jostling to get on the tram home, their last chance to do their marketing before the shops closed for the holiday. She should be here soon. It was starting to turn dark and gas flares were already burning inside the pubs. A lamplighter was using his wand to turn on the gas to the large street lamp outside the Bridge Inn and it cast its warm light onto its surroundings just as a smartly dressed woman stepped under it. He looked past her at first before realising it was Ada, not dressed like he had seen her before in her apron, but instead in a dark blue jacket pulled in at the waist and a matching full skirt with large folds in it, a white blouse with a high collar and blue satin straw hat with artificial flowers superior to any of the street decorations. As soon as she caught sight of him, her face, which had looked anxious, radiated warmth to match the street lamp as she smiled at him. He stepped towards her and, not knowing he had done it, removed his cap. 'Evening miss,' he said.

'Oh call me Ada you daft hap'orth!' she laughed, holding out her hand. He shook the soft, gloved hand gently; how different from the workaday hand he had last held. He became aware of his cap in his other hand and put it back on. Then, becoming conscious of his hands, stuffed them in his pockets.

'I wasn't sure you'd turn up,' she said

He looked into her blue eyes. 'I wasn't... going to let you down.'

Her cheeks flushed. He felt like she was smiling at him almost like a woman does to an endearing child. He had not felt like that before. By some startling process he felt like she had made him drop his guard and landed a tender punch in his ribs.

'Where are you going to take me?' she said, slipping her hand under his forearm.

'Wherever you like.'

She looked around. 'Let's head straight up into town then.'

They went slowly up to Haymarket and High Street, the same

way he had walked with others just the day before. The pavements were thronged and people kept spilling off onto the road, competing with horses, dog-carts, hansoms and four-wheelers on the dusty street. But one sensation crushed all the others – the light pressure of her small hand on his arm. He now wished he hadn't come – he didn't know what to say; and what if someone recognised him, or if it was someone who knew him well enough to stop and talk; who would he say she was – his cousin? But then what would she say? The crowd and noise was both a comfort and a worry – he felt anonymous in the crowd but surely more people meant more chance of someone recognising him. He pulled down on the brim of his cap. She kept pointing out things to him, marvelling at the transformation of the town and how magical the shops looked lit up. She said 'oh ain't that a picture' at the front of the Gas Light and Power Company's building with two large Queen's heads with laurel wreaths around them, bright red drapery, and all lit up with miniature lights. He agreed and wondered to himself how he had overlooked it before. He pointed to the lights on the Market Hall and the floral display in front of the Marples and the gilt figure of Britannia; and they paused to look up blinking at the new lamp on the corner with its famous twenty burners, now done up with striped poles topped with flower garlands and with flowers around the base.

'Are you all right Rab? You seem a bit quiet?'

'No I'm fine, shall we get out of the crowd and get a drink?'

They went into the Westminster Hotel and found a table. Compared to the street, inside it was calm; despite being busy, the waitresses floated round with their white aprons and lace, unflustered, and shoulders of customers instantly relaxed when they seated themselves on the plush covered seats. The places the team ate at when playing away games were usually more spartan – temperance hotels, or small-town station hotels – no padded seats, fancy silver cutlery, and no waitresses with lacy things on their heads.

'Oh it's nice to sit down, I've been on my feet all day,' Ada said. 'I've never seen so many folks in town.'

'No me neither – it's like Bramall Lane out there when we play *the Wednesday.'*

He looked around him at the other tables. No one he knew.

'Hows that horse of yours with the daft name?' He looked into her eyes and felt himself held again.

'Completely better I'd say.'

'That's good.'

They sipped at their lemonade from the elegant glasses placed before them, glasses like if he'd had them at home no one would ever drink from.

'So how was it you learnt about horses, what exactly did you father do?'

'He's a greengrocer now – up in Ecclesfield, so he keeps one himself, but he used to buy and sell a few as well as travelling door to door selling stuff.'

'Stuff?'

'Hardware and pots and pans and wooden things.'

'But you don't live in Ecclesfield yourself?'

'No, I live in Brightside – I'd rather not be havin them know all my business.' He raised his glass and glanced away towards the window.

'So have you been a footballer long?'

He was glad the subject had changed. Her eyes were on him, lively quick eyes, eyes that smiled when she did. 'A fair few years. I joined the United in their first season and turned professional soon as I got chance – anything to escape the pit.'

'You were a miner then?'

'Yeah, a hewer, and horrible it were an' all. Crouching or lying in the dark and wet, swinging a pick, seeing your mates get crushed under rock, no ta.'

She did that smile again. Her pale neck and throat went down under her high collared blouse, pinned at the middle with a silver brooch with a picture of a lucky horseshoe on. He imagined the pale skin on her chest and wondered if the veins would be visible and whether you could see the blood pulsing through them. He wanted to lay his head against her; she would stroke his hair.

'I've never been to a football match.'

'Then you must. The next one will be in August – just an

exhibition match amongst ussens as we prepare for the season.'

'I would like that very much, but I wouldn't know what to do; I couldn't go on my own.'

'Well I'd take you but I'll be on the pitch, so I can't.'

'Perhaps Jim'll take me, though he would be surprised at my sudden interest in watching young men running around after a ball like kids in the street! It does sound rather a strange idea when put like that – and to think you get paid to do it.'

'You should come along and see,' he said, a tinge of harshness in his voice, passion rising as he spoke, 'football could be what saves this country, if ever we have to go to war again, that's what our captain says. People who work in foul, unhealthy conditions can get out and play football in the fresh air and it turns weaklings into men. We're looked up to – we're the fittest and best because we can train and play the game without having to worry about not being able to feed us families. Without football England would be a country of namby-pambys brought up on parlour games. It's more than a game – it's about life. It holds up a mirror to what it is to be alive: strength, character, hope, belonging, failure, pity even. It might not make sense if you just say it's kicking a ball about, but then you're just looking not feeling… '

Her face ashened as he gave this speech; one he had rehearsed and heard bits of before from others in defence of their profession.

'I… I didn't…' she started to say, and reached forward with her now ungloved hand and lightly touched his where it rested on the table – the sensation shot through him – she withdrew her hand again. 'I'm sorry,' she said, 'I didn't mean to tease.'

'Nay lass, I'm sorry, I just get this all the time at…'(he was about to say "at home" but stopped), 'I'm sick of having to stick up for misen and what I do.' He wished her hand was back on the table so he could hold it.

She raised her eyes to his and he even wondered whether there was dampness there.

'No it's me that should be sorry. I can see you are very passionate about what you do and I admire that, very much. If you don't think I'm too silly I would love to come and watch you play.'

She took a sip of lemonade and, having put her glass down, her hand was now resting on the table.

He covered it with his own and stroked the side of her thumb with his own and the smile returned to her face. 'I'm glad we came out,' he said.

'So am I.'

Something had thawed and they talked freely, Ada trying to understand the subtleties of half-back play – how they were the backbone of the team, both defending and attacking, and feeding their own forwards and marking the wings in defence. She asked about the places he'd been, from Scotland to London and Ireland. She seemed genuinely interested and he was happiest talking about football, and avoiding questions about other things.

Back on High Street Ada again slipped her hand under his arm and, Rab thought, leant towards him a little as they walked through the mass of people. The sky was now dark and Coles was indeed more spectacular at night with ruby red lamps around the bottom windows, the windows above that lit in amber, then turquoise on the balcony. A crowd was gathered on Fargate looking up and pointing upwards. They tried to see what was happening past the tall hats and wide brims in front. Climbing the steeple of St Marie's were two steeplejacks, moving surprisingly quickly like monkeys up a pole, draping bunting from top to bottom of the steeple whilst the crowd murmured as if raising their voices might cause a fall. Rab queued at a hokey-pokey stall for ice cream: two little glass cones, sweet and cold and melting quickly in their hands so it was hard not to spill drips. Then they went up towards the new Town Hall where a huge crowd jostled to get a good view. Two huge searchlights were mounted on the roof and their beams swept across the sky, searching out the suburbs past Broomhall, the beams showing bright as they picked out smoke and dirt being kicked up in the Sheffield night air by its multitude of citizens.

'Look, the little fella up there is holding a lamp,' said Ada, pointing at the statue of Vulcan at the top of the tower.

'I think it's an electric one. How the heck did they get that up there!'

As they craned their necks to the night sky, Ada leant against his shoulder. He slipped his arm around her and she nestled in.

They didn't say much as they wandered back. The crowd had dwindled by the time they reached Snig Hill, with just the usual groups wandering in and out of the pubs. He walked her back up Bridge Street and they stopped on the corner of Love Lane opposite her shop shrouded in darkness.

'Well, thank you for a lovely evening Rab,' she said turning to stand facing him.

'My pleasure, Ada. I'll be seeing you then.'

'That would be nice.'

She didn't move away but looked up at him, her lips parted slightly and she took a breath and touched his arm. He shuffled a little closer and still she didn't move, so he leaned towards her and met her lips with his, and he felt pressure on his chest from the softness beneath her blouse. He straightened up and took a sharp breath.

She smiled at him, 'You all right?'

'Yeah. *Kek vafardes na tshuma.*' He murmured.

'Rab?'

He felt dazed. I'm sorry. It's an old saying…. Romany, gipsy speak. It means "no harm in a kiss." He looked at the ground.

'You are a deep one Rab Howell,' she said. 'Say it again.'

'*Kek vafardes na tshuma,*' he said quietly, looking back at her once more, feeling as if he stood before her like a rabbit caught out in the open, away from cover, and she leaned forwards and gave him a more lingering kiss, this time her hand moving down his side.

'No,' she said, 'no harm.' She smiled that smile again and left him standing watching her go inside.

*

That evening Selina bathed Little Rabbi and the girls ready for the next day – they had had the afternoon off school and had spent it getting dirty playing in the street. After tea, while she had tidied up and got the bath ready, she had made them stay in – Lizzie darning socks and Little Selina unravelling some old knitting for re-using the wool.

Upstairs at bedtime her mother told the girls one of her stories about life in the open, beautiful large tents, collecting sticks for the fire or water from the stream, and how her brothers used to put nettles in each others beds or frogs in their sisters' and how they'd end up in fights with blankets and all of them getting into trouble. They had no clocks to live by; they went to bed when tired and woke up when they were not, sometimes waking in the night and sleeping in the light mornings. Selina stopped on the landing to listen before getting her mending together. There was a torn skirt of hers and Lizzie's second best dress was frayed at the edge. She then went into the wardrobe and got out Rab's jacket to put a button back on and took them downstairs.

The fire was going out but it was a mild evening so she let it die down, better to re-light it in the morning than waste coal. She sat next to the dying fire, then started darning the frayed dress. Tomorrow would be a good day – her and Rab going to watch the girls sing to the Queen in Norfolk Park. She would talk properly with him, set things right between them. He was her husband and he loved them and provided for them. She then got out an old button from the workbox, brown like the others on Rab's jacket and started to sew it on. As she did so she saw something slide out of the inner pocket. It was an envelope with what looked like Rab's name on the front written in a beautiful hand. She slid it quickly back in, then, after pondering a while, took it out again. Who would write a letter to Rab, and why was it in his jacket? She took the paper out of the envelope – there were several blue lines of the same pretty writing. She stared at it a while as if by doing so it's meaning would reveal itself to her, but she knew it wouldn't. She heard her mother coming down the stairs and quickly put the letter back and picked up her needle.

The two women sat together in the dim light from the oil lamp, Jemima with her eyes closed, Selina quietly working away with her needle, the sharp point penetrating the tweed and re-emerging, the mechanical movement an accompaniment to her mind's wanderings. It was definitely a woman's hand. It was not official looking. It was personal. But no one who knew Rab would write to him. What woman would write to another woman's husband? And how did he come by it? You wouldn't hand a letter to someone when you could talk to them. And it wasn't posted – the Queen's head wasn't on it. The postman never came round here – except that time when Rab had sent a postcard from Scotland. Someone else wrote that for him.

She looked up from her work; her mother was looking at her, reading her face like she would read a palm. Selina gave a half smile, 'You all right *Dei*?'

'Yes love; just tired. Are you? You look troubled.'

'No, I'm fine, just tired too. All these things going on – I'll be glad in a way when it's all over with.'

'Aye, there's comfort in routine.' She leaned forwards to pick up her blackened pipe from the hearth, heaved herself out of her chair to reach for her tobacco pouch off the mantelpiece and went through the ritual of half filling the bowl. As she got it going, wisps of smoke intertwined with wisps of grey hair that had worked their way out from the plait hanging in front of her shoulder. 'We're going to have to set off for town early tomorrow – it's a long walk in for me these days and they reckon there's no chance of taking the tram – they're all being taken over by the schools by all accounts.'

'And you'll need to get your place early – it'll be thrussen, it was bad enough the other night when we went in.'

Footsteps in the yard and the privy door banging heralded a returning male or two. Dennis was the first to clatter in shortly followed by young Charlie still fumbling with the buttons on the front of his trousers. The women rose and ceded them space, and the two men slumped into the chairs.

'There's some bacon bits and onion left and some bread if you like?' said Selina.

'Aye that'd do nicely,' said Dennis, and a, 'Ta sis,' from Charlie. They sat dipping their bread into bowls of greasy slop – sinking down into the beer in their bellies; their faces saying that, at that very moment, life just couldn't get any better.

Jemima went up shortly after her men-folk.

'I'll sit up a bit longer for Rab,' said Selina.

By the ashes in the grate she sat, still, Rab's jacket on her lap, the letter in her hand; the room, the plain furniture and the dim light gradually absorbing her into their inanimateness.

She woke with a judder as the door opened into the room.

The room was dark as he entered, but as the light from the candle he held invaded the room, he started – seeing her in the chair: expecting the room to be his alone.

'Lina?'

He moved into the room and saw her hands on the envelope.

'Who is she?' she said, her voice cold.

Rab stood struck. How long had she had it? …his other jacket. Damn!

'Who do you mean?'

'Rab. Who wrote this letter?'

Did she know what it said. What did it say? Had she got it read to her?

'Just someone I did a favour for.'

'A woman? A favour?' Her voice was faltering.

No she couldn't know what it said.

'It's nothing…'

'Nothing? Then why keep it in your jacket?'

She didn't know. He sat down and put his head in his hands and waited. His mind raced ahead as he sat.

'Well?' she said. 'What have you got to say?'

He raised his head and wore a pained expression. 'You've hurt me. How could tha doubt me? I'd forgot the letter were there,' he said. 'Just some lass and her brother that deliver summat to the Lane and I told 'em what to do wi' their horse what had the gitts – summat mi dad used to do. And they must've left me a note to say thanks. I dunno what it says do I? It's nowt.' He resumed his previous posture, head in hands. 'Here,' he said taking the letter off her and throwing it on the fire.

Selina rose and put her hand on his head and smoothed his hair.

'I'm sorry Rab. I'm just feeling a bit emotional – what with everything going on – and tomorrow and that. Please don't hate me for being so mean.'

'Go on, get up to bed,' he said taking her hand. 'I'll be right up. I'll just get a drink o' water.'

He held onto her hand as she moved away, and only letting go when he had to. He glanced into the grate – the letter was still there, the grate was not hot. The stairs creaked as she went up and he lifted the letter out – it was a bit crispy and starting to brown on the back where it contacted the ashes, but the writing on the front was untouched.

He ran some water into a cup in the scullery and turned the letter over with the fingers of his left hand. He sat back down in the living room and took the letter out and gazed at the beautiful writing. There was nowhere in the house that was not Selina's domain, nowhere she didn't clean, nowhere safe. He put it back in the envelope, drank the water then used the letter to poke the remnants of the fire, found a piece still hot enough and pushed the letter in and blew on it – it smoked and browned, blackened, and the edges smouldered. He headed upstairs. He didn't need the letter. He could now have the real thing – if he wanted.

Chapter 6

Friday 21ˢᵗ May 1897

The sky was cloudless again the following day. In some parts of the world a cloudless sky is blue, but not in Brightside. There was always a haziness in the air, something up there bleaching the blue out of the sky, blocking out the sun's full strength. The girls were given as big a breakfast as they could eat to keep them going and were sent off to school in their good-as-new dresses with their medals proudly displayed and their hats with the new ribbons. Such levels of excitement as this, being shown by all of Brightside's children, were more than the walls of the terraces could contain; and best of luck to their teachers in marshalling their bodies and their spirits. Charlie went off with his mates. The others left towards midday and went round to Charlton Street where Selina's brother Henry lived with Agnes. Agnes, nursing baby Agnes, was the depository for all the family's – and several neighbours' – unwanted children for the day; here Little Rabbi was to spend the day competing with cousins.

As Rab and Selina wandered into town, children, packed into trams at double the normal capacity, streamed past them like some great, tiny army being mobilised in a hurry – all waving and shouting, especially if they passed someone they knew, which was often, as there was a steady stream of grown-ups and older children all heading the same way.

Rab was pleased at how the day had turned out. He was happy – it was hard not to be, it was warm, and everyone was smiling and comparing plans for the day: each having their own ideas for getting a good vantage point. Selina was being nice to him; he was secure at home and yet had other opportunities for happiness: like he stood on top of a hill with the valley opening up before him and several

65

paths to choose from. Ada was clearly capable of adding something to his life and making him feel whole – filling in the gaps left by Selina. And before long the new season would start and he was in the best shape ever – he felt he knew exactly what he had to do for success and if they added a decent centre-forward they could beat the Villans to the top spot, or win the English cup.

They approached the park from Norfolk Road where they were passed by all manner of vehicles conveying babbling children to the park. It seemed like every brewery in the city had donated its drays for the cause of shipping not barrels but young citizens, and, thanks to its furnaces and dust, Sheffield was a perpetually thirsty place and had more breweries than anywhere in the land. Other merchants and factory owners had also lent use of their wagonettes and carts. Some children even travelled in unaccustomed style in spare carriages of local worthies. Reaching the grand entrance to the Duke's park and entering its cool avenue of trees was wonderful after their hot and dusty walk. Many people had been complaining along the route that there had been no sign of the water carts to dampen the streets, and how they would be filthy before they got there. Rab and Selina didn't know which way to go in the park but followed the stream of people. The Boys' Brigade were out in force and the Empire's uniformed little soldiers were relishing their important job of keeping routes clear and directing people.

They emerged beyond the trees onto the slope overlooking the valley. A man in a straw boater pointed out to them the platform down below where the conductor would stand and the barrier-lined route of the newly built Queen's Drive. They settled on a spot on the slope under some trees and there Rab unfolded the cloth bundle he had been carrying on his shoulder. He set two bottles of herb beer on the flattest piece of grass and they had some snap of bread and a polony, followed by a penny cake each.

Down below, last minute preparations were still being made and a man with a ladder could be seen climbing part way up a flagpole attaching the Royal Standard. There was plenty to watch despite their being early.

'Look at these elegant ladies Rab,' Selina said pointing out two women floating along in large feather-trimmed hats with dresses in flouncy layers of white and coloured silk, and carrying parasols, as if the costumes were wearing the women rather than the other way round.

'And those'll be the ones what's paid for that pretty get-up,' Rab said, indicating two puffed up men in tailcoats and chimney pot hats, parading their silver topped canes a short distance behind the women. 'Sheffield's finest are out today.'

Rab removed his jacket, folded it, placed it on the ground and lay back against it for a pillow, positioning his cap over his face to keep out the sun.

'Rab! Your best jacket!'

'I know. Wake us up if owt happens.'

Selina kept a watch over the shifting scene, the comings and goings, keen to spot the first children arriving. Soon they did: first a little rivulet of white frocks coming up from the town; then joined by ranks of boys in uniform, marching solemnly, a little ripple of applause going up for their efforts. Then the rivulets turned to streams and they kept coming and coming. Selina poked Rab in the ribs with the toe of her boot and he sat up with a grumble.

'Can you see them anywhere?' she said.

'We'll never spot 'em!' he scoffed.

'We might, you just keep a look out; your eyes are better than mine.'

After a while children began pouring into the park from different directions. Some were just little mites, waving their union jacks, being herded along by their teachers to take up their positions at the lowest parts of the slopes; others strapping lads and lasses of twelve or thirteen, who would soon be put to work for the Empire, in melting shops or buffing rooms or in the earth, fetching or carrying until they were allowed a go themselves. Others, well drilled, formed patches of uniform colour on the slope wearing the same blouses with matching hats, or boys in blazers and caps: the ones who would not face work for some time yet, if ever, who would live off the work of the others, run the Empire or make its laws. The upper slopes around Rab and Selina were also filling up with red-faced men mopping their brows, women with baskets containing oven-bottom cakes, pies, spice cake and bottled drinks, and big brothers and sisters, proud yet jealous, in charge of picking out the best spots to sit.

'Ey up! Here comes us elders and betters!' said Rab, as the dignitaries started to move into the enclosure to take up their seats.

'Wouldn't it be nice to have a chair to sit on!' sighed Selina.

'When they make us Lord Mayor tha'll have one love,' Rab replied.

A military band settled into place and started playing, and Rab whistled along to the tunes he recognised and sang the opening lines of one: "Way down upon the Swanee ribber" as did one or two other wags adopting the accent.

At one point a burst of applause started and spread as a man in full regalia drove up.

'It's the Duke!' someone said.

'So that's what he looks like!' said Selina.

'Well I don't s'pose he sits down to his breakfast boiled egg looking like that though,' said Rab.

Seeing the Duke got the children excited and afterwards they cheered and waved their little banners and flags every time someone went past on horseback, no matter who they were.

In the distance they heard a cannon boom. An excited murmur went up through the crowd, the collective wisdom being that it signalled the Queen's arrival. 'That's the railway station.' 'She's here.' 'She's arrived.'

The chattering died down as buglers sounded out to get everyone's attention and the conductor started the bands going: interspersed around the valley were eight brass bands and they all joined together somehow keeping in time. Then the children sang "Auld Lang Syne" and the effect on the crowd was palpable. Many of them had experienced Whit sings in the city's parks, but this was beyond anything they could have imagined.

Afterwards the children cheered and the upper slopes applauded madly.

Selina took hold of Rab's hand and held it in both of hers and shuffled towards him on the grass.

'How many children do you reckon there are here Rab?' she whispered.

'A lot,' I'd say.

She slapped the back of his hand, 'I know that, but how many.'

'Well they say there were thirty thousand there when we played *the Wednesday*, Boxing Day last, and I reckon there's nigh on twice that. Who knows?'

The children were waving their songsheets in the air. Rab counted seven different colours of songsheet, each colour occupying a distinct patch of ground, so the effect was like different coloured flower beds or fields, but in movement. England's future. Sheffield's future.

'Rab?' she said quietly.

'Yeah?'

'Thanks.'

'What for?'

'For three lovely kids, and for looking after us.'

He didn't know what to say, so just smiled at her and squeezed her hand. The bands picked up again while the children took a rest.

'Rab?'

He looked at her again, and she leaned towards him and whispered in his ear.

'There's another child on the way.'

She looked towards him trying to read his face. He thought she looked tired and drawn, 'Are you sure?'

She nodded.

'That's good,' he said and put his arm around her, and looked back towards the valley.

The children sang "Home Sweet Home." Rab felt his cheeks ache, and his nose smart as sensations pulsed up from his chest. His eyes moistened. Damn. He looked away at the trees behind and tried to shift his concentration onto something other. He brushed away a tear with his free hand, as if he were just scratching his nose. He noticed he wasn't the only one doing so. A woman in front had produced a lace handkerchief and someone else was sniffing. He wasn't sure what he felt. Sentimentality? Happiness? That Selina had planted her flag-pole on his chest? He would have to abandon ideas of seeing Ada again now.

Another military band arrived in splendid red uniforms with

spikes on their black helmets. 'That's the Queen's guards, I shouldn't reckon,' said a raised voice. 'Nay lad, it's the Connaughts,' said a tweed-suited man behind, 'Irishmen.' Rab again thought of Ada, and he felt a shiver. Selina looked at him. 'Sun's lost its heat,' he said pulling on his jacket.

A short burst of "Rule Britannia" followed, and everyone looked to see if she was coming but it was evidently just a test, because the conductor stepped off his rostrum. Chattering started up on the slopes again as they waited once more.

Eventually cheering could be heard in the distance, coming from over St Mary's way. Rab had calmed his emotions again.

'She must be coming,' he said.

The cheering and applause got less distant until it reached the fringes of the park and then glittering steel and polished metal could be seen flashing through the branches. Everyone got to their feet. Rab was quite pleased to be standing and rubbed his slightly damp behind. Then soldiers on horseback, resplendent in white, blue and gold, appeared, and a huge cheer went up from all the children as they waved their flags. Next came some carriages and cavalrymen in red uniforms with plumes in their silver helmets. There was a deafening cry as a dark chocolaty brown carriage with red and gold on it arrived at the Royal Standard and stopped. Inside on blue seats sat a small figure all in black. They could see the Duke of Norfolk standing next to the carriage and then the National Anthem was sung by the children, with most of the grown-ups joining in. Then there was another song that Rab didn't recognise, followed by Rule Britannia. Then it was all over in what had seemed like a few seconds – there was another huge cheer and the carriages and trample of horses started up. Rab and Selina looked down as the tiny black figure rolled quickly away out of the top end of the park; the coloured papers and union jacks waving and little voices straining to make themselves heard above all the others.

'That's that then!' Rab said.

'She must've been impressed, don't you think?'

'Aye that she must. I bet she's never heard owt like it. This is what her country's really about.'

They stood looking over the valley, as did everyone else, feeling suddenly deflated.

'Now what?' Rab said. As if in reply groups of children started trooping off in various directions.

'They're off to the tents for their buns and lemonade,' said Selina. 'Then we'll have to try and find 'em somehow and take 'em home."

*

The next day at teatime there was a big post-mortem held on the previous day. Rab, Selina and the girls had reached home late after walking all the way: they didn't even bother waiting for a tram – it was so busy in town. The others had stayed on in town a while after the Royal procession to look at all the decorations and to seek refreshment.

'She smiled at me y'know Granda!' said Little Selina.

'She didn't just smile at you,' said Lizzie.

'She smiled at everyone, but she smiled just at me. She was looking right at me and she smiled, but I didn't stop singing, I just kept on, and she smiled at me.'

'Well I never!' said Dennis.

'Did she smile at you too?'

'Nay lass! Fact is, we never even saw her. All we saw from our side of the street was the top of her black umbrella thing. Two chuffing hours we waited an' all.'

'Still Den, it were a lovely procession, weren't it, with all the horses and uniforms.'

'You just had your eye on them Scotchmen, I know you. You should've seen her – ogling their hairy legs she were!'

'I was not, they just looked smart in their black kilts and red tunics, with those furry hats with feathers in, and the bagpipes!'

'Kilts! Skirts yer mean!'

'What did you like best granda?' asked Lizzie.

'I'd say it were the veterans – from the Crimea. Poor buggers some on 'em, but right proud and still looking like they could sort out a Russki or two if needs be. What a cheer they got!'

'And how were the Duke's buns?' said Jemima.

'They tasted lovely – and we were so hungry and thirsty after all that waiting and singing.'

'They say that he tested them buns himself, and that the first lot, that were ha'penny buns, weren't up to scratch so he ,old the bakers to go up to a penny,' said Jemima.

'Jemmie, tell 'em about the fire at Cole's corner,' said Dennis.

'What was that *Dei*?' said Selina.

'Well we didn't see it ourselves but apparently some of the bunting or paper flowers set on fire and this lad shinned up somehow and put the fire out and got a huge cheer from the crowd. A proper little hero I should say!'

'And a couple o' blokes got killed an' all,' said Charlie.

'That's awful!' said Selina

'One on 'em fell backwards off Blonk Bridge and got drownded and t' other un fell off a roof.'

'Poor sods eh? I hope they didn't leave families behind,' said Dennis.

'We did see three fellas sitting up on a roof wi'a big bottle o'beer and clinking their glasses – sitting on a plank they was, tied on to the chimney,' said Rab. 'There were quite a lot o' folks climbing up anywhere to get a view – trees and what have yer.'

Everyone was quiet for a bit and seemed to be concentrating on their pikelets.

'I've some good news though,' said Selina. 'I'm going to have a baby.'

Rab winced – he hoped it was only inwardly. Why did she have to tell people like that? It came as a shock to hear it said aloud, he had only heard it once so far, whispered.

'Oh that's wonderful love!' said Jemima, giving her a big kiss on the cheek.

'Mummie! Can I have a little sister this time, not a brother,' said Little Selina.

'Here's to the next member of the family!' said Dennis raising his tea cup.

Rab was quiet for the rest of his tea. He resented everyone knowing – when he was not used to the idea himself. It also didn't feel right for them to know his business – not that you could keep such things secret, especially seeing as how they lived on top of each other in a small house where you could even hear what next-doors were up to, but it was still somehow embarrassing to discuss such things at the tea table in front of her parents – what that meant he had done to their daughter. He knew he was being irrational but that just made him more annoyed.

He took Mr Gladstone for a long walk after tea.

By Wednesday all that remained of Friday's dream was the ceremonial arch in Pinstone Street. One of their uncles had brought back a couple of yards of paper flower garland for Lizzie and Little Selina which they draped over their iron bedstead where their medals dangled for years after.

Chapter 7

The fine weather broke and it seemed fitting. Everyone was in a kind of mourning; for one all too brief moment life had seemed full of colour, excitement and anticipation – and now it had gone: a bit like the feeling they had after Christmas with only the damp, cold, and darkness of January and February to come. The skies returned to grey and with the rain the streets turned from dust to mud again; the unpaved roads round Lake Street being particularly bad, especially when the nightsoil men had been round, boots having to be scraped with an old knife blade before you were even allowed into the scullery.

Even when the rain stopped you soon seemed to be wishing it back again, for the air thickened and clung to you – there was no relief. Sheffielders, when they thought that rain was coming, said, "It looks dark o'er Bill's mother." This though was not just dark over Bill's mother but over "everyone's soddin' mother" – the whole sky was the colour of Bill's favourite tankard that the landlord put to one side just for him. But for several days the rain never did come as expected. On days like this the city was again layered in grey – the streets, pavements and yards all coated with Sheffield's patent, slippery coating, made of Mother Nature's dirt, coal dust, horse muck and the secret ingredient: the powdery by-products of turning rocks into blades; the buildings were a darker shade of grey tending to black, unless they were new, in which case they had a few years' stone-coloured respite before blending in with their smoke-stained neighbours; and over the buildings the greyness pothered from Sheffield's thousands of chimneys mixing with the dismal, vaulted, pewter sky.

Then the rain did come and, after days of ducking under washing strung across the living room or knocking into washing hung over the winter hedge in front of the fire, people wished it would stop raining. Rab was like a rat in a box on these wet days. He would sleep as much as he could to pass the time. He felt his muscles turning womanly by the hour, but if he stayed out too long in wet clothes he feared getting the Russian flu that was already claiming souls in the district. He would pull on a pair of football knickers and an old jersey and go for a run up to Wincobank Woods, but that was all over far too quickly; having rubbed down and massaged his legs and got into dry clothes he would find himself in the front parlour to keep away from the women folk, with a whole afternoon ahead of him, the rain relentless. He would play a few tunes, stare out of the window at the wet greyness, pace the room, and occasionally snooze until the kids came home.

When things got really bad there was Armstead Road Turkish baths, where for sixpence he could get an extended version of that feeling seconds before falling asleep when, after winning a match, his limbs were heavy and ached pleasantly. At the baths he left the outside world at the door with his boots, and, wrapped in towels, entered the eerie world of warm and hot rooms before plunging into cold water, then being kneaded like bread by the attendant, wrapped again in towels and left with a smoke in the cooling room. Going back out into the reality of noise and graft was the downside.

Fridays were best on rainy days because the players met up at the Lane. They collected their wages and got weighed, though why they bothered weighing him Rab couldn't tell. Before he got on the scales he would say to George: "nine and half," and it always was. Some of the others, on the other hand, struggled, especially off-season; 'little' Bill being on a seventeen stone upwards trajectory, cursing George and his bloody scales; George giving it back about fighting weights, but knowing he was powerless – it made no difference in any way: there was no one better than Bill, not for three quid a week anyway. They would hang around to play billiards or cards, and to exchange stories of sixes hit, stumps scattered, centuries, hat-tricks, and rumours. A few had already gone: Jimmy Yates, a bit of a surprise, though Cocky had claimed his wing role, George Walls, and John Bowes never properly settled in – no longer collecting pay packets. Then came speculation of replacements and who they'd like to see up front. But one of the best stories concerned the Club Secretary, the now-not-so-honourable Mr JB Wostinholm. When Rab had walked into the clubroom a big huddle was gathered around the billiard table and Ernest Needham was talking in hushed tones with the occasional, 'Nah gi' o'er!' and bursts of laughter. Rab's stomach knotted thinking they were talking about him, had he been seen? – but Mick caught sight of him and shouted him over, 'Rab, come and listen to this!' He got to the table and saw that Needham had a newspaper in front of him; the story started over again for Rab's benefit in the same low voice, now with others adding bits.

'Mr JB Wostinholm was ordered by the court to pay thirty eight pounds for not complying with a notice served on him in eighteen ninety two.'

'Apparently the Philanthropist was dodging his civic duty, the tight old sod, and not stumping up his share to pave the street where he owns some property.'

'He reckoned he didn't have to, 'cause his tenants didn't use the front street and just came in the back way!'

'Like anyone round here uses their front door anyway!'

'Can yer credit it – the bugger! As if he couldn't afford it!'

'Rather see his tenants paddling around in shit, like animals. So much for him!'

'Hey it's not on our street is it?' Rab asked. 'About bloody time that were paved.'

'No, it says Latimer Street wherever that is.

'Up town somewhere I think.'

'Anyway I thought you lived in a painted caravan Rab?'

'Well yeah, of course but I've got to park the damn thing somewhere and find a post to tie the horse to haven't I?' Which brought another burst of laughter.

*

During the long wait for the football season Rab also dreamed and planned. He imagined holding Ada close to him, tried to remember her kisses, her smell, he dreamed of being allowed to touch her magical, red Irish hair. Her skin. He planned his next move. He ached to see her again, be alone with her, but how? He had to see her soon or she would think he wasn't interested, or was just taking advantage of her. He might lose her. But he suspected he would anyway sooner or later: when she found out the truth about him, his family. She might be one of those people who believed in sin, who think that people go to hell. Irish. Catholic? Almost certainly. He'd always thought they took things too literally – too much like the old Romanys believing in spirits and ghosts and other worlds: like Jemima's mother had: like Jemima. He might just have to make the best of it while it lasted, but he had to try or he would never know what might have been. Not yet, but soon – he couldn't hold it off – he would be forced to retire from football. And then what? He didn't want to look back with regret at not taking the chances life presented him. His life in Brightside stretched into the future, struggling to support his family. What could he do? His trade was mining, but he would not be going back underground until they lowered him in a box. Become a counter-jumper, a miserable shop assistant, earning just a pound a week? Sinking slowly into poverty like those he saw around him, broken men with dead eyes escaping in drink they couldn't afford, people looking at him with pity in their eyes – 'Didn't you use to be Rab Howell, the footballer? What was it they called you? The Terrier wasn't it? I remember – and… the Evergreen? Let me buy you another drink for old times sake.' He didn't want to run from anything. No need for drink.

There was the Whit fair coming up. He would love to take Ada to that but he couldn't risk it, too many of the tribe there, what with the horse fair running alongside and everything. Or could he get away on the Bank Holiday afternoon, perhaps to take her to the cricket? Not that he was that bothered about the summer game, it wasn't for the likes of him; he just wanted cricket out of the way: it was the salad; football was the pie – and gravy!

*

He waited one morning on Bridge Street near Ada's shop. He wasn't sure what he was waiting for exactly: something to turn up. He leant against the wall, one foot raised flat to the bricks, and watched. People walked past and wagons rumbled on their way to and from the foundries, a small boy trundled a hoop, and the ironmonger's boy was hanging pots and brushes outside the shop. He fiddled with his pipe, pulled a bit of tobacco leaf out, shredded it and filled Gladstone's head, pressed it down and put it back in his jacket pocket. He was just thinking he would have to go into the shop and face the Bosom when he saw the door to their yard open and out came the horse followed by the reins, and Ada driving the cart. Was she on her own? He couldn't see if her brother was in the back. He stepped out and crossed the road and waved.

'Rab, it's nice to see you!' she shouted down, her voice almost singing the words. She stopped the horse and he stood alongside and smoothed its flank.

'How do you do Ada.'

'I was wondering whether you'd forgotten about me, or if I'd scared you off.'

'Not at all. It was just with, y'know, the weather being so wet and everything.'

'I can't really stop, I'm blocking the road. Are you busy? Jump up if you like, I could do with a man's help.' He climbed up next to her and she drove the horse on up towards West Bar.

'Jim's minding the shop, and mother's ill in bed and our Annie's looking after her.'

'Nothing serious I hope.'

'I don't think so, no – bronchitis – but she's past the worst now, she's got a bit of a weak chest.' Rab couldn't equate what he'd seen with weak. She added, 'It's this damp weather: there seems a lot of it about. It's a worry for us though because it's almost two years to the day since father died – and with a bad chest as well.'

'You could try boiled chestnut leaves.'

'I see. Another of your gipsy cures!'

'I don't know where it's from, that's just what my mother used to use – she used to make up a plaster of them.'

'I didn't guess you were a gipsy, you don't look Egyptian.'

'My family's been here for centuries, probably as English as yours.'

'Except my family's Irish!'

'I knew that, I just meant...'

She laughed and he joined in.

'I'm sorry I didn't come round earlier. I've been thinking about you a lot.'

'Have you?' She paused. 'I wasn't sure how serious you were.'

'I came to see if you wanted to go and see the cricket next. Do you get time off on Monday? We won't need tickets or anything, I'll get us in.'

'I've never been to a cricket match before, where is it?'

'At the Bramall Lane ground – it's Yorkshire playing, should be good.'

'Yes I'd like to.'

He helped her with the delivery, unloading at the Infirmary. It felt natural to work alongside her, like they'd done it before. He got a lift back and when they reached the yard door, he jumped down to the street, like he was half the age he was, to open it. He helped her with the horse and she invited him in. He said he'd better get off. She looked into his eyes and he kissed her; she put her hand up to his face and ran it across the stubble – it was a few days since he'd last been for a shave. He skipped round, gave her a wave and a smile, and went out into the street. He felt he could fly home.

Ada went inside. Her sister Annie Eliza was right behind the back door smiling. 'Who is he Ade?'

'Have you been spying on me?'

'No I just happened to see you out of the window.'

'And then just happened to be lurking behind the door listening?'

Ada took her sister's hands in hers. Annie was two years younger, and like herself in many ways, though Ada could see more of her dad in her. She knew that there was no point trying to bluff her way out.

'He's called Rab, and he's very nice,' she said.

Annie gave a little girlish leap and a sort of squeak. 'So you love him?'

'Annie! I've only just met him! But he is very nice.'

'You do, you do – I can tell!'

'How's Mother?'

'Stop changing the subject Ada McGrail! Mother's fine – she must be feeling better because she's telling me off and grumbling and demanding beef tea! I'd better shift or she'll be banging on the floor for attention.'

Ada went into the shop; Jim was stood looking at her with raised eyebrows.

'Not you an' all! Am I not allowed any life to myself!'

'No Ade, we must know everything!'

She fetched him one across his ear, though it was a stretch up for her these days. 'You're still my little brother, even though you're bigger than me.'

'Yes sis, of course.' And he patted her on the head. 'He'd better treat you nice or he'll have Jim McGrail to answer to, that's all.'

'I don't need you to stick up for me. You might be the man of the house now but I can look out for myself. Anyway he's very nice. A gentleman. He's taking me to the cricket next week.'

Ada left Jim to mind the shop and went into the back room to make a start on a pile of ironing. The flat iron was nice and hot having been warming all the while she was out.

She wondered if this could be her chance to leave home like her older sisters. Sarah was so much older than her that she could not even remember their sharing a roof; then from around the age she left school there had been regular weddings: Maria, Elizabeth, Theresa, and then Emily, who left her with her mother to nurse their dying father and worry about the business. The sleepless nights she had sat up, watching him gasping for breath in the dim candle light, his belly swollen like he was with child. She sat holding his hand wishing it would end soon and feeling guilt and shame for her thoughts.

She knew of course she would feel guilty if she were to leave – she felt it just thinking about it. Why was she always running from guilt? But Jim and Annie could manage without her, and the business would support three better than four. She didn't want to be stuck, the old maid, looking after the shop and her mother, if the other two left before her. She had always put everyone else first, perhaps now it was her turn. She cursed her own selfishness; but she thought of Rab. He was older than her, maybe three or four years but she hadn't asked how old. It was hard to tell – at times his features looked boyish; the fashionable thin moustache made him look mature, but that time in the cafe when she had upset him by being foolish, when his eyes darkened and his brow furrowed, he looked much older. He was not a tall man, though taller than her, but was obviously "well made" under those clothes, lean, muscular. She couldn't wait to see him playing a football match. She felt colour rise to her cheeks. Yet more to add to the list of things she ought to tell her confessor, but probably wouldn't: her confessions were usually about greed, coveting other people's hats, or neglecting her duties to her mother. He didn't talk about himself very much, not about the stuff that really matters, but she had never known boys or men who did. It seemed as though he had a leisurely life though – not having to time his life by the turn of the grinding wheel, the winding pulley at the pit, or shop opening hours. She imagined him sitting by a fire, pipe in hand, waiting for his landlady to bring his tea on a tray, having his room cleaned for him and his bed made. Then in her mind's eye the landlady looked like her and she chided herself for being silly. Fancy him being a gipsy too, what was it? a Romany? That thing he had said, so mysterious! She remembered a skipping rhyme from her girlhood: "My mother said that I never should, play with gipsies in the wood. The wood was dark, the grass was green, and in came Sally with a tambourine."

She remembered the gipsies she had seen selling pegs at the door or the itinerant knife sharpeners, or the fortune-tellers at the fair: Rab was nothing like them. And nothing like the others who had tried to court her: the clerk, the potman, the chargehand – they were all as you found them, as much depth as a puddle in the yard.

Annie came in and slumped in a chair. 'She wants her bed changing now! She's stopped sweating on her sheets and wants clean ones!'

'I've just done 'em,' Ada said, 'In that pile there.'

Annie picked them up and sat on a wooden chair at the table, eyes on Ada as she ironed. Ada felt her sister's eyes on her, she suspected something was coming and picked up an undergarment.

'So will you marry him?'

Ada aimed and threw the linen, landing it on her sister's head.

Annie threw it back and scuttled out of the room grinning.

Monday 7th June 1897

Whit Monday came around. When, first thing, Rab crossed the yard to the privy to empty the pot there was a thick damp fog; it didn't feel like summer, and the smoke had a welcome diluting effect on the privies' stench which hung in the viscous air. After breakfast they went round the corner to Selina's brother Henry's, then they crossed Abyssinia Bridge in a little troop – the cousins running ahead, then falling back every now and then so that the grown-ups could catch up. They passed their old house on Dunlop Street and onto Attercliffe Common and hearing one of the brass bands they waited. The children ran on up to the "rec" to join their schools, while the others, with Little Rabbi on Uncle Henry's shoulders, watched first the Sally Army procession and then the Canada Street brass band. The sun was burning off the fog and everyone's mood lifted with it – it was going to be a good morning for the Whit sing after all.

When it finished Rab said he had to go to Bramall Lane and hurried off without waiting to discuss it.

He called for Ada who was sat waiting in the shop. Almost as soon as she had opened the door to join him, a girl appeared from through the back, smiling coyly.

'Rab, this is my sister Annie Eliza,' and he shook her hand. Annie was still smiling; Rab noticed how her self-consciousness brought colour to her neck, like Ada; though she was not quite so pretty.

'Let's go Rab,' Ada said.

'Have a nice time. Be good!' Annie said. Rab was amused at how this earned her a big-sisterly, thrown look through narrowed eyes. Ada took his arm; she was wearing a wide brimmed straw hat with a frill around it – modest, not like some of the large feathered, holiday contraptions on display around town – and a dark skirt, ivory blouse and lace shawl.

'If anyone comes up to us at the ground, I'll introduce you as my cousin, is that a'reight?' he said.

'If you wish. But does it have to be a secret?'

'It's perhaps easier that way. People talk and if they think I'm courting then they might start wondering if I'm focussed on playing football.'

He realised he'd said "courting." A bigger step than he had planned to take.

After a pause she said, 'Why would they think you're not focussed? Is it that serious?'

'You'd be surprised what they're like. They don't want no distractions – women, beer, gambling. They want everyone in bed by ten during the season and make us spend Wednesday, Thursday and Friday evenings at the Lane to make sure we don't do owt we shouldn't, like drink, like a night out in Sheffield. Some of the lads even reckon they've spies out to check on yer. Best just keeping mi head down.'

'Oh, I see.'

Play had just got under way when they arrived; they found a space on a wooden form. A decent sized crowd had come to watch. Yorkshire were out batting against Warwickshire. Upwards of eight thousand Rab reckoned, quite a few of them ladies, and Ada remarked on how intently everyone watched and concentrated. Men were sat around the cinder track on spread out handkerchiefs to preserve the seat of their trousers from dirt and their own hides from the wrath of matriarchs. They puffed away on their short clay pipes – their "nose-warmers." A cloud of smoke hovered over them and dispersed only when clapping and hat waving followed a Tunnicliffe swipe to the fine leg boundary. He wanted to put his arm round her, but you couldn't do that with your cousin – there were too many people here who would recognise him – club members, committee men. She consulted him on rules but he didn't feel able to talk openly – perhaps it was a mistake to come here. But there weren't many places they could go. They shared some sandwiches and ginger beer. Ada asked him how cricket compared to football.

'Not a patch on it!' he said. 'It's usually cold, wet, and muddy, and noisy and glorious! The crowd don't just clap and go "hurrah" occasionally, they carry you forwards on a wave of chanting and madness.' Ada said she thought it sounded a bit "beastly."

'Oh, I s'pose some might think so, but it's really living – you'll see – you must come.'

Play finished early when rain came down after tea with Yorkshire on three hundred and thirty seven for six, and the crowd drifted away. On the way back up into town, a small huddle of people had gathered as they headed up to the Moor. All they could see over the bystanders were the feathers of two enormous holiday hats bobbing up and down and they could make out shrill female voices. It was an argument.

'Tha dirty little bitch!'

'Tha's the bitch – just look at thi! Get out o' mi way!'

'Whore! Taking another woman's husband off her!'

'I didn't take no one, sweet'eart – he came to me 'cause he hates thi!'

'How dare thi!'

'If tha looked after him he wouldn't go wandering would he?'

Rab and Ada saw the scuffle break out between the gaps in the onlookers and the hats ended up in the dirt.

'Tha can keep him anyhow – he were useless, too pissed to get it up!'

'Let's go and get a drink,' said Rab – he wanted to get away as quickly as possible.

'There's a new café opened on Fargate, the Victoria Tea Rooms.'

'Aye, sounds good.'

'Those frightful women: never saw anything like it,' said Ada.

He didn't want to have a conversation about this. 'Just horrible,' he said.

The café was cool and calm inside. There was a rockery with ferns and a fountain splashing into a little pool.

'Hey it's a bit fancy in here ain't it?' he said.

They were shown to a seat and ordered strawberries and cream, and were brought tea in dainty china cups.

'So not all Romanys live in caravans then?' she asked.

'No, though *gorgios* – that's anyone who's not Romany – think they do. Some still do, mostly in summer, but they won't much longer – there's no point in the old ways no more. The whole world's changing, not just for us but everyone, all the old ways being swept aside. But that has to be good don't it?'

'I suppose. But I worry where we are heading: what with a new millennium. And I don't suppose Queen Victoria can go on for much longer. I can't imagine the country without her.' Her eyes fixed him, 'So have you always lived in a house?'

'No I was born out on the road somewhere, so they say; my folks moved about sometimes when work was tight, making a living where they could, from what they could. My older brothers and sisters were born in houses out in Lincolnshire, I think.'

'So you were born in a caravan?'

'No, in a tent I should think – babies are never born in caravans – it isn't thought clean.'

'And how many brothers and sisters have you got?'

Rab counted out two brothers and six sisters on his fingers. 'But I don't see much of 'em these days, they're all up Ecclesfield way except for my brother Charlie who's just a few years older than me.'

'And how old are you?' she said putting her hand on his.

He curled his fingers round hers. 'Twenty-eight. You?'

'Twenty three.'

He walked her back, when they had reached the quieter streets he said, 'I want to see you again.'

She stopped and stood in front of him and held him. 'Then you shall.' She kissed him. 'Whenever you like.'

*

The next day at about seven o'clock, Jim came through to the back room where Ada was working through the books; invoices, bills and receipts were laid out on the table in front of her. He had his jacket on and his favourite billycock hat perched on his head.

'Right, c'mon,' he said, 'put that pen down and get thi 'at.'

'Give over Jim, we don't shut for another hour.'

'Shut already!' he said, 'locked up and put away. I've had enough. Tha coming to the fair or not?'

Ada put down her work and got up and slapped him on the arm. 'You're a rogue James McGrail!' She got her jacket and her hat off the peg. 'C'mon then.' And she took his arm.

The fairground was, Ada thought, noisy and glorious, to use Rab's phrase. It was packed into the two hundred-odd-yard stretch of ground known as Smithfield market, below the station approach. There were horses for thirty-five pounds and vendors of tackle. Dancers and trumpets competed with the melodies of merry-go-rounds and shrieks from girls on the swingboats, rising and falling. Everything was trying to outdo its neighbour in its show of electric lights, gilding, statuary and mirrors. Colours, feathered hats and squealing pretty faces whirled past in the night air to the sound of steam orchestras. The smell of baked potatoes drifted amongst that of steam engines, fried fish and stale sweat. People crowded around for the free entertainment and those spending money queued to throw things for unattainable prizes and to see the delights of the boxing saloon or to gawp at a collection of incongruous wild beasts in cages, the tattooed lady, the miniature Samson, or the Yorkshire Giantess weighing in at nigh-on forty stones. Ada and Jim bought oysters from a vendor who opened them deftly with a single twist of his blade, a toothless smile and a compliment for all the girls. They went on the American cake-walk, but most of all Ada wanted to see the moving pictures: they paid tuppence to see pictures of the Derby, someone feeding a tiger and some acrobats.

'What will they come up with next!' Ada said, 'How do they do it Jim?'

'Beats me lass – black magic!'

A ghost-show man wearing a mask leapt out at Ada and tried but failed to make her jump; but just after something did – Rab was heading her way! He was with someone but hadn't seen her – yet. She called him. He saw her and looked startled.

'Hello Rab, fancy seeing you here! You've met my brother Jim?'

'Hello again Jim.'

'Well aren't you going to introduce us?'

'Er, this is my brother Charlie. Charlie, this is Ada – a friend.'

'Rab told me about you,' she said. She saw Charlie look at Rab interrogating him with his eyes. So he couldn't have told his brother about her. 'Have you seen the moving pictures? Those things are incredible.'

'No we haven't. We were just going to see what was on at the boxing booth, weren't we Charlie?'

'Yeah Rab,' he said.

'I'll see you soon Ada,' Rab said. Charlie gave a "nice to meet you" over his shoulder as he was towed away by the arm.

'What's up Ada?' said Jim as they walked on. 'It's like he were embarrassed.'

'I know. I think he was. I don't think he can have told his brother about me yet and didn't want to stick around and have to explain to him in front of us.' She was quiet for a bit as they wandered round; she clung to his arm.

Rab was indeed a mysterious one; yesterday at the cricket he hadn't been himself and now today! – he was obviously very shy, and didn't like to show affection in public. Strange that a footballer should be shy in public, when he was used to performing every week in front of thousands; perhaps that was it – because people knew him he was more self-conscious?

'I've had enough of the noise and crush, can we go and get a drink Jim?'

'A nice pint is just what I had in mind,' said Jim, 'must be them oysters what's made me thirsty.'

*

Earlier on, Charlie Howell had dropped by after tea. 'Who's coming to the fair then!' were his first words when he came through the door.

'Can we, Uncle Charlie!' said Little Selina.

His sister-in-law gave him an exasperated look. 'It's too late for you,' she said. 'Your Uncle Charlie will take you another time won't you Uncle Charlie?'

'Oh, yeah, sorry Lina. Your ma's reight. I'll take my favourite nieces another time, promise.'

'Did you know you'll have another niece soon Uncle Charlie?'

'Will I? Hows that?' He looked at Selina; her eyes dropped and so did the penny.

'Oh that's good news!' he said. He slapped Rab on the shoulder. 'Well done mate, didn't think tha'd got it left in thi! Congratulations sis!' he said kissing Selina on the cheek.

'How's our Liza, Charlie?'

'She were bad over t'weekend, what wi' it being so close an' all, but she's better today. She gave me orders to get out o' the house and go and enjoy misen, so I came here to see if my miserable baby brother was up for it!'

'Go on with yer then, get out ot our way!' said Selina.

On their way to town Rab had told him the rest of his news, with one omission; and Charlie told him of how for a shilling he'd arranged seats in a wagonette to get to the Jubilee procession, and had bought seats on a stand on Pinstone Street for three and six.

'Four and six! Flipping heck Charlie! That's more than a weeks rent!'

'I know, I can't really afford it, but how else was she going to get to see it. I didn't tell her how much it had cost.'

They had bought pallid sausage rolls wrapped in greasy paper and went for a drink before heading to the fairground. They looked at the horses and were greeted by quite a few people; sometimes Rab didn't know if they were distant cousins, or family friends, or just football supporters. They wasted tuppence each trying to knock off cocoa-nuts they believed were glued on or wedged in tight on their holders, and a further tuppence was spent at the shooting gallery.

They were just heading to the boxing booth, dodging penny squirts wielded by girls who had had a drink or two too many, when Rab had heard his name... Ada! He had fleetingly wondered what his chances of hiding were, but realised they were non-existent. After exchanging hellos and introductions, he got away as quick as he could without wanting to appear rude. A few paces on Charlie had gripped his arm and held him tight, hurting him.

'What's going on Rab?'

'Nothin's *going on*'

'Oh come off it! Who is she?'

'She's just a friend, someone I met.' He tried in vain to shake his arm free.

'A woman like that cannot be just a friend Rab!'

'*Like* what? What's tha trying to suggest?'

'Tha'd best tell me! A pretty young woman can never be just a friend to a bloke! Tha knows what I mean. So who is she?'

Rab looked down, and tried to release his arm, but it was held in a grip made for holding a pick for eight hours a day.

'Not here Charlie.' He felt like he was under arrest being escorted to the lock up.

'Suit thisen, let's head up to the station, we can sit down there.'

They found a seat at the end of the platform, away from the main entrance.

'So?'

Rab shuffled on the seat. He felt as if his arm were still gripped. What chance did he have against Charlie?

'She's really nice.'

'Nice? Has tha…?'

'No Charlie! I've only just met her, seen her a couple of times, nothing's happened… It's just that…'

'Just what! You mean it might!' Charlie lifted his cap and ran his fingers through his hair, looking up as if for guidance.

'I dunno. I really like her. I want to get to know her better.'

'Does she know tha's married?'

Rab looked down. 'No, I ain't got round to it yet… Has tha never…?'

'Never what? – betrayed Eliza!'

Rab put his feet up on the seat, elbows on knees, palms pressed against his temples. He felt Charlie's hot gaze on him. At last Rab said without looking up, 'she's interested in me, for who I am, what I am – it's like she can see inside me.'

'For God's sake Rab, get a grip man, tha's married! And tha's going to have another child! It's not all about thi – tha's duties to thi family!'

'I know, but I feel stifled, like how yer feel when yer gets to t' pit bottom, and steps out; a whole shift ahead of yer – except I won't be getting back in the cage to go up again.'

'Don't tha love Lina any more?'

'I do but…'

'But what…' said Charlie.

'There's got to be more to living hasn't there?'

'End it now Rab… or tha's gonna hurt a lot of people!'

A train pulled in, the engine stopping right in front of them, steam pressure releasing with a big hiss and immersing them in it's soft vapour and warm grease smell.

'I know tha's reight,' Rab said.

'Yes I am. Now come on, I'm thirsty.' Charlie put his hand on his brother's shoulder, and gave him a friendly push in the direction of the steps.

Rab sighed, looked Charlie in the eye for the first time, gave him a resigned half smile and pulled himself to his feet.

Chapter 8

The weather couldn't make up its mind as to which season it was. Some days you left the house thinking it would be like yesterday, shirtsleeves weather, then had to turn back for your coat. There had been a lot of rain; some of it came as thunderstorms following a hot day when the sky took revenge for the punishment it received from the city and pelted it with its rain, trying in vain to make it clean.

A warm day found Selina on a wooden chair in the yard, a cup of tea on her lap, and flies buzzing around. Her mother had made her take a rest while she and Agnes heaved the men's washing from the sink to the wringing machine. It was their way to wash the men's clothes separately from their own – to wash them together was considered *mochardi*. This made extra work: but Agnes usually brought her washing round too so they were never short of things to fill the set pot. Selina shut her eyes, soaking in the warmth. This had always been the worst time for her – except for the very last day of course: the few weeks when she had nothing to show for the child growing inside her, except for the smell of bacon, when preparing breakfast, sending her dashing to the scullery to wretch over the sink. That time when her body as well as her mind was getting used to the idea of being not just one person, but, wonderfully, having another feeding off her. She looked down. At her side in the shade, Agnes' baby, little Agnes, fast asleep, lay in the emptied drawer from the wardrobe. The sides of her mouth twitched as if in a faked smile, and her hands shot out in a spasm before peace returned to her features. Selina saw herself nursing her own baby for that first time and smoothing its damp hair.

Agnes came and sat on the back step and shooed a fly away from the baby.

91

'At least it won't be hot like this when you're heavy,' she said.

'I was with Lizzie. It was worst at night, not being able to sleep and getting done off Rab for waking him up – it was bad 'cause back then he had to be up for earlies at the pit.'

'Has he got used to it yet – yer being…' Agnes nodded towards her midriff.

'I think so – why do they seem so shocked when you tell 'em?'

'I know, it's like it were nowt to do wi' them!' Agnes laughed and added in a gruff voice, 'bloody 'ell lass how'd that happen?'

'What are you two laughing at?' said Jemima appearing in the doorway with a big basket of washing at her hip.

'Menfolk,' said Selina.

'Allus good for a laugh, I s'pose. Hutch up love while I get past with this washing.'

She set the basket down and went back inside.

Agnes and Selina pegged out the shirts. 'Henry's never keen on me when I join the pudding club – e's understanding and kind – but he gets little affection off me until well after the baby's born – I just go right off him, if you know what I mean?'

'I'm a bit the same – can't be doing with him mithering me, and it don't seem right somehow – not with a baby in there.

'Some say a baby will allus make room for his father, but I'm like you – it don't seem decent does it? She paused. 'What's he up to anyway your fella?'

'Mooching around somewhere as usual. I never know where he gets to – just rolls in at teatime – if he's not here getting in the way. I'll be glad when his football starts again in a few weeks – when they start training again properly – give him something to get on with instead o' wasting time. You see that over there?' Selina pointed to a small wooden lean-to up by the end of the yard.

'What is it?'

'Indeed! He built it – borrowed some tools and stuff off a neighbour – reckons he's going keep a pig and fatten it up for Christmas!'

'That's not so daft, plenty o' folks keep animals round here.'

'Yeah but who'll end up feeding the damn thing when he's off kicking a ball around in Scotland or Brummagem or wherever? And who'll have to boil up the potato peelings, cabbage stalks, and leftovers?'

'We can save ours if you want.'

'We'll see what comes of it eh? He did bring us back a couple of rabbits though yesterday, so he's not entirely hopeless. He wouldn't say where he got 'em from but they came home the traditional way – one down each trouser leg, so I don't s'pose they were from Carnelly's.'

'I s'pose money's tight what with all the holidays we've got this year.'

'A little bit, but I think he just caught 'em for the sport, re-living his youth!'

'Henry's promised to treat me on Jubilee day proper since I missed seeing the Queen. We're going for a picnic and then if you or Jemmie will mind the kids he says he'll take me to a bonfire in the evening.'

'That sounds lovely. Tell you what, why don't we all go for a picnic – then we'll have the kids at ours for the night. We'll make Charlie sleep on the couch and the boys can have his bed and baby Agnes can come in our room. Then you can have your house to yourselves when you get back and not worry about waking anyone.'

''cept the neighbours!'

'Agnes Smith, you're shocking!'

'It's a good idea though – it will stop certain folks from sloping off to the Blucher or the Rubber Boot won't it, and if we get Jemmie on to it the men'll have no choice in the matter.'

Baby Agnes was stirring, so her mother picked her up to feed her. Selina watched the baby kicking her toes out from under the shawl as she sucked greedily. She went inside.

'*Dei*, I'm just going to pop out for a ha'porth of tripe and vinegar – do you want anything fetching?'

'You and your tripe!'

'I'll have gone off it again soon no doubt.'

'You could pick up a couple of bottles of something to wash down the rabbit stew.'

22nd June 1897

Jubilee day felt a bit like any other summer holiday in Sheffield – they were vaguely aware that the Queen would be doing some sort of procession in London, but everyone knew it would be nothing special – not like the spectacle they had taken part in in Sheffield just a few weeks before: for them that had been the proper Jubilee, not this.

Some people known to the inhabitants of twenty-four Lake Street, who the ministers and worthies had deemed to be the deserving poor, had received tickets for a celebration tea at St Clements Hall, where they would partake in their share of the five hundred sheep and eighty-five quarters of beef that had been donated by the Australians. Jemima was scornful of the sheep and their consumers.

How could meat be fit to eat when it's travelled all the way round the world – they could keep it, she had said. 'As for that *mumply* Effie Chafer and her street urchins getting free tickets to a slap up tea – deserving! – they ought to see what she got up to when she wasn't polishing pews or sweeping the aisle.' Whatever they had themselves, they had earned it, or leastways gained it through their own guile, she had said. So, no foreign meat. Instead their basket, which Selina had lined with old shirting, was filled with bread cakes still warm from the oven, pork pies, hard-boiled eggs, potatoes, saveloys, and a big gooseberry tart placed on top; and then the cloth folded over it all. Agnes and her baby arrived with Henry, and the boys Leo and James came clinking after them straddling another basket full of bottles which they threatened to drop, at the risk of ruining the picnic, at any moment. The living room filled up as the picnic party assembled. Finally, they were joined by another of Jemima's brood, Mary Ellen, overtly aware of her charms in her straw sailors' hat, with her Arthur on her arm in his new straw boater, also swinging a basket. They couldn't all fit in the room so spilled out into the yard, the children running excitedly between the grown-ups, and getting into trouble for not minding baskets and not respecting lace trimmings on dresses.

The little Jubilee procession moved on up to Wincobank Woods, carrying baskets, babies and blankets. Mary Ellen and Arthur each held one of Little Rabbi's hands and swung him between them until, falling behind the rest of the party and getting bored of his "again, again," they handed him to his father to carry. Rab had had his mandolin across his back, which he shifted to his front and put Little Rabbi on his back, from where he was rewarded by getting his ears pulled and his cap played with all the way up Upwell Street.

Everyone flopped onto the grass when they finally reached their chosen spot – a patch of grass by some trees overlooking the Don valley and its majestic array of chimneys. Jackets and shawls that had been slung over shoulders on the way up were folded or hung on bushes and the blankets were spread out. Mary Ellen and Arthur strolled off arm in arm, doubtless to find a secluded spot. Henry organised cricket teams which went off to find a flat piece of ground and Dennis took Little Rabbi exploring in the jungle looking for lions, leaving Rab with Selina, her mother and the Agneses.

The women watched as Rab went off with his mandolin and sat against a tree trunk – where he strummed a few tunes before settling down to rest, pulling his cap over his eyes.

'He's been quiet lately 'as Rab,' Jemima said to Selina.

'Oh he does get like that sometimes – who knows what goes on in that head of his? I don't think he's got used to the idea of another baby on the way – doesn't seem real to him yet I suppose.'

A cry of "tea's ready" from Jemima, enough to wake anyone asleep on the hill, brought him back down; and cricketers and explorers came crashing through the undergrowth moments later to excitedly gather around the blankets where food was spread out on cloths.

Dennis spoke: 'Just a few words before we start – thank you Jemmie and your girls for putting on such a spread, and thank you Lord for what we are about to receive. Now we haven't got glasses to fill so let's raise us bottles in a toast to Her Majesty Queen Victoria, Empress of India!'

'Her Majesty Queen Victoria!' everyone said.

'Long may she reign!' added Jemima. 'Now then who's for a bit of pork pie?'

Between mouthfuls of gooseberry tart, Mary Ellen said, 'Did you hear about that lady cyclist?'

'No what was that love?'

'Well it's rather splendid – can't remember her name, but she cycled from London to Sheffield in fourteen and a half hours!'

'Is tha sure tha's got that right lass?' said Dennis, 'A lady tha said?'

'She must be some girl don't yer think?'

'Don't they arrest folk for riding furiously?' Rab said; 'that must've been pretty furious I'd say.'

'Just shows yer how we don't have to sit around all the time looking pretty though!' added Mary Ellen.

'But that is just what you're doing now dearest – sitting and looking pretty!' said Arthur.

'Thank you Arthur dear, but you know what I mean! Things are changing, women aren't fools.'

'That they're not, said Jemima, 'but men are and couldn't run a house, so that's where we're needed – tearing about the countryside on a bicycle don't do no good for no one does it?'

'But life would be dull if it were all graft,' said Rab, 'and if someone can do that and cheer up folks like Mary Ellen then good luck to 'em I say.'

'Thank you Rab, well spoken,' said Mary Ellen.

'Have you been to London Uncle Rab?' said Leo.

'Aye, a few times. To Crystal Palace, to play the Corinthians, the Woolwich Arsenal…'

'Could you cycle there in fourteen and and a half hours Daddie?' asked Little Selina.

Everyone laughed and Little Selina looked cross.

'I've never even been on a bike lass so, no, I don't reckon so. It takes about four hours by train so fourteen and a half hours is going some.'

'I'd like to ride a bike, one like in the song: made for two!'

'I'll go on the front!' said Leo. There followed a little rendition of "Daisy Belle" with everyone joining in.

Mary Ellen dug a bag of cherries out of her basket, and passed them round.

Leo was sat next to Lizzie, 'Bet you can't beat this,' he whispered, spitting his cherry stone about three yards. Lizzie, not one to be easily beaten by a boy, matched him but a stop was put to the game for being "disgusting" before they got to measure exact distances.

After tea Lizzie, Little Selina, Leo and James led the singing of "O King of Kings," which school had drummed into them with discipline that would make sergeant-majors on the North West Frontier puff up their chests. They had all sung this hymn in church on Sunday so they more or less knew the words with the children's help. Rab then strummed a few chords for Arthur who sang "Oh, Dem Golden Slippers" and everyone joined in with the chorus of "Golden Kippers," as had become the tradition.

On the way home Jemima announced that the boys and baby Agnes would be stopping the night at theirs so that Henry and Aunty Agnes could go out on the town. The children were very excited by this. Rab said, 'I'll be back late anyway, we've got a team meeting to discuss the start of training for next season.'

'What on a holiday! Surely not Rab?' said Selina.

'Well yeah, I think they want to keep a check that no one gets drunk and shames the club, you know what they're like about that.'

*

Rab headed into town in the evening. He headed straight round to Bridge Street where Ada was waiting for him. He had gone over in his mind many times what his brother had said to him. He could see why Charlie thought it was wrong for him to see Ada, but he always kept coming back to one thing – he really liked Ada, he certainly wanted her, he might even be in love with her; and that was just nature. He could still love Selina and desire another. In the old days he'd heard that some Romanys had more than one woman and they all travelled together. It just felt right to be with Ada, it was nice; it was his escape.

They ate cake and drank coffee in town before joining a steady stream of people on foot, and in hansoms, heading up Duke Street towards where the bonfire was to be lit at Sky Edge. The sun was already down behind the distant Derbyshire hills when they arrived, and pink, fish-scale clouds flecked the sky. Rab pointed out where the Bramall Lane enclosure was; and over to his right, he saw shadow descending on the wide Don Valley and he looked to where Brightside was – then looked away.

Swifts whistled to each other as they chased, wheeled and dived against the fading light of the sky. A crowd was already several deep around the pile of wood, wood shavings, tar barrels and coal that stood twenty feet tall against the gradually darkening sky. Rab made sure his money was safely tucked inside his waistcoat pocket – this was just the sort of place where you might feel a hand brush against your trouser pocket or a pretty young woman would apologise for bumping into you and, before you realised, your jacket pocket had been emptied, and the contents had passed from hand to hand several times. He pulled Ada towards him. Drifting around was that smell: ubiquitous where crowds gathered, of baked potatoes, beery breath and pipe smoke.

Already across the city smaller bonfires were underway, dotted across the skyline on all the hills, brighter than the dim sky around them. Lights could be made out in the town below.

Then some men in shirtsleeves, looking very purposeful and self-important, relishing their position in the proceedings, started moving around by the bonfire holding lanterns. Soon the light from the lanterns was supplanted by small clumps of flame at the base, and smoke and sparks started to stream up into the evening as the wood started to crackle and the coal spit out its gases. The flames crept up the wood-pile and took hold. Across the city another large fire at the high point of the hill at Mount Zion was throwing out its light as it came to life. Rab felt Ada's arm around his back as the warmth from the fire reached his face. Ada half turned towards him and, placing her hands on his hips, she moved him half round towards her; a gap still between them warmed by the flames. She looked up at him and he saw the flames reflecting in her eyes. He put both arms around her and the feeling, starting somewhere inside him, which shuddered outwards to his limbs, made him hold her tight. He felt the weight of her head on his shoulder as she leant against him. He loosened his embrace, embarrassed at the physical effect it was having on him and moved away from her so that she wouldn't notice. She pulled him back towards her – there was no hiding it – she knew.

Several rockets were let off into the darkened sky, the final one a magnesium star rocket bursting white light into the sky making him feel momentarily very self-conscious as the brightness invaded their night-veiled intimacy.

She still held him to her and turned her face from the sky to him, 'Rab you've come to mean a lot to me.'

He felt giddy, his heart jumping, 'You mean a lot to me too. I need you Ada!'

She moved against him subtly, discretely, 'I know. Let's go for a walk.'

They headed off away from the bonfire and the crowd, out over the fields and climbed across a stone wall.

Chapter 9

With an eye on the beginning of the season George Waller called the players in more often to start getting them into fighting shape. Some days were spent walking out as far as Hathersage and back, others in the gymnasium swinging Indian clubs, lifting dumbbells, exercising on rings, bars and ropes, punchbag work and even going a few rounds with the gloves on. This would be followed by a trip to the baths on the corner of John Street for the joys of cold sponges, hot baths and a rub down, steak for tea in the pavilion and sent home under orders for early nights. No master had ever treated his servants so well in history: looked after better than thoroughbreds indeed.

About half the team, Rab included were sat around waiting for the others to arrive. There was still only one new signing: Henry White a centre-forward from Hibs.

'All in good time,' said George, 'we're working on it. Once the Committee's decided you lot'll be the first to learn.'

Tommy Morren said, 'Does that mean you'll be down at Midland Station, nicking the luggage off any honest footballer that happens to be passing through?'

'You know I'll do anything to get my man,' replied George.

Kenny McKay, who had joined midway through the last season asked them what they were on about.

Rab said, 'Oh this is funny, ain't it Bill, hasn't tha heard it?'

'Go on Tommy, tell "Och Aye" how tha ended up here!' Bill said.

'Well,' said Tommy, weighing up his opening words like a well-seasoned after dinner speaker, 'I'd made a bit of a name for myself havin just won the FA amateur cup with Middlesbrough. One of our team, Phil Baske, had signed pro for Reading and he had put in a good word for me to go and join 'em. So here's me sat on a train heading for Brummagem where I was to change for Reading. The train pulls up in Sheffield and who should turn up in my carriage but this ugly bugger, Waller here, who I once played cricket with once or twice a few year back. So he says to me, c'mon Tommy, you don't want to go down south, the beer's no better than badger's piss. Come and play wi' a proper team and win summat. I says, "but I've agreed to go to Reading," and then he grabs me bag off the rack and jumps down to the platform and runs off wi' it. So there I am shouting "Come back here y' bugger," and the whistle goes, so I have to decide to go wi'out my stuff or get off. And then this stroppy guard's wanting the door shut, so I jumps off and goes after George. "Good decision," he says, "we'll gi' yer thirty bob a week." "Find us a job as a moulder as well, I says, and you've got a deal." So I gets in a cab wi' 'im and comes to the Lane and finds myself playing in a red and white shirt that very afternoon, ain't that right George? So I signed up and here I am, running up and down the pitch wi' that under'and bastard shouting at us day in day out.' There was laughter all round.

'That story gets better wi' each telling Tommy!'

'Right boys,' said George, 'looks like we're all here – nice of tha to join us Cocky! Even the town hall clock keeps better time than thi.'

'Sorry George, train were delayed.'

'Well if tha does insist on living somewhere daft like Mexborough!'

'Yeah, bugger off George!'

'That's two extra laps for thi then whilst we're sitting down to dinner,' Rab whispered to him as Bennett found somewhere to perch next to him.

George continued, 'Since it's a nice day – only warm drizzle, rather than the usual pissing it down, I've a treat for you all.'

'Is it medicine balls instead o' dumbbells?' said Bill, 'I'm in danger of losing my figure.' He patted his stomach. 'I hope we've got a decent dinner.'

'No but I might just leave thi here to do that, whilst we all head up to Abbeydale for a round of golf.'

Everyone set off enthusiastically; what a great idea of George's; ought to do this more often. However, a few holes in, after a few forays into the rough where the grass was long and even more wet, and the damp started to seep past oft-darned socks, the enthusiasm of some paled a little. Rab reached the fifth green in four shots, and was joined by Mick Whitham. It was a bit of a free-for-all – some of the players like Needham, Foulke and Jack Almond were way ahead: Needham by dint of being sickeningly good at anything involving a ball that he should happen to turn his hand (or foot) to, Bill Foulke because he could hit the ball twice as far as anyone else and Almond because of his familiarity with the game.

'Ere Rab, does tha reckon Sugar has his own golf course in his back garden?'

'Well he could afford it, by all accounts – he certainly knows what he's doing with these here stick things don't he?' said Rab, lining up an imaginary tee shot with his putter mimicking Jack Almond. 'He's a'reight though is Jack, you can't grudge him his money, I wouldn't say no if my father left me money in his will, not that I'll get a brass farthing off of him, when the owd bugger finally shuffles off.'

'Watch out, George is about!' Mick said – they could see George not far off on a different hole. 'Act serious.'

They each took three puts to the hole and made to look very earnest. On their way to the sixth, Rab said, 'he's a crafty sod is George, ain't he? Some of 'em think we've just come for a jolly little trip to the golf course for a bit o' fun. But what they don't realise is how George is testing and probing all the time to see what sort of players they are. It's the same when he sends us off on a hike into Derbyshire or doing laps of the track – those that don't get on wi' it, those that don't appear to be enjoying themsens, he's on to 'em, and if they don't get it quick they never seem to last long.'

'Yeah tha's right, he knows what he wants right enough, does George and he gets it too, or it's the reserves – or the door.'

'What's tha been up to this summer then Mick?'

'Keep it quiet – but I've been doing a bit o' work, just to help out a mate – but to stop misen getting bored as well. And I could do wi' the money, I don't get as much as thi don't forget.'

'What's tha need money for – tha's only got thisen to look after.'

'I'm saving up.'

'Chuffing heck Mick, tha a'reight? Not feeling ill?'

Mick smiled, gave a little click with his tongue and placed his ball on the tee, and lined up his shot which went swerving off to the right accompanied by a "sod it."

'Hang on,' said Rab, 'What is tha saving for? Wouldn't happen to be a woman would it? Mick Whitham's not settling down is 'e?'

'Perhaps. Perhaps not.'

'No! Tha's got to tell me now. Who is she?'

'She's called Laura, she's seventeen so we're not rushing into anything.'

'Seventeen! Bloody hell Mick, tha jammy owd sod!'

'Keep that quiet too. I don't want no one to know – you know what they're like, and nowt might come of it.'

'Sounds serious though, if tha's saving up. What's she like then?

Mick told him how they'd met and described her; he was clearly besotted. As Mick sang his sweetheart's praises Rab thought about Ada, and once in the conversation he said, "Yeah I know what tha means," and meant it from recent experience.

Over lunch in the clubhouse, the talk was of strikes.

'So I'm the only one bringing in money now the colliery's on strike,' said Needham.

'Which colliery's that then?' asked Henry White, the new player.

'Staveley, where I live – both my father-in law and brother-in-law work there.'

'What's it about then?'

'What's it ever about? Money. There's this new electric cutting machine and they're using it as an excuse to cut rates.'

There were a few colliers around the table and memories of ninety-three were still fresh.

'The bosses have got to realise that slavery's been abolished,' said Bill. 'Pit men might come up looking like Negroes but they ain't picking cotton! They can't just keep nibbling away at men's wages and expect 'em to lie down!'

'What about the engineers strike in London, and where-'ave-yer, do you reckon that'll happen here too?' said Needham.

Alfred Priest, an engineer by trade spoke up: 'No one seems to think that'll 'appen 'ere. There's no one asking for eight hour days: they earn six bob a day – not bad money – they're skilled men, they've no quarrel with the bosses here.'

'Here I've got a story to lighten things up a bit,' said Bill, 'it's a true un an' all'

'All yours are Bill, whether you've made 'em up or not!' chipped in Rab.

'Well this fella in Lancashire somewhere, probably one o' Rab's mates, I shouldn't wonder, was arrested and sent to prison for a month. He were caught by the police for being drunk and disorderly. He were down on his hands and knees, and his face were covered in blood and scratches. Apparently there were a bet on, and all his mates scarpered when the copper arrived leaving him there. He'd been fighting a rat on a string wi' 'is teeth, and the rat were all covered in bite marks!'

Most of them roared with laughter as the story progressed, and one or two put down their knives and forks and stopped eating whilst such images were in their heads. Rab was glad to be back amongst this. The serious business was not far off; soon there would be a discipline, a timetable, a focus at the end of every week – when Saturday comes!

*

By now Selina had stopped feeling nauseous – the worst part was over. The presence of her baby was starting to show and soon people would treat her with kindness, be interested in her, talk to her in shops about more than the weather and offer to carry things for her – she would not resist. She was having to wear different clothes – but she had sold the skirts she had worn for Little Rabbi and taken in some blouses that couldn't easily be let out again. Agnes had said to go round to theirs to see what she could dig out – she had also pawned some skirts which could be got back again. Selina walked round with Little Rabbi – a minute's walk taking about ten as they stopped for a neighbour to ruffle his dark locks and tell him how much he had grown, or for him to stoop and pick up stones, to point at goodness-knows-what, and for no apparent reason whatsoever. Agnes sat Little Rabbi down with some pots and pans and a wooden spoon. What with these and the stones to put in and take out he was quite happy for some time. Agnes rooted through a chest, found a dress and a blouse and gave her the pawn tickets.

'How did Leo and James get on at sports' day?' asked Selina, when they sat down to watch baby Agnes asleep in her homemade crib, crafted with care and some skill from timber borrowed from the pit.

'Leo was full of it when he came home: he came second in a football dribbling race or something and won a little ribbon – he said he was going to be like his Uncle Rab.'

'Oh don't encourage him will you.'

'Don't worry, he also wants to drive electric trams when he's big.'

'A proper regular job.'

'What about Lizzie and little Lina?'

'They enjoyed themselves too – Lizzie got a ribbon for a skipping race, but Lina didn't, she said she would've if some girl or other hadn't nudged her and knocked her egg off her spoon, just as she was nearing the finish line.'

'Oh I can imagine how she took that!'

'Little does that girl know: the grudge that will be held against her till she meets her maker. If they reach seventy you can imagine little old Selina saying," See that old goat over there – she's the one who knocked my egg off back in Ninety Seven!"'

Little Rabbi looked up at the laughter and joined in, banging on a pan with his spoon.

'I'd never got to speak to you properly since your night out, tell me about it,' said Selina.

'Oh we had a fine old time – we went up to town and had a few drinks then went up to the bonfire – huge it was and there were fireworks and everything – I'd never seen fireworks before. Then we had a few more drinks before heading home merry as you like and straight to bed for...' and she tailed off from a whisper into a silent lip movement and a smirk. She paused, 'Selina, your Rab didn't go up to the bonfire that night did he?'

'No he was at a football thing, why?'

'No, nothing, I just thought I saw someone that looked a bit like him, but it were dark, and crowded. Could've been his Charlie, or some other bloke wi' a moustache.'

Agnes took a sip of her tea. Selina looked at her; what was she on about?

Just then Henry came in. He had his cap in front of him between both hands, clutching it like he had just entered a church.

'What's up love?' said Agnes.

'You've not heard the news?' he said.

'No what is it?' Agnes and Selina's faces both suddenly drained.

'Mundella's dead.'

The women were instantly relieved that it was not something closer to home, before a milder sadness descended.

'He was a good man,' said Henry, 'and a bloody good Member of Parliament. The end of an era.'

'God rest 'is soul,' said Selina.

Teatime was a sombre affair, with those who knew about Anthony John Mundella genuinely reflecting what they had lost, and those who didn't know or care very much, not wanting to get told off for being disrespectful.

'It seems like he's always been our MP,' said Dennis.

'He has though, ain't he? said Jemima.

'Getting on thirty year,' said Dennis, ' – long before we rolled into *Chooreste-Gav*. A good man, one o' Gladstone's finest. That whole generation are fading away.' There was a long pause. 'You kids've a lot to thank him for'

'Why's that Granda?' said Lizzie.

'Because he's fought hard and won the right for ordinary kids like you to go to school, and be educated – not just the kids of rich folks. That's why you girls can read and write and us old uns can't. And it were him what made the gaffers see sense back in ninety three.'

If an uncle had been lost to the family, a stranger looking in wouldn't have noticed a difference in their demeanour. They ate largely in silence with only the occasional thought bubbling up to the surface and forming into words.

'I met him once – shook his hand,' said Rab, 'he came to a match when we played Forest, he were introduced to the team.' The words just hung there unanswered. There was a pause as if they were waiting for an "and," but there wasn't one and they returned to their plates. His interesting encounter thus ignored, Rab lost himself in his thoughts. All this talk of the end of an era – life after Victoria and Gladstone – the end of the nineteenth century – now Mundella. But why the pessimism? Wasn't that just life? People die; we move on. Weren't things better now than ever? He thought of his beginnings in a tent on a heather moor. Ecclesfield. The room they let on Carlisle Street – to the back-to-back with a tap in the yard – to this house. When you reach a high point why do some people always think the only way is to fall back down, why not move on to the next high point. Wasn't that what Mundella and Gladstone were about – looking for the next high point and how to get there? Lizzie, Little Selina and Little Rabbi would ride in electric trams, motor cars like he had seen in London, have electric lights and other electric machines, telephones, watch moving pictures. Then he remembered the baby too, not yet born. He looked at Selina; she looked tired but not so drawn. She had some colour in her cheeks. The baby had settled in – stopped making her sick. The baby was her main focus now, then the kids, then the home: not much left for him. He felt it was like she was only half in this world and half somewhere else; if she could go off and hide for the next six months, somewhere warm and dark and still, then emerge with a baby, she would. She was here though and, he sensed, the best she could do was put on her invisible armour, protection for herself and the thing she was growing inside her. Ada was now the one who held him, who reached him, who excited him. He had called on her when he could after training, or in the evening. They sat, they talked, they became familiar with cafes and luncheon rooms with lemon tinted or panelled walls; they whispered to each other amongst ladies in hats sipping tea, under lofty, vaulted ceilings picked out in gold, illuminated by electric lights concealed behind fairy shades. He stroked her hand under the table, and thought of more.

At night he'd lie on his back, awake, as Selina and Little Rabbi breathed heavily beside him – longing for Ada. Sometimes he'd stand cloaked in the curtains looking out over the dark, still yard and the rooftops, pressed against the cool glass of the window, an image of Ada lying in her bed. It seemed cruel that he could not lie beside her, but how could he ever? That night at the bonfire – the clumsy, urgent fumbling in the dark, like the euphoria of netting against *the Wednesday* last year: over so quick, a now insubstantial memory, leaving him wanting more, wanting the feeling back, to immerse himself in it, and fully.

*

July turned to August, and boys in the street, the same ones who played "bull roar" – setting fire to newspaper in drainpipes to make them roar – found new entertainment: they now conserved their paper to tie into large balls which they would tie with string and swing around their heads like medieval weapons and go around the streets chanting songs. "Vote, vote, vote for Maddison, if you don't vote for him we'll kick your doors in, and throw the rotten Tory in an old dust bin."

Three new Scotchmen joined them in training: David Morton from Millwall, and two Johns: Cunningham from the no longer so invincible Preston team, and Blair from Stalybridge Rovers. Also another North-Easterner, a "nearly Scot," who had played out Chesterfield-way last season. Rab still regarded himself and Mick as the only true Sheffielders in the team. Training went well – they were all fit and ready. Behind his back Rab cursed George Waller for all the boring stuff he made them do in the gym, and all the walking.

'We should be running with the ball, taking shots and corners, not swinging these bloody clubs,' he quietly cursed to Mick through grimaces of pain from his shoulders.

'Well tha knows what he says, and Nudge says the same – it hardens your muscles and makes you more prone to injury, and

108

you'll lose your hunger fo' t' ball.'

'That's a load of crap though. As if you'd ever get fed up with kicking a ball! I got done off him the other day – I came back after training had finished – to practise my free kicks and he caught me at it. It makes no sense!'

Thursday 12th August 1897

The day of the first proper practice session – the Red and Whites versus the Whites in front of a crowd – was fresh after thunderstorms had cleared the dry heavy air in the night. This was it. Rab had his kit ready and his boots, his "Gam-kicks," the ones he dared not reveal the price of, nicely broken in and dubbined. The lucky fairy's foot in its leather bag, suspended from a thong was tucked carefully in his bag. There should be a decent crowd and Ada would be amongst them to see him play for the first time.

In the club-room they had whiled away the hours before the match playing billiards or cards, watching the clock on the mantel shelf going round so slowly. They had eaten mid-afternoon following George's instructions: always three hours before kick off. Needham had been studying the comings and goings at their rival clubs and was holding forth on the prospects for the season.

'Villa have lost Campbell, Welford and Reynolds: all gone back north to Glasgow Celtic, but they've still got more than enough talented players to choose from and have brought players in to replace them. I reckon the biggest shock though is Robinson going off to New Brighton – they must be paying some money them, 'cause they've poached Arridge and Milward from Everton too and players from Sunderland.'

'Well if Robinson wants to go and rot in a non-league club then that's fine by me – perhaps they'll realise he's not the best keeper in England and gi' it to someone who deserves it!' said Bill.

'I can't see Liverpool or Sunderland doing much. They've brought in new players who are a bit untested – Sunderland's had a right clear out and brought in lots of young lads – they've kept their best ones though, Doig, Wilson, Dunlop, and Morgan – who's the only forward from last season.'

He addressed Cunningham, 'What do you think about Preston, Jock – lost a few haven't they?'

'Aye, that they have. They've lost their most promising player obviously.' This received jeers all round. 'But they've lost Orr and Blythe who've gone back home.'

'Well now the Scotch've seen sense and started paying their players...' Needham said. 'Anyhow, I should think they'll be hard-pushed this season. They're weak at half-back especially.'

'What about that other lot,' said Rab, jerking a finger in the direction of Olive Grove, *the Wednesday's* ground.

'They're not much changed. Bell's gone to Everton, but they've brought in a couple of Scots. Can't rule 'em out.'

'I can,' said Rab.

George ran through the new rules with them again.

'Accidental handling of the ball's allowed – so if it justs hits thi hand that's no longer handball – it has to be wilful in the ref's eyes. So some of you gorillas what drag your knuckles on the ground shouldn't be giving away so many free kicks and penalties, with any luck. Talking of gorillas, that brings us to goalies: law ten says they are no longer to be charged unless they are running wi' the ball, so Bill tha'll have fewer centre-forwards bouncing off thi.'

'They allus come off worse nor me!'

'Bill and Bradders, to remind you, no more juggling the ball; you can't take any more than two steps with the ball now or its carrying.

'But bouncing it is permitted, yeah?' asked Bert Bradshaw, the number two goalie.

'Yeah that's allowed. Also the law on tripping has changed. Last year you'll remember that it was a foul if you were running behind your man and put your foot out, whether or not it was a genuine attempt to get the ball. Now if the referee judges that you were not intending to trip there is no foul. Any questions?'

'It seems to me,' said Needham, 'that the referee has got a much harder job judging whether trips were intentional or whether hands were accidental.'

'How ref's'll rule on it we'll only find out as we go on,' said

Waller.

'Aye,' Rab said, 'but at least we won't have players deliberately aiming the ball at your hands to win penalties. I hated that!'

They were divided into the two teams, Rab was in the Red and Whites, the side with the strongest backs and the weakest forwards, the Whites having the strongest forwards and the weakest backs.

It felt good to be in the changing room, lacing on his boots; the smell of warm wood, and linseed oil, a reminder that the willow wielders and trundlers had not quite yet moved aside for the main attraction. George ran through what he wanted to get out of it. 'There's a decent crowd out there considering: three or four thousand, I reckon, so put on a good show, no injuries – Howell I wish tha'd get thisen some shinguards –'

'Don't need 'em George, slows yer down.'

' – so no going in hard, let's see some goals eh? And the new blokes – I want to see what you've got.'

As they ran out onto the pitch, there was a big cheer. Rab knew they were thinking the same as him: football's back!

Ada sat in the John Street stand next to Jim; one of only a handful of women in the crowd. She felt out of place, like she had walked into the smoke room not the lounge bar, by mistake; it smelt of drying wood and tobacco. She looked across at the terraces and the sea of faces each topped by a cap, and a fog of smoke hovering over them. There was an excited chatter all around, and people shouting greetings and waving their hats at each other over their heads.

She listened in on the conversations around her. The team's chances for the season were debated: goals, that's what was needed, they needed a Bloomer, or Johnny Campbell, or someone to net like the Preston front men. The United had the best back line in the country, without a shadow of a doubt, but couldn't hope to compete with the Villans who had scored thirty more goals last year, despite the United's second place. An' Preston likewise: seventy goals to our forty odd. But it was too much to hope that the United's backs could be even meaner. Perhaps, this Cunningham feller, wasn't he from Preston? Aye but not their first string. What about the other new Scotch bloke, Morton, was it. Never heard on him before. Nah, they just got lucky last year. The committee should've got a proven forward. But just look at the bloody money the big clubs spend on wages: five thousand odd for the likes of Everton, the Villans or *the Wednesday*, nearly twice what we pay — how we gonna compete wi' that?

Ada tried to follow what they were saying but struggled. She was surprised at just how serious they all were, how fed up they sounded, how they were sure they were not going to succeed before they'd even seen a ball kicked: the same seriousness that Rab showed.

She wasn't quite sure what to expect next. She wondered where Rab was and what he was doing. Was he as nervous as her? Why was she nervous exactly? It was more than just being in a strange place; it was like something in the very air, some strange energy, was seeping into her skin. A brass band moved round the side of the pitch, playing as they marched, and headed off round the back of the pavilion where she had first met Rab.

'It's a nice evening for it Jim.'

'Aye, but I could think o' better ways to spend a summer's evening. Somewhere where there were girls for a start. But mustn't complain since it cost nowt!'

She squeezed his hand. 'Thanks for coming with me, I couldn't exactly have come on me own could I?

'No sis.'

Applause broke out and Ada looked to see what it was about. A stream of players in red and white jerseys and navy blue knickers were walking onto the far side of the pitch followed by players in white still walking down the pavilion steps. She picked Rab out, fifth in line — she could tell by way he moved, rocking slightly, almost swaggering, whereas some of the others walked stiff and others seemed to shuffle. They seemed to take a long time to walk across the grass to where the football pitch was laid out — Ada noticed them deliberately avoid the rectangle of short grass which was, she now knew, for cricket. They spread out and two of the men came forward to talk to the man she thought must be the umpire. Rab was looking round, he was trying to pick her out in the stand. She stood up and waved her hat – she thought she saw him smile and turn back. She noticed men with flags on the side line, dressed like the umpire, in breeches, jackets and caps.

Her eyes mostly followed Rab throughout the game, except to compare his physique to the others. She gasped when she saw him charged into the first time – she felt he must have been hurt – but apparently not. He also did it to others to get the ball off them, and he stuck to them and wouldn't let them get away, stopping them from giving it to one of the other whites. And when he ran forward with the ball it seemed attracted to his feet like a magnet. Like the others his long sleeves were rolled up past his elbows, but unlike the others she could see his legs; his socks were not pulled up as were theirs. More than once she felt blood rise to her cheeks and felt self-conscious; Jim and everyone else weren't interested in her though, they were all focussed on the game. Rab had the ball at the corner of the pitch and the others were stood towards the middle. Somehow he managed to loop the ball up into the air and get it near the goal; then she was shocked to see someone rise up and hit the ball with their head – did that not damage them? – then the ball bounced into the goal and the crowd all cheered. Jim shouted, 'Bravo,' along with the others, whilst Ada just clapped.

'That was good – a good corner off your fella!' said Jim.

'I would never have believed it,' she replied.

Every now and then the umpire would blow his whistle just as someone looked about to rush forward and try to score.

'Why does the umpire keep stopping them Jim?'

'He's called a referee, and he's blowing for offside. You've always got to have at least three of the opposition closer to the goal than the man you pass to, or it's offside.'

'I see,' she said, though she wasn't convinced she did really.

Ada found that her mind wandered; surprising that amongst all the noise and commotion, you could immerse yourself in thoughts and dreams. She thought of the night of the bonfire and of his and her desire. She felt so lucky to have met Rab; such a strong, charming, funny, man; someone that all these people admired – they called his name like they knew him too. "Get on the ball Rab," "Gi' 'im snuff Rab!" whatever that meant. And yet she really knew the man. And yet he was still so ordinary. She wanted to be with him as much as she was sure he wanted to be with her. She wanted to lie with him as his wife, and knew it would not be long before he asked her. It was worth the wait. Oh how it would be worth the wait!

Three more goals were scored before the game ended: two for each side the result. Ada again thought she saw Rab look towards her before walking off. She would have liked to go and see him straight away but knew she couldn't; she would have to wait. She held Jim's arm as they left the ground and headed to get a drink on their way home.

Chapter 10

The next evening Rab called round to the shop just as Ada was cashing up for the day. He tapped on the shop window, seeing her at the counter and gave a huge grin as she looked up. She hurried over to let him in, 'How are you today Rab, I was worried you might be limping after last night – it seemed awfully rough.'

'That weren't rough! We're all mates – that were friendly. Rough is what you get when it's *the Wednesday*. Then there's real rivalry, a bit of needle.'

She smiled at him like a mother would to a mischievous child – he thought if he hadn't had his cap on she might even have ruffled his hair. 'Did you like the game though, apart from it being "awfully rough"?'

'Rather too much, I'm afraid – too much to be ladylike, I think. I was tempted to shout out like some of the men.'

'No, I don't s'pose there's much ladylike to do wi' it. But it's getting more popular wi' lady spectators these days.'

'Just to admire the skill and occasion of course,' she said wryly.

'What do you mean, what else is there... oh...,' he grabbed her by the forearms and she giggled and half-heartedly tried to pull free.

'I don't know. I can't think what else there would be seeing all those strapping young men running around after a ball!' she said, as she stopped struggling and let him kiss her. 'There was only one player on the pitch I really kept my eye on though,' she said kissing him back.

'I'll help you tidy up a bit, then shall we go out somewhere?'

'That'd be nice. I'll only be about ten minutes. We could go up to the Grand – there's usually something worth seeing there on a Friday night.'

'That sounds good, I've not been to the Varieties for a long time.'

Rab grabbed a brush and swept the day's dirt and debris off the floor into a little pile, then sat down on a crate and watched Ada as she wrote in a ledger on the counter in front of her. Her brow knotted from time to time and she made a funny little movement of her lips to the side. She didn't look up at him so he was able to self-indulgently stare at her, caressing her with his eyes. Sometimes when sitting on a tram he would study people deciding who was the most desirable and guiltily look away when they became aware of his attention – but now he was allowed to stare. Then Ada did look up. 'What are you gawpin at?' she said.

'You,' he replied with a smile.

She turned her back on him without an expression flicking across her face, and rested her book on a shelf instead. So he stared at the back of her head, her hair tied loosely up, her neck and shoulder blades shaping her blouse. He went over and stood behind her, enclosing her in his arms and resting his chin on her shoulder. She relaxed against him.

'You done yet?'

'Yes I think that'll do,' she said closing the ledger and clasping his hands in hers.

They paid sixpence on the door of the Grand for balcony seats. They got drinks then found seats just to one side, overlooking the stage. The stalls and tuppenny pit seats below were filling up as people drifted in from the bar. Bottles clinked and hats wafted, and warm air and smoke rose up and caught their nostrils. Rab removed his jacket and rolled up his sleeves.

'It's smart in here since they've done it up aint't it? Electric lights, plush seats, the lot,' Rab said.

'I've not been here much, only with Annie once or twice.' She looked around and leaned over to look at the people below. A girl with a basket was moving down the aisle selling oranges. 'Have you ever seen anyone famous at the theatre Rab? Marie Lloyd, or anyone.'

'No can't say that I have.' Then he added, 'Though I did once see Lucy the singing pig at the Gaiety – does that count?'

'No it does not!' She slapped him on the thigh. 'I saw Vesta Tilly once – not my sort of thing though: I'd prefer girls to be girls. I would love to go to the proper theatre – y' know where the audience all dress up in evening gowns – and see Ellen Terry – I've still got a picture postcard of her that I had on my wall as a girl – my father gave it to me for Christmas one year. I always thought she was the most beautiful woman in the world!'

'Aren't you the dreamer eh?'

'I'm sorry, I know satin evening gowns aren't for the likes of me. Every girl dreams though.' She came back down to earth, 'Come on, what's on then?'

Rab passed her the programme with a: 'Here you are.'

The curtain went up and the orchestra played a tune that Rab was familiar with from somewhere. Then the chairman came on and banged his gavel asking for order before the first act. He toasted the Queen and then warned the ladies in the gallery to keep a tight hold on their fellers, as he introduced the beautiful, the delightful, Miss Jessie – bang – Heywood! She came on dressed all in layers of white lace, carrying a white parasol and opened with "The boy I love is up in the gallery;" several of the men near to Rab and Ada waving their handkerchiefs in the chorus and getting kisses blown at them in return.

Then there was a father and son acrobat act where the boy was balanced on the upside down father's feet, and then he was thrown around like he was a toy. Two comedians with an Italian sounding name, but who were clearly from no further south or more exotic than Worksop, did little sketches: like a farmer who sees his neighbour digging a hole, and throwing something feathery in, when challenged he said he was just replanting some of his flower seeds. But the farmer says, that looks mighty like one of my chickens! It's all right is the reply – my seeds are inside. Also on the bill were a change artiste and ventriloquist, and other singers. Rab sat holding Ada's hand and the evening flew by.

They waited until most people had left before descending to street level. As they approached the door, Ada holding on to his arm, they became aware of a group of young men, unshaven, not well dressed, wearing shapeless jackets, collarless shirts, their caps pushed well back on their heads. They were staring blankly at Rab and Ada. The one in front with dark strands of greasy hair lying across his forehead: his dark eyes looked straight into Rab's - then he glanced at one of his mates and gave a slight nod. Rab stiffened and moved in front of Ada, ready to land a punch and split the youth's mouth open, thinking they were setting something up between them. Ada clenched Rab's left hand tight, he loosed it and shook it away ready to spring. But the youth moved aside, and smiled a cold smile. 'Ey up Rab!' he said. Rab took Ada's hand and he guided her out into the street ahead of him, his heart pounding; they heard chuckles behind them.

Rab checked over his shoulder to make sure they weren't being followed.

'Just a bunch of nasty, gallows-faced gets!' said Rab. 'Think they're clever. I get this sometimes – usually from supporters of other teams trying to throw me. They'd soon have known it if they tried owt. I've dealt with their sort before.'

'I think I know one of 'em,' said Ada. 'Lives round here somewhere. Our Jim's had run ins with him – a bad sort.'

They went straight back. Ada made some tea, and they sat in the dimly lit living room and spoke in hushed voices so as not to wake her mother.

'I ought to be getting back I suppose,' said Rab after a while. 'You all reight now?'

'Yeah.'

They stood by the door and Rab held her tight.

'I do want to be with you,' he said.

'Me too.'

'I'll find a way.'

She smiled as she looked at him, 'I would not turn you down Rab Howell.'

After she had closed the door behind him, Ada stood in the darkened shop looking out of the window into the street illuminated on the far side by a single gas lamp in her view. He had as good as asked her to marry him, he was just wanting to make sure all the plans could be made. He didn't need to be so meticulous. She didn't care – they could just move into a room somewhere, anywhere, it didn't matter, she could get a job to help out with the money, she couldn't imagine he earned much: he spent so much time doing nothing very much, but so long as she was with him…

She sat on the crate where he had sat watching her. His gaze had made her feel warm, she had pretended not to notice him. She stayed for some time, dreaming, in the dark.

She heard footsteps of someone running. Then she jumped with fright as there was a desperate rapping at the door that shook the whole frame. Oh God! Rab! 'Who is it!'

'Ada, it's me, Freddy, Jim's mate!'

She unlocked the door, he was out of breath and looked sick and was trembling.

'Ada, it's Jim, there's been… a fight – and he's got stabbed. They've taken him up to the Infirmary!'

'Oh God, Freddy, is he dead?'

'No, he's bad though, I mean… it were just his arm, not his body, so he's not dead or owt, but…'

'Will you come with me Freddy, I don't want to trouble mother – the shock could kill her – just as far as a cab?'

'O' course Ada, don't forget yer jacket!'

They headed up to West Bar neither wanting to speak, not knowing what to say, nor wanting to tempt fate, and Ada got into a cab near the cabmens' shelter.

'The Infirmary please,' she gasped at the driver, 'quickly!'

The horse just wouldn't go fast enough. She wished the driver would whip the horse and make it gallop. She was shaken around as the wheels ran over the granite sets up Gibraltar Street. The streets were still busy with people spending their week's wages. A thin drizzle cast a halo of blurred light around the gas lamps.

The cab took her right up to the door past the gardens and flowerbeds that fronted the Infirmary. She rang a bell and a porter answered it. He looked her up and down as if establishing her state of health, 'No visitors at this time, love.'

'It's my brother he's been stabbed, I've got to see him!'

The porter rang a bell and a nurse appeared wearing a white apron and starched white hat perched on her head, ghost-like in the dim, echoing, empty corridor; a solitary gas jet struggling to throw it's light into even the nearest corners. The porter muttered to her and she came over to Ada. 'It's my brother, he's been stabbed, is he alive? Please can I see him?'

'We don't really allow visitors but I will let you in for a few minutes. Follow me.'

'Is he alive?'

'I don't have any information, but he's in good hands. Follow me, please Miss…?'

'McGrail. It's my brother James.'

They got to the end of the corridor. 'Wait here please Miss McGrail.' Then the nurse went through a door. Ada sat and shivered in the cold corridor. She then noticed a man sat hunched across from her, not moving, dressed in workmen's clothes holding some sort of bundle of cloth over his face. It was quiet apart from the man's laboured breathing and shuffling noises from behind the door that she could not distinguish. She was scared: of this place, of the hunched man, the starched unemotional nurse, of doctors, of seeing Jim stretched out lying pale and bloodless his face distorted in pain. The door opened.

'Miss McGrail, you may come in for a minute,' the nurse said. 'The surgeon has stitched him up. He has lost some blood, and is still groggy from the chloroform.'

Ada saw across the dim room her brother lying on a bed covered in a sheet. She hadn't taken in what the nurse had said and walked slowly over expecting to see his corpse. When the head turned towards her she almost buckled at the knees.

'Oh God, Jim! You're not dead!'

'No sis, not that I know. But it ain't half sore!' His left arm and shoulder was bandaged up and his hair looked wet and untidy.

'We've got to move him to a ward now. So I'll have to ask you to leave. As you can see he should recover well enough. You may come back at visiting time.'

She kissed Jim on the forehead and followed the nurse back

down the corridor. She found herself back out in the night air alone. At least he was alive. She hadn't even thanked the nurse, and it dawned on her just how kind she had actually been in her own standoffish kind of way. She pulled her jacket round her, heading towards the sound of a clock tower striking the late hour in town.

Chapter 11

Ada took her mother with her to the four o'clock visiting time the next day. She had been turning over in her mind all day how Jim could have got hurt, who could have done it, and her mind went over the events of the evening and the rough boys in the theatre entrance. She'd barely had time to see Jim in hospital. She'd told her mother that he'd accidentally cut his arm to stop her worrying – she would have been insufferable if she'd told her he'd been stabbed – Ada had her head full of her own worries without wanting her mother's witterings adding to it. New scenarios kept rearing up throughout the day about how it could have been his heart not his arm, whether his wound would heal, blood poisoning, infection, and if he didn't die whether he would lose the use of his arm, whether the police had caught the attacker and whether he would try again and finish Jim off.

They had found which ward he was in and waited in the queue for the doors to open. Ada and her mother didn't speak. They listened to the others in the queue – mostly women in shawls, some of whom seemed comfortable in their surroundings: like the place had become a familiar part of their lives and routine; exchanging gossip as if they were queuing at a market stall, only mingled with more than the usual helping of sympathies, and hopes and disappointments about their menfolk. The doors opened and the regulars purposefully fanned straight out leaving Ada and her mother glancing nervously down the rows of beds looking for Jim, hoping. They looked at beds without visitors where grey men lay apparently without hope or expectation of kinship, and at others where they were sat up, brave-faced, searching the incoming tide of visitors for recognition. Ada picked Jim out, sitting up and, thank

God, smiling at them.

Her mother took charge and bustled over and kissed him ceremoniously on the forehead.

'Which arm is it?' she asked.

'Er, the one with the bandage mother?'

She slapped him on the opposite arm. 'That's for being snydey.' She slapped him again.

'Mother!'

'And that's for getting into trouble and worrying your poor old mother! You should be more careful! I've brought you some clean clothes.'

Jim didn't reply. He knew it was best just to let her run her course.

'So how are you feeling Jim?' Ada said. 'You do look an awful lot better than last night.' Her mother was now the spectator, she had done her job, said her piece: she folded her arms and hitched up her bosom.

'So I did see thi last night. I half wondered if I'd dreamt it. That chloroform is good stuff. But it doesn't half give yer a belting headache!'

'I'd blame that on the beer.'

'I hardly touched a drop last night!'

'Is it very sore your arm?'

'Not half. They sewed it up like you would a split rag doll, but I'm reight. They reckon I'll be in for a couple of days until it knits its-sen together but I can move mi fingers see – the doctor came and saw me today and he's happy enough wi' it.'

'That's a relief isn't it mother?'

'That it is, to be sure.'

'So you going to tell us what happened?' Ada asked after a short silence.

Jim looked at his mother, his lips pulling back against his teeth, betraying his reluctance. 'It were nowt really, but you'll hear it soon enough I s'pose. The police've been round and taken a statement off us. They're taking him what did it to court.'

Her mother's face dropped, 'What do you mean Jim. Taking who to court?'

'It were a fight mother, the other bloke pulled a knife and cut me.'

'Who was it?' Ada asked.

'John Brown, him what lives round the corner, a rat he is.'

Ada recognised the name now, and matched it to the greasy-haired leader of the boys who had stood in front of her and Rab the night before; her unease had been justified, it was like something had been brewing and had ended in this.

'But why did he draw a knife?'

'He's just a nasty piece o' work. We had a few words and instead o' waitin for 'im to strike me I tried to get in first, but instead of fighting fair he drew a knife. Then he ran away like the coward he is. I'll have to go to court later this week the copper reckoned.'

A bell rang signalling the end of the short visiting time. Jim got another kiss from his mother and advice on eating and sleeping: as if he had much else to do. As Ada took his hand, he squeezed it and held her until their mother was joining the stream of visitors leaving the ward. He looked into her eyes with a fixed earnest expression.

'I need to talk to thi sis. Come on thi own tomorrow eh?'

'If I can, I will.' She squeezed his hand back and put on a resilient smile.

He let his hand drop to the bed, 'See thi then.'

She didn't know what to make of this. It troubled her deeply. There was something he was not letting on, more to this episode than he could say in front of mother. She caught up with her mother and took her arm.

'It's a pity your poor father's not here, God rest his soul, to sort that boy out. He'd not have stood for his nonsense. He'd have kept him on a narrow path.'

'Yes mother, he would. But Jim's not a bad sort and he'll learn from this, you see.' Ada thought of her father's temper and his ability to drink that Jim seemed to have inherited, but all she could do was mouth words of agreement with her mother.

*

Ada went with her mother and sister up to St Marie's on Sunday.

She often found an excuse not to, but today it felt right to go. For the last two nights she had knelt and prayed at her bedside – for Jim – and as she took up her place in the church she knelt and did so again until Father Gordon entered and mass began... *Dominus vobiscum*. She looked up at the winged angels watching over them and Christ on the cross looking at her. She felt safe and protected. Here, all around her was perfection; the air was cool and fragranced, a soft light fell on the floor from the stained glass, a calmness and peace contrasted with the world outside. That sense of peace however did not fully penetrate her own mind: her head was full of thoughts she couldn't control. *...et cum viris sanguinum vitam meam....* *In quorum manibus iniquitates sunt...* She consoled herself that God would understand, make sense of the mess of worries for Jim, her mother, having to support them both, nurse them both, keeping the business going on her own and feed them all and pay the rent; and whether business would be hit by spiralling lock-outs and no one getting paid, and then her own receding chances of escaping spinsterhood. She bowed her head when the bell rang for the Elevation of the Host and she felt comforted by God's presence. Everything would work out for the best in the end. There must be some purpose to it all. *Agnus dei qui tollis peccata mundi: misere nobis.* Her mind wandered to thoughts of Rab and her hopes; she dismissed from her mind that she could have committed any sin because surely their love must be God-sent. She looked at the window showing the story of the Mother of the Church, cradling the body of her son: how must that have felt? – her own problems were nothing. *Libera me per hoc sacrosanctum Corpus et Sanguinem tuum...* Surely it should not be taken too literally, she could not see how it could really be the actual blood and body of Christ in the chalice. The thought had always frightened her, and repulsed her. And with mortal sin, if taken too literally, everyone she knew would be condemned sinners: honest ordinary folk, just trying their best with what they'd got, looking out for each other and struggling with the bad hands that life had dealt them, seeking what glimmers of happiness and comfort they could find in their hard lives, scraping together to get by. No well-fed bishop in his palace could condemn them as sinners. God could see into people's hearts and saw you for what you were. *Dominus vobiscum.* Father Gordon went over to the gospel side of the altar and read the gospel. Her mother would be easily persuaded not to trail over to the Infirmary again today; but what was it Jim wanted to talk to her about? *Non ex sanguinibus, neque ex voluntate carnis, neque ex voluntate viri.* He was not a man who had thoughts that troubled him, he didn't discuss things with Ada of any importance. Jim was as you saw him – plain to see, no "side" to him – if he wanted to talk it could only be something business like. Perhaps he had decided to get a job elsewhere. It couldn't be a girl, there was no one in particular; and why would he want to talk to her about that.

*

When she joined the visitors' queue outside the ward, she felt like one of the regulars herself, recognising one or two of the women standing in the same spots, and not feeling overawed by the imposing black temple-like building, long echoing corridors, starched white hats and matching faces, or the smell of carbolic. Now she didn't have to hesitate, wondering where Jim was. She went and sat by him.

'Hello sis, mother not here? Nice to see thi – I'm, fed up in here, despite having some gorgeous nurses to look at and change my dressing. They don't take too kindly to being asked to marry you though. Some of 'em are like the Klondike.' He paused for Ada's puzzled look before adding: 'Cold and very distant!'

She slapped the hand she held with her other hand, 'I can tell you're feeling better!'

'Yeah, they might let me out tomorrow.'

They were quiet for a while. Ada could tell Jim was thinking something over.

'What was it you wanted to talk to me about?'

Jim didn't speak, it was as if he couldn't find the right words. 'Jim just spit it out – they'll be ringing the bell before you say anything at this rate.'

'You've got to stop seeing Howell,' he said softly.

'Rab?…. Jim what are you saying? What's Rab got to do with

anything? Why are you saying that?'

He again looked pained. He spoke quietly, holding back his emotions. 'He called you Howell's dollymop… his hussy. That's why I hit him. I was standing up for thi.' His eyes started to water.

'Jim, no! You can't… but he's just a no good… he was just trying to wind you up.' It was hard to speak such words in a hushed voice.

'Well he succeeded, didn't he!' There was a bitter edge to his voice now. 'He said he'd seen Howell out with his wife and kids!'

'That's rubbish, he's just making it up! And how does he know who Rab was with, even if he did see him?' Now Ada was flushed and angry.

'He was wi' 'is mates, all of 'em laughin at me, I just lost it and then he pulled out a knife and there was blood everywhere. I thought I'd had it.' A tear rolled unchecked down his cheek. 'Tha sure about Howell? I won't have him hurt thi.'

'Yes I'm sure. You just forget about it. I know what I'm doing. Rab's a good man… unlike John Brown.'

'Anyway don't worry I've not told the Police what were really said, and I don't s'pose he will either – it'd make him look bad wouldn't it – everyone'd think he got what was coming if they knew he'd set out to provoke a fight, insulting my sister, and had come armed wi' a dagger. I told the coppers I'd challenged him about why he'd knocked my hat off a few week ago – which is true he did. He should still get done for carrying a blade around – the snide little wreckling – thinks he's the hard man. As it is, it makes him look better if it were me what started it.'

'Why not teel the truth? That he insulted me?'

'No, I've thought it through. I've not had much else to do. I don't want to drag thi into it – and what if what he said were true – thi name would be dirt. And it'd bring shame on mother.'

'Jim, it's not true, so tell the truth.'

'It's too late now it's done – I've signed a statement.'

The bell rang and Ada got to her feet in response. She looked into Jim's eyes.

'I'll perhaps be home tomorrow, if not make sure someone comes to see me, to stop me going mad, eh?'

She gave a half smile, 'Yeah, see you Jim,' and she joined the procession of women heading for the door.

She didn't look anyone in the eye on the way out and, once outside, leant against a wall not knowing quite what to do next as people descended the steps past her, getting on with their lives when hers seemed to have stopped still. It couldn't be true could it? A wife and kids? He wouldn't be so cruel to her. It was probably a sister and nieces or nephews – he had a lot of sisters after all; and then why would you believe anything someone like Brown said? Should she say anything to Rab; he would be calling round after tea? Or would he be angry, feel betrayed that she could think him a liar?

The streets were dark and hostile as she made her way home: both emptiness and approaching people feeling threatening.

Chapter 12

Selina had already got up and gone downstairs with the children by the time Rab got out of bed on the Saturday morning. He pulled on his trousers and opened the curtains; cool air blew in through the raised sash as he pulled his braces up over his vest. Patches of brightness were breaking through the white clouds and some pigeons, white and grey, wheeled round in the air up from the river and settled on the roof over the back of Moses Street. Pointless things, pigeons: stupid. You feed the damn things better than your kids, treat them better than any woman, keep them at their peak, coo sweetly to them – all they do is let you down and they fly round rather than coming home and winning you the prize. Best keeping your money on the ground.

He still had not answered the question that had been on his mind all the way home the night before and which he had fallen asleep thinking about. How was he going to find a way to be with Ada? He had wondered about the idea of a trip to Castleton and stopping over at a hotel – he could use the pretence of stopping over with the lads at special training – but he wasn't sure how Ada might react to such a brazen plan. It was getting complicated – but it really shouldn't be – what was more simple than a man and a woman liking each other and wanting to spend time together? Perhaps he could arrange to miss the last coach back, so they'd have to spend the night. This desire was driving him mad and now Selina had shut herself off, there was no outlet for this want of affection. She made him feel ashamed of his body and its ways. The nearest he came to a caress was once a week getting his back scrubbed. He had more physical contact from bloody George Waller's big sodding hands pummelling him like a loaf of bread before it gets baked. The stiffness from Thursday's match had settled in. Strange how no matter how fit you keep it always takes a few games for your body to get used to it. He prodded a couple of bruises on his shins and leaned against the window frame to stretch tight calf muscles, leaned his head from side to side and headed down for breakfast as the smell of bacon was already drifting up.

'We need everyone out of the way this morning – we're going to whitewash the slop-kitchen,' said Jemima. Rab had half wondered what the mangle and all the other stuff was doing out in the yard.

'The rest of the stuff we'll put in here – there's not much in until we've done the marketing later. We'll also give the floor a good scrub, eh Lina?'

'Yeah, and Rab, you'll have to either lend a hand or get the little un out of the way – we don't want him under our feet or getting whitewash on his clothes.'

'But I've got plans for the morning, can't he go round to your Henry's?'

'No they've gone round to her mother's – I'll take him out if you like and you can do the painting instead.'

'No, he can come wi' me. I'm due at the Lane this afternoon though.'

'It's only for an hour or two.'

Rab set out for Brightside Lane with Little Rabbi in tow. Rab took his hand to pull him along faster.

'Where going Da-da?' said Little Rabbi.

'To the shops. You be a good boy and I'll get thi some spice.'

'Spice! Spice! Choc-choc!'

'If tha's good. Come on we ain't got all day – get on!' Rab bent down and Little Rabbi leapt on to his back.

Rab bought half an ounce of tobacco and, seeing there were not many in the barber's, went in. There was someone sat in the chair and a man behind a newspaper in the waiting seats; the smell of damp hair and bay rum in the air. Walter looked round as Rab entered and waved his razor in greeting, gesticulating towards the seats against the wall, slicing the air like Saladin flashing his blade, 'Nah then Rab! I'll not be long, sit yersen down.'

'A'reight Walt.'

Walter had hair that was a poor recommendation for his trade: thin, grey and lazily combed back. His one good eye was always busy, making up for the one rendered useless in a grinding accident. He bent down to approach Little Rabbi's height, and tickled his chin, 'And would young sir like a shave?' Little Rabbi recoiled at the blade and hid behind his dad, causing great merriment in the stout razor bearer who, despite the chuckling, steadied his hand to continue scraping the white soap off the man's throat.

'Just a penny shave for you will it be today Rab?'

'I thought I might as well have my hair cut too.'

'Nice and trim ready for the new season eh? Don't want it in your eyes when you go up for a header!'

Rab let Little Rabbi onto his knee. Walter's Saturday boy came through from the back with a jug of hot water and, having placed it down carefully, picked up the broom and pushed the black and white hairs across the dimpled linoleum into a little pile.

'Here Rab, Bill here says his lad's been gi'en notice today of a lock-out at Cammell's. Bleeding disgrace don't yer reckon?'

'I don't understand much about it. I thought there was no quarrel in Sheffield.'

'That's right but the gaffers are making one ain't they. A quarter of all the engineers are being gi'en notices today. They're wanting to hit the Society and break 'em so as they can't pay out strike pay to thems in London and where-'ave-yer.'

The seated man lowered his paper, 'It's bloody suicidal – they're always bleating about trade being driven from the country and yet what will this do to trade? The men have no wish for a feight – they want to work and yet are being locked out!'

'That's right!' said the man being shaved, the sudden movement causing Walter to stay his razor, 'And it'll only get worse. My lad says the Society men won't stand for it and it'll lead to 'em all walking out – then where will we be? We'll have kids goin hungry again and all for nowt. It's bloody stupid.'

Little Rabbi had now shuffled off Rab's knee and was sat on the floor patting the pile of hair like it was a small animal, re-shaping it, lifting it up and putting it down again.'

'So why would the bosses do it then?' asked Rab.

'Tha knows what I reckon,' said the man with the newspaper, 'the Employers Federation have got together and have decided it's make or break time – they're out to get the union and push down wages – sweat the labour, and they can't do that while the union stand in t' way. They've been planning it a while, but waited until after the election so as not to ruin their boy's chances: that hoity-toity Hope.'

'Aye, related to the Duke o' Norfolk weren't he?'

'Aye nephew or summat – not that that did any good 'cause Maddison were going to get in no matter what – but hoity-toity's vote would have been wiped out altogether by a lock-out. Anyhow, it's all about bringing labour back under the thumb of capital – sweeping away all the progress us workers have made these fifty odd year. And if that means starving thousands in the process they'll do it – anything so that they can get fatter and build bigger bloody mansions in Ranmoor. But they'd never say that – it's all "unreasonable demands overpricing British goods," "greedy, lazy workers," "troublemakers."'

The end of his speech was marked by a crisp parenthetical flicking up of his newspaper. Walter went back to finishing his shave; he then got a wet towel and wiped the man's face.

'You next then,' he indicated to the man with the newspaper.

'Nah, let this fella go first. I'm happy sitting reading, and it keeps us out o' the house.'

Rab sat in the chair. 'Here little un,' said Walter, 'I've a job for thi – come here and help us put soap on thi dad's face.' He handed Little Rabbi the shaving brush and held his arm to direct the soap approximately where he intended it.

'Funny Dada!' said Little Rabbi, before scuttling off when Walter produced the razor and started slapping it up and down the leather strop.

'So if there was a poor shopkeeper with a bob or two to wager, who do yer reckon he should put it on for next season then Rab?'

'I'd say he should put it on the butcher's tab and get a nice few decent beefsteak suppers that's what!'

'Oh come along now, who's got the best chance.'

'Well I s'pose you'd get good odds on someone like Sunderland, since they did so badly last year, but it'd still be money wasted. It's our turn this year – providing our for'ards do their job. Some 'uld say you can't rule out the Villans neither, but that's not advice on what to do wi' thi money! Good beefsteak – never wasted on that!'

'Try not to get it everywhere!' – soon after Little Rabbi was walking along painting his face with a chocolate bar, a rather vain hope of Rab's that this would be kept a secret. He produced his pocket handkerchief and wiped his face and hands as best he could.

'How's it possible to make such a mess? Come on, I've got a surprise for thi.'

He went into the butcher's and waited while two customers had been served; little wrapped parcels being dropped into their baskets.

'Morning Bob – you got my order as agreed?'

'Yes Mr Howell, come on through.'

The butcher led them through the back room into the yard. Over to one side, the butcher nodded towards a crate, 'These do yer?' Rab looked in and pushed Little Rabbi closer; the little lad cautiously peered inside: 'piggy-wiggies!' Two one-stone weaners with big ears and long lashes looked up at them with their weak eyes. Rab picked one up squealing. 'These'll do just great, won't they eh?' he said half to the shopkeeper and half to Little Rabbi who was trying to get to the other pig.

Rab carried the, at first, wriggling weaners home in a sack slung over his shoulder, but they soon stilled. He put them into the little shed he had made and put a straw bale up against the opening to stop them getting out. Little Rabbi kept saying "piggy-wiggy! piggy-wiggy!" insisting that he should be allowed in the shed with them.

'No Rabbi, the piggy-wiggies need to get used to their new home. Tha can see 'em again tomorrow. He lifted Little Rabbi back over the fence enclosure much to his disgust and he stood and rattled the fence repeating "piggy-wiggy!"

Selina came out to see what was going on.

'Looks like my fence is good and strong leastways!' said Rab.

'You've gone ahead with yer plan then?'

'Yep, lovely little pair they are – but nice big uns they'll be by Christmas! All for a few scraps and peelings. I'll fetch us a little barrel to tip it all in.'

'Don't you go leaving it all to me though! I've got enough on looking after the kids wi'out looking after swine too. And I'll have nothing to do wi' slaughtering 'em neither!'

'Don't worry I'll do my bit, just like tha'll no doubt do thi bit when it comes to eating 'em! I'm going to call 'em Freddy and Jack. There'll be pork at Christmas and bacon and ham till Easter! And as for slaughtering, we'll get a pig sticker in and I'll help him – that way he can take away all the bit's we don't want – we could even make a bob or two selling bits to those what wants some.'

Chapter 13

After tea on the Sunday Rab said something about going for a training walk and went out the back. He said good evening to Freddy and Jack who were shoving straw around their enclosure with their snouts. It was a pleasant enough evening. One or two children were out in the street already, without having let their tea go down. Two boys in long trousers were playing pitch and toss up against a wall. A man leaned against a passage entry, and didn't acknowledge Rab as he passed. Looked like he's on the look out for someone Rab thought; not someone he knew from round here. Probably keeping an eye out for the police for some blokes out the back, or a bookie's runner waiting to take money or provide odds.

When he reached Bridge Street he found it much quieter than on a weekday: no factory workers coming or going, no clanking of metal, no hissing, none of the deep rumblings that seemed to come from the earth itself rather than being generated by men above ground. Instead of the shambling men in grimy jackets and sweat-stained caps, and women with head scarves and blackened aprons, there were less burdened figures heading to church or for Sunday walks, clean limbs bearing clothes that had spent the week hanging with their friendly mothballs or at the pawn shop, where they would return after their own Sunday airing. Rab tapped a few times at the shop window with a half crown and waited. He lifted his cap in greeting when he saw Ada come through, but she didn't smile back like he expected.

'Come in Rab,' she said locking the door behind her.

'Everything all right Ada love? You look out o' sorts.'

'I am. It's been a bad weekend – I've hardly slept.'

'Not your mother is it?'

'No she's fine. She's sat in the back, knitting. Let's go out and I'll

135

tell you about it.

'We're going for a walk mother,' Ada said as they went through to the back door.

'Eh up missis,' Rab said in response to her mother catching his eye. She replied with a terse "good evening." Whatever it was had settled over the household: he saw her sister sat by the window reading, and she didn't even look up, never mind cast him a flirtatious smile.

'Shall we head out past the river?' Ada said, and then fell silent as she walked along on Rab's arm. Rab didn't know what to say. He always thought it best to say little when the other sex had moods, otherwise you'd say something trying to help and somehow get it wrong and end up being the inexplicable cause of it all, even when it was nothing to do with you in the first place.

They got as far as the Iron Bridge and stopped. Looking up towards Borough Bridge, factories flanked the river on both sides – the river running through a blackened brick gorge. A four-wheeled cab, a "growler," rumbled over Borough Bridge, the driver erect and bowler-hatted looking straight ahead, eyes on his horse. Rab put his arm around Ada and looked down at the water making patterns as it's flow was interrupted by hidden stones underneath. She was waiting for him to speak first.

'So you going to tell me about it?'

She pulled away from him, creating space between them. 'It's our Jim – he's been stabbed.'

'Stabbed? he's not...?

'He's all right. It was on Friday night – that punky who we saw outside the Grand – it was him.'

'I knew he were bruising for a feight. I should have leathered him!'

'Then it might be you in the Infirmary, not Jim. Jim hit him and he pulled a dagger. He's lucky to be alive.'

'So he's still in hospital?'

'He's got stitches in his arm – here, where the blade struck, but they might let him home tomorrow or early this week. He's got to go to court on Thursday probably.'

'So they got him? Him what did it?'

'Yeah, I think so – they know who he is leastwise.'

'I'm sorry to hear what's 'appened Ada. If there's owt I can do to help, y'know.'

'Thank you Rab. But I don't think so.'

They were quiet again. Just beyond the corn mill Trinity Church's bell rang: its doleful note threatening damnation to those lurking indoors.

'So when did it happen?'

'Not long after you left I suppose – one of his mates came round to find me, and he'd already been taken to the Infirmary. I thought I'd find him dead when I got there.'

'Shall we head up to the countryside up Shirecliffe way – there's a footpath across the fields at Pitsmoor or we could go to the new park at Roe Wood?'

'Yes I would like some fresh air.'

As they headed up the hill they moved away from factory buildings and jerry-built back-to-backs: the houses getting newer, the stone it's proper colour, proportions more suited to humans than animals, and with small gardens in front. Ada was still quiet, but Rab didn't mind that. He was happy with Ada at his side, just like other couples going for a Sunday walk in the country; commenting on things they saw: a rose bush, a scraggy dog; or practical conversation about which way to head was enough for him. Half a mile up from the river they crossed a stile and fields were before them.

'If we head up this way we can follow the path up to Shirecliffe Hall, then we can decide which way to go after,' Rab said.

'If you only looked ahead you wouldn't know you were in Sheffield,' she said.

It was true, ahead was countryside; look back and you only saw the industry that encrusted the valley bottoms. Once he had seen a girl, ever so pretty a profile – pale skin, fair hair curled under a hat decorated with fruit and flowers, cute nose – then when she turned he saw the scars on the other side and a drooping eye socket; he had hoped his face hadn't shown his shock: how she must have hated the look on people's faces.

They started to climb steeply then stopped for a breather on top of a small heather covered hill. They looked back on the city: no it wasn't ugly, not from here. You had to admire what these people had achieved, what they had built. It was a city without airs or graces, pledged to ends other than beauty, a take-it-as you-find-it kind of place, that said to its visitors "aye an' welcome, love. Don't mind the mess, come thi out into t'garden."

'It's some view,' he said. 'Worth climbing the hill for – not pretty like the Peak District but still it's got summat.' He bent down and picked her a sprig of the purple heather. 'Lucky heather?'

'What makes it lucky?'

'The gipsy that picks it of course,' he said grinning.

She smiled back at him. 'This must be the closest bit of heather moor to town,' she mused. 'It's a while since I got out of Sheffield.'

'Would you like me to take you out to Castleton? We could see some decent sized moors – purple stretching into the distance. We could get the train most of the way or go on one of those Old Times coaches.'

'That would be nice, yes.'

'We could go next week?'

'I'll have to see, there's Jim to look after and he'll have to go to court.'

'Maybe next Sunday then? Can't your mother and sister look after Jim for just a day?'

'I'll have to see Rab, no promises.'

He thought she was rather short with him – still out of sorts. She asked where Bridge Street was and they worked out where it was from the Town Hall, St Peter's and the chimneys.

Rab stood in front of her and pulled her towards him. 'Gi' us a kiss then, eh?' It was as if she hesitated. He put one hand in the small of her back, the other behind her neck so that he could insist, but she turned her mouth away from his and struggled free from him.

'Rab, I can't!' She turned her back to him.

He went to her side; tears were rolling down her cheeks.

'Come here lass. What's up wi' yer?' He put his arm round her and she sobbed in his arms. He held her for several minutes, saying nothing, stroking her back gently until the tears subsided.

'I'm sorry,' she said. Rab was hopeful he'd now get his kiss but she put two fingers up over his mouth and held him back.

'Rab, I'm sorry, I've got to ask you about something.'

'Of course lass – owt you want.'

'Do you love me?'

'Yer know I do. What is it?'

'When that lad stabbed Jim, it was Jim who struck first.'

'I wish I had hit him – he wouldn't have got back up to pull a knife!'

'No Rab, listen. Jim hit him because he insulted me.' He was about to speak but she put a finger to his lips again. 'He hit him because he said I was courting a married man.'

It was Rab's turn to avert his face; he did not want her to see his eyes.

'Rab?' Ada burst out sobbing this time hysterically. 'Rab? Say something!'

'I can't.' He turned back, reached out to put his arm round her but she struck him away, then sank onto her knees. Rab just stood looking down at her as she sobbed, making noises like a snared animal. He stood and watched as her shoulders heaved. She looked so small. He knelt down next to her.

'Ada, I'm sorry. I can't help misen. I love yer.' Now he felt the shock of copious tears coming to his own eyes. He could not remember the last time that had happened. He put one hand on her shoulder, wanting some physical contact and cried silently next to her. Minutes passed. He was glad no one else was around. Eventually she looked at him, saw his tears. She touched his hand.

Rab spoke. 'I'm sorry. I've just fallen for yer. What could I do?'

'You could've walked away. Told me the truth.'

'I've never lied to yer Ada.'

'You have Rab. Everything was a lie!'

'But how could I…? you would never have seen me again.'

'No, and that would have been better for both of us. Kinder to me.'

'I've been a fool Ada, I know, but it's loving you that's made me risk it. I can't be happy wi'out yer now.'

'Well you'll have to be, because it's over. It's wrong! You've really hurt me Rab. I can't be happy without you either.' She broke out sobbing again. 'What have you done to me?'

He had been selfish. He had known it couldn't last, he'd just hoped something would work out – he didn't know what. And now this is what he'd done to her.

'Ada, I'm sorry.'

'I believe you, but it's too late for that.'

Her red, tear-filled eyes looked up at him, he blinked away his own tears which he could do nothing about.

'Tell me the truth now, Rab Howell.'

They sat on the grass side by side, but apart, and talked; midges oscillating over the field around them. He told her in flat tones about his family, about his home, his children. Ada sighed as he spoke and occasionally took deep breaths to stifle little sobs. He finally got to the bit about another baby on the way and she broke down again.

When she quieted once more he said, 'I still want to see you.'

'Well you can't. How does it look?'

'I don't give a damn how it looks!'

'Don't be ridiculous Rab! And I won't be a married man's whore!' she threw at him through renewed sobs.

'Ada, how could you! You're not. It's you I love. If we could only run away together I wouldn't turn back.'

'Don't you still love Selina?'

'I don't think I do. I've been wi' 'er for nearly ten year, so I have respect for her, she's a good woman, but if I could be with you, I wouldn't miss her.'

'Rab it's a sin. We must not see each other again. We will have to get on with our own lives.'

'Ada...' He was about to plead again.

'No Rab, just give me a hug. Then take me home before it gets dark.'

They walked back in silence, not holding hands, across the darkening fields and through the streets, the air now damp and clinging, and forming into a light drizzle. Windows glowed from gas lamps inside cosy rooms. Not a single word passed between them until they arrived back. He could make out in the now dim light that her face was blotchy from crying and her eyes bloodshot. They entered the yard through the small door.

'Don't come back Rab. Go to your wife. Look after your kids. Don't think of me!' Tears filled her eyes again. She moved to the door, latchkey in hand, 'And Rab... hope the season goes well – and I hope you get to play for England again.'

Rab just stood there helpless and watched her go inside. He was alone in the yard looking up at the house, eyes blurred, mouth dry. He remained several minutes on the spot. He heard the horse stamp in the stable; he turned and let himself out into the street.

Once in the house, without removing her hat or jacket, Ada went straight up to her room which overlooked the yard. She stood back from the window. There was the dark figure of Rab standing rooted below, watery through her eyes, like he was waiting for something. She felt the urge to rush back down and throw herself at him and tell him it would be all right. She watched the statue in the gloom. The she saw him turn and leave. She would not see him to talk to ever again. She pulled the curtains, undressed in the dark and climbed in between the sheets; now she would never get to share her bed. She felt alone in the world. She cried quietly to herself as she went over the evening in her mind. Then she thought of the times she had spent with Rab and imagined him in a house with children, children she would never have, him in another bed, with his wife with a swollen belly. She prayed for forgiveness and prayed for help. It was late into the night before fatigue overtook her and she slept.

When he had left Ada's yard, Rab stood in the street not sure whether to go right or left. What next? Needing to sit down he dropped onto a door step and cradled his head in his hands. It was all wrong. You shouldn't have to sacrifice everything – people always telling you to give things up, do your duty, forsake pleasure and idealise misery as if it were some sort of virtue. The saintliness of living a life of drudgery and boredom. Where was the virtue in hewing black, stinking rock, filling or hauling corves, not seeing daylight or breathing clean air, or living with someone who no longer drove you to passion, someone who no longer sought you out for yourself amidst the mess of life going on around. Ada had perhaps started off as a curiosity, a challenge; he had perhaps been selfish – he should have listened to Charlie, but it was too late by then. Ada made him live, and he wanted more of life, more feeling. What a waste to go from day to day, not feeling, not taking what life had to offer – in walking past bilberries without tasting – did that denial make your life better? He was wasting his life, soon his football career would be over and then what would be left? A cold home, and grinding into old age down the pit, day in day out until it ended, bitter, full of regret at what might have been. Had he meant what he said – he would have run away with Ada? He had said it without thinking, because it seemed the best thing to say. It hadn't occurred to him before, but yes he had meant it. It would mean he would no longer wake with Little Rabbi's hot sweaty hair pressed against his cheek, the beautiful girls running to meet him in the yard after a trip away. He would miss them, but they had their own lives, he had his. Having a half-dead father around would do them no good. Selina was their mainstay – it was impressive how she adored them, got them ready, kept them clothed and put meals on the table. He was not a vital part of the machine, not the engine, or drive wheel, or the pulley – it would still work without him. The children would have been sad at first perhaps, but, like when their rabbit died in ninety three, well… was skinned and butchered, they would soon forget. At times like this he could see the merits of oblivion brought on by drink, he had seen it many a time, but it never made their problems go away – just made them poorer and less capable, less fit.

The two and a bit miles home took longer than their usual half an hour or so – something vital had gone.

Chapter 14

The days shortened and it was that time of year when stumps chalked on walls started to fade through lack of maintenance and were replaced by large white rectangles, when sticks drilled in to the ground were no longer a ball's width apart or were replaced by discarded jackets or caps for goalposts; when the price of a pig's bladder shot up to a farthing. As he walked home through the streets of Brightside, Rab felt lifted to see knotted balls of rags being kicked on the still dusty streets by determined scruffy little boys seeking goal scoring glory and adulation. The streets also had more men in them than usual, some of the younger ones also playing football. Others in small huddles tossing coins against a wall, frittering away penny stakes while they still could, one always on the look out should the coppers be out to cause them grief and deprive them of their innocent pleasure of gambling. For these were engineers, locked out or walked out from Vickers, Cammell's, Brown's, Firth's, Jessop's, Edgar Allen's: all the giants of Sheffield's industrial age. Rab shook his head; the poor buggers, nothing to do and no money to boot.

Training for the season had intensified – both at the Lane and away from it. George Waller had the team in most days, if only to keep an eye on them and keep check on their diet and weights. Rab spent the time between the hours spent under George's direction walking and running around Tinsley or Wincobank. After a session in the gym, face down on George's rub down table, George inflicting pain on his legs, stretching and pummelling, Rab would be ordered to rein back a bit, 'You'll over-harden your muscles Rab!' or, 'A bit of fat is a good thing – shows your body's getting enough.' Rab, face buried in a towel, would grunt his consent, fully intending to do his own thing anyway. He had been doing this long enough to know his own body. Anyhow he had to keep busy, keep his focus on that first match proper – Derby – the Peakites – the legendary Steve Bloomer and John Goodall – he was their equal, or should be, though he never got the credit, not flash enough, not from the right background.

He tried to push Ada out of his mind, and Jim, and their trip to the Police Courts. He had to get on with it, make the best with what he'd got. Not for him like some people – who lived their life just waiting for the next one, believing that the worse this one was the better the next would be: they wallowed in pain, grief and deprivation as being heaven-sent, sharing in Christ's suffering. He wanted to shake them and shout, 'Wake up, live your lives! This is it, here and now – there won't be another chance!' Selina was a bit like that, she too was happy to wait patiently, doing her best, accepting what came her way, believing that there was some point to it all, that better was to come. And yet hadn't Ada talked of sin? But somehow she was different, she had a lust for life, for living. Somehow, all her eggs were not in the basket of the afterlife. If he kept running he could leave thoughts behind in the woods. Another swig of Quinphos tonic at bedtime, 'good for depression of the spirits and brain fag,' the man at Thompson and Cappers had said. He had gone in for some embrocation and the man must have seen his long face and general demeanour. 'Give it a go,' he had said.

The team did some ball work, though not enough for Rab – not much dribbling but lots of quick releases of the ball as favoured by Needham. There followed some shooting, and some corner taking: the new forwards trying out their heading and ability to stay upright against Bill, as they attempted to contact the ball before Bill's fist punched clear, or his bulk swatted them away. Evenings were spent in the club room as they built up to the match: some of them thirsting for the beer this policy was designed to prevent. For Rab it was just what he needed: company and something to do, even if only billiards or cards.

Wednesday 1st September 1897.

The last time he had run out onto the pitch Ada had been sat up in the stand; he had picked her out and then she'd stood up and waved her hat. Not many here today – mid week, tipping it down, but not cold. He had nodded to John Goodall and his baby-faced apprentice when they passed him earlier on in the pavilion as they talked to the other Goodall – Archie. They might have well been walking past the caretaker – did they even recognise him? – never mind that he'd played alongside them for England – what was it, three years ago? They'd soon remember Rab Howell.

Nudge wins the toss – kicking with the wind towards the Shoreham Street end. New blokes Morton and White up front. Blair alongside, no Tommy. This is it. Good, happy god of gold!

From the off, there's pressure on both goals, Goodall cleverly slips a pass to the tallow-faced Bloomer, who switches feet, but Bill's not beat that easy. Sugar strikes low and hard, goalie dives full stretched to deny it. Then Morton goes off injured... how the hell! Ten men versus Derby, Bloomer and the Goodalls. Now we'll see what we're made of. Forward with the ball, hold, hold, past the man, easy does it, release. Go Cocky. Cuts inside, shoots; in off the far post!

Keep 'em close, don't let 'em pass it, check the man. That's it Goodall, pick thisen up! Remember me now? Rab Howell.

From half time Bloomer pressing for his 'rightful goal' – welcome to Bramall Lane, tallow-face. Clear our lines, shift the ball away. Morton back on but not much use, hobbles about in midfield. Bill thumps it long. Nudge runs then quick pass. White loses it. Back to defend. Tallow-face shoots. It's heading in – not if it can be stopped. Push it past. Ref blows. Penalty – hands. Yeah, but stopped that sod scoring. Goodall – Archie lines up – and fires it wide. Fucking brilliant. All our fans behind the net love it. Love Rab Howell. Nothing through our back line now. Harry does the same thing – palms the ball away. Ref blows. Goodall – John, this time puts it in past Bill. Brother Archie shakes his hand, sick inside.

Now United back on top, Cocky crosses ball, Sugar runs forward past his man, hoofs it. In it goes. Goalie arguing it didn't go in. Must have gone through net. Ref talks to linesman – the cheating sod of a linesman says it didn't go in. Well he's Derby's trainer what d'yer expect? Two thousand fans shout words we can't use or we'd be out on our ear, Nudge wouldn't stand it, Tooth-yanker would get to hear. Still evens. Not long to go. Twenty five yarder from a free kick, Needham, the Prince, strikes it, hangs low, wet and heavy, goalie reaches it – ball nice and greasy – in it goes. U..nite...d! U..nite…d! U..nite…d!

*

Routine and physical activity soothe the mind. At the end of a training session lifting dumbbells, twenty minutes skipping, sprinting or kicking a ball, Rab would be at the baths or getting a rub down and be surprised to realise that his mind had been clear all that time of his worries and conflicts. What a blessing. Like a rest by the side of a moorland stream to a traveller, when the clear water refreshes, cools sore feet and equally the stream's melody bathes the mind. Three days after Derby, it's Preston away: Deepdale Road. The Invincibles, just look at 'em, fat and sluggish: beaten three-one. Cocky and Freddie linking up well, Rab cursing the ref for denying his goal. 'What a shot that were,' he said, 'old man Trainer definitely saved that behind his line. Should've been four-one!'

The following week the United walk out at the Bramall Lane Grounds in front of eleven thousand, followed by the claret shirts of Stoke. Maxwell, their top scorer doesn't mess around and after three minutes quietens the crowd with a goal, then Harry heads a cross into his own goal off the bar and they're two down after five minutes. But the United aren't beat that easy and the game ends with a four-three win: "Och-aye" getting two, his hat-trick disallowed for offside. But worryingly the goals were not coming from the centre-forwards.

Chapter 15

Monday 20th September 1897

As soon as Selina and her mother emerged arm in arm from Chapel Walk they saw, through the thick iron railings, a crowd already gathering in the front of the Wesley Chapel, despite their being early. People were gathering in groups or leaning on the wall on the pavement outside, waiting, and their numbers were gradually swelling. Selina and Jemima went in through the gates and found a space where they could perch against the railings and take the weight off their feet. Her baby was asleep and still, safe inside, but she still felt an inner turbulence.

'For some reason I'm really anxious *Dei*, excited but somehow scared.'

'I know it's a bit like I felt waiting for the Queen to arrive, but why scared? He's only a preacher and you've seen plenty of them before.'

'I know, it's just who he is – you know one of us – and famous too.'

'*Dordi!* He's just a Romany *chal*, a Romany *rashi*, a brother. He's been through what we've been through, he understands us.'

'I think that's what makes it worse.'

The forecourt was full by now and a policeman by the front gate was stopping anyone else from entering. Then the large wooden doors behind the columns of the portico entrance opened and people jostled to get in. Jemima had her sharpest elbow at the ready to ensure her daughter and granddaughter weren't on the receiving end of any jostling. They went into the vestibule and, as most people were streaming into the main part of the chapel, they headed up to the balcony and found a seat at the front, halfway along.

Down below, people clattered into the wooden stalls like cattle in pens on market day and were chattering like they were taking up seats for a pantomime rather than with the air of self-conscious saintliness Selina had often observed as they took their places at Sunday service at her church. She looked across at the five groups of pipes on the organ, looking itself like a temple within the bigger temple. The organist softly playing a hymn that was all but drowned out by the cattle. Before long there were no seats left and Selina could see people taking up standing positions at the back. She removed her shawl and folded it on her knee. The door to the vestry opened and a group of men and women filed out and stood in a line at the front; it was then she noticed others also standing at intervals several pews apart around the chapel as if watching the congregation. She immediately picked out the Gipsy – like an Englishman can always instantly pick out another Englishman in a foreign place – so it was with Selina. She did not need to study him to reveal the gipsy; but she studied him to try to reveal the man. He was not tall and was thickset, not unlike her father. He wore an ordinary-looking suit, collar and creamy coloured necktie. His skin was not dark like some gipsies but neither was it white, not dissimilar to her own. There was nothing ostentatious about him. His hair was black and wavy and he wore a heavy, dark moustache – not fashionably trimmed like Rab's. But it was his eyes that shone out, dark hazel eyes, large and bright; glinting gipsy eyes that saw beyond what they looked at. The minister climbed to the pulpit and surveyed the whole congregation, high up enough to see all those on the balcony and to look down upon his flock – or was it herd – below. He held up his hands seeking a hush which gradually descended. He welcomed the congregation, old and new faces. 'But I know you have not come to listen to me, so I'll hand over to our esteemed guest preacher, Gipsy Smith, the Missioner for the Free Church Council, and one of the country's greatest evangelists. He has been to America and the Colonies and preached to thousands. God has given him gifts of the most wonderful kind, a simple gipsy boy, who God found and turned into a saviour of souls.'

The Gipsy took his place at the pulpit. He looked around and Selina felt his eyes look upon her. It was not like in her church where the pulpit felt distant – here he was right amongst them. Total silence fell.

'I must take issue with the words of your minister, dear to you though he may be. I do not feel I am one of the country's greatest evangelists, nor am I a saviour of souls: it is God that wins souls, I am just God's vessel, a vessel unto honour: not a very large vessel perhaps. I was born in a tent and could not read or write when I reached out for Christ. But if a small vessel cannot hold much it can stay under the tap and it can overflow a lot, overflow with the glory of God, overflow until from us will stream channels of blessing.'

He again paused and cast his eye over everyone.

'Ask, and it shall be given you; seek and ye shall find; knock, and it shall be opened unto you. For every one that asketh receiveth; and he that seeketh findeth; and to him that knocketh it shall be opened. These are the words of the Son of God as he gave his sermon on the mount.

'This does not mean that all you have to do is kneel and pray and you will receive. The Lord will not hear any who have not done His will. They who do not know how to ask – they ask amiss. The almighty said: "If my people, which are called by my name, shall humble themselves, and pray, and seek my face, and turn from their wicked ways; then will I hear from heaven, and will forgive their sin, and will heal their land."

'The promise is not to any people it is to "my people." So this morning I ask you to look into your hearts and find out if you really, and truly, and wholly, have surrendered and obeyed, and by faith in Jesus Christ can honestly say you belong to God.

' "My people" – if you are doing the will of God intelligently, if you are obeying God's commandments, then you can ask things of God, and you will get them. There are many people labelled God's who don't belong to Him at all – God knows better than to answer their prayers. They ask for things, and if the Lord answered their prayers they wouldn't know what to do with the things when they get them. It would be moral and spiritual suicide for the Lord to answer some prayers.

'The man who is out of harmony with God can't ask the right things in the right way. If you want to get the right things, first of all, get right yourself. Begin with yourself. Begin with the person who wears your clothes. Begin with the person who is sitting where you are sitting. If you are right with God, you can't help knowing it. If you do not feel it, something is wrong – something is wrong with you. When you get near a rose you know; when you get near a violet bed, you know; when the world is flooded with the glory and magnificence of God, you know.'

Selina knew now exactly why she had been afraid. She looked at the ashen face of her mother. How could she know if she was one of His people? She did not know!

'There are moments when my Gipsy heart cries out for the woods – there is still something of the wildness of my youth left in me – and I am glad of it. If I were to be born again, I would want to be born a Gipsy. I have stood in the woods in Spring – in the month of April. I have seen the primroses, the hawthorn, the fern, the green lush grass – standing in it up to my knees. I have smelled the perfume of the flowers – perfume that would make you think it had been wafted by the wings of angels, from the hills of Paradise. Once as I stood thus I saw an old trunk. Not a branch remained on it. The limbs had all rotted off. It was not even covered with ivy. There it was in the midst of this beautiful Spring's bridal bouquet – barren and ugly. And I thought I heard that old trunk say, "I don't believe in Spring." And I answered, "No, poor thing, you are too dead to believe in anything." There are people in our churches who are like this old trunk. Their lives are barren – their souls are stripped of brotherly love, and of kindness. They are not "my people." '

Selina saw tears rolling down her mother's cheeks. Inside her the baby gave a kick.

'I carry with me a picture.' He held up a small photograph. 'It is a gipsy tent. There is a father and five little motherless children, without a Bible, without school. Nobody wanted them. Who does want a gipsy? Nobody. Outsider, ostracized, despised, and rejected. But God looked on that poor father and those five motherless little things and saw them in their ignorance and heathenism, hungry for God. And He looked again, and He said, "There are six preachers in that tent." And He put those arms that were nailed to the tree round the father and the children and saved them all; and I am one of them.'

Now tears came to her own eyes, and she saw that many around her cried too.

'Think of what it would mean for your home if you, my brother, took Christ home with you. Your wife and children would have a chance they have never had before. If both of you husband and wife bow at His dear feet together, what joy there will be in heaven and on earth! It would mean your home for Jesus. You will give Christ a chance with every child in your home by taking Him there.

'When Jesus said, "Ye must be born again," did he say it to a drunkard? No. A harlot? No. A murderer? No. A poor gipsy? No. I think if Jesus were to come and speak a message to a gipsy tent, knowing its past and how much it has been despised, how little people have cared, and how little people have done to save its occupants, He would speak very tenderly. To whom, then, did Jesus say these words? Listen. A church member. So you see it is possible to be a church member without being born again.

'Your psalm-singing and your hymn-singing, and your church-going, and your offerings, and all the rest of your religious paraphernalia, are so much mockery because you have not walked the straight and blessed path of obedience and trust. Your drinking and your gambling must go, your pride, your selfishness, your meanness, your bad temper, your un-Christlikeness must go. Slay to the death your love of pleasure, your love of show, your love of appearing more than you are. God wants you to be as sweet and as lovely and as transparent as the breath of heaven's own morning. That is God's purpose.'

The gipsy looked at her, she was sure. It was as if a look of recognition passed across his face. He must know her to be Romany. It was like he was speaking to her. He knew about her and was speaking of her failings, her sins, and that of her husband, of her father. Rab's pride and single-minded pursuit of that game of his. Her father's drinking. And they were so far from finding Him! She felt as if a lantern was being held up to her sin. And yet he was not accusing, he was beseeching; there was no vitriol in his voice, only love.

'What brings you here today? Deep down in your conscience you know, there is a real cry in your soul for God. You have often heard your minister preach. Maybe you have been hearing him for years. Perhaps you sit in the gallery or away back in one of the pews, or near to him, and every time he preaches and you hear him, you go home and say, "My pastor is right; I ought to be a Christian, I know I ought," and you feel beneath the powerful pleadings of your own pastor, beneath the pleadings of the evangelist, you know God's claims, you admit them, you feel them. They are right, they are reasonable, and you ought to surrender.

'I can believe there are scores and hundreds who mean to follow Jesus. Who will leave all to follow Jesus? Who will sacrifice everything for Jesus' sake? Who will take their stand for Jesus, and who will go home and say to their friends, "I have come to tell you what great things the Lord hath done for me?" Jesus calls to you. Will you follow?'

Her tears turned to sobs and around her others were moaning or falling onto their knees. Down below, people were walking forward to the communion rail and kneeling, asking to be saved. Others were making their way into the inquiry room in the vestry, seeking conversion.

Suddenly the Gipsy began to sing: 'There's a hand held out in pity. There's a hand held out in love. It will pilot to the city, where our Father dwells above.'

His voice, pure and clean, penetrated to her core, overwhelmed her; she got to her feet and was helped to make her way towards the stairs and down to the vestibule by one of the mission workers. 'There are people waiting to speak to you in the inquiry room sister, go and talk with them and they will help you seek Christ.' But, reaching the bottom of the stairs, Selina turned away and went outside and sat down on the steps, gulping in the cool evening air. The baby kicking her from inside, her head aching, the pure melodious voice of the Gipsy still resounding inside the building.

'Are you all right?' Quite some time had passed before she heard her mother's voice. She looked up and nodded.

'I couldn't find you. I looked up and you were gone. I thought you'd gone downstairs to kneel with the others. But a young man pointed me out here.'

'I couldn't take it any more *Dei*. I feel tired. I feel awful. Wretched.'

'He made me feel ashamed. There was no need to treat folks so harsh. Some of them things he said! I would be cross, but he seems so nice. He cares about us.'

'I'm sorry *Dei*. It's just too much. Can we go home?'

They walked slowly and quietly down towards the tram stop.

'Do you not think he could be related to us *Dei*?' Selina said at last.

'I don't think so – I've never heard anyone mention him that way. *Poori-dei* would've known, God rest her soul, she knew all the families going way back, it seemed. He is a Smith though, so it is possible.'

'What did you really think of what he said?'

Her mother paused. 'I think he must be right in what he says. he knows something: has seen something that he needs to tell everyone.'

'I think so too. I feel like we should go back.'

'No love. Let's leave it. You're tired. Our Henry said he's here all week. We can always come back another time. Let's think on, eh?'

The two women went about their work the next day washing their own clothes; then, once they were hung out to dry, they would iron the ones they had washed yesterday. Selina could still hear the Gipsy's voice ringing out in her head: the melody of that hymn being her first waking consciousness when she heard the knocker-upper tap on next door's window. "There's a hand held out to you, to you. There's a hand held out to me, to me. There's a hand that will prove true…"

Only when the children had been sent on their way to school and the menfolk had gone did she feel able to let the tune out of the confines of her head, out into the steamy scullery air, as she turned the ponch in the tub. As the words quietly sang out, she felt something stirring – something lifting from her. It was something more than happiness – it wasn't just enjoyment of the moment –

such as happened naturally every now and then. This was forward looking, more a feeling that everything would turn out all right, that. … was it hope? or was it — faith. The thought of that word suddenly made her stop what she was doing, stop singing, and she stood over the tub holding onto the handle of the ponch. Her mother came through from the living room.

'Don't stop singing; I was enjoying that… Lina love is everything all right?

Selina turned and smiled at her mother, framed in the doorway. 'Yes *Dei*, I'm fine. In fact I'm better than that.'

'You had me worried. I thought the baby…'

'No, just something occurred to me.'

'What's that?'

'I don't know exactly. Will you come back with me to the chapel? Last time I went to see him – now I think I'm ready to listen.'

'I wish I could have put it like that, love. I'd like to go and listen too.' Her mother gave her a reassuring smile. 'Let me help you with that, I've finished tidying,' she added.

The water got progressively murky looking, as they took clothes out and put new ones in; scrubbing, rinsing and wringing.

At teatime, the women announced their plans.

'The children can play out after tea, but not for long, because we want to get them ready for bed early – me and Lina are going out.'

'Out! Where?' said Dennis.

'We're going back to see Gipsy Smith, Dad.'

'But you've seen him already.'

'And we're going again, Den,' said Jemima.

'What's the attraction of this gipsy preacher – he must be good looking or summat.'

'It's his message we want to hear Dad. He knows what he's talking about – he makes it sound so true. God is working through him.'

Dennis made a snorting noise at the back of his nose, not unlike Jack and Fred out in the yard. 'But you hear all that stuff every Sunday! *His message!* Anyhow I'm not stopping in to see to the kids. Our union branch have organised a gang to go over to Cammell's to join the picket outside.'

Selina looked towards Rab. 'It's all right,' he said, 'I'm not going out. I'll see 'em up to bed.'

The children had been quiet. 'What are you talking about?' said Lizzie.

'And who's this gipsy?' said Little Selina. 'Is he from the old days? Does he have a *vardo* like Grannie Lizzie?'

'He's a preacher, love. He's like us – he was born in a tent and never went to school, but one day he found God and now spends his time telling others about God,' Selina said.

'He found God? Was God lost?'

'No God wasn't lost, but perhaps the poor little gipsy boy was,' said Jemima.

'I don't get it!' said Little Selina, and went back to her task of trying to cut the gristle off a lump of stewing beef.

'So why are you going back Mummie,' Lizzie asked.

'Because he is wonderful to listen to, love. He explains about God in a way that we've never heard before.'

'Can I come?'

'No love, not tonight, it's too late. Perhaps another time.'

'So what's going on at Cammell's then?' Rab asked.

'There's some knobsticks in there…'

Little Selina laughed, 'Knobsticks! What's a knobstick?'

'A blackleg, a strikebreaker, a spineless man of no principles, who'd sell his own mother for a shilling.'

'They're not nice then!' said Lizzie.

'No they're not. Anyhow, up from London they are. The gaffers have put 'em up in the works on a night-time and have 'em working the machines of the locked-out engineers of a daytime. We're off to go and lend a little friendly persuasion to the argument. When they get tucked up in their little camp beds they'll hear us singing 'em to sleep – and I dare say there'll be one or two trumpets to play 'em a lullaby! Since they arrived the crowd outside just keeps getting bigger and noisier. There could be nigh on a thousand there tonight.'

'Well you be careful and don't go getting yourself arrested, do you hear?'

'Yes Jemmie, dear. I hear.'

*

'....Jesus has not forgotten the women. Some of you even say that religion is all well and good for womenfolk. Well it's a blessing some of them have got a bit of religion. They don't get much comfort from the men they have to call husband. It's a blessing some women have got Jesus to look to, or I don't think they could live at all. Have you forgotten that you promised God at the altar to take care of her, to shield her, love and honour? Forsake everything for her? Have you forgotten? Because one day God will make you remember. Poor suffering woman, weeping woman, you hair grey long before it ought to be, your face pinched and your back bent, and you do not have a moment's peace, and in your sleep you dream of misery, full of tears and disappointments and agonies. Jesus knows my sister. God help you to make him your friend. When sometimes you smile and you are forced to smile because others are there, when you have sorrow enough behind, storm enough behind that smile to wreck Her Majesty's navy. He is with you. If you will but let him, he will kiss your tears into jewels. The sun of his love will light up your face once more and if the wrinkles do not go, He will make them beautiful, and if your back does not straighten He will give you grace to bear the burden and the flowers of paradise shall bloom again in your poor, wasted life, for as it says in Isaiah, "the wilderness shall blossom, it shall blossom abundantly." Oh mothers! Oh sisters! For the sake of our Lord and for your children's sake and for your husbands' sake, open your heart to Jesus. Let him take the throne-place in your heart. He will stand by you. Serve him, follow him! He will say "woman thy sins are forgiven thee."

Selina and her mother again had cheeks wet with tears. Now Selina had no fear. She felt her heart was open, she felt a presence. More than once it was as if the Gipsy spoke directly to her, looked at her, implored her.

Then he told the story of a small girl not much older than her Lizzie, who had been with her mother to one of his missions. 'She was a beautiful child and gave herself to Christ. Afterwards she

156

thanked me and as I bent down to talk to her she kissed me on the cheek. Several weeks later I saw her mother stricken with grief. She told me her beautiful daughter had gone home to Christ; suddenly struck down with a fever. Her mother said she had gone home with a smile on her face, telling her mother and father to dry their tears because she said she heard the angels singing and just before she passed over she said, "I am here Jesus, I am one of Gipsy Smith's little converts, I am ready, I am coming!" And she went to be with him forever.'

The Gipsy closed his eyes but Selina did not see; she and her mother were on their knees sobbing, holding each other.

This time they made their way to the inquiry room after the service. They found themselves kneeling next to female mission-workers.

An elderly woman, dressed in black with an old-fashioned bonnet spoke to Selina.

'Would you like to read this line from the gospel of St John?' Selina shook her head.

'Shall I read it for you then?' Selina nodded; she felt very small and childlike kneeling there.

' "If we say we have no sin, we deceive ourselves, and the truth is not in us. If we confess our sins, he is faithful and just to forgive us our sins, and to cleanse us from all unrighteousness." Do you believe that he will forgive you?' Selina nodded. 'Then bow your head and confess your sins to God.'

Selina thought back to when she had stolen from fields as a child. She had used Romany *hockabens* to get money off foolish people when she was young. She admitted she was selfish and jealous of others' things? Too fond of nice clothes – of trying to appear more than she was.

After a while she lifted her head. 'Do you feel you have been forgiven, child?'

'I don't know?'

'Are there any prayers you know that you would like to say?'

'I can't think of any.'

'Then how about one from the Psalms, it begins: "Out of the depths have I cried unto thee O Lord. Lord hear my voice: let thine ears be attentive to the voice of my supplication." How about I read it and you repeat it after me?'

After, Selina said, 'I think I understand now.'

'No don't think – it is not with the head that one finds religion – it is here,' she said clutching her breast. 'In your heart.'

'Yes,' said Selina, 'it is; thank you.'

Selina waited outside the vestry for her mother. Jemima emerged smiling and she took her arm. They stepped lightly towards the vestibule. Just as they were about to go out of the door, Gipsy Smith himself descended the stairs from the balcony. *'Kooshto raati!'* he said with a smile.

'Kooshto raati! Pariko toot,' said her mother, as if there was nothing unusual; and they went out.

'Dei – he spoke to us in Romany!'

'So he did! I didn't think anything of it.'

'So he did know.'

'Yes, I suppose he must.'

'Should we have stopped and said something.'

'I wouldn't know what to say.'

'No, I would be too embarrassed. But what a great man. How do you feel?'

'It's hard to say – but I feel very different.'

'Me too.' She squeezed her mother's hand as they walked out onto the pavement.

Chapter 16

Selina woke feeling elated and was attentive to Rab at breakfast. Both she and her mother took great pleasure in their work about the house all day. And at teatime, when Rab came home from training he was sat down to tea and buttered pikelets as soon as he got in. The women had decided to talk to their husbands separately about coming with them to see the Gipsy. Dennis had said he had more important things to do – there was a rumour that the London blacklegs might be thinking about leaving. 'I don't want to miss seeing them off on their way,' he had said.

Now, Rab slurped his tea and said he had to be at the Ground the following evenings of the week ready for the Bury match, and that once a week in church was enough for him.

Selina hid her disappointment, it wasn't even once a week he went, and what was it Gipsy Smith had said, something about imagining if husband and wife took Christ into their home, what joy there would be in Heaven and on earth!' She went back to her needlework. Rab put down his teacup. Later on he leaned over her and whispered:

'You don't fancy a bit of an early night do you?'

'No, I ought to finish this.' How could he? She was trying to get him to open his heart too, and all the time he was having lustful thoughts. It is indeed a blessing some women have got Jesus to look to.

Rab got out his pipe and smoked in silence for a while before retiring on his own.

The home game against Bury was tied at one a piece, as had been the previous game way to Forest.

Away at the Molyneux grounds was also drawn, a match in which

159

the United couldn't afford to idle on the ball for fear of being flattened by the big aggressive Wolves. If you weighed the two teams the difference would have filled two more gold and black jerseys, even given the head start Bill Foulke gave them. More than once Rab found himself face down, tasting the Black Country mud, even when he was nowhere near the ball. Rab sprang back up, but after one such challenge Harry did not: and Harry doesn't stay down for nowt. Only Bill's fine display of goalkeeping kept the parity of scores. Davy Morton was ineffective up front, no better than Henry White. That forward position was going to be their downfall, Rab said when he caught Needham on his own after the game.

Monday 4th October 1897

Blackburn Rovers were in town that following Monday. Rab was making his way from one tram terminus to the other, his kit bag slung over his shoulder, when something shouted by a newspaper seller attracted his attention.

He went over. 'One penny please,' said the seller.

'No ta. I don't want to buy one. What was that thing you shouted?

'Handsworth man attacked with hammer!' he said in his same sing-song voice only quieter.

'No, not that – the other thing.'

'Oh you mean: "Lyceum box office opens – Sir Henry Irving – Miss Ellen Terry – Read the details."'

'Yeah that were it. Thanks.'

Rab took a detour down George Street, past the Theatre Royal and to the Lyceum. Decorators were putting the finishing touches to paintwork. He watched a gentleman in a felt hat go inside and followed. He found what looked like the box office.

'How much is it to see Ellen Terry?' he asked the woman.

'Between one and six and seven and six, unless you want a private box. Which production would you want to see?'

'I just wondered about seeing Ellen Terry that's all.'

'She is beautiful isn't she.'

'I don't know. What should I do?'

The woman looked at him quizzically, 'Well there's Shakespeare's "Merchant of Venice" on the first night, that's the eighteenth, then there's "Madame Sans Genes," then two plays on the Thursday: a little Ellen Terry pastiche, "The Journey's End," an' "The Bells," one of Irving's finest; then "Madame Sans Genes" again, then the final night is "The Story of Waterloo" and "The Bells" again.' Rab didn't really understand what she was on about.

'What is best to see Ellen Terry?' he said.

'Well, either "Madame Sans Genes" or "The Journey's End" which was especially written for her I think. Rab caught the word "Madam" again but the other bit made no sense, so he said he thought "The Journey's End."

'And what price tickets do you want?'

'Not the cheapest, but not the pricey ones neither.'

'The Upper Circle is five shillings or the balcony is three an' six.'

'Yeah that one,' said Rab. 'Look I ain't got it on me so I'll have to come back, can you write it down for me, the Journey thing and those seats.'

The woman scribbled on a piece of paper and handed it to Rab. He folded it in his jacket pocket and headed to the Moorhead tram.

As he was going past the window of Roberts Bros he stopped at the window that was dressed with women's fashions. He smiled to himself at the audacity of it. It was bold, but it was such a neat idea. Could he get away with it? It would be risking a lot of money that might just get thrown back at him, but surely it was worth a try. He had, after all, a few quid tucked away at the Club, a few sovereigns in bonus payments from cup matches that he'd asked them to save for him for a rainy day. And wasn't it raining a bit? He blew out his cheeks, 'You old dog,' he said to himself, chuckled, then went into the shop. At the ladies outfitting department an assistant came over to him as he shuffled awkwardly.

'How much is a nice frock?' he asked.

'Who is it for, and what is the occasion?' said the girl.

'For a lady, for the theatre,' he said.

'Well yes I imagined it was for lady,' she said. 'Your wife

perhaps?'

'Yeah, that's right.'

'Well,' she said, 'a nice gown with silk skirt and bodice would cost upwards of five pounds.'

'As much as that?'

'I'm afraid so, we could always find sir a cambric gown… cotton, for less.'

'No, that wouldn't work. I'll order one of those that you said.'

The assistant smiled. 'Won't the lady be coming in to be measured?'

'No it's to be a surprise.'

'Well do you know her size?'

'About this high,' he said, holding his hand out flat.

'We would need her waist and other measurements as well sir.'

'Oh!' he said, 'I suppose she's a bit more rounded than yourself, but not much.'

The assistant laughed. 'Wait here sir.' She went to fetch another assistant and Rab saw them talking in collusion and laughing. Then they both came over.

'Is she about this size?' the first assistant said as her friend stood blushing as deep a colour as Rab felt he was himself.

'Yes I'd say so.'

They helped him choose a dress made up of a steely blue, pleated, satin skirt with a simply-embroidered bodice, the short, pleated sleeves reflecting the pleats on the skirt. They had first suggested pink, but decided for him that that would be unsuitable, twittering on about the importance of eye and hair colour when choosing a material. They also chose silk gloves and an opera cloak to match. They were, he thought, very charming and kind. In fact, they were largely just launching themselves enthusiastically into their roles, enjoying spending several weeks' worth of someone else's wages. He arranged to collect his order the following week and trotted to the tram fearing his diversion would make him late.

Over a fiver! For someone who didn't gamble, that was a tidy sum of money to wager. Still it might pay off, and at the very least it would make a decent apology for having treated her badly. Perhaps if she would not have him as a lover she could still see him as a friend and then you never knew… a dog that wanders will find a bone, as they say.

He had tried to forget about her, it was after all an impossible situation, but she was there in his dreams at night and he'd wake and realise that the overwhelming happiness he'd just experienced was an illusion. Then, unable to sleep he would creep downstairs, the cold oilcloth on his bare feet as he tried to avoid the creaky stairs, and would wander around before he was able to creep back up and use the chamber pot. He thought he had seen her once or twice in the street and his pulse quickened, only to discover it was someone else. His mind also caught him unawares, playing tricks on him: he'd see a dog chasing a pigeon like a thing possessed, or a motor-car in Birmingham and his mind would say: "have to tell Ada about that," before the reality struck.

Dinner was at twelve noon on the dot. Rab sat next to Mick Whitham: 'Harry's bad luck's turned out good for you, eh Mick? Chance to show 'em you've still got it.'

'We'll see, but I don't think I'm a match for a fit Harry Thickett these days. No my star's waning I reckon. I could move on and find another club that would value my experience, but let's face it who'd have me, and I don't want to flit – besides I'm getting reasonable money playing for the reserves and then there's my other interests.'

'Oh yeah, how is the beautiful young lady?'

'Sh! Keep your voice down. It's going well – I'm happy.'

Rab put his hand on his friend's shoulder and gave it a squeeze.

John Almond, in his new centre-forward role, scored United's second and, up until Blackburn equalising, the game seemed well balanced; but then Needham went on to get a hat-trick – the third goal of which Rab had thought was his, until the goalie saved, then Cocky had a strike, only for the blessed Needham to pick up the rebound and fire in.

This five–two scoreline was replicated at Gigg Lane on the Saturday.

When Rab got home that night the house was dark. He threw his bag down in the scullery, lit the candle by the door, ran some water into a glass bottle, then looked around for something to eat. Finding some bread and a bowl of dripping he went and sat at the table, digging down into the dripping to get to the jelly layer. He heard the stairs creak and the living room door opened. Lizzie appeared, night-dress crumpled and dark hair falling across her face and shoulders, blinking in the candle light.

'Daddie, you're here. I'm thirsty.'

He pushed the bottle across the table and she sat down, elbows on the table, leaning on her hand.

'We won again. I nearly scored. First half shot, a right stinger, but it was saved.'

Lizzie looked at him and smiled thinly or sleepily.

'Granda took us to see the cycle parade – you missed a treat. Father Christmas was there, all dressed up in his furs – but riding a bicycle! He looked so funny! And all the bicycles were decorated and there was a pirate called Blue Beard, a clown, Punch and Judy, Hindoos, savage princes, and all sorts. There were loads of people all clapping. Laughing and cheering, and brass bands. Oh and the devil on a bicycle too! Scary! Granda gave us a whole shilling each to put in the collection tins for the poor children of the engineers. My brother cried when he had to put his in, because he wanted to keep it! Funny Rabbi!'

Rab listened and smiled and passed a bit of dipped bread to her.

'I made the fifth goal – picked up the ball and went past two or three before I passed it to our inside-left who smashed it past the goalie.'

They sat quietly each thinking their own thoughts. Lizzie looked at him, yawned, got up, and kissed him on the cheek. '*Kooshto Raati*, Daddie!'

'Yeah to you to!' He finished the bread.

Chapter 17

Rab sat down on the wooden seat of the tram with a satisfied sigh-cum-groan. His legs were tired and a little bruised, but he'd come off lightly compared to Sugar, Fred and Cocky. He wasn't shy about getting stuck in but you could never accuse him of not playing fair: Langley had deliberately gone for Cocky to slow him down. The "Clash of the Blades" they called it. There must have been well over twenty thousand at Olive Grove, cheering and hooting, and United's bugler did a fine job to keep going throughout. The way they had defended their early lead – despite everything! What a job he'd done on Freddy Spiksley, he'd been on him at every pass and cut him out of the game. Oh how they loved him! How they had cheered him at the end! Red and White colours being waved; and all the pats on the back. Jack Earp and his men beaten at home by the better side! He got off the tram at Moorhead and strode across to Roberts to collect his parcel; five foot five and a bit, going on six foot.

Rab stood at the corner of Love Lane, looking over the road, cradling a big paper parcel. He had not quite worked out the next bit. The gas jets were on in the row of shops and singing was coming from the pub three doors down. If they were football fans they were not from the other lot. He struck on the idea of getting someone to deliver a message. If only he could have written one. He watched several boys go past and then saw the right one: nice looking, shod, blond hair stuck out beneath his cap.

'Here, does tha fancy earning a ha'penny?'

'What for mester?'

'Just running a little errand – nice and easy.'

'Go on then, what d'y want?'

'See that shop over there? The greengrocers?'

'Yeah, that's McGrail's.'

'Yeah, that's it. Well go in and tha should find a lady called Ada. Make sure tha gets Ada, got it? No one else, or tha'll not get thi ha'penny, tha'll get a bunch o' fives. Now, when she says she's Ada, gi' 'er this. Don't say owt. Then come straight back here. Got it?' Rab handed the boy an envelope containing the ticket for the Ellen Terry thing and watched him cross the street and enter the shop. A moment later he emerged grinning, and, dodging a dog cart, crossed back over.

'Gi' us mi ha'penny then.'

'Not yet – was it her?'

'Yeah, Ada, I've seen her before. Mi mam shops there sometimes. Gi' us mi ha'penny mester.'

'Just a minute – I'll let thi double it if tha likes.' Just then the shop door opened and Rab saw Ada look out into the street. He ducked back round the corner and pulled the boy with him.'

'Oi gerroff us!'

'Right here's a ha'penny. To get the other tha's got to take this parcel over and gi' it to her an' all. Don't drop it, or squash it!'

Rab looked round the corner: she must have gone back inside. The parcel was hard to hold; the boy took the string and holding his hands high so as not to trail it on the ground, made his way back over to the shop. Rab watched. The boy scraped the parcel over the step into the shop. Rab waited. The boy came running back and he was given another ha'penny, and sent on his way pleased with such easy takings.

Rab kept his eye on the shop. Should he go over? Surely she must've opened it? Why wasn't she looking out again? Still he waited, unsure what to do. Then Ada came out of the shop, hat and shawl on. She was heading straight for him. She had looked across the street to where he was standing but perhaps she hadn't seen him, and was concentrating on crossing the road. He came out of hiding and waited for her to cross; a cab trundling past. No; she glanced at him again. His idea wasn't going to work.

He spoke first as she reached the kerb, 'How did you know I was...'

'Little Arthur told me where you were. You'll have to take it back,' she said looking straight at him without the slightest warmth in her face.

'Don't yer like it?'

'It's not a case of whether I like it or not, you'll have to take it back.'

'So what have yer done with it?'

'Well I couldn't leave a thing like that lying around – I took it upstairs before anyone saw it.' Still cold eyes, unchanging expression. This was not the Ada he had dreamt of this last month or so.

'At least try it on eh? It don't have to mean owt. Just a theatre trip wi' a friend, just by way of an apology from me for treating you bad. In fact, the other ticket I've got,' his hand went unconsciously to his inner pocket, 'if you don't want me to go wi' yer, you can take someone else – a girl friend or Jim. How is he by the way? I've been wondering how he's doing.'

'He's better, it's healing up at least, though he still can't use his arm properly. He's back in court on Friday.'

'Well then a night out on Thursday is just what you need to take your mind off things! I'll come round for you in a cab before seven and if you decide to go, fine, if you'd rather someone else take you I'll just hand over the other ticket. But don't decide now. Try the dress on. Only... ,' he hesitated, '... if you do decide to go wi' someone else... can, ... can I see you in the dress first, then I promise I'll never call again, but I'll at least always remember the last time I saw you?'

Ada stood looking at him unmoving. Had her face softened a bit? She was not fighting back now. Was she tempted?

He made to go, then stopped. 'Ada?'

'Yes.'

'Nah, nothing, see yer Thursday.' He spoke in what he thought was a serious way – but kind. He reckoned he'd said enough. He was still up in the game; if he said too much he might spoil it – give her a reason to go on the attack. He turned and walked away without looking back.

Ada looked down at her hands; one of her nails was broken and they had dirt in them. She looked up at Rab, heading down the street, then crossed back over to the shop.

'Thanks Mother, I'll take over again,' she said, 'you go back to what you were doing.'

She served a few customers more; then, after a lull of several minutes, she closed the shop for the night and headed up to her room with a lamp.

The brown paper parcel was there on the bed, the corner gaping open revealing the satin beneath. It had been obvious what it was as soon as the paper had ripped. She put the catch across the door, put the lamp on the table and stood looking at the parcel. She moved closer and reached out at the perfect fabric shining blue through the hole in the drab paper in the lamp's glow; her cracked nail still dirty, despite washing. She grabbed at the string around the parcel, threw it under the bed clattering the chamber pot, then sat down on the bed. She took the ticket out of her apron pocket and studied the print. It was too cruel! The last few weeks had been so, so hard. Looking after her brother and the shop and deliveries, her mother fussing around, Annie off all the time with her new feller. And the void within her. To begin with she had cried so much that turning the pillow over made little difference to the dampness; but when the tears dried this hollowness was left – her days just a series of things to do, functions with no purpose. Endless days, from rising early to retiring late, with unrefreshing sleep between. She had been so happy, so alive, and he had played with her, and lain waste all her vitality, her hopes, her future. A trip to the theatre with a friend! Just taunting her with what she had lost, what she could never have: the ragged, shoeless child at Easter outside the shop window, elaborate chocolate creations within. She put the ticket on the bed and fetched a small, faded cardboard box from her bottom draw. She sat back down and lifted the lid. On top was a piece of heather, dried but the flowers still retaining a reminder of mauve. She closed her eyes; they pricked beneath the lids. She placed the heather on the bed – she should have just thrown it away – and took out the other things: postcards from Ireland, the seaside, a portrait of Lily Langtree, and the picture she was looking for, a bit bent at the corner: Ellen Terry, arms up, hands resting on her head, wearing long gauze-like sleeves, gazing straight out at her with sad eyes. She was coming to Sheffield. She put everything back in the box, with the addition of the theatre ticket.

The parcel lay untouched under the bed except for, in the morning, being kicked further towards the wall. Ada was more short with Jim than usual; he had got used to being waited on, but he couldn't expect that to carry on. His arm wasn't back to full strength but there was nothing wrong with his legs. She knew she was taking it out on him, but he just put up with it. Perhaps he would have noticed the difference in her mood had he not been so wound up, by trying to avoid John Brown who was out on bail, by thoughts of oak-panelled court rooms, judges in wigs, sticking to his story, and everything else that his forthcoming trip to the City Quarter Sessions entailed.

The stabbing had been in the newspapers, so everyone knew why he had been going round with his arm in a sling. She was fed up of customers asking, not out of concern for her brother or the family, but wanting juicy details so they could tittle-tattle over their suppers. And none of this would have happened had *he* been more honourable and not made her fall in love with him. She had been humiliated and she felt as if people could see her shame, as if it were written on her face. The other day she was walking into town and a group of boys on the pavement did not move and let her past – she had to raise her skirt and step out onto the mud-smeared road as they laughed at her. It was then she realised it was Brown's gang. Her ears felt hot and the roots of her hair tingled. She hated them, and struggled to turn that hatred into pity like she knew she ought.

She confessed at church that she had been seeing a married man, even though unknowingly. She told her confessor about her overwhelming sadness and how she could find no purpose. The priest seemed more interested in talking about her lust as if she were somehow dirty and she came away with her Hail Marys, and a sense of disappointment that she had not received any comfort for her spirit; angry at the man behind the screen. She felt let down by God as well as by her confessor. She had always scorned the idea of a horned devil at work putting temptation before mankind. But she could not understand why this cruel thing had happened to her.

On Wednesday night she knelt at the side of her bed and prayed, but there came over her a sense that she was talking to no one but herself. She couldn't ignore the decision she would have to make – tomorrow he would turn up, full of hope. Ellen Terry, the real Ellen Terry – and she would never again get the chance to see her, never. He said she could take someone else, and he had meant it, she knew. Perhaps it was no more than a kind gesture to apologise. After all, was it not possible that he just couldn't help himself from falling in love with her as she had with him? Could you ever stop love? But then, even if he had fallen in love with her, he could have been a gentleman and turned away – that way he would not have hurt her too.

She would get the dress out. Just to look at it. She closed the latch on the door and quickly pulled off the string and paper before she could change her mind. The folds of smoky blue satin fell to the floor – she held it up by the bodice then laid it down on the bed. It was as if a light source in addition to the lamp had been let into the room, and all the other colours were not real like this one. She sat down on the small wooden chair by the table. How much must it have cost? She would try it on, no one would see. She tidied the paper away and came across two small parcels that she had missed before. She opened the larger, flat one and took out a grey brocade cloak; the smaller one contained silk gloves of the same colour. The satin was cool against her skin as she stepped into the blue folds. She couldn't tell without getting someone to fasten the bodice but it seemed to fit. Remarkable that he had managed that. She pulled on the gloves and slipped the cloak over her shoulders. She could not see much in the small mirror on the chest of drawers and by the lamplight, but she tried to stand as far back as she could to get an impression of the effect. She had no shoes to go with it, but her best ones would do: they wouldn't be seen underneath the skirt and petticoat; and would it be acceptable to not wear a hat if she tied up her hair?

When she pulled back the counterpane, she lay awake a long time. Each time she opened her sleepless eyes the dress draped over her chest of drawers still shone in the faint light entering through the window.

She awoke in the morning to the noise of tapping at the door and her mother's voice questioning why the door was locked; it had been late yet again when she finally got to sleep, so she was still dead to the world at her usual waking time. She told her mother she would be down in a minute. She opened her curtains and the early morning light made the dress look even more incongruous in her small plain room than it had by lamplight. There was no uncertainty in her mind as to whether she would go: it was as if she had decided in the night – all her dreams having resolved the previous evening's doubts. As she put on her everyday clothes she smiled as she remembered the story of Fair, Brown and Trembling told to her when she was a little girl by Grannie Flannery. She was Trembling and the old henwife had put on her magic cloak and snipped a piece of rag from her clothes and asked for a beautiful robe. All she needed were the honey-bird and the milk-white mare to take her to Mass. The void she had lived with was now filled with her own fairy-tale and thoughts of Ellen Terry and the theatre. She confided in her sister Annie Eliza; she needed her help in getting ready that night. Annie was both shocked and thrilled at the adventure, especially when Ada showed her the dress.

'But what will you tell mother and Jim? It's not like you can sneak out in a dress like that.'

'They need not see who I'm going with, if you help me. When he arrives – you must keep a look out – send him down the street and get him to send the cab back empty. We'll just not tell them anything.'

'Oh this is so exciting! Just like a story in the weeklies!'

'So you'll help me then?'

'Yes of course, but you'll owe me one Ada McGrail! You'll have to cover for me in return.'

*

Rab pulled up outside the shop before St Peter's marked the hour. The lamps of the cab cast a little light onto the pavement where he saw Ada's sister. As soon as she had seen it was him, she rushed up.

'Go round the corner, get out, and send the cab back!' she said before he could even think of opening the cab door. 'Go on! Go!' she said half to him, half to the driver who flicked the reins. Rab wanted to question her, but, having done her job, she turned straight back.

He did as he was told and got out by the brewery. He stood there feeling a touch ridiculous in his borrowed billycock hat; silver half-albert dangling his Birmingham cup runners-up medal from his waistcoat; handkerchief tucked in his jacket pocket. He gave a little shiver; it was turning colder and there was that dampness in the still night air that seemed to penetrate clothing.

He didn't have a hope – it was a big gamble of a month's wages – a hoof from outside the twelve-yard line that would need a bit of a bobble to go in; and it meant getting done off George, and probably Nudge as well, for not turning up at the Lane for a sober evening of card games and billiards. He'd think up his story later. He chewed a loose bit of nail off his thumb, then had to suck it when it bled. She probably didn't want to see him and perhaps was going to take up his offer of going with a friend – had that been a wise thing to offer? It was a neat move though, asking to see her one last time in the dress! He was curious to see her in it – he couldn't picture it in his mind at all, from seeing it in the shop to what it would look like on Ada.

The black four-wheeler stopped in front of him and the door opened.

'Don't just stand there gawping. Are you coming or not?' Ada said.

Rab grinned and jumped up and sat down next to her, perching on the edge of the seat, since fabric consumed most of it. He looked her up and down and just carried on grinning, unable to speak as the cab pulled away.

'Well?'

'Ada, you look magnificent! You look a proper lady.'

'Thanks Rab, but I'm cross with you for spending all this money and for coming round the other day. I'm cross, and you're not forgiven.' She looked serious, eyes straight on him, but was there a hint of a smile in her eyes? 'But the money's spent and it would be a shame to waste it. But there's nothing between us. There can't be. You get that into your thick head, Rab Howell.'

'Right you are.' Rab carried on smiling. 'But you do look summat else! Does it fit a'reight?'

'Annie had to make a few adjustments but it's fine now. How did you do it?'

'Lucky gipsy guess – and a bit o' help from two nice shop girls.'

'So how have you been?'

'Pretty terrible. What about you?'

'Terrible too.'

'I'm sorry…'

'Don't. We must move on. How's the football going?'

'Good – we're top of the league – for now.'

'I heard.'

'And I've been selected to play in the Sheffield against Glasgow game.'

'And that's good?'

'Yeah, the best players from United and the other lot play against the best Glasgow eleven – it's a good match.' Rab's eyes kept drifting towards Ada's neckline, where through the front of the cape he could see a glimpse of pale skin at the top of her chest. 'What did y' mother reckon when she saw yer?'

'I don't know, I just rushed down the stairs and out before she could get a word in. They don't know who I'm with, Annie saw to that.'

The cab pulled up behind others on Tudor Street and they got out. The pavement outside the main door was covered by a glass canopy, where men in chimney pot hats assisted ladies out of carriages with whom even Ada couldn't compete in their puff of silks, feathers and furs. Rab went from feeling over-dressed to under-dressed. The building was not like a Sheffield building. It was clean and bright with classical columns and decorated with stucco flowers, leaves and cherubs; a statue surmounted a copper dome holding aloft a bright electric light. It was like the building had been lifted out of Shaftsbury Avenue and dumped in Arundel Street.

Rab offered his arm and he puffed up his chest as a silk glove rested on it. They showed their tickets and were directed through the foyer, climbing the stairs and wandering past mirrors and fancy electric lights, feeling a little as if they shouldn't be there. If someone had shouted: 'Oi you, what do you think you're doing in here,' he wouldn't have been surprised.

He offered to get them a drink from the circle bar but she was anxious to get seated. When they entered the auditorium they found their seats and for several minutes they just looked around trying to take it all in: hangings, curtains and upholstery were all done in red velvet with silk cords and there was polished brass everywhere. The walls and ceiling were decorated with plaster mouldings, picked out in gold; electric lights making everything glow. The stage was framed by an arch made up of swirls of gold through which the crimson plush curtain could be seen.

Just in front of them was a sort of wall and in front of that the "carriage lot," the residents of Nether Edge and Ranmoor, were gathering in the expensive seats; seats upholstered to match the upholstery of their occupants. Rab looked around – where they were sat the arm rests were brass rods; other people taking their seats around him were dressed in their ordinary Sunday best, not like the lords and ladies in front. In fact Ada should have been sat in front in her gown. He cursed himself – if he'd raised the stakes by another two and six a seat they could have been in front too. But then he'd have felt even more out of place amongst that lot – he wouldn't have dared open his mouth and given himself away. But then, as it was, they could have watched ten football matches for what he'd paid. 'We've a good view from up here at least,' he said.

'Isn't it. And nice comfy seats too!' Perhaps he'd done all right after all.

It was warm and Rab took off his jacket and folded it on his knee. Looking straight ahead Ada slipped her cape off her shoulders. He tried to look out of the corner of his eye – that pale skin above her... Oh if he could just rest his head there, touch it with his lips… She caught him looking at her and he looked quickly away with half a smile, but he just wanted to stare, to take his fill of her, in the full glare of the electric lights.

Gradually the place filled as the uppermost four or five layers of Sheffield society, responding to the bell in their designated saloon or bar (so that they could avoid mingling), settled into their strata. Those in the cheap seats perched on benches in the pit or in the gods, some on more padded seats, and others in seats so grand that they were no longer seats but 'fauteuils,' a word which would not have been understood except by those people who 'moved in society' and whose own suitably proportioned 'derrières' were parked on one.

They watched the orchestra take their places down below, then everyone stood for the Anthem. The curtain rose and there on the stage was a room as elegant as the rest of the theatre with a sofa, a table, and a fireplace; then another room next to it with a bed. A door at the side opened and in came a woman dressed in a beautiful gown. Rab felt a thrill as his hand was grasped sharply; then, just as suddenly, let go as Ada started clapping along with everyone else. He leaned over, 'That 'er then?' She flashed a quick smile at him and settled back down. He caught a whiff of flowery scent from her neck and took advantage of the dimmed lighting and her rapt attention to sneak a look at her – she had a silk choker round her neck with what looked to him like pearls on it, and, with her hair tied up, he could follow the curve of her neck from her ear down to the pleats at the top of her dress and round. She glanced quickly, her face lit up, and he smiled back.

Rab then found himself drawn in by this character on the stage – she had been to a ball and had returned alone; her husband saying he'd gone to his club when really she suspected he'd gone off to Lady Fairfax – he was a footballer too then? He smiled. Where had he heard that old story before? She'd been dancing with Captain Maramour – bloody stupid name that – and felt guilty.

'Oh! Why is it so terribly wrong, and pleasant to be admired?' – 'Tha's reight lass!' he thought to himself.

Her husband no longer took delight in her; no longer even quarrelled; they just lived apart – this was obviously her room, and her husband slept elsewhere in the house. Rab thought of the eight, soon to be nine, he had to share his small house with. The lady on the stage talked about wanting appreciation and intimacy; she was just not sure about falling for this other man who was not her husband.

'I wonder whether he too, like my husband, has a brilliant talent for infidelity? Two years of enchantment and then a lifetime of etiquette. That is a happy marriage.'

Suddenly in burst her Captain – who begs her to run away with him and pleads for her love. It's clear she doesn't love him though and answers coolly. But Rab still thought she was tempted and was urging her on – let yersen go lass, live a bit! He thought it was funny how she kept talking to the audience to tell them what she was thinking whilst this daft captain feller stood there not hearing what was being said.

She begged him to leave – what if her husband returned? Then off stage there's the sound of a door and footsteps and she hides the Captain in her bedroom that she calls a 'boudoir.' She says to the audience: 'Let me escape tonight and I'll never speak to a man again. Tomorrow I go to a convent.'

In walks her husband – all starch and whiskers: probably one of those amateurs, an old time Corinthian or summat, Rab thought. He wants to get back to the happiness of their perfect days together – what rot! – and says he's never really loved any of the other women – don't fall for that one love yer should boot him out and run off wi' that captain feller!

From the moment Ellen Terry had come through the door, Ada was entranced. She forgot everyone around her and where she was and what she was wearing. *The* Ellen Terry was right in front of her, talking to her. She followed every movement, every pained expression, every gesture. Just her and Ellen Terry. She rose a little in her seat when the captain entered and relaxed when he was hidden away, then was drawn back in when she spoke to her husband – what a rat he was to cheat on her.

He asked her whether there is any way a woman can tell whether a man loves her?

176

'Yes, if he is cold one moment and kind the next. If he calls her every name under Heaven from an angel to a scorpion, if he contradicts all she says, hates everything she likes, and likes everything she hates, and if he makes her life now a rapture and now a misery and now the weariness of death – she can make up her mind that – '

'That what?'

'That he worships the ground under her feet,' she said mimicking a man and then laughed a harsh laugh. All too often that is how it is, Ada thought. The husband talked of their reading poetry together in the old days and how he could still find her favourite volume of poetry with his eyes shut; he made for the bedroom to find it. Ada leaned forward. Ellen Terry stops him and says: 'You lost the right to talk sentiment to me: I must at least enjoy the distinction of being the one woman you do not make love to.' He asks for one more chance to prove himself, says he could find the book blindfold. She sees her chance and blindfolds him and makes him promise not to cheat. She opens the door and she gestures to the Captain who ducks under the husband's outstretched arm and escapes – stopping only for a bow before leaving the stage. Ellen Terry then laughs and then sobs – and the husband comes out clutching the book. 'What is the matter dearest?' he says.

'I am so glad – you did not find – the wrong book.' She then falls into his arms and the curtain falls. Ada let out a little gasp. Not the end already – she felt a pang of grief. She jumped to her feet like everyone else was doing and clapped. The curtain rose again and there she was – but somehow a different Ellen Terry – she could now see that his was the real one – different from her character. She shouted out a couple of 'bravos' and only stopped clapping when the curtain fell and the lights came up. She sat down and looked across at Rab who was wearing his daft grin again.

'You can buy me that drink now.'

'So which one was Henry Irving?' Rab said as he brought two sarsaparillas back to where she stood.

'Neither of them. He's on next, it's a famous play of his.'

'So is your mate Miss Terry in it an' all?'

'Sadly not – wasn't she just wonderful though? You really believed everything she was going through.'

'She should've run off with her fancy man though don't you reckon?'

She scowled at him. 'Don't you go getting any ideas!'

The curtain call for Sir Henry was if anything longer than that for Miss Terry. Rab felt exhausted when the last of Sir Henry's long deep bows was over – almost as exhausted as the actor himself.

'He don't half throw hissen into it!' Rab said as they rode back in a cab. 'Queer feller though ain't he?'

'Well he had to be all smiles one minute, then sobbing with grief the next, then tormented for his sins the next. It's like he really is Mathias isn't it?'

'Clever how he gets is come-uppance in the end though! The rope, the rope, cut the rope!' Rab said clutching his neck and gurgling. Then, seeing Ada laugh he continued: 'No! The bells. The bells again!' He received a slap on the arm. 'It was reight clever how they did that dream bit.'

He kept his eyes fixed on Ada looking for an opening, but none came. If only the ride had been longer. If only he could tell the cabbie to just drive on and not stop until he said, but this was real life not some novel.

'We're here Rab. Don't get out. Thank you, I've had a wonderful evening. One that I shall never forget as long as I live. And I think you are forgiven. But that's it now. It has to be. I wish things were different.'

She leaned forward and kissed him on the cheek. He didn't move just muttered, 'Aye me too.'

Then she left him.

'Just drop us off round t'corner, eh feller?' he said to the cabbie.

Chapter 18

With the end of October came the first fogs of autumn. A visitor to London might have found the fog there to at least have some compensations: the sensation of walking around with your ears muffled and not being able to see more than a yard ahead lent a certain adventure and sport to the endeavour. Any visitor to Sheffield though had no such romantic notions of its fog on stepping off the Great Central or Midland train. In Sheffield, the air felt abominably dirty; its dampness clung, fell to the ground and created that thick mud, treacherous to horses, which that leapt on to your clothes like filings to a magnet. Sheffield fog was a thing to be endured, for it would only pass when it was ready, sitting over the town like a beast over its half-eaten dinner. Its soupiness was full-flavoured. And, above all, no one would escape the sore throats and the melancholy that it brought with it. And it stank – it seemed to capture and to hold every smell released by industrial process, man and animal alike. It then blended them, ripened them and fermented them, so that ladies would stay indoors, and all but the hardiest and most downtrodden pulled their mufflers or neckcloths up over their noses.

Real hardship was now manifest all around the neighbourhood, as out of work engineers and their families lived on handouts from their neighbours and supplemented their potato and swede diets with the bread and soup they queued for. They were not alone in their suffering. On the hills above Sheffield, the Earl of Wharncliffe and his guest Balfour and others found it too foggy to play golf and had to settle instead for shooting one thousand one hundred rabbits and a hundred and fifty brace of pheasant, most of which, entertainment over, were piled up and left to rot. Back amongst the blackened bricks, money was collected in boxes, and brassy

179

instruments attempted to blow away the fog at parades of the Newhall, Tinsley Victoria or the United Grimesthorpe bands marching from Ellesmere Road Temperance Hall to town. Attempts were made to raise funds and spirits: glees were sung by Attercliffe Clarion Glee Club, charity concerts, magic lantern shows, and lectures on things like 'A Trip to the Moon,' were held at Liberal Clubs, and there were special football matches between locked-out engineers and publicans: sometimes combining the fancy dress of the preceding parade with the match itself. Rab and some of the United team wandered along after training to join the five thousand or so spectators to watch such a game at the Sheaf House Ground. The players were given many a pat on the back for their unbeaten run and they all felt obliged to empty the change from their pockets into collection boxes or to buy buttonholes or oranges from the women touring the ground. A Great Dane, that his owner said ate three blokes Rab's size every day for breakfast, had a collecting box round his neck and Rab had little choice but to put in a thruppenny bit he had been holding back.

Escape from the gloom was provided by the away matches. A thousand supporters accompanied them to Goodison Park where they swelled the crowd to thirty thousand. Everton and their fans were confident they would be the first to lower the colours of the United, especially on taking the lead only four minutes in. But it was the thousand who cheered their boys the loudest, the opposing supporters being seized by despair, as the red and whites outplayed the blues; Bennett finishing the game with a fourth goal, taking on and beating four men; such quality raising cheers from all parts of the ground. Plaudits turned to stones aimed at Bill Foulke, and the referee had to stop the game to caution the crowd – Lawrence Bell, the *Wednesday* player of the season before, tried to take on United's custodian in an aerial challenge to knock him off the ball. The unfortunate Bell lay prone on the earth after the mountainous goalie landed on him. Bill picked him up like a baby and handed him to the trainer at the side of the pitch. Rumours of his death later proved to be unfounded.

Towards the end of November, storms came and swept the fog

out of the skies and the mud off the streets. Then December brought the first frosts. That cold air flowing down across Sheffield's hills from Scotland and beyond brought fear to some of its inhabitants. Cold exacerbating the hunger; that little food which seemed to suffice when it was mild, no longer satisfied. They feared a harsh winter of frosts that penetrated window panes, that froze the privy middens so that they could not be dug out for weeks on end, that brought lasting stillness to their elderly as they lay in their beds or sat through the long days in front of embers that faded with them. They stiffened their backs, prayed or cursed the unrelieving grey skies.

Then there was the daily choice between food and coal, and if food it were, then uncooked it would have to be. Into the evening and early morning when twilight's cloak was thrown over the woods around Attercliffe and Brightside, neighbours would bump into each other and exchange a knowing nod, or quiet "'ow do" as they stripped the ground of fallen branches and hacked down saplings to take home as fuel enough to raise the heat in a kettle sufficiently to mash some donated tea. Then, every time the cold air stilled, the fog started to congeal once more.

On undedicated streets like Lake Street, the smell and the filth was not just in the air but became part of the broken ground which it permeated and infested so that even a good downpour would not cleanse it, for bubbling up it came again straight after. Then sometimes the stench would be overlayered with carbolic when some typhoid-worrier attempted to combat the work of the nightsoil men, who had scraped and shovelled their special recipe from ash pits and privy middens into a workable pile for trundling away to the tip on their creaking, leaking carts before the good citizens emerged for the day.

Selina was by now a very peculiar shape, not nicely rounded, not ripening like a mellow peach: her belly stuck out tight, at right angles from her lean frame as if she and the child were not one harmonious peachy whole but existing in polarity alongside one another. She was now tired and unable to walk very far and was of limited help around the house, her back sore after standing for very long.

'I'm going to have to go round to our Sarah Ann's soon *Dei*; whilst I still can. I can't leave it much longer.'

'Well you just say when you're ready, and I'll help you and carry your bag – we'll not have that far to walk: just from the bridge to Snig Hill, then from the tram stop up to their house. It's a shame you'll be *poshaley*, and not be here for Christmas though.'

'I can't risk it – she could even come out on Christmas day.'

'In a way it was easier when all you needed was a separate tent. Then you could just burn it after.'

'Well, I can be nice and quiet up at Sarah Ann's and you'll not have to look after me as well as the kids. She's only got Archie to sort out, now all the others are grown up.'

'But how they'll miss you! We'll have to bring them up to Walkley to see you every week and at Christmas as well.'

'I'd like that; I shall miss them too. You'll have a lot on though *Dei*. Will you manage, what with looking after everyone, and the house, and those blasted pigs?' As if they had heard their name used in vain, a squealing noise came from outside.

'Yes I know how to look after things here; and Sarah Ann knows how to look after you which is more important. And you can rest without Little Rabbi, or big Rabbi for that matter, bothering you.'

Saturday 11th December 1897

Selina left on the day Rab was away at Stoke. It was easier with him out of the way. She had packed a few things into an old canvas bag, including a small tin containing a little lock of hair from each of her children, and a bottle of her mother's rose water, which looked a little cloudy but still smelt sweet, and two meat pies to share with Sarah Ann and Albert Lovell. She asked her mother to climb up and get her money tin off the scullery shelf. She had been putting away a penny or two since the summer as her Christmas fund. She slipped the tin into her bag and put on her hat and fawn woollen mantle.

'You got everything?' her mother asked.

She looked around the living room. 'I think so; I don't need much. I wish I didn't have to go. You'll make it look nice for Christmas won't you?'

'You know I will. It will be just perfect. Roast pork and apple, proper wax candles in the candlesticks, a nice log on the fire.'

Selina wiped a tear from her eye.

'Come here love,' said Jemima, 'don't you worry about us we'll be just fine.' She placed her hand on Selina's belly. 'You just concentrate on keeping this little one safe.'

'I know, I will,' she said opening the back door. 'I want to stop in town and buy a little something for the kids for Christmas.'

'Well you've picked a day for it,' Jemima said as they stepped out into the cold, driving rain, 'you'd better take the umbrella.'

They walked slowly past the brewery, Selina unable to go as fast as the weather would have otherwise dictated. Outside Boots at the bottom of Snig Hill was a man dressed as Father Christmas with a scarlet cloak, fur cap, and white beard: 'Ladies, please do come in, out of this rain and sample the pretty things we have.'

Inside there was a counter for medicines, but opposite that another counter and a display of Christmas cards and novelties. Selina looked at the ebony hand mirrors, but when told the price settled for hairbrushes at seven pence. They picked up and stroked purses of the softest leather – crocodile and monkey skin the assistant said. There was a variety of picture frames; and they wondered at the array of perfumes in pretty bottles. Selina also bought soap for her mother. At Wilson's they looked for a toy for Little Rabbi; there was too much choice: Noah's Arks, horses and wagons, magic lanterns, and, for just under a shilling, battleships with guns and turrets. There were miniature kitchens with tables and stoves that the girls would have loved. For five and a half pence they bought a small walking elephant.

'He'll love that,' Selina said, then burst into tears. 'I won't see his face when he opens it!'

Her mother put an arm round her, '*Ei*, you already have Selina love! *Mantchi too*! Let's pay for this and get you on that tram. There's no point upsetting yourself.'

'Yes, it's all a bit much. I'll leave you some money to buy the menfolk a shirt each.'

'Aye and that's better than having to lug everything around.'

'And the children must have a shiny penny, an orange and a walnut or two in their stockings.'

*

Stoke were third from bottom of the league; this was to be the day that the United, who had not won since the Everton game at the end of October, would pick up two points. Instead their unbeaten run came to an end on a pitch with more mud than grass and so many puddles that all that was missing was a few ducks.

When Rab got home that night he found some bread and cheese and some cold tea on the table, and his bed taken by the three children. He was now on his own in the girl's narrow bed. He had forgotten that Selina was moving into her sister's for her confinement.

The following Saturday, Bolton came to the Bramall Lane Grounds and so did the fog. The teams changed and came onto the pitch but there was not a hope of being able to play. The referee would not have seen the ball go into the net from the twelve-yard line, never mind the supporters seeing anything resembling a football game. Everyone went home disappointed; Villa went two points ahead, and people started to feel that the natural order was reasserting itself. The United were on the wane. Next game up was *the Wednesday*, just after Christmas.

A few days before Christmas, the older Mr Gill came round to the house at Lake Street carrying his equipment including buckets and a cloth roll of Sheffield's finest butchers' knives. Rab had decided to go for just one of the porkers and keep the other for later. Water was coming up to heat in the set pot: for scalding purposes. Gill removed the large jacket that hung loosely on his broad shoulders, hung it on the back of the scullery door and rolled his shirt sleeves up to reveal forearms as thick as a child's thigh and as ruddy as his cheeks.

'Which one's it to be then Mr Howell, sir?'

'We'll go for that un I reckon, he's got the edge on t'other – he's a greedy sod is Freddy, always first to the slops and meal bucket.'

'Right you are.'

Gill noosed Freddy and led him squealing in protest into the yard where a short trestle awaited him.

'He's a nice un sure enough: looked after him good I'd say.' He flipped the seven stone pig over onto its back in a swift movement. It was surprised to find itself upside down in such an undignified position and squealed in alarm. 'Help us hold him down a bit while I tie him will yer!'

Rab could sense the accusation of betrayal in its voice as it changed from an angry squeal into a roar of fear. Inside the pen Jack crashed the sides in panic as he answered his comrade's cries. The pig thrashed against the rope then, without ceremony, a thin pointed knife went into its throat: the steady stream of hot blood being deftly caught in a bucket held with the other hand. Freddy's sense of betrayal was now complete – his roar intensifying with the agony, as he thrashed against his restraint. Another precise incision and the bellowing stopped, the steaming, dying breath now sputtering out of the wound of the severed windpipe. The blood kept flowing for what seemed an inhumanly slow death. Gill sensed Rab's discomfort – 'have to do it nice and slow so as not to spoil the meat wi' blood.' The beast convulsed again then grew stiller with each rasping breath until the flow ran to a trickle. 'That's him done.' The thick forearms then set to on releasing the cascade of innards, and their stench; then the scalding, scraping, hacking and sawing. Two symmetrical halves were then taken inside over his shoulder and the kitchen table was then used until Freddy no longer resembled the fine beast he was, but a pile of joints slowly losing the warmth of life. After his hard work Gill washed, then retrieved his jacket, and went away whistling a music-hall song, his payment in blood: the head, body parts and an assortment of lard and offcuts for sausages all wrapped in a canvas sheet.

Rab slumped down in a chair feeling queasy and drained. He gladly accepted a cup of tea from Jemima who now took charge of the next stage of the operation, planning which of the joints piled on the oil cloth should be kept, which to take to the family and setting aside the hams and loins for curing.

The next day the slops that had been boiled up for Jack contained remains of his former companion's trotters from last night's stew.

*

Saturday December 25th 1897

Anyone crossing the yard and catching sight inside the end-terrace house on Christmas afternoon would have seen what they thought was an idyllic Christmas-day scene, as the family crowded round the table, swelled in numbers by others: Henry, Agnes and the boys, perched on chair arms or upturned crates. Dinner had been roast tenderloins and crackling, then Christmas pudding with a shiny silver thruppence inside, that the finder wasn't allowed to keep since it had been used in the family every year since before the first Jubilee. A fire was roaring, the gas mantle was lit for a change; holly sprigs that Rab had collected decorated the room. Everyone was in their Sunday best and the children were rosy cheeked from sitting on the rug by the fire playing with their new toys: the girls had squeaking India rubber dolls, gratefully received from Uncle Henry as had been a toy horse for Little Rabbi which was talking to his prized elephant. Henry's boys had tried and failed to convincingly perform conjuring tricks out of the box they'd received – to everyone's greater amusement than if they had in fact succeeded. Rab had saved his present for the tea-table: a large, beautiful pork pie which he had placed on a plate which brought a cheer of anticipation but which when tackled with a knife proved to be made of wood. The lid was then lifted to reveal chocolates and sweets inside the box. 'Typical lack of bloody substance!' muttered Dennis under his breath.

*

They all went on the tram to see Selina on Boxing Day, picking it up from the terminus. As he boarded, Rab recognised the bookie's runner he'd seen before, crossing the street behind them, and wondered to himself that there should be business for him even on Boxing Day.

When they saw their mother the girls were very quiet and would not leave her side; Little Rabbi had innumerable kisses on his hair and face that he had to wipe off. He had insisted on bringing her the elephant that Father Christmas had brought him – in fact it was now his constant companion – and she sat down in a corner with him to play elephants in the jungle. Sarah Ann was thrilled at the arrival of so many guests and she set the table with her best lace tablecloth and crockery. She laid out all manner of cheeses, pickles, pork pies (real ones), and even opened a tin of ox-tongue and some salmon in their honour. When he finally got near her, Rab gave Selina the present he had bought her, as she presented a cheek for him to kiss. She unwrapped the potted meat and the jar of preserved cherries from their brown paper and handed them straight to her sister for putting on the table. Albert Lovell insisted on opening a new bottle of Scotch whisky then proceeded to drink most of it himself from a bone-china teacup as he fell to regaling them with stories of the old days and something about Jesus and how the flounder got his crooked mouth. Rab barely spoke to his wife all afternoon: she was absorbed in the children and was evidently enjoying having the company after being in the house on her own so much, waiting.

'Have you everything ready for when the baby makes her mind up, Selina love?' asked her mother. 'Is there anything you still need me to fetch?'

'No *Dei*, I don't think so. When it starts I'm going to go round to a friend of Sarah Ann's who lives on her own – she can let us have her house for a bit while she's at her daughter's in Rotherham.'

When he took his leave of her Rab got a "goodbye" and a kiss on the cheek, much the same as the others, 'Thank you for coming Rab. Bring the children again soon won't you?'

He walked down the hill after the others feeling very lonely. It was already getting dark; the remnants of the meagre December light slipping away. The wind sprayed rainwater out of an over-

187

brimming gutter onto his face; he turned up his collar and pulled his cap down tighter. His mouth was dry and his tea hung heavy in his stomach. The ox-tongue and cherries churning there came to his mind; he felt he could wretch. Nothing he did was right – he couldn't stand living with this constant scorn – he was always being judged and always being found guilty. He couldn't set the rules himself and say himself whether he had followed them; the rules were set for him and he would break them without knowing. The constant blowing of the whistle for things he didn't understand. So he'd try and follow the new rule to the letter only to find it had changed since the last time. And when he got it wrong, the love Selina once had for him – and she did, once she had admired him, revered him even – every time that love seemed to shrink a little more. It was further poisoned by those around her, adding little drops to the roots to make it slowly die. He thought her love in recent years had not been for what he was but for what she wanted him to be; he could not be himself but had to be this other – for then he would be loved. He couldn't go on with this; life did not lay there; it was slipping by. He had to do something about it. As he turned the corner, there was Little Selina waiting for him. 'Come on Daddie slowcoach,' she said, slipping her warm little hand into his and pulling him along. She smiled up at him, 'I love you and Mummie,' she said. Little haloes formed and grew around the street lamps' globes of light and shivered as he blinked. He stroked her hand with his thumb.

Chapter 19

Monday December 27th 1897

The Wednesday had beaten Stoke four nil on Christmas Day and were now just two points behind the United in fourth place. All over Christmas their followers were convinced they were about to catch up. There was only one topic of conversation in the town: who would get the upper hand the Lane-ites or the Grove-ites. On that Bank Holiday all human traffic, mostly of the male kind, seemed to flow in one direction only from midday, as thirty seven thousand citizens made their way towards the Lane. Their progress was punctuated by stops at the numerous refreshment establishments along the way, as being stuck at home for two days solid engendered as strong a thirst as a shift at the furnace. The women they left behind were mostly resigned to it: they had given up arguing some time since about spending those sixpences on food or shoes. That there was to the male, but denied to them, a necessity of life, a right, to get out of the house, did at least have the upside of one less cluttering the place up. However, the evening return was for some a source of dreaded anticipation, of unpredictability: so much hanging on whether a leather sphere had passed between which posts and how many times, and consequently whether sorrows were drowned or feats celebrated.

The noise was deafening as the teams filed out. The very air itself was thick; football fighting sorrow for the souls of men. Rab came under early pressure from Spiksley who was considerably more lively now than his namesake, the remains of whom was packed in salt in a barrel in the cellar. Harry Thickett had to work hard alongside Rab to keep him quiet. But it was the United who scored first; Cocky Bennett, back from injury, rasping a shot at the goalie

Massey; then Jack Earp, trying to clear the rebound sliced the ball in, much to the one half of the crowd's enjoyment.

Just before half-time all *the Wednesday* supporters leapt into the air and waved their hats when a free kick went sailing straight in, but the United half of the crowd had their second big laugh of the afternoon when the referee disallowed it since it had been an indirect free kick. It was Spiksley who equalised into the second half when having got past Rab and created an opening for Kaye, went on to smash in the clearance from Bob Cain.

A surprisingly clean game finished one all and both sets of supporters went away with both praises and grumbles: the midget half-backs did their job, gave 'em no space to play: no better in the league. John Almond was under par they said, but before Christmas he'd been doubtful with influenza so fair play to the gent.

They had another game two days later against Liverpool. On his way to the ground in the morning Rab had been looking in shop windows at their Christmas displays as he stayed close to the buildings to avoid the wintry showers, biting wind, and annoying small children trying to sell matches. He puzzled at the ladies' footwear in the Public Benefit Boot Company: flimsy satin things and pink leather slippers that would neither keep a woman's foot warm nor dry. In John Atkinson's window were ferns and flowers that looked real but couldn't be really. Also there was a life-like model of a lady, not unlike that Ellen Terry he thought – wearing a fancy yellow frock. Other clothes and jewellery were in the same window. He had just a few minutes to spare, so popped in.

The Liverpool game was a miserable affair in front of a mere four thousand hardy, and less post-Christmas-broke, supporters, where, one by one, the players' kits became indistinguishable as they fell in the mud – the blue and white quarters turning the same colour as the red and white stripes. Liverpool's winning goal came from a Thickett own goal as he strained to clear a cross. Everyone concluded that the United's neat passing game was not good in the mud – they had floundered whereas Liverpool's kick and rush tactics – hoofing it long – were more successful. Again the United forwards had been disappointing – Almond had still not regained the form he showed way back at the Everton game.

The newspapers had never been of much interest to Ada. She didn't have time, and stories about wars in Soudan or wherever didn't mean much to her. She knew of boys going abroad and not coming back, but squabbles played out in South Africa with Germans or with Russians in the Mediterranean didn't seem part of her life. She read the occasional story about the Engineering dispute, skipping over the long political pieces and speeches. The theatre and pantomime reviews she had always read, but she had recently started looking out for the football reports in Monday's paper, when for her the back two pages had never existed before. She found herself listening out for the scores, shouted out by newspaper vendors on Saturday night, or asked customers coming in late on in the afternoon. She noticed when the United fell off the top spot in the league; looked out for the name Howell in the column to see how he had played. It was Monday's paper she now wrapped the muddy leeks in before dropping them into Mrs Cousins' bag – she had felt something akin to pride when she'd read that the half-back line had been masterful and had taken the sting out of their opponent's attack.

Annie brought her in a cup of tea and she warmed her dirty fingers, clasping them around the cup. A boy came in the shop – a letter for A McGrail he said, on a special errand he was – feller came in his mother's stationers shop and asked her to write it out for him. She pulled the piece of paper out of the envelope: "Meet me at Victoria Cafe at six." There was only one person she knew who could be so audacious, so lacking in manners! Of course she wouldn't go, what a cheek. She folded the note and put it in her apron pocket.

She knew she was kidding herself. The thrill of a secret encounter swelled as the afternoon went on – like the draw of the bottle of brandy in the sideboard calling to the bored unloved woman, or the tap-room to many a man. Every glass was to be her last. Her life had dragged on through the foggy days and cold empty nights. No henwives with cloaks for her and no princes to carry her away and make her forget. Christmas had been the usual family and church rituals played out; the joys of young nieces and nephews mingled with sadness and sense of loss; tin drums confiscated before dinnertime, her mother shedding quiet tears over her Christmas pudding. The thought of "whose turn is it to have Aunty Ada this year" was abhorrent to her.

As she pulled on her hat and fastened her shawl to head up into town that evening she knew she was raising the stakes. She could well be gambling away her last remnants of happiness on a ridiculous venture, but, right at that moment, she didn't care. She was conscious of every rise and fall of her chest, every beat of her heart, every pulse through her veins rebelling, rising up with nature against her sense of propriety – against convention. She desperately hoped for an opening, something almost miraculous to allow herself to yield; turning aside from the little voice of logic, of piety. What was it if not the strength of love?

Rab got up from where he was sitting by the door when she entered the tea rooms; a big smile on his face. 'I didn't think you'd come – but you have.' He thought she seemed very calm and controlled.

They sat at a table by the fountain and ordered.

'Have you been playing this afternoon?'

'Yeah, we lost. It were awful – like playing in a pigsty or a cow's field!'

'Liverpool wasn't it?'

Rab smiled, impressed and flattered by her knowledge.

'I'm sorry for getting in touch again. I have tried to stay away, honest I have, but I just can't. I'm just not happy wi'out yer,' he said, 'I've got you this…' he pulled a small box from his pocket, 'a late Christmas present if you like.'

'You shouldn't have.'

'I know I shouldn't have, but I did. I wanted to. It's French.'

She took out a silver bracelet; each linked section made of intertwining scrolls and leaves, and put it on her wrist. 'Thank you it's beautiful. But I haven't got anything for you though.'

'Don't matter, you being here is enough for me.'

Ada poured the teas and sat looking straight into Rab's eyes; he lowered his and spoke as if speaking to the teapot. 'I don't want to upset yer by owt. I know y'said not to come round again but I can't carry on. I love yer Ada, and miss yer; every day I wonder what you're doing. Everywhere I go I keep thinking I see yer, but it's always some other girl. I want to find a way, yer know, to be with yer. I don't care what people say – they can think what they like. Folks should be allowed to love who they want.' He looked up from the teapot.

Ada sighed. 'But it won't work will it. Your duty is to your wife and kids.'

'But she doesn't love me anymore and I don't love her, and I'm no good for the kids, I'm just this hollow thing moving about the house, they're better off wi'out me dragging 'em down.'

'So what are you saying?'

'I don't know Ada. I don't know.'

'Well perhaps you'd better think of something. I can't be seen with you – if people knew… I can't do that to my family. I can't hurt them any more. As it is I nearly got Jim killed!'

'But that wasn't your fault.'

'But if you play with fire…'

'How did Jim get on in court?'

'The jury didn't believe him. Brown got off – self-defence they said. And all his mates came forward to lie for him. Jim's story didn't stand up really – but if he'd told the truth…'

'I'm sorry Ada. I understand.'

'Look, I'd better be getting back. I just said I'd nipped out on an errand.' Ada got up to her feet. 'I'm in on my own tomorrow night. If you want to come round…? We could talk some more. Mother's staying at our Lizzie's and Jim and Annie will be out seeing in the New Year somewhere.'

'I'm supposed to be at the Lane – we've a match the next day.'

'Well if you can't…'

'No, no. It's fine. I'll come round after tea.'

'One other thing – that note you sent – you didn't write it yourself?'

Rab looked up at her, 'I told myself I wouldn't lie to you again so I won't – I got the woman in the shop to write it – I can't, see.

Never got on at school. Hardly ever went. Not for the likes of me.'

She put her hand on his hair like he was a child – she had not touched him since the theatre. Involuntarily he closed his eyes for a moment.

'You should've said.'

He watched her leave the tearoom and leaned back in his chair like he was surveying the scene. He filled his pipe, then gulped down the last of the now cold tea, before heading out into the street.

∗

When Rab left his yard and crossed Alfred Road, shoulders hunched with the cold, muffler wrapped round twice, he kicked a small piece of coal, then bent down and popped it in his pocket. The bookie's runner was on the street corner again, collar turned up on his Ulster, cap pulled down on his brow.

What was it Ada wanted? What was he going round for? He watched the tram come up from town and turn round at the terminus. Couples, arm in arm, got on in front of him; a group of lads heading into town to celebrate and several others followed behind.

Ada opened the door. He presented the coal and a piece of green stuff he'd plucked out of a hedge.

'One of the Jocks at the Lane said this brought good luck – supposed to be a tall dark stranger so you'll have to imagine the stranger bit!' he said with a grin.

'Get yourself in quick you daft lummox!'

They went into the living room where a warm fire blazed in the grate, onto which the small lump of coal and the greenery were dispatched. A shadeless oil lamp on the table doubled the light from the fire. The room smelt faintly of boiled cabbage.

'I'll get some tea mashing,' Ada said, and got some cups off the dresser.

Rab sat down in the armchair, his cap in his hands, which he appeared to examine. He looked up at Ada and caught her eye, he smiled, and she went on with making tea.

She then sat down across the rug from him and their eyes met.

'A bit blowy out there,' Rab said.

'I'll pour the tea.'

Rab sat balancing his cup on his knee staring at the fire. Ada sipped her tea and he felt her eyes on him, studying him. The bit of hedge was now just a line of white ash across the top of the coals; a small piece of coal fell through the grate into the ash pan below – must have just been emptied because of the noise it made. He was content not speaking; what could he say? Just sitting there quietly was happiness. He drained his cup.

'Do you want a top up?'

'No ta.'

'Let me take that for you then.' He passed the cup. Now he had nothing to do with his hands. He took his pipe out and scratched away at some black scorch marks on the bowl.

Ada was sat back down still watching him. 'So what are we going to do Rab?'

'What would you like to do?'

'It's not for me to say.'

He fingered Gladstone's broken nose. He glanced at her then back to his pipe again.'

'I dunno Ada.'

'This mess was not of my doing. You're the one with decisions to make.'

Rab hung his head as if staring at the scrubbed flags for an answer. Her tone of voice was quite harsh. He didn't know what he was expected to say.

'Well you'd better think of a way out, or we decide to stay miserable and not see each other. We can't go on like this!' She finished with a sob in her voice. He got up and kneeled in front of her chair, taking her hand – she made to withdraw it but he kept hold.

'Please don't love! I don't want to make you miserable. I just don't know what to do. I want to be with you. That's what I want. It's just...'

'Just what... just your wife and kids?'

'Yes... no! Don't be mad at me. I want you, not them. I just don't...'

'What?'

'What can we do? Why should it matter? Why can't we just get a little house in Heeley or somewhere and live as we choose? I could support us both.'

'Oh Rab! This is so cruel. We would be living in shame and would be shunned by everyone – I would never see my family again – they would disown me.'

'I don't want to bring disgrace on you, but we would have to live in secret – discovery would lose me my job.'

'But we couldn't keep it a secret. We'd live each day in fear of being found out.'

'You're right, we couldn't keep it to ourselves.'

'Hold me Rab!'

He put his arm around her and pulled her onto his knee and there they sat on the rug by the fire holding each other.

Ada got out some bread and cheese and a piece of polony and they ate some supper; sat close, holding hands when the meal allowed.

'Shall you stay and see the New Year in?' she asked.

'I'd like to if I may.'

The bells of St Peter's rang out at midnight as Rab and Ada sat quietly by the dying fire, still holding hands.

'Happy New Year Ada.'

'You too Rab.'

'I'll be getting off in a minute then.'

'You could stay if you wish.'

'You mean...'

'I've only a small bed, but if you don't mind that...'

That night Ada laid her heart upon his warm heart, mixed her breath into his.

They were in darkness and neither knew how sound the footing of their next step would be.

Chapter 20

As Rab walked into the living room at Lake Street on New Year's day, Jemima was clearing away the breakfast things.

'Where did you spend the night?'

'Happy New Year to you an' all!'

She stood, hands on hips, scrutinising him.

'I went round to one the lads' houses and we saw in the New Year and it were too late to get a tram so I slept on the floor.' Rab knew she was trying to read his face, so he didn't hang around. 'Can't stop and chat,' he said, then re-appeared a minute later with his kit.

'Do you want anything to eat?'

'No ta!' then he shut the door behind him.

Notts County. Back up after a few years in the second division. Should set the United up nicely for back-to-back games home and away to the Villa. These three games could decide the season. Nice little trip to Nottingham, not far, should be easy enough, what with them bumping along the bottom; only won twice or something according to Nudge.

Rab picked up his wage packet then rolled into the club-room where he saw young Harry talking to Needham. He looked around the room; Tommy must still be injured. No – there was Tommy as well.

He slung his bag down and headed for the fireplace. Needham caught sight of him and intercepted him. 'Pick up thi bag and come with me,' the captain said, his face unmoving, his eyes cold. Rab thought it was a prank in the making so sauntered after him, waiting for Bill to spring something funny.

He followed him into one of the offices.

'Shut the door Rab.'

Rab did so, still grinning. 'What's up Nudge? Why so serious?'

'Because it is serious, that's why.'

Rab looked at him: moustache neat, not a hair on his head out of place. Needham's left eye held his gaze, his right eye looking somewhere over his shoulder. Rab often wondered whether having eyes that didn't look at the same thing was why he passed so well – looking at the target as well as the tackle flying in. Rab's smile faded under the steely gaze.

'Tha's not coming,' Needham said.

'What?'

'We're taking Harry instead of thi.'

'What? Why? He's just a kid. He's got nowt on me.'

'I can't go into it. Just get thisen away home. Tha's to be back here for a committee meeting at seven o'clock on Tuesday night. Don't miss it.'

'But Nudge…'

'I can't say any more. Tha'd better go. I'll tell the others tha's injured.' Needham opened the door and waited for Rab to leave. He headed down the steps; Needham stood at the top watching him go, as if making sure he did. What on earth? Dropped like that. No explanation? Committee meeting, Tuesday? What could it mean? Nothing good.

He wandered up into town. A wag wearing red and white favours said, 'Ay up big fella, tha's goin t'wrong way!' Rab didn't even acknowledge him. He went over each word that Needham had said and remembered the expression; that cold eye. He had seen this when people had turned up drunk to training. He hadn't showed up last night but he'd done that before and talked his way out of it – it's not like they had to keep and eye on him to keep him out of the boozer. He secretly feared they'd found out about Ada. Could that be it? But how could they?

The weekend dragged. He was sullen, and snapped at the children; only despising himself more when he did so and making himself more miserable; a knot getting tighter and tighter the more it was pulled. How tempting it would be to take himself away to a snug and drink to forget. He ate little, having no appetite. Even the weather was unkind – windy and rainy – affording him few opportunities to get out and walk and clear his head. He played some tunes to stop himself from screaming, as his head was bursting with thoughts about what had happened and what he'd say to the Committee: all beards and whiskers sat in a row, making him feel like he was at school being made to stand in the corridor for whatever was the latest misdemeanour, making him feel like the dirty gypo, ignored, spat at, despised. They had no longer looked down on him when they saw how good he was at football. But here he was out in the corridor again while down in Nottingham some chipper bastard, who didn't have enough hair on his chin to shave, was in his place at half-back. He couldn't even find a reason to hate him, other than he was too bloody perfect all round. Part of him hoped they lost. Then they'd have to have him back.

On Sunday they went to see Selina, who sat in her chair: Madonna, to whom they paid homage. Rab sat at the table sipping tea, saying little as the others twittered around.

*

He was there far too early on Tuesday night, as if by arriving early he could get it over with faster. He walked round the ground and then self conscious that he might be seen, walked up towards Sheaf House and back. He asked the time again – quarter to seven. He threw up in a corner just next to the Anchor brewery, which did not make him feel any better as he had expected, before heading up to the committee room where he was told to sit outside on a chair by one of the clerks.

It was cold in the unheated corridor and the only light came from the committee room through windows high up in the panelled wall separating him from the room. Should he take his cap off or keep it on until he entered the room? He took it off and turned it in his hands. Inside he could hear the Philanthropist's voice, none of the words distinguishable, the occasional scraping of a chair and coughing. He waited, and waited.

When he was called in to the room filled with cigar smoke a

wooden chair awaited him across the table from his superiors; a fire blazed at one end and gas jets lit the room casting shadows across the floor; large windows looked out onto the dark ground behind where the committee sat. They had all turned out to greet him: Wostinholm himself, giving his best benevolent Father Christmas impersonation, though the eyes gave him away, Stokes, the Tooth-yanker, looking as pompous as ever, Beardshaw, known as 'Baltic,' with his wild eyebrows twitching over his spectacles, Hodkinson, Bingham, and others he didn't know. He was honoured.

'Take a seat Howell,' Stokes said, moving his hand with precision to indicate the chair.

Wostinholm spoke, 'You've been a good servant of his club and you have not gone without ample reward, ample reward indeed. But your behaviour cannot be condoned. Deplorable. Deplorable.'

Everyone's eyes were fixed on Rab; watching him, scrutinising him for his response. He shuffled in his chair. He wasn't sure whether he was supposed to speak or not. He was far from clear what they knew, what was being suggested.

Wostinholm continued, he had evidently just paused for effect. 'The team managed perfectly well without you on Saturday, as you will be aware. Splendid three one win. Young Johnson fared admirably well, so our success doesn't depend on you, Howell, if you choose to continue in this vein.'

Rab would have liked to have argued that Johnson had not yet had to face real pressure, hadn't shown the grit it needs to come out top against the likes of Wolves or Aston Villa. Without him they wouldn't succeed.

'Not only did you fail to attend the club-room as directed on the night before the Notts County game; no indeed. This rule is made for the best of reasons – to keep you young fellows from the temptation of the music hall and the public house which as we all know are too numerous in this city of ours – a scourge on us all, the enemy of hard work and sound principles. There were nods and mutters of approval from some of the others. How long have you been married Howell?'

'Nigh on ten year, sir.'

'Quite, quite! Keeps a man steady does marriage. Children?'

'Three sir and one on the way any day now.'

'Good, good. And you have been converted? You know, from whatever religion you people have… to Christianity?'

'I do my best – and go the church on Sundays, sir.'

'Then you know what a higher authority than myself –'

(Only one up though, in your own opinion of yersen, Rab thought.)

'– has to say about the sacredness of the bond of marriage. To be even seen to be associating with ladies, let alone entertaining them when they are not of ones own family is a very serious matter and would, if known, bring scandal on this club and the disapprobation of your fellow professionals.'

Rab's worse fears bubbled up – he didn't understand everything that the Philanthropist was driving at but he clearly knew something…

'Your conduct as a professional must be to the highest standard – you represent Sheffield United Football Club: that is all of us in this room.' Again there were nods and grunts of assent from the beards and whiskers. 'Not only in your conduct on the field of play but also in how you conduct your life off it too. How long have you been with us Howell?'

'Longer than anyone still in the first team sir – eight years.'

'Quite. All the more reason to exhibit exemplary behaviour for the younger players – who look up to chaps like you to… to… set standards, and if those standards slip then we will not tolerate it, will not tolerate it in the slightest. Is that understood Howell?'

'Yes Sir.' (It wasn't but it seemed the right thing to say.)

'Quite frankly, were it not for one or two of my colleagues, I would cut you loose now, Howell, but others caution against too hasty an action which might disrupt the team at this crucial stage in the season: providing a different course can be charted. You need to provide a satisfactory explanation and if that is acceptable then you need to determine where your commitment lies, Howell. Is that understood?'

'What exactly am I being accused of sir?'

'I thought I had made that abundantly clear Howell. Have you not been listening to a word I've been saying!' Wostinholm sat back with a jerk, a look of exasperation on his face. He shot a vituperative glance to Stokes on his right, removed his handkerchief from his pocket and dabbed the build up of spittle away from the side of his mouth. He then leaned forward ready to launch an assault but was stopped by Stokes who leant forward himself.

'Let me speak plainly Howell. It has come to our attention that you have failed to attend here as you were told and instead were seen with a young lady. You are a servant of this football club and it therefore behoves us to look to your welfare. We take it on ourselves to know what sort of person we employ – for the good of all our team. It has been reported to us that you have been spending time alone in the company of this lady. As Mr Wostinholm made clear –' saying this he made a deferential nod to the man next to him who returned it with a benevolent smile, '– that cannot be tolerated.'

Rab looked along the line of beards and whiskers and tried to control his expression to keep it blank. There was the taste of vomit in his mouth and though he was not hot, his armpits were soaked under his jacket. How did they know? They must have been spying on him. Spying? The bookie's runner came to his mind, who he'd seen near his house. Had he been followed? No one spoke. All eyes were on him.

The Philanthropist had regained his composure, 'Well Howell, what have you got to say for yourself?'

'Things are perhaps not as they seem sir.'

'Well kindly enlighten us... it seems clear to us that the evidence of your, shall we say... misdemeanours, and of your lack of commitment to this club is convincing to say the least.'

'My football means more to me that anything sir.'

'But your conduct Howell! Your conduct!'

'It's true I have been to see a young lady.' There was an audible sucking of breath somewhere down the line and the Baltic eyebrows danced above their spectacles. Rab continued, 'I can see how that looks and it was perhaps foolish of me, but it's not what it seems. She is the sister of a friend, and he was attacked in the street, you might have read about it in the papers, unprovoked it was – with a dagger – he was badly injured and wasn't able to look after the family – his sisters and his ailing mother – she's very frail.' He was warming to this – the thought of the Bosom being described as frail! 'I helped out a bit that's all and his sister has come to regard me as a friend, no more than that.'

There was whispering along the line. Wostinholm bent his ear to Stokes then spoke again.

'Highly inappropriate for a married man to visit a young lady un-chaperoned on New Year's Eve whatever the circumstances!'

'I apologise for my foolishness – for letting myself be… for how it looks… when it's nothing of the sort. It won't happen again, sir, if that's what you want from me.'

'No Howell it won't – if you want to stay with this club.'

'That is what I want sir.'

'Then you will give your word that there shall be no more of this nonsense!'

'Yes sir.'

'Go and wait outside Howell.'

He sat back down in the cold corridor and waited for what seemed a long time. Just how much did they know? Spying on him! He'd heard of this sort of thing before – it was well known that drinkers got caught – but actually having someone lie in wait – he must have been followed on New Year's Eve. And he'd not left till morning – surely no one would spy all night? Would they believe his little explanation? What else could he have said.

He was ushered back in.

'You have given your word that you will put a stop to this, this … association, whatever its nature. Therefore we'll hear no more said about it. However, this is your last warning Howell. Your attitude and commitment to the club has been found wanting, but your duty is to make amends on the field of play. We all have a duty towards the team; that must come first. You may be aware that the team have been sent away on special training for the week. You will report to Mr Stokes at eight o' clock in the morning at Midland Railway Station. He shall escort you to Matlock where you will rejoin the team for preparation for the match here on Saturday. From Matlock you'll travel straight back to the Bramall Lane Grounds so you'll need all your kit with you. Clear?'

'Yes sir. Thank you sir.'

The train jolted and pushed through the rain along the steep-sided valley. He wiped a wet circle in the window; he could make out the canal, or the river – one had been on one side of the train, one on the other, but now they seemed to have switched. Opposite him sat an old lady, toothless, with a face not unlike a tortoise, dressed in black with an old bonnet on her head with the ribbons dangling down untied. Looking out of the opposite window a young man sat expressionless; almond eyes, long drooping moustache, high forehead and smooth skin – the sort of smug face that just deserved to be slapped; Rab smiled to himself, and looked back out of the window. Even in winter it was still green; it was good to be getting away from it – just one thing to think about: the Villans on Saturday. He knew nothing about where he was heading – he was just getting away from where he'd been. The Tooth-yanker had said little other than to make sure they were on the right train and made their connection, before getting into his first-class carriage at the front. Thank God he didn't have to sit with him! They stopped at small stations and went through tunnels as the valley closed in.

He'd got away with it. The committee had, even if not convinced by his story, decided they needed him for success. It was going to be hard to see Ada now though – he closed his eyes and tried to conjure up the first few hours of the New Year – he hadn't dared to call round on his way home last night – and now he was miles away.

At Matlock station he dropped his bags onto the platform and waited for Stokes. A porter followed Stokes, bringing his luggage; Rab followed behind him, his bags on his back. Stokes saw Rab into a hansom, 'I have made other arrangements for my stay, but I shall be along to get reports into the team's progress. This represents a considerable investment into you chaps, to get you in the finest shape possible for the challenge ahead. Make the most of it Howell. Chesterfield House please driver!' Rab again thanked his luck that he did not have to share a cab with Stokes as he thought he might.

The horse slowly pulled the cab up the steep hill out of the town up to Matlock Bank then pulled off the road up a drive and past a gatehouse. Rab saw the large house at the top of the drive and looked around as the grounds stretched out in front. Over on one of the lawns he saw a group of men doing some sprinting – it was the team. He wasn't sure what sort of reception to expect from them. At the top of the drive he unloaded his bags and sat on a seat on the veranda as the cab wheeled round back down the drive. He could see Needham inciting his men to one last effort as George Waller stood watching; then they were slapping each other on the back and sauntering up towards the house.

'Just look at thi – bloody typical, missing all the graft, turning up just in time for thi dinner!' said Bill with grin.

'Nah then Rab, how's the thigh Rab?' Needham asked.

'It's fine now ta Nudge,' Rab replied, thanking him especially with his eyes. 'Just a bit of a dead-leg.'

'That's good – glad tha's here – tha's going to love it, ain't that right boys?'

'Oh Yeah – especially the nice warm baths!' said Cocky.

Rab looked puzzled; he didn't get the joke that everyone else clearly did.

'And I hope tha's thirsty – lot's to drink,' said Bill. 'Here tha's not smuggled in any bottles of owt tasty has tha?' he said patting the sides of Rab's bag. 'No don't s'pose tha has. All us bags were searched and my bloody bottle were confiscated.'

'Tha knows the rules,' said Waller, 'tha's here for one thing only – not a bloody holiday.'

'I know George. Only kiddin.'

They went in and Needham helped Rab with his bags.

'Careful with that un, it's got my mandolin in.'

'Good, tha can entertain us with some tunes. There's not much to do in the evening and there's no going out allowed. I'll carry this up to thi room – tha's in wi' Tommy, Bob and Bill.'

'Oh bloody hell Nudge!' Rab said smiling.

'Well someone's got to share wi' 'im. And I took my turn last time.'

'Ere Nudge, thanks for covering for me.' Rab felt a surge of warm feeling for his captain – he was straight and you could always rely on him.

'So tha's made thi peace then.'

'Yeah – promised to put the team first an' that.'

'I thought tha'd had it.'

'Seems not. How much did they tell thi?'

'Not much, just that it were serious and they knew why tha'd not turned up when tha was supposed to. I don't really need to know any more. Anyhow it's good tha's here – young Johnson couldn't get released from work so he'll not be able to put in the work before Saturday.'

'Well thanks again Nudge. I'm right on board... as ever. Tha can count on me.'

'That's good – let's get some snap!' Rab threw his bags down on the floorboards next to the plain iron bedstead and followed Needham back down.

Rab found out what the joking had been about. There was a strict regime – Matlock's famous water being at the heart of it. They were woken early and had two glasses, followed by sitting in a tin bath and having to endure some brute of an attendant pouring cold water on them, or having a cold douche bath. They were spared being wrapped in cold, wet sheets: a procedure that some of the other residents were treated to – apparently the more awful they were made to feel the more efficacious the cure. There was one exception: John Almond was singled out for special treatment. He appeared under the weather probably owing to the fact of his influenza the fortnight before. He also made the mistake of coughing within earshot of an attendant. His treatment was discussed with Waller and Needham who concurred that ill-health was perhaps a contributory factor in his poor form of late. His fate was therefore determined and special treatment prescribed: missing some of the physical training in favour of the beneficial effect of being wrapped in wet sheets "like one of Rab's pyramid building ancestors", or sitting in a steam box – with his pink head sticking out like a strawberry. Once, when the attendant was out of the room, he returned to find a small mound of shaving foam – cream on the strawberry – on John Almond's head, deposited as he sat captive in his box. Of course Bill was nowhere to be seen and entirely unaware that the unfortunate incident had taken place.

After their cold baths, the team went for a stroll around the grounds before breakfast. Before dinner they did some running work, to trees and back, around stones placed on the lawn, copious amounts of water to drink followed. Then George would lead them in a long walk up over Matlock Moor or down to Matlock Bath and along the Derwent. More water to drink when they were out, and when they returned for tea; then early to bed.

Four miles out from the house on Wednesday, stuck in the middle of nowhere, the clouds swelled and burst – their take on this was that it was as good as being wrapped in a cold, wet sheet so must be doing them the world of good. 'Bet the Villa aren't getting spoilt rotten like us eh?'

In between the exercise and water, quiet time for digestion afforded them periods when they could sit in the drawing room. They would play cards: little stacks of brown coins being slid businesslike across the table in games of Nap; and an equally serious air prevailed over the billiards table. There were newspapers and pictorial magazines which Rab would flick through to look at things like pictures of monkeys smoking pipes, contortionists, natives from around the Empire being made to look foolish, or other strange pictures that made no sense to him. Rab also played requests on his mandolin or went out onto the veranda for a smoke. Stood with Mr Gladstone overlooking the darkened gardens and grounds, a vixen's eerie shrieking over to his left, echoing round, he felt calm. They were a good bunch of lads in there – as good as you get. If he were out in India being attacked by screaming tribesmen, these were the blokes he'd want at his side or watching his back. They'd do the job on Aston Villa – we may not have a barrel of money like them, or like Liverpool or the other lot, he thought: we've got something much better.

Stokes put in occasional appearances in the mornings and spoke to Needham and Waller and watched them training – but having him there took any fun out of it that there might have been. No piggy-back or wheelbarrow races, no larking about. He also informed them on Friday that the committee were pleased with reports of the training and had decided to keep them there for another week until the return game at Birmingham. All they would need in the morning would be their kit bags. Some of them moaned about this once he had gone, but to Rab it seemed another week away from problems and dilemmas. Like his life outside was on hold while he was there in Matlock.

Saturday 8th January 1898

Stokes returned on Saturday morning with a two-horse brake to take them to the station. None of them had touched a football since the previous Saturday – 'hungry for the ball! I've bloody well forgotten what one looks like!' Rab said.

They ate on the train and arrived in Sheffield around half past twelve. The station was chaotic – a large crowd of supporters were there to cheer them. Who could fail to be lifted by several hundred men and boys, and the odd woman or two, worshipping them, treating them like royalty, and singing "hi hi clear the way for the rowdy dowdy boys!" as they made their way to the forecourt and their waggonette.

Sitting in the changing room they could tell that a fair sized crowd was building in the ground as the Sheffield Prize Band played. Ralph Gaudie, up from the reserves, was in the first team ahead of Almond.

Villa's Charlie Athersmith was the first to put the ball in the net, receiving a long ball over the heads of the United midgets and using his speed to get ahead, but Needham had been through this with the United backs who had pushed up and played him offside so it didn't stand.

Every time the United went forward to attack the Bramall Lane end there were loud cheers, none louder than when Bennett went past first one, then another claret and blue jersey, then past Evans and Crabtree to smash it into the roof of the net. The sound from the Shoreham Street end swept solid across the ground. Had mankind ever combined voices to make such a noise before, even as armies had met across the battlefields of Europe? Repeatedly the half-backs blocked, and Rab felt the warmth of adulation as he stopped the Villa attack from the left with only Bill left to beat. Brilliant saves by both goalkeepers, particularly by Whitehouse kept the score one to United until the end of the game.

Tea was taken in the pavilion after the game and a glass of beer was savoured by some as much as if they had just crossed a desert. Then at six o'clock they were heading back to the station, accompanied by further adoring supporters, to prepare for going through it all again in Birmingham in a week's time; a match that would live on in the memory of all who were there that Saturday at Aston Lower Grounds. The story would be repeated over – and improve each time in the mind of the teller – to bored wives and wide-eyed grandsons. It was amongst the first of those sporting occasions where more people remembered being there than the capacity of the ground allowed.

Chapter 21

In a small two-roomed house in a blackened brick courtyard in Greaves Street, where humanity was packed in so that no rumour was secret, no slap across the face unremarked, no illness personal and no shriek of pleasure not shared, a scream ripped through the damp air; a scream of pain that sounded like life was being torn out.

In the washhouse across the yard, the domain of the footsoldiers in the fight against dirt, a group of women with big pink hands stopped their scrubbing and looked at each other, a flash of anxiety crossing their course features, 'It's her at number two!' 'Ah!' was the reply. The screaming stopped only to start again just minutes later. This time the scrubbing continued, 'When I had our Marion...' '... nearly the end on us...' 'ee it were bad...' 'should'a kept thi bloody legs crossed then!' the screaming went on through the ponching, scrubbing and wringing until at last a different cry was heard, shrill and tiny, and those hard women softened just a little.

Selina lay on the bed, face flushed, hair wet; and next to her wrapped up in flannel, a small equally pink and wet haired creature looking at her, filling her whole existence, a happiness so big that it could shatter the windows and burst walls. She had created this life, this tiny girl who would love her in return, who would depend on her. Sarah Ann wiped her face and hair with rosewater and she closed her eyes and lay back on the pillow. 'If I don't make it through, you will call her Edith,' she said, the effort of opening her eyes even to stare at her daughter too great.

'Don't be silly, you're just fine. It went well.' Selina smiled a faint smile. She nursed Edith and they both dozed. They awoke and stared at each other. They cried and slept. Her sister; her aunt;

keeping watch over them. It went dark outside and grew light again. In the darkness she had seen her baby's eyes open by the light of the fire and cradled her until they both fell asleep. Selina had oatmeal porridge and beef tea. When she at last made it out of bed she was not sure what day it was.

Sarah Ann saw to the burning of soiled sheets and towels. Selina was by then recovered enough to be able to get about the little terraced house that had become her retreat. She sat by the window, the net curtain pulled back so that she could see out into the yard. She could hear sparrows chirruping, and she then watched them as they flew onto the privy roof. She waited for Edith to awake for her feed. It was a long time since she had last cradled her and she was impatient – she lay in the drawer peacefully, not moving. Several times she had put her ear up close to check she was still breathing or risked waking her by stroking her soft pink cheek. She thrilled at the thought that her big children were coming and could meet their sister for the first time. She knew that Little Selina especially would have been bursting all week to come. It was nearly four weeks that she had been away, but soon she would be strong enough to go home – how nice it would be to be able to cook for them and wait for them coming home from school; to sleep in her own bed. Poor Little Rabbi wouldn't take kindly to having to give up his place in bed next to her. It would be cosy with all six of them in the room. They'd have to find a mattress for him now – that would slide under their bed. He was no longer her little baby. A tear spilled over her lower eye-lid. They grow up so fast. She tried to imagine him kissing her cheek, his snap-bag over his shoulder, off to the works or the pit: or a soldier with his kitbag going off to the Empire. She wept openly now and was caught by Sarah Ann bringing some tea. 'Lina love?'

'Oh it's nothing – I always get like this – it's babies that does it. I'll soon be out of your way.'

'We can stay here as long as we need to, Hannah is grateful to us for minding the house while she's away and Albert and the others can look after themselves for a while. It is a pleasure to help out with my beautiful niece.'

There was a commotion at the door and Albert came in, 'Look who I found strolling up the road – bunch of vagabonds – and not a peg to sell between 'em!'

Before the women could utter a "shh!" in rushed a clatter of boots and a rustle of pinafores as the girls embraced their mother. The baby gave a little cry and the girls turned to the noise and squealed and woke her up entirely; and they cooed and fussed as Edith screwed up her face and howled.

'Your sister Edith,' Selina announced.

The girls watched entranced as their tiny sister latched onto the breast, the doll-like hand pressed on the pale curve, feet kicking beneath the shawl.

'Your Daddie not here?' Selina said.

Edith paused and looked up, then carried on.

'No he's away on holiday.'

'Lina!' chided Lizzie.

'That's what Grannie said!' replied Little Selina.

Jemima, who had been stood back surveying the scene, with Little Rabbi shyly holding her hand, came forward. 'He's away at Buxton or Matlock Bath or somewhere with his football – lording it at a hotel – special training he calls it: just swans off one morning and says he don't know when he's back and we ain't seen nor heard on him since. What were it Den, nearly a fortnight since?'

'Aye must be nigh on.'

'Well I suppose he must be coming back for matches? Selina said.

'I suppose so love. Don't know if he's playing at home or away though today.'

Edith let go from her task and started crying. Sarah Ann started shepherding everyone out of the room to give them some peace. 'Let Little Rabbi come over and see his sister first,' Selina said.

He was pushed forward – Selina held out her hand to him and he edged forward cautiously. 'Say hello to her,' and he leaned forward and said hello. Then like an overlooker satisfied with the quality of work being turned out he smiled at his mother and followed the others into the living room, leaving her and Edith in peace.

She stroked her baby's hair and settled her back down. Perhaps Rab would buckle down to a proper job soon, Selina thought. He was thirty now – he couldn't keep mucking about like some kid for much longer. Sometimes he was so quiet that you didn't know what he was thinking – just sitting there in the background whilst everyone else talked. Once he'd got a proper job and spent some time at home things would be so much better. Perhaps he too would then find Christ? Him and his football! What if one of these days he got really badly hurt, then he wouldn't be able to hold down a job at the colliery. The best he might get would be a guinea-a-week surface job. Her dad couldn't support them all, and he would need looking after himself eventually. Perhaps by then the girls would be bringing in some money – but that wouldn't last long before they upped and left her. A tear fell into Edith's ear – but the baby didn't flinch from her sucking.

*

Rab slipped straight back into the Matlock routine. Some of the others had been quieter than usual on the train back, but that was perhaps to be expected after the highs of the day and the crowd cheering them onto the train. Others grumbled and cursed the committee – they had wanted time off to go and see their families. 'They could've given us Sunday off at least,' said Bill, 'Johnny'll be asking his mother who's that strange man?'

'You just want to cuddle up to the lovely Bea for the night,' said Cocky.

'Ah, and who wouldn't!' said Bill, '– though if anyone puts their hand up I'll kill them with a single blow.' He closed his eyes and didn't open them again until they changed trains.

Some of them wrote letters home or postcards, which were posted on their way out for heel to toe work in the afternoon. 'Does tha want me to write one for thi Rab?' Needham asked him, looking up from the desk in the drawing room.

'Nah, it's a'reight – I've nowt to say.' He would have liked to have sent a postcard to Ada, but how could he? She would start to

213

think something was amiss before long. It was out of his hands.

That night he woke after a dream where he had been playing football but he could no longer run, like his legs were made of lead, and Charlie Athersmith was getting away from him, then Ada had come onto the pitch holding hands with Little Rabbi and then kissed him on the cheek; and everyone knew. And then a baby walked on and spoke to him though he couldn't understand – a walking talking baby – how could that be, and somehow the baby was Selina. Whilst still half asleep he tried to get back off, but all the water-drinking had had its effect; he tried to ignore it. His mind wandered onto how he was going to sort out his life. He imagined leaving – getting up in the night and kissing Little Rabbi and the girls goodbye whilst they slept and sneaking out quietly. What if Selina died in childbirth? Perhaps she already had. He sickened himself! But would that make it harder or easier? He listened to the others breathing heavily. He had to clear his head of such thoughts. He got up to use the chamber pot. He made out an upright figure on Bill's bed. 'Tha awake too little un?' Bill whispered.

'Yeah. All that bloody water!'

'Want a bite of apple pie?'

'Where'd tha get that?'

'I snuck it in my pocket at tea on Sat'day. It's still good. Got a drop o'beer too.'

'No ta. That what's keeping thi awake: thi stomach?'

'No. Just that when I'm awake a little biting on 'elps us get back off.' There was a long pause.

'Rab?'

'Yeah?'

'Tha not missin thi missus?'

'Not really. Go and get one of them cold shower baths – that'll calm thi down.'

'Fuck off!'

'I didn't mean owt, just jesting.'

Bill lay back down. Rab lay awake and tried to think of something calm but his mind went round in circles. When he got to sleep it seemed like only moments later when he was awoken by the clink of the water jug and glasses.

They trained hard and well. They filled their lungs with cold air as they strode quickly back from Bakewell, where they'd got off the train; any access to puddings being strictly banned. They could keep up a fair pace without getting out of breath. They felt their hearts beating regularly and strong, their muscles glowing. They occasionally talked in small groups. Rab made an effort to talk to Bill after their conversation in the night, but it went unmentioned and Bill seemed his usual self. Sometimes they just walked in silence, each in their own thoughts. Saturday loomed large in their minds. They all knew that Villa had not lost at home since they moved to their new ground. This could be the key game of the season. Lose and the Villa go above them, win and they were three points clear.

Saturday 15th January 1898

Nerves showed on everyone's faces as they waited for the Birmingham train on the platform at Derby – the Tooth-yanker patrolling the platform with his silver-topped cane, like a schoolmaster marshalling a group of schoolboys to church. Rab just wanted to run out on the pitch, get the waiting over. Bill was the last one into the carriage, running, puffing theatrically.

'Lads, lads! I've just heard the funniest thing! Everyone gathered round as the train pulled away. 'I was just up the platform, having a good pinch of snuff when this young lady wanders along (as he spoke Bill traced her curves with his hand). Fur trimmed cape thing, fruit on her hat – yer know the type. Well, then this train backs up and two guards are on the platform. One shouts to t'other un: "Ere Wilf, jump on her when she comes by, take her behind the coal heap and cut her in two, then bring the head end up to platform two!" The young miss jumps up and down and screams, "Murder! Murder!" I says to her "they mean the train, not thi lass!" Everyone fell about laughing. 'She nearly swooned into my arms!' Cocky slapped Bill on the back, 'Bring the head end up to platform two!' Rab unbuttoned his jacket shaking his head. 'What would we do without Bill eh?' he said to Bob Cain who sat opposite him.

'Well the air in our room would be more breathable I know that much! Reeking auld blatherskite!'

They took an early lunch at the Queens Hotel before heading to the grounds. The streets were thronged on the way to the Witton Lane enclosure even though there was still some time to kick off; it was clearly going to be a large crowd, mostly wearing claret and blue favours, but there were quite a few Sheffielders too. They had seen them streaming out of the station and, as their brake progressed along the streets, small groups wearing red and white shouted out to them: "Good luck boys!" "Show 'em what yer made of United!"

The mood in the changing room was serious, even Bill's light-heartedness was muted. Half past two slowly approached.

'Is Lewis in charge again Nudge?' Tommy asked.

'Yeah: they wouldn't want to give a match like this to someone less experienced.'

Needham called them round. 'Right men. We all know what we need to do: they might think they're lords and masters out there. They must be confident. They've not lost here yet. But we're every bit as good as they are because we are a team. Not one of us is better than the rest. Every man has his job to do and that's to put in every effort from start to finish and to help out his mates. If someone's better placed than you, get the ball to 'em and get it there fast. Then when a ball's loose get to it smartish. If they think they own the ball we'll show 'em and nick it off 'em. You've been first class this week, now let's get out there and do it for each other and for all our supporters who've come wi' us.'

Filing out onto the pitch, band still playing: trooping off. Bloody hell, look at 'em all. It's packed! Even up on the top of the stands, on the roofs; mad bastards! No one speaks. No wind or rain, good. Nudge sorting out the toss. There's the United fans – quite a few thousand of 'em too. Forty odd thousand, gripped in anticipation.

Ralph kicks off, and all forty odd thousand roar and eddy. Back and forth. Whitehouse fists away Johnny Cunningham's spinning shot across goal.

Athersmith gets away, cross comes in, steady… clear it for a corner. Harvey shoots wide. Push back at 'em, long dropping shot by Nudge just grazes bar. Nice one Nudge! Back at the other end, Bill and the earth meet as he stops a low one. Then they hit the bar.

Pass it through to Cocky. He gets away, defender clatters him. Bloody hell ref! Ball through from Tommy, chance to shoot, dropping in… bugger it! Just saved! Athersmith knocks ball down wi' 'is hand – ref not seen it – Bill tips it over the bar. Nudge says "Keep poppin' those free kicks onto heads Rab. Good stuff!"

Not long to half time. Fred and Ralph break quick, Ralph gets ball and lines up shot. In dives defender. Batters into him. Ralph lies motionless, blood streaming from smashed nose. Carried off senseless. There's a point to prove now.

Defending back. Steve Smith breaking down left. No yer don't. Lying looking up at sky. Searing pain; blood red sky. Nah, it's nowt. Blood drips onto ground; red on green. George says, "Come on I'll sort it."

Mops at cut. Smears grease over eye. Och-aye's hit the post. George says, "Tha'll do, on tha goes Rab!" Ball placed for free-kick. Whip it in – Crabtree fists it off the line. Penalty! Ref doesn't see it. Should've been one nil at half time.

Back in the changing room, George Waller was busy. He moved between towels and cups of lemon barley tending the cut over Rab's eye where blood was seeping out again, making it sting with alum salts and grease; rubbing Cocky's knee, keeping it mobile; and checking up on Ralph, who was sat, still ashen, pail of vomit between his knees. 'Nil all is good boys. Don't stoop to their level, don't get distracted, play your game and we'll get one. Cocky's been slowed down; we'll keep pushin it through the left, Bob and 'arry get the ball across to me. Stick at it!' urged Needham.

Ralph doesn't come out. Ten men. First corner of the half, Nudge gets on the end, Whitehouse pushes over. Corner again. Damn, that was crap! Villa break. Sort it out fellas! Athersmith's speed shows. Bob checks him. Back with Villa. Shot comes in high. Lunge forward to breast it down. Hits arm. Penalty, shit! "What's tha playing at! Fucking hell Rab!" Bill shouts. Just like the other night. One nil to Villa. All the crowd shouts, sways and surges. Songs of Villa. Pressure on them now. United push up, noise from Sheffield end. Bombard their goal. Then Ralph comes on, trying to smile in response to cheers – he shouldn't be on really – he's not right. Ten and a half. Half-backs lining up smoothly – crankshafts on an engine. Again Freddy just inches wide.

Cocky and Och-aye force a corner. Nudge hanging back off twelve-yard line – delivered straight to his feet – bangs it low and hard – defender fists it away. Penalty! Ref blows! But instead places ball outside twelve-yard line. Nudge argues: gets nothing off him. Everybody knows it were inside! Free-kick comes to nowt.

Back in defence Smith is dangerous, but take him out again and again. He picks up a long pass from Devey over by corner flag. Bill makes to out sprint him – no chance tha fat sod! Smith crosses. Three Villans in attack, goal wide open. Get a foot in! United supporters loved that. Saved thi there Bill. "What the hell tha playing at Bill!" No reply.

More United free kicks. Superbly placed. No one can get their head on 'em. Ralph keeps trying. What a trooper. United still going strong. Villa tiring. Here come the dirty tricks again. "Keep at 'em Rab" says Nudge. Push up, ball at feet, past the man. Through to Och-aye, on his head, towards the goal; then Johnny leaps and puts it past Whitehouse. Fucking brilliant! United supporters turn to cheer now. Not long to go. Quick burst from Villa. Bill redeems hissen: ball heads past him to top corner – tipped at full stretch. Seventeen stones-worth of grasshopper! "More effort United!" shouts Nudge, "One more push!"

Och-aye dashes in, takes the ball off their feet. He's going to score! Ball blocked. Ralph, Fred and Johnny all rushing in. Johnny blasts it. No one saw it fly in – so fast it flew. Handshakes all round. Back in play for seconds only when ref blows whistle for full-time.

Up in the stand, in the two-shilling seats, chocolates rained down on the silk top hats of the Villa committee as their former owner experienced a momentary loss of self-control as she waved the box around in the air.

Down on the pitch, hands were shaken and backs patted. Needham picked hanging shreds of skin off his knees. The whole crowd gave them a standing ovation. They realised what they had seen. Ralph Gaudie who had sunk onto his knees at the final whistle, having to be assisted off the pitch by the shoulder of John Cunningham.

Some supporters hung back to escort them to the hotel at the station. They were to have three nights at home before setting off back to Matlock. On Monday Rab and some of the others were to play in an English versus Scotch game as part of Bob Cain's benefit: mostly United and *Wednesday* players in either side. 'Why does he get a bloody benefit match?' Rab said to Needham, 'Haven't I been here a lot longer nor him?'

'That's as may be Rab, but there are those that think tha don't deserve it – tha'll have to keep thi nose clean, show more respect, then tha never knows.'

When they got back to Midland Station at a quarter to ten, hundreds of supporters were still there to cheer and applaud them.

Rab melted away into the evening. He didn't want to go home; nor did he want to admit that he was scared. Matlock seemed safe – he was woken at certain times, fed, and told what to do, when to go to bed – it was prison-like but somehow it made him feel free; he only had one thing to focus on – and that was the next game. All the excitement of the day was now gone – he was now just some bloke with a bag, walking home to a small house where he would be regarded as a disappointment, where he would not talk about the day or what he had achieved – where no one would be bothered if he did, and where the cut over his eye was not a badge of honour but a cause for disdain. He had just been worshipped by forty-odd thousand and was going to where he would be just judged on the two guineas he brought home each week. He also did not know what to expect; wasn't sure who would be there. He would have liked to have just gone round to Ada's but he couldn't take the risk. He checked his shoulder to see if he was being followed. There were plenty of people about; how could he know? He caught a tram to Brightside.

The house was dark when he let himself in. The fire was dying. He lit a candle and sat down – he felt he was sat in someone else's house – he'd only been away, what? twelve days and yet it seemed longer. The house was quiet except for some banging coming from next door's. A shiver went through him – he ought to feel good after a day like that, but he didn't. He felt miserable. He had made a mess of things and there was no one who would understand, except one and she was out of reach. He put his head in his hands and thought he would cry, that, somehow, that would bring a release – but nothing came: there was no release. He sat for a long while then went up to bed. The two girls were in his bed… his and Selina's bed, Little Rabbi had been relegated to the girls' small bed. He stood for a while not knowing what to do. Then he scooped Little Rabbi up; his eyes opened and he looked at Rab but didn't awaken. He placed him in a small space between the girls where he shuffled in without being noticed. He stood and looked at the three of them now that his eyes had become accustomed to what little light there was. Perhaps one day they might understand him and forgive him. He got into the small bed, which was still warm at the top from Little Rabbi. He lay trying to ignore the banging and voices coming from next-door's bedroom. It was well into the night before he slept.

Chapter 22

Those first damp and foggy days of January were the bleakest of the year for most folk. Christmas, and the distraction it brought from reality, were gone; as were the colours – the reds, greens and golds vanished, and the backdrop to their lives returned to black and grey. The pork pies eked out of impossible household budgets were gone and only the well-off had a Christmas cake large enough to last through to Epiphany.

For the families of locked-out engineers, practical gifts had, for some, allowed their stomachs to forget, all too briefly, their pangs; and now the handouts of soup, temporarily enriched by seasonal charitable additions of extra barley and meat rather than just boiled carcases, were again being bulked out with water.

No more the groups of choir singers on the streets warming your heart with carols, or brass instruments warming the air with tidings of joy. In their stead the animal sounds of a child with whooping cough, gasping for life on the other side of paper-thin walls, or out in the street the silence surrounding the horses' hoofs as it pulled away its light load of another measles victim. Eighteen Ninety Eight also brought with it no such excitement as the prospect of a Jubilee, as had lifted spirits twelve months previously. On the contrary something seemed on the wane; something fading with their Queen, as if the Jubilee had been no more than a last farewell, not just to a monarch but to an era and a sense of optimism and national courage that she seemed to embody.

Ada had tried to throw herself back into routine, buying produce at the wholesale market, keeping regular hours in the shop and looking for new customers to expand the delivery business to, in order to make up for the dwindling sums in the cash register. It was to be expected after Christmas – some had blown their money and would try to squeeze a number of meals out of one cabbage, stalk and all. Their better off customers, who had spent well before Christmas, were still eating through their overstocked larders. Then there were the increasing numbers of entries in the strap-book – some of her customers, she knew, would pay it all back as a matter of pride. For them they could only live with the embarrassment of having things on tick if they balanced it with a fierce determination that they would pay it back, to maintain their self-respect. Ada knew these women well, they were serious-minded women who kept their houses clean no matter what, whose steps saw the donkey-stone every week, and who would never be in such a position if they were able to exert the same control over their menfolk or their menfolk's employers. Then there were the women who were just desperate and despairing, who just wanted a few potatoes for the next meal, women who were trying to keep their families out of the workhouse but who couldn't see beyond teatime. Ada was letting more of these into her book, but she knew she had to be hard: if McGrails was seen as a soft touch, news would spread and they would be inundated.

On New Year's Day she had been in a good mood, though it was hard to rationalise. Her future was no less uncertain. Nothing had been resolved the night before; if anything, as wisps of ideas were snuffed out one by one, things seemed more hopeless and she had willingly allowed herself to sink deeper into the mire. However, there was one thing to cling to – like a gold-rush miner she had scrabbled around and held a small nugget in her hand. It was a sense of security, a knowledge that, no matter what, she had a safe place in Rab's heart, even if she could not be with him – and she chided herself for even imagining she could, tutting audibly: "Don't be so ridiculous Ada McGrail!" If one day she were to be the spinster Aunty Ada, she would at least always know she had been truly loved.

She had looked for his name in the Telegraph's match report for the Notts County game, but to her disappointment he wasn't there. Then a wave of fear, a cold nausea, came over her as she read a comment in an adjacent column about his "conduct," that it "cannot be condoned" and that he was "in the bad books of the committee." It said no more, but she felt an overwhelming sense of shame – she immediately assumed that what couldn't be condoned was her, what else could it be? – as if she had just read one of those reports of a high profile divorce case naming her as the other woman. She passed the day afraid of someone whispering behind her back, of shunning her publicly, or of a policeman coming to the door. Is that what happened? she wondered. After all, the newspaper writer must know something. But how?

She felt ill and wondered if she were going down with something, and the feeling continued the next day and the day after. She didn't eat well and slept fitfully. But then no one whispered, no one turned their face and there were no policemen; although when Ned Jones – whose mother had always shopped at McGrails – now Police Constable Jones – walked past the shop, she froze whilst counting out change, such that her customer said, 'Has tha seen a ghost love?' and Ada had to start afresh, 'I'm sorry Mrs Ward, that's three, and three's six, and six is twelve.' Only towards the weekend did she settle and realise she wasn't ill.

She attended Mass and prayed again for forgiveness, for a sense of release. But the inner shame lingered. She found little comfort, and her feelings of love for a man who was forbidden, remained resolute. How could she follow the path that was set out for her by her religion when there was such conflict in her, a conflict between what is said to be right and what felt right, a conflict between good and... well, good – surely? If Rab had only met her first; was that their fault? How was this God's design?

On Monday she read that Rab was reinstated in the team having trained well in Matlock. Matlock? Very nice! She felt much better – perhaps she had over-reacted, perhaps he had done something else to upset them. He was always going on about what sticks-in-the-mud the bosses at the club were. Still, this risk of shame hanging over her was not something she could live with. She knew of women who "carried on" – how awful that sounded! – with married men for years, apparently oblivious to what anyone thought or said – like something feeding parasitically off their host – but that filled her with horror. She would have to take her love, fold it carefully, wrapped in tissue, and put it away in her wardrobe, safe, like her gown, locked away, cherished but preserved; archived.

She heard about the excitement of the match at Birmingham, third or fourth hand, when she emerged into daylight from St Marie's on the following Sunday. Men in morning coats, like small boys in their enthusiasm, discussing penalties and goals. She let her family walk on ahead as she eavesdropped, standing with her back to them, wanting to turn and ask them questions, but she knew that was an impossibility. 'Rab's found his form,' they said. She felt a frisson and turned round. They caught her eye and she suddenly felt how foolish she was and hurried away towards Fargate.

That same Sunday morning after the Villa game Rab sat at breakfast feeling superfluous and being largely ignored; his eye swollen and partly shut. Earlier, Little Selina had squealed when she had first opened her eyes and saw him. This woke him with a jolt and, at first, he didn't know where he was and tried to swing himself out of bed to the left, but hit the wall. Little Selina went to sit on the bed next to him and the other two followed. They told him about their new sister, Edith. 'She's like a real dolly – we've only seen her once and she cried and then she slept.' They poked at the cut over his eye and asked if it hurt but they didn't know what else to say and Rab couldn't think what to ask them or what he could tell them that would be of any interest. He just looked at them for a while and tried to smile. Then they heard breakfast preparation noises downstairs and Lizzie said, 'Come on Lina let's go and help Grannie.' Rab watched as the girls quickly put on their pinafores and pulled a pair of short trousers and a wool jersey onto Little Rabbi. They had disappeared out of the door when Little Selina popped her head back round, 'Missed you Daddie,' then disappeared again. Rab settled back on the pillow again, no enthusiasm to go down himself.

He sipped his tea and spread some bacon fat on a piece of bread as the others went about family life around him. Another girl. He felt empty; he knew he should have felt otherwise.

When they went to church, he went for a walk instead up into

Wincobank Wood, hoping to get a view across the city and beyond, but it was cloudy and misty and he struggled to make out anything beyond Tinsley or Attercliffe. Jemima hadn't said much to him other than to ask him for money towards the housekeeping and for shoes for little Rabbi. He had pacified her with a half sovereign and a small pile of half-crowns. She scooped these off the table into her apron pocket without a "thank you," and had little else to say to him. Dennis hadn't spoken to him at all, not that he did much anyway. From brother-in-law Charlie Smith he had had a grunt by way of greeting: at least he seemed to bear no grudge.

In the afternoon they went to pay homage to the Walkley Madonna. Rab gave Little Rabbi a piggy-back as the girls ran on ahead, talking nonsense. Little Rabbi's new found shyness of his father had been overcome by a stronger emotion – that of reluctance to conquer the hill under his own effort. He had tried his granddad first and then his grannie, but got short shrift. Rab tried to get Little Rabbi to talk but he didn't seem to want to and Rab thought he couldn't blame him for that.

Selina was sitting by the window in the parlour and the baby was in the wooden drawer on the table asleep. She had only just got her to sleep so everyone was instructed to be quiet. When the others had withdrawn to the living room, Rab stepped forward to have a look inside the drawer out of a sense of duty. The baby had wispy dark hair and a screwed up blotchy face. The skin on its hands was dry and flaky and looked diseased; *mochardi*.

'What have you done to your eye? It looks awful,' she said.

'Oh it's nowt,' he said, touching it. 'I gather you've called it Edith.'

'Yes it suits her, do you like it?'

'Yeah, it'll be right enough.'

'You've been away?'

'Yeah, they've had us all in Matlock for special training. It's working too – we're still top and edging ahead now.'

Selina said, 'We'll be fit enough to come home soon.'

'That's good for you then.'

'Yes.'

'I'll keep an eye on the baby if tha wants to join the others,' Rab said.

'I will, thank you. Call me if she awakes.'

Rab sat in the chair by the window, warm from Selina. He looked out, then closed his eyes.

'Dad your tea's ready!'

Rab woke. Lizzie was poking his shoulder. 'You been asleep?'

'No love. Just resting mi eyes, that's all.'

'It's all right, she's still asleep. I'll stop here while you have yer tea.'

Monday 17th January 1898

Monday afternoon was the Scotch versus English benefit for Bob Cain. In the changing room, Johnny Cunningham, sat in a blue and white *Wednesday* shirt grinning up at Rab, 'You sure yer not one of us, Rabbi?' he said in his thickest Glaswegian, rolling his 'r' for extra effect, 'Wi' a fine Scottish name like Rabbi you oughta be.'

'No, I'm as English as Her Majesty!' Rab said, 'and thank God too, I would not wear one of those if I was at the North Pole in nowt but mi pants!' He smoothed down the sides of his United jersey, looking smug.

The game wasn't up to much but, after a bit of arithmetic by Fred, they reckoned afterwards that Bob would pocket more than a hundred quid. 'Not bad for an afternoon's work that Bob!' said Bill.

After tea in the pavilion they were all told to be at Midland Station for three o'clock the following day to get the train back to Matlock in preparation for the visit of the Wolves on Saturday. Rab had been thinking. He caught a tram into town and sat so as to make sure he was the first off – he leaned against the railings of the Crimea War monument and observed the other passengers getting off. He tried to watch each of them disperse then cut across to Union Lane which turned into Norfolk Lane – both narrow and straight. He walked quickly, keeping an eye over his shoulder – no one coming his way – most folks would stick to the main streets, just the odd worker or two. He went past the theatres and down Mulberry Street and out onto a busy stretch of High Street. He went into the Norfolk Market Hall by the front entrance, here he bought some crocuses planted in a porcelain bowl: green shoots pushing out of the peat. He went out the side entrance, then crossed quickly to Castle Hill where he waited to see if anyone followed him. He went down Waingate and instead of going straight round Bridge Street he cut down Millsands then ducked into Mill Lane and the jennel, where again he waited. He raised the collar on his jacket and pulled down his cap before looking out into Bridge Street. No one loitering or watching the shop, so, checking his shoulder again, he made straight for it and was through the door. Behind the counter was… the Bosom.

'Evenin missus! Don't know if you remember me? Friend of Ada's.' She stood there not flinching, arms folded supporting the weight of her greatest asset. She raised an eyebrow as if to say, 'And so what?'

'Is she in? Only I just wanted a quick word, just in passing. Nowt important like.' To his relief, Ada appeared at the door at the back, 'Come through Mr Howell,' she said. 'Thank you Mother.' He sensed her slowly shaking her head disapprovingly as he went past, following Ada through.

They went into the living room, where he had last been on New Year's Eve. She closed the door behind them.

'For you,' Rab said holding out the crocuses in the bowl.

'Thank you Rab, I love to see the first flowers of the year. Not long before these'll come through.'

'Sorry I've not been to see you. It's been… difficult.'

'You've been in Matlock.'

'You know?'

'Yeah, I read it in the paper… I also read something about you being in the bad books of the committee.'

'It said that! How…? What else did it say.'

'Something about "conduct that couldn't be allowed," nothing else. What did it mean?'

'How the hell did that get in the paper! It must've been one of them bastards on t' committee spreading gossip! How dare they!'

227

Rab felt sickened. 'They've no right. They treat you like they own you. Like a dog.'

'What did it mean Rab?'

Rab sat down. 'Any tea going?'

Ada filled the kettle. As she went about making tea Rab tried to compose his words. It was as if Ada understood the process in his mind – he loved her for that. She took a cup through to her mother in the shop – they had at least as long as it takes to drink a cup of tea he thought.

'I think they've been spying on me. Checking up on me, where I go, who I meet. They've been known to do it wi' blokes what like a drink or two. I think they've seen me with you.'

Ada put her head down and looked at her hands, her face very grave.

'It's a'reight though love, I've made it up wi' 'em and I've been careful – no one's followed us here now. I don't think they know much really, but it's made worse 'cause I've missed club room nights, and they think I'm not respectful enough or summat, that's all. But they know they need me – especially after how I played Sat'day.'

Now it was Ada's turn to weigh her words. 'But we can't go on can we? If we're followed? Knowing that someone might be spying. I can't bear the thought that someone might be watching the house right now.'

'They're not interested in you.'

'They are if I'm with you. And what if they catch you?'

'Well I've had a final warning – if there's owt they take exception to they'll finish me.'

'Then we can't take the risk can we? And what if people start talking? When I read that in the paper I feared that scandal might follow. I've been miserable Rab.' Tears filled her eyes. He leaned over to her and gently caught the tears with his thumbs.

'No Rab, don't... besides mother could come through.'

He sat back. He looked at her and tried to look into her eyes but she kept them averted.

'Rab you know I love you?'

She looked up and he nodded. 'Well that has to be enough. We have to take comfort in that and just get on with our lives because it can't work can it?' She held him now, with her eyes. 'Well can it?'

He shook his head. She was right: it was foolish to think they could go about unnoticed.

'I wish I could at least write to you, but I can't.'

'I can read about how you're getting on in the papers,' she nodded to the paper on the table. 'It sounded quite some occasion on Saturday. How's your eye?' She reached up and touched his eyebrow, stroked her finger over the bruise; her touch went through him like a shiver; down his back.

'It's nowt really, though it looks summat. It was a cracking game. One of the best. If we only play half that good, we'll finish champions.'

'I hope so.' She got to her feet. 'Thanks for the flowers, I'll think of you when they come out.'

Rab got to his feet as well. 'Ada...'

She leaned towards him; she didn't want words. He returned her kiss.

'Take care Rab.'

'How many final goodbyes is that?'

She smiled a thin smile. As he was about to leave she told him to wait and returned with the scissors from her sewing basket and some blue-green thread. She loosened her hair and bound the thread round a small strand, then cut off the inch-long lock of hair and handed it to him. He went out the back, neither of them speaking as they parted.

Saturday 22nd January 1898

The low winter sun that had been in Rab's eyes in the first half had gone down when the teams made their way over to the Norfolk baths on John Street after the game. In the sky, grey clouds like puffs of smoke, above that salmon pink letters, and higher still a small, pale, curved blade of a moon. Bodies were tired, sore or both; but it was the Wolves team who walked most heavily, feeling they should at least have got a point for their efforts.

Rab emerged from under the water in the slipper bath. 'Get a bloody shift on Rab!' It was George grumbling from over the partition. Then Bob Cain spoke up, 'Come on yer wee chanty-wrastler, the floor's freezing out here man! You're supposed to be getting the muck off, nae ha'en a swim! ' He wrapped the towel round him and got out, 'nearly done lads.' He quickly started pulling on his clothes that were laid on a little wooden seat attached to the wall. 'Here George,' Rab shouted over, 'Thought I'd got mi first goal, Nudge laid that free kick up nicely for me. Did tha see the shot! Only just got his fingers to it!'

'It's a shame all thi nearly-goals don't earn us bonuses Rab, Harry Thickett said, 'We'd have two hundred in us bonus pot not just the one.' 'Ach! Don't make me laugh – that hurts,' said Bob.

Rab emerged half-dressed.

'Let's have a look at thi before tha goes in,' said George

'Don't reckon there's much to see gaffer.'

'Yeah but if it 'urts just laughing. What about breathing?'

'Aye that too.'

'Do a deep breath for me.'

Bob winced.

'We'll get the doctor to check that out, could be broken ribs.'

'Well the bastard didn't half batter me – talk about playing the man!'

'In tha goes.'

He then examined the bruise on Thickett's back. 'I reckon that's sore 'cause it's right in the kidney, but I still reckon it's just a bruise, Harry. I'll gi' thi summat to to rub into it.'

'I got him back for yer though,' Bob shouted, over the noise of running water. He set out to take yer out o' the game, so he'd a better run down the left. Little tap to the ankle slowed him down.'

'Who went at t' back after I was carried off?'

'Nudge dropped back,' said Rab. 'Makes yer sick – he can play anywhere, and do it well!'

The relief of victory, steam, free flowing water and the temporary absence of the formalities imposed by dress, added to the knowledge that they had a week at home before an easy home match – first round of the Cup against lowly Midland Leaguers Burslem Port Vale – all combined to put the players in high spirits. Amidst splashing water, there was talk, not always gentlemanly, of how they would spend the coming week – there was apparently "catchin up" to do, which could have been taken in any one of a number of ways. Rab was now amongst those urging haste on those still inside the tiled cubicles – meat and potatoes back at the pavilion having an increasingly strong pull. He didn't share their boyish excitement at going home.

They headed back in small groups; the now chill air, as they emerged wet-haired, making them walk quickly up Bramall Lane.

Chapter 23

Selina sat by the window sewing some lace onto a robe for Edith while the baby slept and she waited for the event of the week – her visit from her family. As she had recovered and Edith gained in strength, her mind turned to fretting about leaving the little retreat in Walkley and her sister's warm care. Here she felt safe; away from people; away from infection. She hardly had to lift a finger: her sister doing all the chores and being ever present, apart from the occasional short trip back round to her own house. She didn't want to burst the bubble. But she was torn. She missed her house, her mother's company, and running the household.

Edith murmured and seemed to grab at imaginary flies; she covered her over with the blankets again.

In recent days her thoughts had also started turning to worries about Rab, and the effect her absence was having on him. But her worry was intermingled with an irritation, the two emotions ebbing and flowing so that at one moment worry was to the fore, only to be replaced by irritation. She struggled to make sense of it. When he had visited her with the others last Sunday, he had again made no effort to talk to her. He just sat there with his mind apparently elsewhere. He had not held his new daughter and seemed afraid of using her name. The week before that she had felt pride in her husband, when he had sat with Edith to let her spend time with her other children. But then Lizzie had told her afterwards that he had been asleep. It was as if he feared intimacy. She had known women who had neglected their babies, appeared barren of love for them: women who having grieved for lives cut too short, too often, seemed to fear falling in love again; that lack of love bringing their

232

fear towards prophecy. Was Rab afraid of love too? But then, was he punishing her for something? And what was the meaning of his Christmas presents? Nothing for her – for her alone: nothing special. There had been a time when he had bought her dainty handkerchiefs, trinkets or Nottingham lace, not preserved fruit! And her birthday had just gone by, unmarked. Once she was able to return home she would work on him, get him to hold Edith. Get him to church. If only she could have got him to see the Gipsy, to be touched by his power. Instead she would have to wait. To pray.

Her mother, father and her children arrived. She kissed and caressed the girls and Little Rabbi. They sat with her for a while, but then, having to be quiet, started to look bored. 'Why don't I take them round to Albert; they can play with their cousin for a bit before tea and you can sit and talk,' her sister said.

'Why is Rab not here?' Selina asked once they were sat on their own.

'He's away again I suppose,' her mother said. 'He never said he wasn't coming back yesterday but he didn't. Off he traipsed to his football and that were it.'

Selina sat quietly for a moment, as she tried to make sense of it. 'He should at least have said.'

She changed the subject: 'Tell me what's going on in the world? I don't feel part of it here.'

'The dispute's over,' Dennis said, 'They've bloody well caved in – poor bastards! Starve the womenfolk and the childers, and wait for the men to go back tails between their legs!'

The women said nothing, they sensed that what was coming was not meant to be a conversation, and sympathetic words would not help – a fly can't fly into a closed mouth. When he was self-righteously angry like this, trying to soothe him just made it worse. Then he'd just turn on them for not appreciating how awful things were, for trying to make disaster seem unimportant. It would not do to belittle deep commitment. No. Sympathy or kind words would not help. When the time came just agree.

'Colonel bloody Dyer and the Federation's got 'em where they want 'em – on their bloody knees!'

In the pause for breath, the women shook their heads and tutted at the unfairness. 'There were a meeting Wednesday, they've agreed to go back on the old terms. Not even wi' their dignity in tact! It's a disaster for all on us. Knocks on t' head any hope of eight hours for a generation, never mind skilled men keeping skilled jobs – now they've seen bloody blackleg labourers operating lathes why would they go back to paying engineers to operate em? While the bosses are banqueting at Town Hall or t'Cutlers' Hall – ten courses: turtle soup, lobster, pheasant and what-'ave-yer – they grind honest men's families under their feet – obey or suffer! And they make out the men what's standing up for their rights are lawless by getting the Watch Committee to order the police out on horseback, pretending that they need a display o' armed force to keep order! That Keir Hardie were right the other day – we need our own men in Parliament, labour candidates. I've had enough wi' liberals – half hearted men!'

He sat back. He had blown himself out. He spat on the fire and picked up the teacup that had been placed beside him; the blackened phlegm sizzling on the grate.

After Saturday's cup-tie, the committee had decided to dispatch the team straight back to Matlock on the next train, rather than let them have a couple of days at home. No one had been bold or foolish enough to give voice to whatever objections they might have had. The fact was they all felt they deserved it. They had settled into the game and early on they had had chances but no goals – but surely it was only a matter of time. Then just quarter of an hour in, Burslem attacked quickly and Foulke could only push the low shot round the post. They failed to clear the corner and Bill couldn't keep the shot out. Only a penalty late on in the game earned them a replay at Cobridge the following Wednesday. United's forwards had no sting in front of goal. Too much "catching up" had been indulged in. Training had been relaxed and the Potteries men had had the greater thirst. Some put it down to luck, or the red and white stripe effect (because Burslem had the same colours, the United, as the home side, had worn white shirts). They had missed chances, and several times hit the upright. They had had the best of the play but it just wasn't their day.

Rab tried to see out of the train window, but it was too dark outside to see much. From a corner he had sent a sharp header on target, but their goalie pulled off a clever save. Heading back for Matlock was good, no distractions, no catching up; they would not be caught napping on Wednesday.

The previous week at home had dragged. Satisfying sleep had eluded him. Most mornings he still felt tired when the others went downstairs, so he had stayed in bed, emerging to slurp down some tea and thrust any remaining bacon in two slices of bread before heading out to training. Or, on mornings he wasn't due in, he would go back to bed and doze.

When the rest of the team had gone home after morning training and dinner, Rab sometimes hung back and went onto the pitch; one man alone with a couple of pigeons, where thousands stood and roared. It was calm, all sounds being distant except for his own breath and the thud of his boot on the leather as he curled it into the area or it bounded across the mud as he tried to break his record length for throw-ins.

Afterwards, he had called by at the flower stall in the market: pretty little bunches of primroses were displayed.

'They're ready early – it's been that mild,' said the stall-holder.

'I'll give you sixpence for some if you'll deliver them for me.' She wrote down the name and address. 'Any message?'

'No. No message,' he had said.

He had picked up a bit of a thigh strain against Wolves, he couldn't recall how, bit of a dead-leg maybe, the sort of thing you could run off. Now sat on the train chugging up the valley to Matlock, it felt warm above his right knee. Then the back of his other leg cramped tight and he leapt up banging his knee on the table. Tommy jolted awake and others started laughing as he hopped about "like a Zulu" trying to quickly stretch the muscle. The pain went off and he sat gingerly back down, keeping his leg out straight for if the spasm came back again.

'Nowt a few cold sit-baths won't sort!' he said.

If anything Burslem Port Vale were even more up for the replay than they had been walking out at the Bramall Lane Grounds. They now had behind them ten thousand over-heated potters who completely boiled over when their side beat Foulke after just three minutes. Bill raged against having been fouled but the referee dismissed all appeals. A gale blew and even balls hit on target sailed over the touch-line and sometimes out of the ground. One of Bill's goal kicks was even blown out for a corner, so strong it raged against them. In the second half Bill came half way up the field to assist the attack. Port Vale had everyone back and continually cleared and blocked. Just before time Harry Thickett scored playing up at centre-forward. Extra time followed, as did hail and snow, lashed sharp against bare skin by the wind. Then the inevitable happened, Vale broke away quickly leaving Bill stranded in the middle of the park. Simpson, at left back for the injured Cain, managed to clear the first shot; another forward, rushing in, followed up and slotted it in.

The journey back to Matlock from the Potteries was bad tempered. Players blamed anyone but themselves; the blame had to be deflected away. The referee was awful – their forwards impeded Bill for the first, their second was offside – Cocky's goal wasn't offside – Bill should've done his job and stayed in the net – not thinking he could do others' jobs up field better than them – Nudge was under par – Tommy should have put that header in – they shouldn't have been forced to play extra time by the referee. Needham had to step in.

'It was simple. We lost because we deserved to. We all could have played better, me included. We could have trained better, we could have passed better, we held the ball too long and our tactics were flawed, here and at the Lane. We didn't adapt. They deserved to win. They stuck to their plan. Both times they scored early, then defended their gains. We can all learn from today. Now shut up. We sort it out at Liverpool on Saturday.'

That is just what they did. They came away with a four nil victory.

Rab had stayed behind in Matlock – despite his protests to George that he was fine – he couldn't run properly, his thigh was heavy and he was ordered rest and treatment. Young Harry Johnson was called on, and Logan, a six foot Scotch lad kept his place in preference to John Almond who kept Rab company receiving treatment at the hydro. Rab knew he should have been pleased when they rolled in triumphant that evening, but he wasn't. He had half hoped they would lose, or perhaps win but only just. To make matters worse, Young Harry had scored and was keen to tell everyone all about it again. Big Jock Logan had scored twice. The pair of them made Rab sick – going on about it. If it wasn't for his bloody leg! They also told how Cocky had been hacked by the Liverpool back and how in return he later saw to him so that he too had to be carried off the field. There was also much talk of the merits of the Professional Players' Union. Needham had not been along to the conference to set it up before Christmas, but they had met Bolton's John Somerville after the game.

'We could do wi' someone on our side, if you ask me,' said Bill. 'Look at all the money we bring in and how little o' that makes it to our pockets – and the money what changes hands these days when players move clubs – hundreds o' pounds! We should get a bit o' that an' all. We're not cattle, to be bought and sold!'

'That fellow Burrows we've been trying to get from Woolwich Arsenal,' Needham said, 'they're refusing to release him without a substantial fee. And he's an amateur!'

'It's disgusting!' Bill said. 'They think they own players' flesh and blood!'

'My mates who played for Scotland last week, said they were nae going to play against Ireland unless they got paid – just before kick off an' all,' said Bob Cain, 'One pound they demanded – and they got it! I'll ha'e a bit o' that!'

'Well personally speaking, what persuades me most is the widows and orphans fund and that disablement fund,' Needham said. 'At present we are at the mercy of our clubs' charity if summat goes wrong. I believe our committee would do the right thing by us and arrange a benefit or whatever, but what if you're at a small club, the likes of Gainsborough, or Newton Heath? I think we should all sign up on Monday when we see him again. Just about every other team has. Shall we have a vote on it?'

Rab travelled with them to Sheffield on the Monday and had to watch the Bolton game from the sidelines. The crowd was disappointing for a Saint Monday. Rab watched as Johnson, in his place, twice shot on goal early on; and he muttered, "that's rubbish Johnson," when he misjudged his man or tried to tackle too early and failed to stop a pass. "Inexperience that." He had to admit the boy got back well though. He struggled with his conscience, and again didn't want to see them do too well, and applauded more for show than with enthusiasm when first Fred, then Jock Logan and Cocky scored. Then Och-Aye did a little link up with his countryman Logan who got the fourth. They met with John Somerville after the game. Rab pledged himself along with the others to the Players' Union – once they had received their entry forms and the rules. He'd leave all that to Nudge to sort out. He didn't join in with the banter: he couldn't join in with their buoyant mood. He ate his tea quickly and making his excuses, left as soon as he could. He suspected this is what happened at the end of a career: injury, battling with pain, and frustration. Like those dreams he had where he was on a steep slope and couldn't climb it, couldn't find a handhold, always slipping backwards, downwards. Then denial and self-doubt battling it out for supremacy, self-doubt getting stronger, feeding off the other emotions. And, rearing up above you, forming a bitter symmetry as one career pushes out another, feelings of jealousy towards the ones squeezing you out – those who you used to beat, those who once looked up to you; envied you. Then there was the fear. The fear of letting the supporters down, letting the team down, letting George down, of missing a tackle and not being able to get back and put it right. Where had this self-doubt come from? His self-belief had always been so strong; you make a mistake, you put it right, you improve, you get better, stronger, you don't let it happen again.

He tried to spend as little time at home as he could. He was required to go to Bramall Lane every day. George manipulated his leg, applied warm mustard plasters, gave him exercises to perform, and rubbed his legs down with Wilson's "anti-stiff." 'What's that stuff George?' Rab asked.

'It's summat I've not tried before, it's says it "imparts strength to the muscles by drawing blood to the part." We'll do some running wi' thi after the weekend – that means tha's not coming to London for the Hotspurs game – we'll have thi reight for the following Sat'day though – that's more important.'

'We shouldn't be playing friendlies though should we, eh? We should still be in the Cup.'

'No point looking back – what's done's done. Tha knows better than most not to look back at what's gone wrong, but to get on wi' what's in front of thi. Notts County, week on Sat'day, that's all tha needs to think about.'

Rab was heartened by George's prognosis. George believed he would be back a week on Saturday – he wouldn't have said that if he didn't think he had a good chance of being picked. "Notts County, week on Sat'day, that's all tha needs to think about," he repeated in his head as he stretched and slowly lunged as George had showed him.

12th February 1898

On the following Saturday, whilst the team were in London, he spent the morning at the Turkish baths. And in the afternoon he went to watch the reserves, where his friend Mick was washed-up, playing the Black Watch team. He disliked watching football, but disliked even more the thought of sitting around at home, while he knew the team were away playing somewhere. As he stood watching, he found his muscles twitching as he went for tackles in his head, rose slightly for headers, and mentally lined up the free-kicks.

He had not been in a rush to get back home all that week. He had found things to do in town in the evenings: magic lantern lectures, a cinematograph show in the Montgomery Hall; or at the Albert Hall he saw a prize fight from the United States: Corbett versus

Simmons. Preparations were being made for Selina's return with her baby. Soon it would be swallowing up all the life in the house, diverting all the talk in its direction, sucking in all the energy.

Chapter 24

For Selina, it was time to start thinking about moving on from the little, warm room where she had hidden; resuming life in the real world again. There was no longer any good reason to stay at the small house in Greaves Street. She was to go round to Albert and Sarah Ann's for a few days before her mother came to take her back home.

Albert took Selina's arm on the short walk round to his house, whilst Sarah Ann carried Edith in a basket. Her first proper trip had been to register Edith's birth. The registrar filled out the ledger. He asked her for the occupation of the father: 'coal miner,' she said before making her mark on the record where she was told.

Friday 18th February 1898

At the end of that week Selina and her mother walked slowly down Alfred Road in Brightside towards the back gate leading into the yard at the back of Lake Street. Under her shawl, Edith slept, warm against her, the motion of the tram, its creaks, rattles and groans having sent her to sleep. It seemed so long since she had been here last – a lifetime away! She had to get back in a routine sometime though, so, when her mother came round as planned, she had gone with only a private twinge of reluctance.

'We ought to get some paint on that door,' she said as they pushed it open into the yard. 'It's funny how you don't notice it after a while when you're here all the time.' Then, indicating the wooden enclosure: 'Still got that blessed beast!'

'Yeah well Rab's not been around much to deal with it. It'll be getting too big before long. And I'm sick of feeding it slops.'

'Is he here now, Rab?'

'He's around somewhere, he's been around more than usual the last couple of week. Don't know what time he'll be back.'

'Did he not say?'

'If he did I can't say as I recall.'

They went inside. In front of the fire stood the bath containing cold water and pit muck.

'The idle beggars! They could've at least emptied it! Right I'll sort this out and get you sat down with a cup of tea, and then I'll go and bring the kids back from Henry's.'

Selina sat in the armchair whilst her mother shook coal out of the scuttle onto the fire, then shuffled to and fro with jugs of dirty water from the bath before dragging it into the scullery.

'If you make up a drawer to pop her in, I'll start on tea, *Dei*,' Selina said.

'You'll do no such thing!'

She might as well enjoy it while she could, she thought. In a day or two there'd be no stopping and there'd be a procession of visitors too, all expecting cups of tea and a little something to go with it.

'It's nice to be home *Dei*,' she said as her mother set a cup and saucer next to her on the table. 'You'll be glad of a bit of help again I should imagine.'

'And the company love.'

The children crowded round their mother and the girls cooed over Edith; then they were all sent out to play before tea. In the evening, the two women sat mending, the others having been sent to bed or down to the public. Tiny Edith was upstairs in the middle of the big bed. The women looked up at each other when the back door opened. Then came the thud of a bag onto the scullery floor and they knew it was Rab.

'Evening!' he said, then sat down at the table. 'You back then?'

Selina smiled. 'I'll pour you some tea shall I?' she said.

'I'll do it love,' Jemima said.

Selina sat by the fire; Rab at the table hunched as he blew steam from the tea.

'I'll get off up in a bit,' Rab said, 'I'm jiggered.'

'Mind out for Edith when you do. And don't trip over Rabbi either, he's on a mattress on the floor.'

'I'll not bother yet then if the baby's there.'

Selina felt another pin prick – why was he so scared of being alone in bed with her – with his baby? Was it to punish her – using Edith to get at her? She felt like her little pin-cushion – into which he had been sticking more and more pins, every thoughtless remark, every time he ignored Edith. It couldn't be the old Romany instinct in him: regarding newborns as *mochardi*; never happened with the others – funny time for new-found respect for the old ways!

She watched him drink his tea. He sat uncomfortably, like he was in someone else's house. He got out his tobacco pouch, then went out to "take Mr Gladstone for a walk." He always said that and it had ceased to be amusing a long time ago.

Rab stood alone on the bridge, the glow in the little clay crucible under his nose the only warmth around, the air and river below cold. He tried to remember back to when he and Selina first set out. It was his house then; Selina was his – not as it was now, living under someone else's roof, not his rules, where Selina was more daughter than wife. A horrid house in Carlisle Street, but it was theirs, just the two of them to please; and a baby on the way. She had, back then, often been at her mother's – but was always there when he got home. Had she been the first to realise that there was no longer an exclusive connection between them? Had she run back to her mother and father, and just towed him along? Then it had been convenient to be in Dunlop Street near to her parents where they could help out with small children, but had she been running back to them even then? And though they had all moved in together at Lake Street he and Selina had still had their moments: moments when they were together, when they had poked fun at her mother and father and their ways; but now they all just laughed at him. When had she last been truly his? He didn't know. When the baby sparked into life? – when she last came to him after the Glossop match? Had she given herself to him then or had he just taken?

243

The damp started to penetrate his bones. He returned to the house, and found his father-in-law sat brooding by the fire, Jemima tidying round, and Selina upstairs checking the children. He went straight up. Selina was lying in the dark on the bed. He removed his boots, and placed his trousers and shirt on the chair, his jacket over the back, and climbed onto the narrow ledge of bed on his side. At his back, the baby snuffled and slurped, sounding not unlike his father-in-law never closing his mouth between mouthfuls.

Saturday 19th February 1898

The next morning after the baby had been fed and while Selina was helping her mother clear away after breakfast, she had passed the baby to him to hold. He held it. Its glazed blue eyes staring at something, mouth twitching, flaky crusts of skin in its hair. He felt nothing. He knew that was wrong. He should feel something. White posset erupted out of its mouth: 'Here it's….' He passed it back to its mother.

He had slept badly. He had woken in the middle of the night with a jolt after his fist had come down hard on the pillow – in his dream he had been fending something off – something small and savage – then he realised his blow had missed the baby's head by inches. He had then crept downstairs and sat shivering in the dark, watching the glow from the dying embers in the grate.

Now Selina had her baby over her shoulder, it's eyes looking vacantly ahead, as she carried on clearing away one-handedly. Rab sat back down at the table. He would set off early, as soon as he was ready; clear his mind. His thigh felt better: perhaps he'd walk in, nice and gentle, loosen up; sit in the clubroom and wait for the others to arrive. Notts County. Last time he'd been dropped: New Year's Day. He remembered that day walking away from the ground: from where he was supposed to be. He had to play well this afternoon. He wanted that first goal; he needed it; it would make him feel better. He wanted the others to shake his hand, and pat him on the back. He wanted the supporters to sing his name. He had his chance back; to show he was still better than Johnson – a boy that couldn't even grow a proper moustache. Notts County. Bottom of the league; the right match at the right time.

'I'll be off in a bit then,' he said. 'Are there any biscuits I can take?'

'No,' said Jemima. 'There's only a few left and I'm saving those. I thought you had slap-up meals beforehand.'

'No, I meant to put in mi bag for a biting on – we're away after today's game until Tuesday.'

'Typical! Your wife just gets home with a new baby and you bugger off! Where is it now?'

'Matlock again; special training. It's important, we're getting to the crunch time of the season.'

'Important, my eye!'

Selina had her back to him. She didn't look round but she stopped what she was doing. He could sense her suffering – disappointment, anger, betrayal; he didn't know which. He just wanted to get away from it.

When he had left, Selina said to her mother, 'I just wanted us all to go to church tomorrow with Edith for the first time. All of us as a family, and receive God's blessing for her. Show her to Him. Arrange a baptism. Pray for her future. Together.'

Jemima looked out into the yard. After a long pause she said, 'I'll get the butcher to come and take that wretched pig away, for whatever he wants to give us for it. I can't be doing with it any more and I don't want the faff of salting pork again.'

There was a decent sized crowd at the game, all looking forward to another four goals from their boys. Foulke made an early save from a rasping shot, to loud cheers, and Tommy and Cocky both had shots saved, as the crowd oohed.

But it was not long before their mood turned and they cursed their wasted sixpences. The County winger skipped past Harry Thickett, pushing the ball past him. Bill rushed out to clear with one of his trademark kicks, but he too was dodged. Then Bob Cain flew in and would surely hoof it out, but missed. A County forward picked up the ball and shot against the post. The rebound, collected by a forward before Rab could get back to help, was tapped in. Rab had watched the whole farce unfold. Could he have got back quicker? But it wasn't his fault.

They had to contend for the rest of the game with eight thousand pairs of eyes picking out every mistake, eight thousand full-throated opinions, eight thousand footballers who could have "bloody done better than that!" The crowd looked for players to blame; each of the eleven on the pitch did the same. Rab knew the only difference from back-to-back four nils was him. He mustn't make mistakes, give them a chance to drop him again. The crowd picked on Cocky, his crossing was poor: to County feet, he kept the ball too long, or tried to get rid too early. Rab had a header on target from a corner but the goalie made a great save.

At the end of the game there were boos. They filed off the pitch in silence, resenting the joviality of the County players. Rab tried to avoid eye contact in the changing room, as the recriminations flew, as they all tried to deflect pressure from themselves by turning it on others: he didn't want to see the contempt in their eyes. Needham railed at them all for their lack of professionalism: they should just listen to themselves! Cocky sat in the corner, head down. Rab went over the game; he should have got back faster. Was he any slower than usual? That ball should have been directed closer to the corner of the net.

Tuesday 22nd February 1898

Cocky was dropped for Tuesday's game against Everton; Rab was secretly relieved that Cocky had been scapegoated, not him. Ralph Gaudie was back in. He had recovered from his ordeal at Birmingham some time since, but something had happened – it had been whispered that he was finished, that the Committee would not have him back, but Rab didn't want to know about it.

It was Shrove Tuesday, a half-day holiday in Sheffield, so there was a good crowd, and they were starting off in a better mood, having already celebrated finishing work early in traditional fashion. The pitch was heavy; frozen underneath and thawed on top. It was difficult to play, slippery, but they tried to play fast. They worked

246

better together and the crowd stayed more positive, and appreciated their effort. The team had bucked their ideas up after Saturday. A good hollering at, that's what they had needed. It finished goalless, the sides cancelling each other out and exhausted. Rab thought he should have played better; he knew he was capable of it. If only he could have put in one of his chances, like the Rab Howell of old.

At tea there was talk of a player in Leicester, in prison for manslaughter committed during a game: 'Some tackle that must ha'e been eh?' Bob Cain said. But Needham was appalled that anyone should joke about it. Rab didn't join in. He felt like he was on the edge of it all, looking in. He looked at Needham, but he was being ignored he was sure. Rab was convinced that the strategist's mind had already written him off. Johnson had made his mark scoring at Liverpool. His mind was already thinking Needham, Morren, Johnson: not Needham, Morren, Howell. He would have to fight like hell; but doubt kept bubbling up. He didn't hang around for a smoke after tea.

He went away with something heavy inside him; he checked to see if he was being followed and stopped while a man in a shabby overcoat and worn bowler hat went past him. Something bad was going to happen, he sensed. What? He went past unlit doorways and passages uneasily – half expecting someone to leap out. The dark had never bothered him. No it wasn't the dark. He chided himself. He was being pathetic. But still there was something rising in his chest, a fear like that he felt when stepping out in front of thousands – but this one couldn't be controlled by chasing a ball. He broke into a trot, moving felt better, but then his thigh twinged and he had to stop.

He reached Lady's Bridge and saw the Brightside tram ahead; there was a queue of a dozen or so people moving, shuffling, in anticipation of its arrival. He came to a stop as people moved on around him – he was finished, washed up, he couldn't get it back. What was there left? What was there ahead of him? He couldn't go back to the house. A wave of fear came over him, a dizziness; he leaned on the parapet, shuddering, his chest closing in and squeezing his breath. Christ! Was it his heart? He bent over, his hands on his knees. No not here! People went past him on the pavement: old men with canes, women in headscarves, couples arm in arm; horses pulled their loads into town and out.

'You all right love? Can I help you?' He looked up. It was an elderly woman in an old-style bonnet, face lined where she smiled, bright blue eyes, a face seemingly moulded by habitual compassion. A woman who would smell of gingerbread.

He consciously filled his lungs and straightened. 'I'm sorry, I didn't mean...' He managed a smile.

'So long as you're all right love, that's all.' She lightly touched his arm. He nodded. He wanted her to stay, to hold his hand. He wanted her to take him home, but she moved on. He felt ridiculous. He looked around to see if anyone was looking. People continued to come and go: just getting on with their business. He turned and looked over the parapet; the water rippled over the weir. Like the sea's edge at the bottom, without the lulling rise and fall of sound. Daylight fading fast. His breathing slowed. Was it his heart? Had the gingerbread lady saved him? He had never felt that before. The sense of fear eased as he was drawn by the hollowed out shapes of water striking a stone. He watched as a brown leaf drifted closer to the weir, then reaching the edge it accelerated down into the froth. His eyes searched for it, but it was gone, dragged down, lost.

He wouldn't go home. But what could he do? Ada's was just round the corner; he wanted to bury himself in her and it would be all right. Except it was impossible. Instead he headed for the only place he could think of: his brother Charlie's. He would walk – he couldn't face the people on the tram.

The streets thinned out away from town and he was alone as he made his way slowly from one pool of gas light to another.

A lamp was lit in the living room as he entered Charlie's yard. He stopped as he saw through the window: Charlie and Eliza sat still by the fire; Clara was sat at the table, lit by the lamp, hunched in concentration. He tapped on the window and felt guilty as Eliza, startled, looked around. He waved through the window and tried to put on his cheeky smile.

'What's up Rab?' his brother said opening the door.

'Nowt. I just… can I come in?'

'Hello Uncle Rabbi!' Clara said as he came into the room. 'D'y like my picture?' She held up a half-finished painting of a bowl of narcissi that were on the table.

'Yeah it's champion. Nice little box of paints tha's got there.'

'Yes, these are the paints you and Aunty Selina got me for Christmas.'

'Are they? Oh.'

Charlie pulled up a wooden chair from the table to face the hearth.

'How's tha going Liza?' Rab asked.

'Middling thanks. I'm glad it's been mild so far – and I think we're past the worst too… signs of spring. How's Lina and the new baby? I bet she's beautiful like Little Selina and Lizzie were eh?'

'Yeah, I s'pose. Seems reight enough.'

Rab's face must have given something away. Charlie said, 'Time tha went to bed miss.'

'But father, I've not finished, and it's still early.'

'It'll keep. Off tha goes.'

She rinsed the brush in the jam jar and said her goodnights, kissing each of them on the cheek. Rab noticed Charlie glance at Eliza. 'I'll be off up too, I think, my eyes are tired,' she said. 'There should still be tea in the pot Rab, and there's a pancake left and cold meat and cheese in the pantry.'

The two brothers sat quietly as feet moved about upstairs, and the iron bedstead in the room above them creaked. Charlie got out his cutty and a short length of twist – he tore some off and passed the dark brown tobacco to Rab who also got his pipe out.

'So what's up then?' Charlie said.

'Can I stay the night?'

'What? What's happened?'

'Nowt. Well, it's hard to explain. I can't go back. It's too much.'

'Not go back home? What's too much? What about the baby and Lina and the kids?'

'I know. It's just… I feel like I'm going mad Charlie. The house just suffocates me and I might as well not be there.'

'Here it's not that ginger lass again is it?' Rab just stared ahead. 'Bloody hell Rab.'

'No it's not like that.'

'No? What is it like then?'

'That's off.'

'Off? – tha means it were on?' Charlie was speaking in a hushed voice but everything else about his speech and demeanour was shouting.

'No. Well it can't be. I realise that. It's nowt to do wi' 'er. I just can't go back to the house. It crushes me, and I just end up hating misen. And I can't get my mind straight. It's like there's summat in there that I can't get rid on. Please Charlie, it's just for a bit until I get misen sorted.'

Charlie looked at him with furrowed brow, puffing to keep his pipe alight, his features softening behind the smoke. When he spoke it was gruffly: 'It's not up to me, it's Liza's house. I'll speak to her in the morning. In the meantime tha can kip on the sofa in the front room. It's not reight warm, I'm afraid. Fire's not been lit in there since Reverend Hartley were round in the New Year. I'll get thi a blanket, and tha can use what cushions there is.'

It was still dark when Rab awoke the next day – shadows were cast across the floor from the gas lamp outside on the pavement, its light penetrating the thin curtains. He was still in his clothes and even had his cap on, it had been that cold in the night, and his body ached and there was a banging in his head like his blood was pounding against his skull. He heard the fire being raked in the next room, coal being shaken. He got up and stretched. As he pulled on his boots he heard low voices and listened: 'How can he stay here?' 'It'll not be for long – just till I sort him out – get him back home.' 'But what about our Lina?' 'It's her I've got in mind. It's like he's not thinking straight. He'll come round. He's a good man.' 'I know but he can't behave like some child, running away from home.' There was a banging of pots. 'Well I can't be doing wi' 'im under my feet all day.' Rab sat back down for a while in the dark shivering, only going through after Charlie had knocked to tell him that the kettle had boiled.

Clara was pleased to see him still there and over breakfast he asked her about her job in the stores and she moaned about being on her feet all day, but she was proud of the nine shillings she brought home to her mother.

Charlie was away early and Clara not long after.

'I'll be off an' all in a minute, Liza.' Rab said. 'Here let me help wi' that.' He set the large panchion on the table for her. 'I'm sorry for dropping on thi like this Liza love. I am grateful. I just can't go back to the house. It's like my head'll explode.'

'I don't understand Rab. You're welcome here, but you can't stay.'

'I know – it's not for long. I just need to… to sort summat.' He rapped his knuckles on his forehead. 'I've got a reight bloody headache.'

'Sit down. I'll make you some meadowsweet tea before you go.'

'Thanks Liza love, I will sort summat, promise.'

Chapter 25

Saturday 26th February 1898

Selina sat nursing Edith – the baby was not herself: she wasn't feeding terribly well and was grizzly and feverish.

'What do you think is the matter with her *Dei*?'

'Not much, I don't reckon. She's feeding a bit isn't she and no diarrhoea? Probably just a little cold.' Jemima rolled her pastry and lined the pie tins with it.

'Do you want me to have her for a bit, while you go and get some fresh air?'

'No I'd rather sit with her,' Selina said. 'Do you think we should get her some tins of baby food – they had some "Bonnie Baby Food" at Masons – she said it strengthened the blood and makes strong bones and muscle.'

'I don't hold with it – leave that to *gorgio* babies, if you ask me. She'll wean when she's ready, like the others.'

There was a tap at the window. Selina saw her sister, Eliza, her hands cupped round her eyes peering in, behind her stood Charlie Howell. Jemima let them in. 'This is a surprise!' she said.

'We came to see out little niece,' Eliza said.

'She's a bit colicky – we were just wondering if she's perhaps got a cold,' Selina said. 'It's nice of you to come.' She passed Edith across to her sister to hold and helped her mother get some tea on, glancing across to her brother-in-law, sitting quietly next to Eliza. He was cooing at her and offering his little finger for her to hold; a contrast between her perfect small soft white hand and his finger, bent from being broken in an accident, rough and pitted, and with pitman's fingernails. So much like Rab and yet so different, she thought; steady, that was what he was. Had she always liked Charlie best, and being jealous of her older sister, settled for the closest thing to what she had?

When they were all sat down, the pies in the oven and a pot of tea mashing on the table, Charlie spoke, 'Rab's not very well.'

'What do you mean? How do you know?' Selina asked. 'We haven't seen him for a week.'

'He's stayin at ours, has been since Tuesday night. Summat's been troublin him. He says he can't come home – he hasn't fought wi' you or owt?'

'No... no... I don't understand.'

'No, nor do we,' said Eliza. 'We don't really want him at ours, he should come back here. You know what he's like though, he won't talk about it.'

'Where is he now?'

'Out at a match,' Charlie said.

'Just wait till I get my hands on him!' said Jemima. 'Not had any bloody money off him for a fortnight, and all this time he's just round the corner.'

'Don't be too hard on him; money won't be on his mind. He's not reight in himself some'ow. It's perhaps the shock of a new baby.'

'Shock! I'll give him a bloody shock! It's her that gave birth, not him. Shock! *Dordi*!'

Charlie decided to keep his peace and change the subject: 'My other nieces and nephew not in?'

'No they're playing round at Henry's,' said Jemima.

'We'll perhaps pop there after then, and go back over the footbridge.'

Selina sat shocked, not listening to the small talk. Had he walked out on her, leaving her with a new baby? He had certainly been behaving oddly, from what little she'd seen of him: very distant; uninterested. But she couldn't have been troubling with his moods: the baby came first, then the children. He was supposed to be a man. Where was his courage? His strength? Yesterday it had been ten years to the day since they had their church wedding; eleven years married altogether. She didn't expect him to be all spooney, like they were at first. She was all too aware of his apparent indifference to Edith, but did she not devote herself to him, to providing a good home here: settled, warm, food on the table? And what of Lizzie, Lina and Rabbi – why would he rather be at Eliza and Charlie's than here? What if he never came back? She had visions of knocking on the door of Fir Vale workhouse with three children and a babe in arms.

She walked round to Henry's with Eliza and Charlie, leaving Edith asleep. 'I'll come for the fresh air, and bring them back for their tea,' she said.

She stopped for a bit and watched Charlie mucking about with all the children; seeing how many could climb on him before he collapsed. Then Eliza wanted to head back before the colder night air fell. Charlie dug in his pocket and gave each of them a penny. Selina wept quietly. Agnes saw her and sent the children back home by themselves.

'You three run back for your tea, I need a word with your mother. You boys go and play in the yard for a minute,' she said to James and Leonard. She sat Selina next to her and got her to tell what the matter was. While Selina spoke, Agnes sat quietly and listened. Selina finished by saying she couldn't make any sense of it.

'I don't want to interfere,' she said.

'But what?' Selina looked at her and dried her damp cheeks with her handkerchief. 'What is it Aggie?'

'You don't think there's someone else do you?'

A wave of fear and shame hit her. How dare she suggest…?

She no longer wished to share her emotions with anyone; even with her closest friend.

'Only… last summer,' Agnes continued, 'I did think I'd seen him with someone at the bonfire.'

Selina tried to remember back then but couldn't. Then she remembered the letter she had found that time in Rab's pocket.

'I'd better be getting back,' she said. 'You were mistaken, it couldn't have been him.'

'No, no. I dare say. Look don't worry, he'll be back like Bo-Peep's sheep. Ignore him, he'll come round, and be dragging his tail. You see.'

That same evening Charlie persuaded Rab to go with him to the pub. He asked him about the game, a friendly against *the Wednesday*, it being cup weekend and *the Wednesday* also having been knocked out in the early rounds. Rab was not very talkative but Charlie persisted, 'Tha shouldn't let bad results get thi down so much Rab.'

'Oh, I'm not bothered about that, we only had a handful of first team players on the field – I'm more fussed about how I played misen usually. I can be happy if the team's lost and I've played well. No, I'm fine.'

'We went round to tha's today.'

Rab looked up from his drink.

His brother continued, 'Edith's beautiful – tha's a lucky man tha knows. Why don't tha get back home Rab?'

'Tha wanting rid on us?'

'Nah, it's not that. It's just tha should be wi' thi family. They're missing thi.'

'I'll sort summat. After next weekend. We're away at Sunderland. They're our biggest threat now. And we've still got to play 'em twice. I need to focus on that.'

'What's that got to do wi' owt? Rab – thi family needs thi.'

'I can't do it Charlie. I can't deal wi' it and concentrate on mi football. Just gi' us a bit longer eh? Please. I can't explain it any better than I have. She's not Selina Howell any more. She's gone back to being Selina Smith – it don't feel like my house.'

Some of Charlie's mates came in the pub. Rab didn't know them but he could tell they were miners: like dogs bred for a purpose they were small and wiry but heavy across the back and they walked differently, shoulders forward. Charlie raised a hand to them.

'Nah then Charlie!' one of them said. 'Tha gonna win on Sat'day then Rab?' It wasn't a question that expected a reply and was followed by the more important business. 'What can I get yer both?'

'I'll be getting back Charlie, I'll leave thi to it,' Rab said.

'Oh come on have one on us Rab.'

'No ta.' He left them knowing he'd breached a code of conduct. Charlie wouldn't mind.

As he walked down the street in Darnall back towards Charlie's house Rab turned up his collar and pulled his cap down tight as the cold north wind blew sleet onto the back of his neck. The air was acrid as chimney pots struggled with the wind for possession of and mastery over their choking emissions. The wet pavements reflected the light from the street lamps; the sleet making them more than usually slippery, giving the flagstones a speckled texture. A day off tomorrow. He'd perhaps go to church with Charlie, Eliza and Clara; then on Monday it was back to Matlock in preparation for Saturday's game. Only two nights on the sofa.

With his head down he didn't notice a figure approaching. It was not until he was almost upon the man that he realised – he saw a pair of boots in front of him, stationary. He looked up. There, obstructing his route was Dennis, grim-faced. He went to step round him on the road side. Nothing to say.

A firm hand on his shoulder half spun him round as he tried to pass.

'No tha dun't. I've been looking for thi!'

Rab looked him in the eye. 'I've nowt to say. Get thi hand off us!'

'But I've got summat to say to thi, tha little sod!'

'Say it then and be gone!'

'What the hell's tha playing at – walking out on thi wife and kids, eh? Who's the *lubni* tha's running round after?'

'Get on thi way – I've nowt to say. Tha's had too much to drink again Den.'

'Cheeky get. I see tha's not denying it then – the famous footballer with his *lubni*!' Who is she then thi whore?'

'Fuck off back home. It's none of your business.'

'*Mandi maurova tooti!*' Dennis leaned forward; eyes wild. 'She should never have married thi!'

'No she probably shouldn't; we'd have all been a lot happier then.'

Dennis moved forward, clenching his fists.

Rab sneered. 'Oh, gi' o'er. Tha's *motto*, old man.'

Dennis lunged and swung a fist at Rab's head. A look of surprise that he hadn't made contact went across Dennis' face as Rab leaned back; Rab then instinctively responded with a well aimed fist to the lower ribs as the older man was caught off balance. Dennis tottered and sank to his knees on the edge of the pavement.

'Go home!' Rab said. He took one look at his father-in-law kneeling, head bowed, and turned and walked on.

A few paces on, he heard a noise then felt a searing pain in his backside as a boot made contact. Dennis had flung himself at him with a flying kick. Rab turned. Dennis was glowering at him, slightly hunched as if catching his breath.

'Tha cowardly bastard!' Rab raged and without thinking smashed his fist into the other man's jaw with a dull thud: Dennis collapsed onto the wet pavement. The jolt had gone through Rab's wrist and his elbow joint and he felt the sting in his knuckles. This time Dennis did not get up; he propped himself against a low wall, fumbling for his handkerchief; humiliated. A window sash scraped up and a woman in curling papers stuck her head out into the darkness: 'What's going on out there?'

'Nowt, missus, it's all over,' Rab said. It was. He kept an eye over his shoulder though as he went, just in case, this time. It was painful to walk.

He got to the house and washed his hands in the scullery, running his bruised knuckles under the cold water. He'd had worse.

'You just missed Dad,' said Eliza, as Rab entered the living room. 'He wanted a word with you.'

'I know. I bumped into him just now.'

'Is everything all right?'

'Yeah, we just had words that's all.'

Eliza gave Rab some supper. He felt his sore right knuckles under the table and wondered how Dennis would explain himself when he got home and Jemima saw the state of his clothes and his swollen jaw. He'd probably be too proud to admit who'd done it to him. Then he took a candle through to the front room and curled up on the small horse-hair sofa, trying to avoid putting weight on his bruise. His heart was still pounding – it was definitely over now. He could not bear to look at that man again, never mind share a roof with him. He felt for the bruise on his backside, it was the left side and the bone in the middle.

He blew out the candle and lay in the dark; eyes open. He pulled his knees up to his chest and tried to feel like Ada was holding him, but instead he just felt alone. Later he heard Charlie come home, and low voices in the living room. Then later he heard them climb the stairs and the sound of feet on the boards above his head. The house went quiet. At some point that night he slept.

Chapter 26

There were fourteen of them on the three o'clock train to Matlock on the Monday, including reserves. Needham wasn't with them; he had been at his father's bedside in hospital all weekend. However, concern for their captain's welfare or that of his father was secondary in most of the players' minds to thoughts of how this would affect Saturday's game, what with Tommy Morren missing too, him having been called up to play for England in the International in Belfast. Johnson was a good stand-in for one; but both? And such a crunch game too. Bill tried to reassure them all that Needham wouldn't miss the game – a herd of elephants wouldn't stop him he said, but Rab could sense the tension, everyone was afraid of losing this one. This game could decide the championship; win it and they'd go seven points clear, lose and Sunderland would close the gap to three.

Friday 4th March 1898

On the Friday, Charles Stokes was already at Midland Station when the team arrived for the train north. Rab observed him nodding his head and moving his lips as he counted them all in: just the sort of man who makes his wife fill out a little book of all household expenses and then checks them every week.

Needham's father had died. The word was that it was gangrene: he'd been injured by a piece of iron falling on his foot down the pit. But, as Bill had predicted, their captain was there to lead them, though looking pale and drawn. The team to face the Wearsiders was likely to be same eleven as for the two Villa games – the first time since that they had all been picked.

259

Bill was hard at work trying to lift spirits. He pointed out to Cocky Bennett that he had a bit of thread on his jacket. Cocky pulled at the short length of red cotton and it increased in length – it wasn't until it was several feet long that he discovered a reel of red cotton thread inside his pocket.

Then once on the train and settled in their seats he took the stage again:

'I've got a good one for you. There's this flea at the circus on the front leg of a brown bear and he hops over to his mate: "Here come on," (Bill spoke in a high squeaky voice), "let's go and have a game of golf old chap." "Golf!" says his mate who was just taking a bite out of a hyena's leg, "Where in the realm of Barnum are we to play golf?" "Why ain't that obvious? Over on the lynx of course!" Most of them laughed, but Harry Thickett looked bemused. This made Bill roar even louder, "Oh Harry! Thickett by name…" and then a play scuffle broke out which ended in Bill's tweed cap being held hostage out of the window as the train rattled through deepest darkest South Yorkshire.

It was a long journey to Sunderland and seemed to involve a lot of throwing of bags in and out of guard's vans. Attempts were made to pass messages from one compartment to the other by shouting out of the windows; then at almost every station there was a change of personnel between compartments – like some sort of bloody daft parlour game George said.

As they crossed the Wear in the evening to reach the Roker Baths Hotel, Rab looked out from the brake, high up on the bridge. Down below in the gloom, picked out by lamps was the dark seething, scarred landscape: waste tips, railway sidings, wooden jetties reaching out to the river, coal trucks, cranes, chimneys, the ugly, sprawling colliery perched on the river's edge, and menacing ships with grimy sails whose masts reached up to the parapet of the bridge. If the Don were a gentle but sullied maiden, this river was a course, pox-ridden whore, lifting her foul skirts at passers-by.

Saturday 5th March 1898

They had kippers for breakfast and walked on the sands at Seaburn in the morning. Snow still lay in patches from the night before, white flecks against the black of the coal dust sands. Their breath hung, adding to the stillness of the fret and the hush of the gentle breakers that wrapped them as they hugged the sea's edge.

No one mentioned the game. Rab felt sure that, like him, they all had it on their minds and their conversation was an effort to drag their thoughts away. He couldn't easily join in the small talk – the feeling that everything was stacking up against him loomed so large – it was all going wrong. As he walked briskly behind the others on the firm wet sand he became conscious of the movement of his limbs, the strength of his legs. It no longer gave him confidence – now he just worried – if he was fit and strong now that meant it could all go wrong and he'd get injured again. But at least the bruise that Dennis had given him had gone. In the week he had been so committed to training that George had ordered him to slow down. He had to outperform everyone, especially the younger ones. He'd wanted to do more ball work – he and several of the others had vented their frustration at George. His timing was out and he needed to get back to where he was before, to practise through-balls, free-kicks and tackles. He needed to do it over and over until he got the touch right. He knew he wasn't ready – he would not have time in the game to get it right, he wasn't as sharp as he wanted to be. However, there had been no way: you had to be starved of the ball, so you'd be hungry for it. Not over-harden your legs.

They sat around in the drawing room; then, after dinner, the brake made its way to the Newcastle Road grounds. Rab leaned across to Needham: 'Here Nudge where's all our supporters? Wouldn't you expect them to be milling about by now? All we've had is locals having a go at us.'

'I don't think there'll be many.'

'What? there's bound to be a few hundred at least. After the game last week I'm sure Ambrose Langley said that they'd had a thousand here just a few week ago?'

'For some reason the train companies haven't laid any excursions on today.'

'Tha's kidding right, Nudge?' said Fred.

The captain shook his head. 'I daresay there'll still be some that's made it – and it's all about the way we play that counts, not the noise our supporters make.'

Rab had been suppressing his nerves all morning, and walking by the sea's edge had helped, but this shook the loose ground he was standing on. No supporters! Sunderland at once felt very foreign, hostile. Their supporters always brought a bit of home with them.

'I bet some *Wednesday* supporter in the railway offices nobbled the excursions!' Bill said. One or two laughed but most seemed to share Rab's mood.

The approach to the ground was busy even though it was a long way off half past three. Sunderland supporters looked something like their own, sporting red and white – but so very different. They somehow didn't move, didn't behave like theirs: there was something outlandish about them, something more fierce, barbaric. They were not sober in their attitude like a Lancashire or a Midlands crowd, who behaved soberly even when they themselves might not be. Or was it just him? He looked at his feet and tried to ignore their taunts, popping eyes and lewd gestures. He had been to Sunderland before, but this was somehow different. It had never felt threatening like this before. There came to his mind that time when Mick, after a game in Middlesbrough, had stripped to the waist to take on those rival supporters who waited for him to question his tackling skills. Good ol' Mick had made his point that day; dumping several of them in the duckpond.

Their changing room was a wooden hut in a corner of the ground. Rab left getting changed as late as he could; only when the others were nearly ready did he get into his kit, saving his jersey for last as usual. The football ground was already full as they sat on the wooden benches. When they had been before there had only been a few thousand; nothing like this. But being second place, taking on the league-leaders, had clearly generated a great deal of interest in the town. Rab put a towel over his head and tried to think of something calming, of being on Wincobank Hill, or by the Don. He held the little leather bag containing the fairy's foot, and now a lock of red hair, and passed it from hand to hand. Then there was a loud bang right beside him making him jump and shaking the hut – someone had kicked the hut outside where he sat. He looked around at his team-mates trying not to show the fear on his face and put the fairy's foot safe in his bag. Now the whole place was rocking and there was more banging.

'It's only some idiots trying to get on the roof for a better view.'

The banging continued and Rab felt he was going mad. His mouth suddenly salivated and he went outside to retch. A group of lads pointed and laughed at him, and said things he didn't understand, in their dialect designed by God for mockery. He didn't look at them but went and sat back on the bench inside.

The banging got louder and then was joined by a creak and the screech of splitting wood.

'Get out quick, the roof's coming in!' It was George who spotted it first and they all made for the door. A number of youths jumped down off the roof laughing as some officials tried to get them down.

'We'll start our warm-up early then,' said Needham. They went out onto the field to jeers from the crowd. There must have been four times more than he'd ever seen here before thought Rab, and not one of them ours. The pitch was in a terrible condition – large patches of straw and sand had been strewn to level it out and fill in divots. The banking behind each goal was already full and only the grandstand seats seemed to have spaces. A brass band paraded in the centre of the pitch as they went through their warm-ups in front of one goal and then took some shots at Bill; the people behind the goal whistling, making clucking noises and shouting "fat chicken" at him. Rab tried to shut it out and concentrate on cleanly contacting the ball on the right part of his foot to loft the ball in.

When to huge cheers the Sunderland team filed out, Needham led his men into the centre of the field.

'This is a tough challenge, but we are not top for no reason – you are the best there is. Play as you can and we'll win, but we'll have to put in a superlative effort and be on our guard. Every man must deny himself and work as one.

'Doig plays the ball to his wing men not through the middle – Rab, you and me need to push up to challenge early before they turn, that'll leave you Harry to stick to the man coming through to pick up the centred ball. Stick to our game, push it wide and go for the space behind their backs.'

Still more spectators arrived; the banks were already a seething mass of faces. Then as the captains were tossing the coin, Rab heard screaming and shouting. Some spectators suddenly jumped the barriers and went up to the edge of the pitch. It was like a dam bursting: a small breach then the whole thing went. People were running round the touch-line and a number even crossed the pitch. One went past Rab, tongue lolling and making a bizarre sound as he ran, like a savage. Within seconds there were spectators on all sides right up to the touch-line. Rab looked round in horror. About a dozen policemen were trying to keep order, struggling in vain to keep people back. Needham was talking to the referee. It was supposed to have been John Lewis again but for some reason he hadn't made it; Rab didn't recognise this one. He couldn't hear what was being said above the noise but he could tell the captain wasn't happy. He was shaking his head and pointing at the perimeter. Hugh Wilson then went over to them and also started gesticulating. The singing was loud and tuneless. Rab felt his chest tighten as fear welled up again. He looked down shocked as his left leg juddered uncontrollably – he jumped on the spot. He thought of the gingerbread lady and tried to conjure up the Lady's Bridge weir in his head. Next to him young Harry Johnson looked down at the ground and kicked the few blades of grass he could see.

Needham places ball on centre spot, shakes his head and walks back, claps his hands and shouts at team. Enough. Let's get it over.

Ralph Gaudie kicks off. Savages roar. Possession lost, back down the hill to defend. Morgan swings in balls from the right; Bob Cain clears. Concentrate on the game! Crowd eddy back from flag for corner, make room for their man; ball headed wide.

Nudge gets ball away: "Leave it to me!" Freddie – long shot. Bastard John Doig; thumps it straight down left. Coming fast, get a foot in, slow him down. Sliding in mud. Young Harry runs up to clear, scuffs it. Wilson gets through. Good work Bob. Bloody hell Harry! Bob gets it out again; everyone at United end, down hill. Sunderland full-back on halfway line, hoofs it back in. Check back. Morgan takes ball past Bob. Shot comes in. Bill doesn't collect. Where's Wilson? Clear it! Ball spins. Mud slips under foot. Hit the ground. Huge cheer. Bill retrieves ball from net. "Bloody hell Rab!" he screams, "that were going out!" Can't look at savages. Clown! Fucking clown! Bill slams ball down. No where to hide. Sweat runs cold down sides; down arms. Hemmed in on all sides by foe. Oh Christ! Should've left it Rab. Don't get flustered Rab. Better luck next time Rab.

Got to redeem it. No errors now. But this mud. We push up. Savages spilling onto pitch. Ref blows. Stops game. Savages jumping about. One bloody lone policeman walks the touchline.

Needham shouts. We'll get one back! Keep possession! Gaudie shoots inches wide. Fast passing. Jock Cunningham dribbling run, must score, shoots over bar. Jeers from savages. Ball fed down left. Wilson. Outside unchecked. A better tackle! Bill's trademark long kick. Nice passing: Ralph to Freddie and back. Must be! Hits bar, headed clear for corner. No room to take it. Savages jostle. Fuck off they say. Not far off half-time. Cocky takes another corner. Ball cleared. Control it, lob it back in. Jock goes up for it. Goal! Total silence except for the half dozen United committee men and reserves clapping, ridiculously. Jock's forehead mud spattered. They shake his hand; pat his back. Walk back for retake, head down.

Young Harry goes for Wilson. Wilson skips past him. Cross comes in. Blocked. Push up. Left-winger shoots. Offside.

As they head off at half-time, Bill came alongside Rab, 'Did you not see the ball was going wide?'

'I thought Wilson was coming in, I had to clear.'

'Well that worked didn't it. Buffoon!'

'If you were so bloody sure it were out why didn't you shout to leave it!'

Needham patted Harry Johnson on the back and encouraged him. They congratulated Cunningham on his header. No one mentioned Rab's ball in that gifted it to him, or the times he'd rescued Harry. Needham just referred to conceding an "unfortunate" goal while they drank their Bovril; he was confident they could get something out of this game. He addressed Johnson: 'We'll try pushing you out right and see if we can link you up with

Cocky – we need to work the right more.' No one spoke to Rab; but then no one said much.

The crowd on the pitch again. Ref trying to get it clear to re-start. John Lewis would have called this off. Idiots.

Wilson gets ball from kick off. Where's Harry? Nudge cuts in, gets touch. Wilson through. Shit! Can't get back. Bill stays on his line. Fires it in from fifteen. Savages spill onto pitch, run across Bill's goal. Screaming. Taunting. Bill shoves one over on his arse.

Stop them scoring again. Get the better of Billy Dunlop. Defending. Always defending. Hoofing down hill. Whistle blows. Savages running in front of Bill again. What's Nudge playing at. Harry's just watching game. Throw-in: threats from savages. Taps on shoulder, pokes in back. Bloody funny that. Fucking hilarious. Twat! Useless Linesman. Ref stops game again.

Ball through to their right wing. Ref blows offside. Still he crosses ball and shot goes in. Savages cheer: idiots. We had yer!

Back defending again. Jim Leslie through, pushing up to line. Foot in! And again. Ricochets into net. Savages leer and scream through net. Hats twirl in air. Bill furious. Others look blankly. Contempt, disdain in eyes. Know they're defeated. Let them down. Frantic efforts to recover respect. Cocky dribbles through, passes; pick up ball and shoot – just wide. More pressure both ends. Free kick. Chance to score – bastard Doig leaps and clears from under bar. Then all over. Make for stripping room quick, as savages laud their men.

The United were grim-faced in the changing room, grim-faced in their suits, grim-faced in the brake on the way to the hotel where tea was laid on. The Wearsiders still making their way home gave mock cheers as they went past; they were closing in on the United. The town's publicans braced themselves and rubbed their hands – a win like that was even better for trade than a heavy defeat.

Rab was not a part of conversations that took place. He felt on the edge of the team – not where he felt he had always been – at the heart of it. No one used to strike up a conversation without making sure he was listening: him Nudge and Bill at the centre, the others revolving round. Now it was different, he was not included. He was now one of the smaller wheels, on the edge, several drive belts away from the prime mover.

He replayed the goals in his head as if the outcome could have been different, but each time he just relived the same emotion; there was no alternative outcome he could find no matter how he searched. Had he been in the wrong place? Had the ball been going out? Had he misjudged his kick? Had it just been that he'd lost his footing? He heard the cheers and jeers, he saw their faces, their eyes. Was the second one his fault? The third? What had happened – he just could see himself tussling with Jim Leslie and stopping a shot, then the ball was in. Where were the others? Where had Bill been; and where was Bob? How could that have been his fault? Someone else must share the blame. How had Leslie got the ball to start with? His memory played him false.

'Don't look so glum Rab,' said Needham.

'I'm not it's just…'

'Don't worry about it, we all play badly sometimes.'

Rab wanted to take him on, shout at him, but he couldn't find it in himself. Badly? He hadn't played well, but no worse than most of them! Johnson had played badly; he'd made a few errors that were inexcusable. When others made mistakes it was nothing; when he slipped it was have a go at Rab time. Put him down to make themselves look better. He'd played his best but it was out of his control. If the championship were to be lost it wouldn't be down to him – though he knew they were all thinking they'd lost because Rab were shit. Needham himself was to blame for the second goal – that finished the game off – where had he told Harry to position himself? How come Wilson was unmarked when he ran forward? It was like everyone had thought: where's Tommy? In bloody Belfast, that's where!

They stayed in Sunderland on the Saturday evening, some of the players taking the opportunity to slip out quietly for refreshment: warm sodas being ordered from the station bar as they waited for their train in the morning. They then travelled to Middlesbrough for a friendly against South Bank which had been arranged for the Monday: George Waller, Ralph and Freddie renewing old acquaintances, which ensured a convivial atmosphere before during and after the game. So convivial in fact that more warm sodas were required before breakfast the next day. Ralph and Fred met up with family members – they were on home territory and swelled with pride at bridging the gap between the two clans. Rab felt part of neither. That old feeling of belonging, of comradeship, was not there. He felt he was watching them all dispassionately from outside as introductions were made and hands shaken. Rab observed how changed Needham seemed in just a few days; he was now his usual self – sharp, and oozing self-confidence, enjoying being the centre of attention. Him and George were deep in conversation with one of the South Bank players – a forward: tall, well-constructed, dashing, and sporting the most impressive of moustaches.

Chapter 27

Tuesday 8th March 1898

It was teatime when Rab pushed open the door to Charlie's house. He instantly knew something was wrong: there was no friendly greeting to welcome the returning traveller. Clara glanced at him, something in her eyes as she was sent up to her room.

'Sit down Rab,' said his brother.

'We've heard what happened.'

For a brief moment Rab thought this was perhaps a remarkable display of sympathy following Saturday's result, but that didn't quite fit. He stayed silent.

'Henry came round wi' thi things. He told us what tha did to Dennis.'

Rab made to rise from his chair. He didn't want to listen to this.

'Sit down Rab. Just listen – tha's left us little choice. I've found thi a room to let. Tha'll like it, it overlooks the river. It's a widow that lives wi' 'er son. It's a decent room. Four shilling a week wi' attendance, less if tha don't want so many meals.'

'What did he say about Dennis?'

'Only that tha bust his jaw open.'

Eliza bit her lip and looked away towards the window.

'It weren't like that, he were the one what...'

'I don't want to know Rab, he's our father-in-law, tha shows him respect. He's an old man.'

'Ah, but he still kicks like a young neddy!'

'I've had thi stuff sent round there already.' Charlie rose from his chair and went to the door. Rab picked up his bag and followed him outside.

'Selina didn't want thi going round and upsetting the kids, making a scene.' Rab didn't speak. 'Perhaps things'll blow over. Gi' it time and she'll have thi back, but we can't keep thi here, not after what's happened.'

'He attacked us Charlie. I didn't do owt except defend misen.'

'It makes no difference. Tha shouldn't have done it. Eliza's really upset. His face is a reight mess: it's not good for her. We can't be fallin out wi' the folks over this.'

Charlie told him the address, just off Attercliffe Road.

Things were just getting worse. Everything was against him now, and he'd just been thrown out by his brother, his best friend. Sent to some dismal lodging house.

The terrace was indeed by the river; overlooking huge hills of coal and coke on the opposite bank. The breeze carried the aroma of metal industries, the Lumley Street refuse destructor, the bone mill and the river. He reached the door to the house and fantasised about it being opened by the gingerbread woman: Mrs Feather – it would fit. At least the name suggested someone soft and gentle. The door was opened by a middle aged woman, small and neat, in black but wearing a white apron. Not the gingerbread woman and rather more metallic than feathery; the sort of woman who would equate a failure to change nets every fortnight and to scrub the step every Saturday with being a loose woman. A cat, black and white to match its mistress, rubbed round her legs. She let him in.

'Your brother has vouched for you Mr Howell, and he convinced me to let you have the room before I'd even met you; but he seemed a nice enough young man.'

She spoke as if to imply that the specimen before her was somewhat less than "nice enough" by contrast.

'Yes Missus. He's as good as they come is Charlie.'

'I understand you're a footballer.'

'Yes Missus.'

'Normally I'd be looking for someone in a steady job, but my son, my other son, Willie, who works as a clerk in the Ironworks, he said he'd seen you play and persuaded me against my better judgment. It's four shillings a week up front – your brother tells me you don't always eat in; in which case I'll knock a bit off. I'll show you the room.'

It was the room at the back, looking onto the yard. There was a single bed, a wardrobe, a washstand and a few framed prints, cut out of magazines, of broken castles.

'It's my son's room: our Edward, who's in Africa with his regiment. It's only while he's away you understand.' She paused as Rab saw thoughts go through her mind. 'You're a single gentleman I take it: because I cannot allow lady visitors for any reason whatsomever.'

'That's fine by me.'

'And I don't approve of late hours.'

'Nor do I. Though sometimes I don't get back from matches or club commitments while eleven.'

'Your things are over in the corner.' She indicated two sacks on the floor by the window.'

'If Edward comes home on leave I'll have to ask you make other arrangements.'

'Of course. I don't know how long I'll be…' He didn't know how to finish the sentence.

'I'll leave you to settle in then. I've some cold ham and potatoes if you want some supper.'

'Thank you, I would like summat. Shall I come down?'

'Yes, down to the living room at the back.'

He tipped the sacks out onto the bed. There were half a dozen shirts, collars, an overcoat, a suit, a pair of black serge trousers, some underwear, his mandolin and a pair of boots. He picked up a brown paper envelope from which fell brass shirt studs, and a small medal made of bronze – an enamel shield on the front and some writing including his name on the back – from when they lost to Villa in the Birmingham Cup. He pulled a piece of woollen cloth from the envelope, white with three rather foolish looking lions with red eyes embroidered on it – the badge off his jersey from when he had represented his country. Nine goals they had scored, one of them his. And yet they'd never picked him again. Face didn't fit. Like Bill – best goalie by far but only picked once, last year. Better a college boy than a pit man. He found his white England cap in the pile, put it on and sank back on the bed. That was it – all the

271

possessions he had in two sacks and one kit bag. He wanted Little Selina on his knee, to call him "silly daddie."

*

That week he got up when called by Mrs Feather, went to training and headed back to his room where he'd lay on the bed staring at the ceiling till teatime. He trained hard, too hard: but it felt like a waste of time. There was no joy in it, no sense of achievement, no warm feeling of relaxed, tired muscles, of getting fit for a contest – of strength. He felt numb, nothing – the exercises being no more than monotonous repetitions. Not even the release of kicking a ball. After Cocky and Ralph had openly argued with George's methods and been disciplined for their efforts there was no chance now of staying behind to train with a ball even if he could see any point to it. It was clear he was being squeezed out – ignored more each time he turned up: as if one day someone would turn round to him and say: "Tha still here?"

They were playing Glasgow Celtic on Saturday in a match that had been dubbed the Championship of Great Britain – everyone hated the presumption that the English Championship was already won, that the United had already been anointed when the fixture was decided upon: damned ill omen that. It was sure to come back and bite them. Then the following Saturday they were down at the Crystal Palace representing the English League against the top amateur side, the Corinthians, in the Dewar Shield. Rab had assumed he wouldn't be playing on Saturday – that he would never play again – but he got no indication from Waller or Needham either way, perhaps he would be given a chance after all.

He found he got on well enough with Mrs Feather – she kept herself to herself and didn't expect any more of others. She cleaned his room while he was out and had a fire made up for him if he said he would be back during the day. Her son, who liked to be called Will, but was Willie to his mother, was equally quiet. At first he plucked up courage to ask Rab polite questions, but getting only the briefest of responses soon gave up and just kept glancing up at Rab over his teacup, before being hushed out on his way to work by his mother. Or, in the evening while Rab sat on his own at the table eating his tea, the son would read bits of the newspaper to his mother: anything that took his interest or anything about overseas campaigns where there might be a mention of the elder son's regiment, such as talk of war with France over West Africa, or Anglo-Egyptian campaigns. 'Our Edward might be there,' she would say. This was a new experience for Rab – whole newspaper articles being read out, bringing to life the world beyond. If anyone on the train to matches read the paper it was silently or only snippets about England's latest batting collapse in Australia. There were the almost daily updates on what was believed to be Gladstone's slide towards death – something to do with his nose apparently. His nose was being operated on by something called Rontgen rays but the boy could provide no explanation as to what this was. 'Is there no limit to what they can do these days!' his mother exclaimed. As he smoked his pipe with the damaged nose, Rab felt somehow responsible for this. He'd have to get a new one with the Queen's head on perhaps. Rab even managed to chuckle for the first time in a while, almost startling himself – there was a story about a Danish consul on the way from London to Newcastle who wanted to be in the first-class carriage. He got off the train when it stopped just outside London to make his way along the platform, but failed to get back on in time – he ended up hanging on to the outside of the train as far as Peterborough being unable to attract attention. The carriage was "built for the convenience of those inside rather than outside passengers" according to the newspaper! Then there was the story about a new second moon that had been sighted – it was believed to be two and a half times further away than the old moon and was only given to shining occasionally. Rab told the boy he'd keep a look out for it.

Saturday 11th March 1898

Mrs Feather poured his tea and dolloped thick porridge into his bowl, much thicker than he cared for, having been sat in the pot

273

since her son had had his half an hour before – but he wouldn't say anything. She busied around the kitchen while he ate. Then, as soon as he put his spoon down from the last mouthful, the bowl was whisked away and switched for a plate with two rashers of bacon, an egg and a slice of bread. He took the hint and ate quickly, the cat looking up at him uncleanly with its penetrating eyes.

Once he had finished he said: 'Right I'd best be off then,' even though he was not due at the ground for another three hours. He shouted "Ta Missus," pulled the door behind him and headed for the Attercliffe tram.

In town, he whiled away time in the Fargate café where he had been with Ada. He could capture something of her by sitting at their table, trying to remember her words, her scent. He was ashamed at what he had done. He had followed his desires, his passions without thinking of where they would lead, what damage he would do. Those passions were animalistic and should have been mastered. Charlie had known that. He had claimed her for his own when he had no right to. He had stolen her love and now it couldn't be returned. Perhaps, some day, a real gentleman would come along and... no he hated the thought. He realised he would rather she pined for him than that. O what a brute he was! But what was so wrong with wanting to love, to live?

Could he even go back to Selina? Only if she wanted him, wanted him as he was and didn't want to maintain this edifice to keep him in – where he had to fit in with her standards, with her parents, with this way of life she tried to weave, where he had to have his role and had to stick to it, where threads were wound around his chest. If they could start again, just the two of them with the kids in a new place with a front garden with woodbines growing round the door and a back garden dug over for vegetables, with some animals. Perhaps then they could at least co-exist and he would be happy enough and would see the kids grow up. "Fucking idiot!" he muttered to himself. He paid for his second breakfast and headed to the Moor. There he stopped to see what was going on: a number of people were standing looking at something. The road was closed and a gang of navvies were digging pits. He went on his tiptoes to look over a man's shoulder.

'It's for t' trams,' a man explained to his wife. 'Thems is vaults for storing all t'electric in.' There were one or two sage nods.

'Ar. Reckon tha's reight,' said another.

Rab was at the pavilion early and was sat on his own with his pipe when Needham arrived.

'Ay up Nudge, how's tha doin, and how's the family? – terrible business.'

'We're coping Rab; thanks for asking. I fear for mother though – it were such a shock for her. She blames herself; but the stubborn ol' bugger wouldn't go into hospital, and what with his diabetes an' all...'

Rab looked into the fire. There was quiet. Needham shuffled in his chair.

'Rab, I've got to ask thi summat. Mr Stokes had me in his office. They know tha's no longer living at home. Thing is they're thinking it's a repeat of what happened before.'

Rab glanced at him then back at the fire as if ignoring his captain.

'There's no other way of putting it – they think tha's seeing someone else.'

'I don't see as how it's got owt to do wi' them, but it's not true.'

'But they know Rab!'

'They're right, I'm no longer at home. I left, but I'm living in lodgings. There's nowt else going on. They've a fucking cheek!'

'Tha'd better button thi lip, Rab. They pay thi wages – show some respect. Tha knows tha's to tell 'em if tha changes address.'

'I'll go to the office to tell 'em. Look Nudge, it's been a tough few weeks, that's all. I'm sorted now.'

'That's shown on the pitch. If tha don't keep things steady in life, it affects thi game.'

'No, it hasn't affected me. I still give everything.'

'I meant at Sunderland.'

'I know what tha meant, but that weren't just down to me.'

'No, it's a team game.'

Bill came in with his arm on Harry's shoulder. 'We up for beating the Jocks then?'

275

'Aren't we always,' Rab said.

There were fourteen of them around the players' table at dinnertime: eleven plus reserves. After they had eaten, Rab learned from George that he was in the team. He looked out of the window onto the empty pitch; he felt he could look forward to walking down the steps onto the grass – there wouldn't be a huge crowd, but enough. And there was no pressure – not much at stake except his own performance; a chance to make up for last week. Things hadn't gone great for him since the Wolves game really – then he'd got injured. Good ol' George had thrown him a lifeline.

Three quarters of an hour before kick-off he made his way down to the changing room with the others and started to go through his routine: sit down in his spot – where he'd always sat for the last eight years – almost to the day it must be, near the end of United's first season. How nervous he'd been that day even though it was only a friendly against Halliwell in front of no more than a thousand or so. Then to score and get the pats on the back and the applause! And two weeks later he'd scored again, against Nudge's old side when the beloved was still an unknown kid. He was always on the score sheet back then, when he had been a forward. That had all changed when Billy Hendry came from Preston's Invicibles and moved him to half-back, made them play scientific football and the combination play that Needham now delighted in. These days he just helped others to glory and the goals he grabbed for himself were precious.

Having settled, he next stood back up and got out his kit and arranged it in order: boots on the left, then socks, never shinguards, then knickers. Then he hung up his beautiful red and white jersey. If he could play well today it would be a turning point. He would not let Sunderland catch them. He picked up his left boot and started adjusting the lacing. He looked over his shoulder as Needham walked in; Johnson was behind him.

'I'm sorry Rab – there's been a change of plan. Take a rest from this one. It'll do thi good.'

Rab looked into Needham's left eye which fixed him coldly.

276

Something snapped. He flung his boot to the ground at Needham's feet. It scuttered away and hit the wall.

'Good? What bloody good will it do me! That's just crap and tha knows it! It's Stokes ain't it, poking his nose in. Judging me! I don't know you!'

Needham's expression didn't change; not a flicker. Everyone looked at the ground. Johnson who had come in smirking, looking pleased with himself, looked shocked. Rab tore up his things and stuffed them in his bag. He was humiliated in front of everyone. Cocky quietly handed him his boot which he had fished out from under the bench as he stormed out.

'Fuck off!' he shouted back to no one in particular.

He left the pavilion; eyes were looking at him going the wrong way. He started running away from them. He crossed the road and back, to avoid some *Wednesday* fans on their way to Olive Grove for a reserve game, and kept running until he reached St Mary's Church. He jumped over the wall and slumped against a gravestone where he could not be seen from the street. For what they had done to him he hated the Wearsiders with an intense, visceral hatred that if examined with the head made no sense, it was clearly a madness in him; but this was not a thing of the head: only the heart could see. It sought release through futile violence but, being hidebound, the pressure could only vent internally. The pathetic gypo struggling against forces divine and mortal ranged against him to mock and jibe at his efforts! He clasped his head as if to hold it together. And how could the only ones on his side treat him like that? He winced as he relived the humiliation and imagined their reaction afterwards; saw them laughing at the clown, shrugging off his impetuousness as what you'd expect from a queer foreigner! And Johnson sitting in his spot, hanging a shirt where his had been.

He heard the cheers as the teams came out – every one of them a further insult to him. They were cheering even though he wasn't there, Rab Howell, longest serving player, played more matches for United than anyone else – ever. Forgotten. No testimonial. All sorts of fundraising being done for Mick, as well as for Bob Cain: a smoking concert, a match. But not for the likes of him. Eight years counted for nothing.

In front of him was a gravestone filled with writing. So many words: this person was missed by someone. Would anyone remember him by a stone; would they have anything to say about him? The sounds from the ground sickened him; he had to leave. All the supporters would be in by now. Up on the side of the church a stone face gurned down at him; its grimace with lolling tongue reminded him of the Sunderland supporter. "Fuck off!" he shouted up. A woman, just coming out of the entrance looked at him aghast as he fled.

He found himself walking along, he knew not where, like so many others walking blank-faced, eyes too unhappy to be kind – undone with misery, all life sucked out from them, being beckoned towards their eventual demise.

Where to go? He had told Mrs Feather he wouldn't be back for tea. He couldn't go back yet. As he went past the Yellow Lion, he followed a sudden impulse to go in; it looked warm and inviting. He approached the polished mahogany counter of the public bar. Beyond were glass shelves lined with bottles and cut glass decanters in front of a silvered plate glass in which he caught his sorry reflection. The bar maid smiled at him, flashing her lovely white teeth, shaking her untied mane of curly hair; a pendant which looked like it was made of little diamonds, but obviously couldn't have been, drawing attention to her chest. She was lovely.

'What can I get you sir?'

'I don't know... something strong.'

She poured a whisky and handed it to Rab smiling as if conscious of the effect her teeth made. He paid and gave her a few coppers extra.

The whisky tasted foul, burnt his throat and gullet, but had an almost immediate effect on the pain: it numbed. He coughed a little and the girl laughed at him, sparkled, then went to serve some more customers before coming back to be with him.

'Not seen you here before.'

'No I... I'm not a drinker.'

'I see. Signed the pledge have yer? And what's that you're

drinking, Adam's ale?' As she spoke every word rang out happiness.

'No I'm just…'

'Down on yer luck?'

'You could say that.'

'I'll pour you another then.' She could be no more than seventeen, Rab thought, watching her closely. He was conscious he was staring, but she didn't mind. She leaned forward to pass the glass to him, her breath sweet, and she stayed leaning forward, the pendant swinging in front of her chest; this time her eyes on him as he drank. This glass didn't taste as bad. She took more money off him and gave him a peck on the cheek.

'You must come and see Susie again sir. I like you.'

A man with long, white whiskers entered, ruddy cheeked, gold albert in his waistcoat with a large seal fob dangling from the middle. Trailing smoke from his cigarette he waved his hat at the girl revealing a balding pate. The girl immediately left Rab and went over to serve the whiskered man who squeezed her round the waist and dropped a small stack of pennies into her hand. She put one of the pennies into the slot of the polyphone which stood aginst the bar and wound the handle; it began to play "Sweet Rosie O'Grady"; one or two less than sweet voices joined in when the chorus came round: "And, when we are married, How happy we'll be; I love sweet Rosie O'Grady, And Rosie O'Grady loves me."

Rab, sitting alone, felt sick. He had been dropped like a stone for a regular customer. He had been duped – he'd just fallen for the publican's favourite trick – getting a fine girl to tease money out of the customers. Lure them in. He noticed for the first time in the corner a small boy, aged only three or four, sat on the knee of a man. The man was forcing the young lad to drink from his pewter: the boy turned and screwed up his face to the laughter of adults – one of whom looked like the boy's mother. Rab felt sickened and headed for the door. 'Come and see me again love!' the girl chirped. Out in the cool air he felt worse and his head was banging. He'd walk to sober up, and stop for some fried fish on the way.

He didn't go straight into the house but went over the lane and stood by the wall at the river's edge. The opaque, brown, dead, water swirled slowly about twenty feet below, as it made its way towards the buttress of the bridge. The scene was dominated by the black hills of coal and coke opposite, food for the hungry furnaces of the valley. The wind direction had changed and the air was rich, the stench drifting from the smouldering colliery tip or perhaps the destructor. Salmon Pastures, that was its name! Mrs Feather said her father had fished there as a child; when salmon was so abundant that it was poor man's food. He pulled the little leather bag from where it hung round his neck. He emptied its contents onto his palm: the small lock of hair that Ada gave him, and the fairy's foot. The soft evening light made the lock of hair glow – it was so vivid it could have been taken from a squirrel's tail. He brushed it against his cheek then put it carefully back in the bag.

He turned the tiny fairy foot over in his fingers. It was, as he well knew, just a mole's hind foot; given to him by an old gipsy woman for luck. Fat lot of good it had done him! She was a great-aunt or somesuch, to whom he was presented as a boy. She had stroked his small white hand in her rough hand, brown like old, polished oak – said he would break hearts when he grew up. He held the object in his palm then launched it into the river below – watched it form a tiny hole in the brown water. Then it was gone.

Chapter 28

When Mrs Feather shouted him for breakfast the next day he didn't respond. Dark thoughts had punctuated what sleep he snatched; when all was quiet outside he had lain awake contemplating how everything he touched turned to shite: his relationship with Selina, his family, now Charlie. He turned events over in his mind: if only the railways had run trains to Sunderland, if only John Lewis had been ref, what if he'd not stuck his boot out when that ball from Morgan swung in? But every time he went over it again the outcome was the same. It was as if he were vainly searching for an answer – if only he could figure it out – but he knew he was just torturing himself, destroying himself: that thought only made it worse. He had achieved nothing in his life and what was the point of life if you left no mark: if it just came and went like that of an insect?

Later she knocked on his door saying they were going to chapel. He said he wasn't feeling very well and she said if he wanted it there was some bacon and bread on a plate in the kitchen under a bowl to keep the cat off. He heard the door close, felt the vibration travel up the walls. The house went quiet. He lay on the bed, a dull ache on the sides of his head, and tried to sleep some more – to make it all go away. His mind felt blunted – like thoughts in a dream that were more feelings than clear notions; there was no direction, no meaning to it. It was like moving through a dim wood, eyes covered with a gauze, ears muffled, legs shackled, arms bound. There was no comfort in sleep to be found. He rose and washed under the tap in the scullery. As he scrubbed his hair, the cat came up and rubbed against his legs; he started and banged his head on the tap. He cursed it and called it a *mochardi* creature; it hissed at him as he heeled it away.

He filled a bottle with cold tea, took some food which he wrapped in paper and put them in his pocket. He wasn't sure where he was going but he would wander about and not return until teatime.

His lodgings were not far from the Turkish baths which he headed for instead of training on Monday – he couldn't face them, he was not sure he ever could again. He sat surrounded by steam; the sense that he felt of being removed from the world easing his brain, and something still felt alive in him when the attendant scraped and pummelled his body.

In the woods where the celandines carpeted the ground, or on the hill as Spring moved on around him, he had a vague notion that something should happen, but that Rab Howell was somehow other, and this... this was just here and now, did not seem to reach beyond the beetle on the ground or that catkin. The days of the week were of no relevance. A small boat that lost its moorings in a storm, now adrift on the sea.

Wednesday 16th March 1898

Mutton stew and bread was on the table in front of him. Mrs Feather and her son sat babbling over the newspaper. There was a knock at the door. The boy was sent to answer it and returned.

'It's a gentleman for you Mr Howell.'

'Did he say who he was?' his mother said.

'No mother, I forgot to ask, but I thought I recognised him from somewhere.'

'You finish your tea Mr Howell. I'll show him into the front parlour to wait.'

Rab ate without hurrying and then went through, it not having occurred to him to be curious as to who it was.

Stood by the empty fireplace, warming himself on an arrangement of red paper roses in the grate, was Ernest Needham.

'Rab.' Needham spoke his name, conveying both a greeting and an inquiry in the inflexion of his voice.

'Nudge, I didn't think...'

282

'I owe thi an apology Rab. I handled Saturday very badly, and wanted to tell thi, and put things right.'

'It's too late Nudge, it's all over.'

'What is?'

'Everything. Nothing can be made to be how it were before.'

'That's not true.'

'Ain't it? I'm finished aren't I?

'No Rab, it's not like that.'

'If tha can't be honest wi' us, tha'd better just go now.'

'All right. Can we sit? I will be honest wi' thi. The fact is that Harry is now first choice at right half.' Rab knew it, but hearing it was like a stab in the chest. He avoided Needham's gaze and fixed on the glass dome containing a basket of wax fruit, grapes, pears and apples, that stood in the window. 'It's not just been my decision – there were a mix up on Saturday and Mr Stokes insisted on Harry playing. I'm sorry for not having seen it coming and spoken to thi beforehand, and I were wrong to tell thi in front of the rest of the lads.'

'I bet you all had a reight good laugh at us after.'

'No. No one laughed. They all thought tha were right to react the way tha did. Most on 'em had a cob on wi' me. They're on thy side Rab.'

'It's no use. I can't go back.'

'Tha should Rab. I'll tell thi for why. Look, I've been thinking and I'm bein honest wi' thi. If tha keeps training and keeps in shape and show a good attitude, I reckon we can get thi into a good team.'

'What? What's tha on about?'

'The Committee think tha should move on for thi own good as well as that of the team. I'm not going to judge thi on thi private life but they've spoken to thi family and the Committee have made their disapproval plain.' Rab shook his head slowly, avoiding eye-contact. 'But there's good news,' Needham continued. 'We've spoken to Tom Watson at Liverpool by telephone. He's a fine trainer, one of the best, a good club secretary, and is building up a good side there. He's interested in signing thi – it's thi experience he wants – to play alongside his youngsters, to steady the side. We told him tha'd do a good job for 'em.' Rab looked up, Needham was being sincere, not stringing him along – he wouldn't do that. 'But if tha drops out o' training, that'll frighten 'em off. Come to training Rab.'

'I don't know as I can face the others.'

'They want thi back too. Like I said, most of 'em said tha was right. Anyhow, unless tha turns up that's it, they'll sack thi.'

'So when did Watson want me?'

'Nowt were said, it were all tentative; sounding us out. But it could happen sooner rather than later. I put in a good word for thi – tha'd slot straight in there – well tha's seen 'em for thisen. They've struggled to keep a toe-hold in the first division but now Watson's there, tha never knows, they might come good some day.'

Needham stood up. 'Look I've got to go – it's Mick's benefit concert tonight.' Rab felt another stab. Needham must have read his reaction, though he didn't know he'd let it show. 'Tha don't need a benefit yet. There's years left in thi. Tha's still one o' the best half-backs in England.' He held out his hand. 'Tha'll train tomorrow?' Rab took his hand.

'How did Sunderland do on Sat'day?'

'They won two – one.'

'So they're a point behind.'

'It won't matter – it's in our hands. We have to stay confident.'

'But the home game against 'em will decide it.'

'Possibly. We've written to 'em about getting it postponed because it's on the same day as the Scotland International and I'll have to be on England duty.'

Rab let him out, then stood still behind the door. Something had started up; a wheel had turned.

'Mr Howell there's some pudding if you want it!' Mrs Feather called.

He went through.

'Who was that man Mr Howell?' Will asked.

'That? That was Ernest Needham.'

'What at our house! *The* Ernest Needham?'

'There is only one.'

*

284

Rab went to training and went through the motions. He had no enthusiasm but he had given his word; put his fate in Needham's hands. There was nothing else to do; he had been stuck, drifting and there was only one person offering a guiding hand. He had to follow; hear him.

On the Saturday that the United were in London to play for the Dewar Shield against the Corinthians, Rab went on a whim to the English Cup semi-final at Bramall Lane between Southampton and Nottingham Forest. He thought it would be interesting to watch a game as a neutral with nothing at stake, just to watch other styles of play, and test the idea in his mind of not being a United player. Unfortunately, Southampton's red and white stripes spoilt that notion of neutrality and, like many other locals who had turned up to swell the crowd to capacity, he found himself willing on the Southerners who as a result had as big a following as the Forresters.

The United returned from London with injuries to Gaudie and Johnson. Training had some purpose for Rab again; he was told it was likely he would play against West Bromwich Albion, but it was not the same as of old. He still felt on the edge, yesterday's man. It showed mostly with Bill: what had been said, had been felt, had formed something tangible between them, blocking respect and fellow feeling. The victory he was working for did not feel his; it felt theirs.

It was confirmed at clubroom night on Friday that Johnson would not travel in the morning – he was still getting shooting pains in his leg. They had to be at the station for half past nine the next day.

Saturday 26th March 1898

It was one of those days trapped between winter and spring where the seasons fight it out for supremacy. One moment the sun would be warm, then the sky darkened and a snowstorm would lash down sending shivers through every living thing. Prematurely discarded overcoats would be fetched out, buds and bulbs, that had foolishly believed the promises of spring, were dashed, and icy winds tugged and nipped at petals and skirts. Then all would be still again leaving patches of snow, shredded leaves and horizontal crocuses.

Tommy Morren had sent a message that he was ill. There was no way of contacting Harry Howard of the reserve team in time. Ralph Gaudie was with them: so he could slot in to Tommy's position. Also on the platform was the athletic, impressively moustached forward from South Bank, George Hedley.

Needham had to have words with some of them as they waited for their train: there was still chatter going on about 'bloody Sunderland.' The Wearsiders had refused to agree to a new date for the fixture scheduled for the following week. The talk was that Needham had asked the England Committee not to select him, though there was no doubt he would have to put his country first. Both Doig and Wilson had said, however, that they would play for Sunderland rather than Scotland.

'If anyone mentions Sunderland again before the end of today's game, I'll make sure they are disciplined. Your job is to focus on beating West Brom.'

The weather at Stoney Lane was even worse than it had been in Sheffield. There was now a constant gale blowing, which brought in waves of snow, then sleet, then hail. As a result only a couple of thousand had turned out to see the game. When they warmed up it became clear that Gaudie was not fit and couldn't play. Big Neil Logan would have to play at half-back, all six foot of him, incongruous between Rab and Needham.

To Rab only one thing was important: his own performance. His emotional attachment to the team had withered; he would run through walls for his captain though. He didn't want to let him down. First blinding snow whipped across the ground, then icy cold rain, then stinging hail. The Throstles pushed hard, still not having given up hope of the title themselves. Rab showed no lack of effort throughout but he had a tough time against the quick feet of Ben Garfield. He hadn't played for three weeks, didn't quite have the edge he thought afterwards, when they contemplated their two-goal defeat. Logan had been a disaster at half-back, there was nowhere to hide, no letting up. But nonetheless it was a game of missed chances. Everyone was convinced that their first was offside. The second was off a stinger from Garfield which Bill had saved only for the ball to drop perfectly for one of their forwards for an easy poke in. Everyone conceded that they were not at their best when playing in storms and on heavy pitches. The following week's Sunderland match had assumed an even greater importance.

*

It wasn't until training on Tuesday that Rab saw Needham again – on Monday he had been in Wrexham with England. Everyone now knew that Needham would be in Glasgow on Saturday and that the Wearsiders would field a full strength side against them – not releasing their players to play for Scotland.

'Can you believe such a lack of sportsmanship?' Bill fumed. 'Just you see, our supporters will sing about hating Sunderland for years to come after this! If they steal the title from us, I'll personally go up to Sunderland and tear down their town hall brick by brick!'

'Aye, and I'll come and lend thi a hand!' Cocky said. 'Here Nudge, is it true that the Corinthians have offered us their players to make up for it?'

'Yeah, but there's only really G.O. Smith who'd fit the bill but he'll be up in Glasgow too – no, we'll do this on our own – we've got to this point – we've three games left – it's in our hands.'

'Joe Smith in a United shirt – that's something I'd like to see!' said Bill.

Needham had a word with Rab on his own.

'There's good news Rab. Tom Watson wants thi; and Mr Stokes has agreed. It is just a question of getting the Committee to rubber-stamp it now. Saturday will be thi last payday. Mr Watson would like to meet thi: they're playing at Trent Bridge if tha can make it.'

'I'll not be playing here then? I thought with thi up in Scotland...'

'No tha'll be a Liverpool player in all but name by then.'

'I'd still do a job for you.'

'I know Rab, but Harry will be back and Tommy's going to be fit and wasn't selected for England because of doubts over his fitness at the weekend. The other Harry can play.'

'But that makes no sense – let me play!'

'It's not my decision Rab! To be honest, it's not just a football decision.'

*

Friday's training was done on the pitch – passing balls in triangles, taking free kicks with half the team attacking the other half defending. When work was being done with the defence, anticipating the movements of Leslie, Morgan and Wilson, Rab was shoved like a spare part into attacking. When setting up formations for the forwards, Rab was asked to fill in, in defence, while Harry Johnson or Tommy Morren took the corners or free-kicks. He was moved about wherever told to go by George or Bob Cain, who had assumed the captaincy in Needham's absence. He was useful to them only to make up the numbers with two others from the reserves. Rab did his best to put on a front, tried to wear the mask of the old Rab, but there was nothing in it for him. He wondered if they even knew this would be his last day – no one said anything – if they did know they didn't care or were too focussed on the following day's game to reflect on whether they cared or not. Everyone got on with the job in hand in serious fashion, no joking or mucking about.

The team felt they had put in a good session afterwards; they wanted Saturday afternoon to come right then. Rab left the pitch feeling flat; he didn't share their emotions; nothing mattered. Did he wish them well? He wasn't sure; he had felt comradeship with these men. Once, he would have done anything for them: if they had been fighting Dervishes together on the banks of the Athara river, he would have laid down his life for them. How could that bond have dissolved so quickly? Soon he might be gone and they were moving ahead on a different path, leaving him behind without even turning to wave farewell: a path towards something so important that those who were no longer on it didn't matter; those who fell made themselves unimportant by doing so. Yes, he still had respect for some of them, but others he resented. He wouldn't have laid down his life for any of them now.

Saturday 2nd April 1898

It was cold but fresh in the morning when he left for town. Bramall Lane was preparing for a big day, a day in which he had no part; people going about their business, each contributing to the preparations for the event – a whole pyramid of clerks, tradesmen, cooks, and officials; all working together to support the success of those eleven men who would walk out that afternoon against Sunderland in a contest for two points, worth four. He felt in the way, like a man sat in his chair smoking after his tea, whilst his wife tries to tidy up and sweep around him. He collected his wages: four half sovereigns and five florins in an envelope, then went down the pavilion steps and onto the edge of the pitch. Happy Jack was repainting the chalk lines – the six-yard rings around each post. Cocky had once been chased round the pitch when he'd said they did those lines by getting Bill to sit down in his goal then painted round his arse. Jack had his head down and apart from his whistling it was still and quiet. Rab felt the ghosts of this enclosure chill his spine – the cheers, the songs, the crunch of game-winning tackles, the goals and joy, the agony and the hurt. He bent down and plucked a piece of new spring grass from the pitch. He pulled the leather bag from under his shirt and put the grass inside, but stopped. 'Fuckin stupid!' he muttered, and flicked the grass into the air instead. He went back round the pavilion and headed to the station; no longer Rab Howell of the United.

*

He was at Trent Bridge before the Liverpool team arrived – they were probably still having their dinner at a hotel somewhere. He was waiting at the entrance to the grounds when a brake pulled up and he recognised the Anfield men. Tom Watson was the first off: bowler-hatted, big black moustache, stout and moving somewhat stiffly, but still athletic. The team unloaded kit bags and fell in behind Watson whose black moustache preceded the party. He then noticed Rab for the first time, stood watching them, but without any recognition.

'Mr Watson, sir, you wanted to see me.'

'Rab Howell! I didn't recognise yer without yer red and white stripes on man! Forget the Mr Watson sir bit, call w' Tommy!' He shook Rab's hand vigorously and Rab tried to hold his own; he smelt the alcohol on his breath. 'You going to join us then! Welcome, welcome! We're going to do great things, aren't we lads?'

'Way aye Tommy!' one of them said mimicking the affable Geordie.

'Cheeky buggers, this lot Rab,' Rab squirmed as Watson put his arm on his shoulder. 'And they reckon they're good. Well they are – my boys. But they'll get better. I want you to teach 'em a thing or two, knock the cocky sods down a rung or two, eh?'

Rab was introduced to them and shook hands with them all; though he knew many of their names already.

He sat with them in the changing room, and, when they went out, Watson made a point of sitting in between him and the two reserves to follow the game.

'So are your boys going to beat my old team this afternoon?'

'I don't think they are *my boys* any more are they?' Rab said.

Watson laughed and slapped Rab on the back. 'Too right! Too right! You've got the measure of it already! Look I'd be interested in your take on this game – where you think we're weak; how the game plays out; that sort of thing. You're just the first I wanted to bring in this summer. I've got feelers out for others too. I can't wait for next season!' He rubbed his hands together.

'Sounds exciting,' said Rab

'Oh it will be!'

Liverpool lost three goals to two, but Watson made his players feel positive nonetheless. It was clear to Rab that Watson had already moved on in his mind to next season; and, whatever it was that Watson had, it seemed to be infectious, because Rab found himself almost looking forward to September as well. He had hope that gradually the void within him was filling drip by drip.

Watson's presence filled the whole room and the players clearly loved him, although there was obviously a hard edge to the man too: you wouldn't want to get on the wrong side of him. There was more beer at tea than Rab had been accustomed to seeing, in fact it didn't appear to be rationed at all. Rab went with them to the station – they would be changing trains at Sheffield. Watson asked Rab when he'd be joining them. 'I hadn't thought about it,' Rab replied.

'Well I'll sort out lodgings for you – what do you need?'

'Er… just a room will do.'

'What no family?'

'No, it's… a bit awkward.'

'Well not to worry, that makes it very easy – how about tomorrow then? Just check in at the London and North Western Hotel at the station and tell them I sent you; then on Monday morning get a cab to Anfield. You can play on Good Friday then – we've a trip to the seaside – Grimsby Town – just a friendly, how's about that?'

'Er… great, Mr Watson… Tommy.'

'We'll sort out the papers when they come through from Sheffield – we'll see you right money-wise, don't you worry about that.'

'Thank you. And thanks for giving me another chance.'

Watson raised a quizzical eyebrow at him. 'Good man. Howay lads, here's wor train.'

Rab shook hands with Watson on the platform.

Outside the station a couple of happy drunks in red and white mufflers staggered along.

'What were the score lads?' Rab asked.

'One nil to United. Johnson scored – mag…nicifent it were!' They hadn't even recognised him, as if final confirmation he was no longer one of theirs.

On Sunday morning Rab told Mrs Feather he was leaving that evening. He'd be in for dinner but had to get away before tea. He got out four shillings by way of a week's notice but she wouldn't take it off him.

'I'll be sorry to see you leave,' she said, 'you've been no trouble.'

Mrs Feather brought him up his washing, ready ironed and folded, and she said she'd pack him some bread and slices of cold beef for the journey.

In the afternoon he went round to Charlie's. They were just finishing their Sunday dinner when he got there.

'Rab! Good to see thi again. How's it going?'

'I'm good Charlie. Better than in a while.' Charlie took him through into the front room where they could be alone.

'Tha's not been to see Selina?'

'No. Look Charlie, I've come to tell thi I'm leaving. I'm going this afternoon to Liverpool. I'm playing for them next season.'

'Liverpool!' Charlie paused while it sunk in. 'But that's miles away! What about thi family?'

'I dunno. I've got to go – it's a second chance. Tom Watson the Secretary there really wants me – I can put it all behind me and start afresh.'

'No! Tha can't! It's not that easy. Tha's married.' Charlie's eyes were on him; intense. 'She'd still have thi back.'

'But it wouldn't be me going back; it'd be some grovelling, trembling thing. And if I did go back, then what do I do Charlie? I'm a footballer. I've got to play football. I can't stay here no more – there's no job for me. And she only wants me back on her terms if at all. I'm not like thi, Charlie. I can't get a steady job. I can't go back *down*. While I can still play, I've got to. It's my only chance. If I stay here I'm finished. I can't be what she wants me to be. Tha's got to see that?'

'Yeah… it's, I dunno… just sad.'

'I know.' Rab said hanging his head. He looked back up at his brother. 'I thought I should go and see the kids before I go; try and explain.'

'I don't think that's a good idea. It'd only upset 'em. They're settled – tha just turning up, then leaving again will make things worse.'

'What have they been told?'

'Not much, I don't think. Just that tha's had to go away.'

'Well that's true now. I'll follow thi advice. But Charlie, will tha make sure they know I'll always love 'em no matter what.'

'Yeah. I will.'

He collected his bags at Mrs Feather's and caught the tram back in to town. From Lady's Bridge he walked round to McGrail's shop. He hadn't had time to think but he had decided he couldn't just disappear without a word. Being a Sunday, the shop was shut. Upstairs was in darkness – he knocked and got no response so he tried the gate to the yard – this was bolted from the inside. There was no one at home.

It was gone nine o' clock when he arrived at the hotel in Liverpool. He did as Tom Watson had told him and was shown to a room which, with breakfast included, cost more than a week at Mrs Feather's, and it didn't even come with a view of the city. He trained hard and well and was accepted straight away. When he spoke out, the others were told to shut up and listen because "they might learn something." It was a strange feeling: being treated with such respect.

He stayed in the luxurious surroundings of the hotel – they would find him lodgings once he'd settled in and knew what sort of place he wanted.

Sat eating his toast in the dining room on his second morning, he reflected on not having seen Ada before he'd left – he had to at least tell her he'd gone away. So he got directions for the post office with a view to sending a telegram.

On Thursday, the team met up in the morning to travel to Grimsby on the quarter to nine train. Tom Watson came to talk to Rab.

'Well it's official – you're a Liverpool player now, bonny lad – the papers have come through. You cost us a small fortune: one hundred and fifty pounds!' He lowered his voice, 'And there's a small "douceur," as they call it, for you as well.'

He slipped a small bag of coins into Rab's jacket pocket. 'Don't tell no-one mind!'

Rab was taken aback – he hadn't really reckoned on any money changing hands, never mind so much. A hundred and fifty pounds he was worth! That made him smile.

Ada was minding the shop – Wednesdays were usually quite busy, as Saturday's marketing was proved insufficient and the day after was half day closing. She had settled into her routine again, and was looking forward to the Easter weekend and the special time this was in the church calendar. She was starting to feel that something in her mind was settling – she missed Rab but it was not quite so raw; it was not so physical. She had closed that down and her yearning was, she believed, spiritual and that could be tempered by other spiritual sustenance. Easter was a time of renewal; of hope. From now on, the shop would have more than just root vegetables, leeks and sprouts. She ran her hand over the damp, fresh, bunches of watercress and traced her finger along a delicate pink rhubarb stem.

A boy in uniform entered the shop. 'Telegram for A McGrail!' he said in a matter-of-fact way. She thanked him and gave him a penny, trembling: for people like her, telegrams were never good: they always conveyed news of a death or serious illness in the family. She pulled out the slip of paper and read it, mouthing some of the words to make sense of them: "flitted to Liverpool… change trains at Sheffield…" She folded the slip of paper and sat down on an upturned crate – just when everything seemed to be achieving some sort of balance once again!

Good Friday 8th April 1898

The Liverpool team were staying at the Dolphin Hotel in Cleethorpes. They arrived mid afternoon and having dumped their bags went straight out onto the promenade to take in the sights and walk on the pier. They visited the grotto in the pier gardens, rode the switchback and ate salty oysters in an oyster parlour on the way back to the hotel. Tea was accompanied by beer and singing – Tom Watson himself putting in some fine solo performances including one about a riotous football match between the Swifts and the

Macalvenny Wallopers which went down well with his audience. Rab tried to imagine The Philanthropist or the Tooth-yanker breaking into song anywhere outside of the chapel, never mind singing about football, drinking and fighting. The thought made him laugh quietly to himself and he wistfully wished there was someone there who he could share the joke with. Such things that were illicit at United were expected here – several times Rab had received scorn for turning down drinks. It was as if enjoying yourself was an integral part of being in the team, not a by-product or something to be done almost guiltily.

*

Rab went through his usual rituals in the changing room: boots, socks, space for the absence of shinguards, knickers, but this time the jersey was not red and white, not even all white, but, of all colours, blue and white! It was unnatural and looked strange hanging on his peg. He'd start a quiet rebellion, suggest there was a gipsy curse on blue and white – red was a much more auspicious colour he'd tell Tom. He smiled and loosened the bootlaces.

It was a glorious day – just right for football – bright but not hot, blue sky and white clouds drifting across the ground, seagulls calling high above. Liverpool won three – one and Rab felt he had commanded the half back line. Tom congratulated him on his start. 'Just you see Rab, just you see!'

They didn't dwell long after the game in order to get the last train back across country, which left at half past five. It was only when he was sat on the train that Rab realised he had forgotten about the other games going on that day. The United were away at Bolton, Sunderland away at Bury. Both would surely win, leaving the gap at three points, with two to go. He didn't want them to win without him, but he hated Sunderland intensely now, it was all their fault. Part way through the journey he shut his eyes and dozed, he was tired – the Liverpool lads weren't all to bed, lights out for ten, like the United.

When he awoke it was dark outside. Some lights low down

pricked the darkness and an almost round moon hung above. He tried to work out where they were, but it wasn't until the train started slowing that he recognised the approach to Sheffield: Darnall, the colliery and the refuse destructor. It felt as if he should be getting ready to go home, but instead he would just be changing trains.

Ahead was a corridor of light: Victoria Station. Steam billowed against the window and flecks of soot came in through the gap in the window and brushed his face, stuck on his eyelashes. The others got to their feet but Rab still sat next to the window as the platform came into view. Steam enveloped the train as it slowed. He could make out a number of people on the platform in the gaps between the steam. A lone figure stood next to a large trunk with another bag on top. The train drew to a halt and the steam drifted away. The figure was small, well dressed, neat, with a blue satin straw hat with flowers on, red hair just visible beneath. She hadn't seen him; he banged on the window; she turned and smiled.

'Who's that lovely lady then, eh Rab?'

'That?' he said with a wide grin, 'that's my wife.'

Epilogue

Rab and Ada went on to have five children: Leo, Madge, James Joseph, Marie and Percy Vincent.

Rab was instrumental in Liverpool's 1898-1899 season when they just missed out on the Championship on the last day of the season. He was selected for England in the international against Scotland at the end of that season, when England won 2-1.

He was a first team regular in the 1899-1900 season, but played only a fringe role in Liverpool's Championship win in 1900-1901 after which he was transferred to Preston North End. His career was ended when he broke his leg in September 1903 playing for Preston. Preston asked Sheffield United to come to Deepdale to play a benefit match for Rab but they declined, saying they could not "accede their way to the request." Instead Liverpool played the fixture on 31st October 1904.

After retiring from football, he and Ada ran a greengrocer's shop in Preston and made deliveries. He died in July 1937 aged 69. He is buried in an unmarked grave in a cemetery in Preston.

On Good Friday 1898, Sheffield United beat Bolton 1-0. Sunderland lost to Bury by the same score and Sheffield United secured the English Championship for the only time in their history... so far. Come fill me again!

Rab Howell… perhaps owes some of his inexhaustible vitality to his lucky parentage. Certain it is that no man is more untiring. … He rejoices at meeting the best of forward wings, and should the outside man indulge in dribbling he sticks to him like a leech. — Ernest Needham, Association Football, 1900

Glossary

<u>Romany words</u>

Archaic spellings, often used by Victorian writers, have been chosen to make the words easier to read, for English speakers. Apologies to Romani speakers.

Beng te lal toot! The devil take you!
Bokalo shan? – Are you hungry?
Chal – lad
Chobben – victuals
Chooreste-gav – knife town (Sheffield)
Dei – mother
Dordi! – an exclamation like 'Look!' or 'gracious!'
Ei! – an exclamation of grief
Gorgio – Non-Romany
Hockabens – tricks, deception
Hotchiwitchy – hedgehog
Keiringro – house-dweller
Kooshto raati – good night
Kooshto doovel – Good Lord
lubni – whore
Mantchi too! – cheer up!
Mandi maurova tooti! – I'm going to kill you
Mochardi – unclean (in a ritual sense)
Motto – drunk
Mumply – derogatory word usually applied to non-Romanies, slovenly
Opre woodrus – upstairs
Pariko toot – thank you
Poori-dei – grandmother
Poshaley – confined (women)
Rashi – teacher
Rinkeni – pretty
Rokkerpen – romany talk

Shoonta! – Listen!
Swegler – tobacco pipe
Tan – tent (can mean 'place')
Vardo – wagon

<u>Sheffield dialect</u>

It is hard to capture the true sounds of dialect speech, and still be legible. Compromises have been made.

Adam's ale – water
Addle – to earn
A'gatewards – home
Agin – against
Cob on – "to have a cob on" – to be cross
Crozzled – over cooked/dried up
Donkey stone – soft sandstone used for whitening the front edges of stone steps
Dunno – don't know
Feight – fight
Flit – to flit, is to move house
Gerroff! – get off!
Get – git (bastard)
Gi'– Give. So, "gi'o'er" = give over!,
Ha'porth – half penny's worth, useless person
Hutch up – move up
Jammy – lucky
Jennel – a narrow passage/through route
Laiking – playing
Lummox – clumsy person
Lundy – very clumsy
Mash (tea) – to brew
Mebbes – may be / perhaps
Misen thisen hissen – myself, thyself, himself
Mither – to pester
Nah then! – now then: a form of greeting
Nowt – nothing

Owd – old

Pikelet – small oatcake, similar to a crumpet

Pitch n' toss – a gambling game where coins are thrown at a mark and each player only gets to keep those that land heads up

Posset – baby's slight milky regurgitation

Ponch – an implement for agitating clothes in a dolly tub

Pot-sitten – dirt in pores of skin

Punky – chimney sweep, dirty person

Reight – right. A' reight – all right – used as a greeting

Saint Monday – a Monday where the weekend is unofficially extended

Scarper – run away

Scrape – margarine or dripping applied thinly

Set pot – large iron pot used for heating water, usually fired separately from the range

Sileing – raining hard

Slop-kitchen – scullery

Snap – food taken for eating in the middle of a shift

Spice – sweets

Summat – something

Tha – thou (see also thi) this term are still used for the second person singular instead of 'you.' in Sheffield the 'th' sound is not as pronounced as in other parts of Yorkshire, being almost a 'd' sound. This has given Sheffielders the nickname Dee-dahs, in others parts of Yorkshire.

Thi – thee/thy

thrussen – crowded

us – pronounced 'uzz' often used for 'me' or 'our.'

were – often used for was

wi' – with

winter hedge – clothes horse

woodenly – awkwardly

wreckling – runt

<u>Latin mass</u>

Ne perdas cum impiis, Deus, animam meam, et cum viris sanguinum vitam meam. In quorum manibus iniquitates sunt – *Take not away my soul, O God, with the wicked: nor my life with bloody men. On their hands are crimes*

Dominus vobiscum – *the lord be with you*

Agnus Dei, qui tollis peccata mundi: miserere nobis – *Lamb of God, who takest away the sins of the world, have mercy on us*

non ex sanguinibus, neque ex voluntate carnis, neque ex voluntate viri – *not of blood nor the will of the flesh nor the will of man*

libera me per hoc sacrosanctum Corpus et Sanguinem tuum – *deliver me by this Thy most sacred Body and Blood*

<u>What the Jubilee banners really said:</u>

She has wrought her people lasting good.

Our steel shall guard and loyal hearts shall praise.

Welcome to Victoria, Queen and Empress.

Acknowledgements

Helen for wise counsel (as always) and Helen, Gaby and Joey for their support and tolerance. My Dad for inflicting a following of United on me and my Grandpa for doing it to him. My Mum for not questioning our Saturday madness. Janette, Robin, and Ian for reading drafts and providing advice, suggestions and encouragement; Cheryl and Greg for that plus. Sheffield Libraries Local Studies and Archives – what a fantastic service! – without this resource I could never have even attempted this. Kevin and Scott McCabe. Jackie at the Vintage Carriage Trust. Glossop Library, and Sunderland Local Studies Centre. Marion and Nick, Rab's granddaughter and great grandson. Graham Phythian, author of Colossus, the story of Bill Foulke. John Garrett, Supporter Liaison Officer and Historian at Bramall Lane. Dawn at the National Railway Museum's Search Engine. The staff at the British Library. Pam at Preston City Council Cemetery Office. Emma at Northend Print. Pauline at Fast-Print Publishing. Linda Lee Welch for an Off-the-Shelf workshop that gave me the confidence to start this.

About the author

I live in Sheffield with my partner and two children. I spend Monday to Thursday on the treadmill, Fridays researching and writing, Saturdays (from August to May) watching my hopes crumble and turn to dust, and Sundays waiting to do it all again.

I am currently working on a novel based around an infamous Victorian court case at Leeds Assizes.

If you enjoyed reading *The Evergreen* I'd really appreciate it if you'd write a review on Amazon: just a line or two would be great.

My website www.theevergreen.co.uk contains more stuff about Rab Howell, pictures and background to the novel. You can get in touch via facebook.com/SteveK1889, Twitter.com/SteveK1889 or e-mail me at stevek1889@gmail.com